ONCE UPON A DEMON'S HEART

ALSO BY K.M. MORONOVA

DARK FORCES STANDALONES

Leave Me Behind

Bulletproof

DARK FORCES DUET

Your Knife, My Heart

My Blade, Your Back

Once Upon a Demon's Heart

K.M. MORONOVA

PENGUIN BOOKS

PENGUIN BOOKS

UK | USA | Canada | Ireland | Australia
India | New Zealand | South Africa

Penguin Books is part of the Penguin Random House group of companies
whose addresses can be found at global.penguinrandomhouse.com

Penguin Random House UK,
One Embassy Gardens, 8 Viaduct Gardens, London SW11 7BW

penguin.co.uk

Penguin Random House UK

First self-published by K.M. Moronova 2025
Published in the US by Bloom Books, an imprint of Sourcebooks, 2026
Published in the UK by Penguin Books 2026
002

Printed and bound in Great Britain by Clays Ltd, Elcograf S.p.A.

The authorised representative in the EEA is Penguin Random House Ireland,
Morrison Chambers, 32 Nassau Street, Dublin D02 YH68

A CIP catalogue record for this book is available from the British Library

ISBN: 978–1–804–96258–9

Penguin Random House is committed to a sustainable future
for our business, our readers and our planet. This book is made
from Forest Stewardship Council® certified paper.

FSC www.fsc.org MIX Paper FSC® C018179

For those who believe punishment is the
only salvation for their mistakes.

Faultore
Alzhor
Florum Forest

Devicit
Gates of Mortem
Fallen Ridge

Content Warning

This is an adult dark romantasy book. That means the themes and vibes in this book can be very grim. Tears may be shed for fictional characters while reading this book, and the cliffhanger will give you great despair. (You've been warned, my friend.)

Reader discretion is advised.

Explicit sex, language, violence, war trauma, aspects of active war, heat/alpha urges, knotting, noncon knotting, degradation, hate fucking (aggressive), death, gore, and breeding kink.

Playlist

My Blood—Ellie Goulding

pain's my only home—Zevia

no more—kny & STÖY

Hollow Hands—Nilu

When It Ends—Avery Lynch (feat. JORDY)

bad luck—We Came As Romans

Mean It—Gracie Abrams

remedy—Alexa Cirri

Gale Song—The Lumineers

Last Of My Kind—Shaboozey (feat. Paul Cauthen)

Breathe In, Breathe Out—David Kushner

Goodbye (Arcane League of Legends)—Ramsey

Go Tomorrow—The Newton Brothers

Persephone—Tamino

World Notes

LORE:

I use a mix of lore in this book, some of which comes from the Roman gods and their respective mythology. I use the names and roles of some of the gods in Roman mythology, but beyond that are things I've made up.

ROMAN GODS:

Venus: Goddess of love, beauty, desire

Jupiter: King of the gods

Mercury: Messenger of the gods

Pluto: God of the underworld

Apollo: God of the sun

Ceres: Goddess of agriculture

Neptune: God of the sea

CHAPTER 1

ALIRA

"*With gilded blood, pray upon a demon's heart, for it very well might save you.*"

The house mother at the orphanage always told us ludicrous stories of lore. Of dragons, wisps, and forest spirits in the Eastern lands. But the one about wishing on a demon's heart stuck with me the most.

Half-gods bleed gold, that's a given. We are taught this from the time we can talk, but what I couldn't figure out was why a demigod would even be close enough to a demon to pray to it. I'd never even seen one before. For all I knew, they were as mythical as the wisps and unicorns in her stories.

I would lie in my cold cot at night and stare at the ceiling, wondering, daydreaming of these creatures she spoke of. Letting my mind run wild with what any of it really meant.

Unfortunately, those naive thoughts and ideas of what the world could be beyond Alzhor were dashed for me from a young age. My first brush with a demon ended smeared in death.

Because, you see, the demons and demigods have never gotten along. Not before the war, and certainly not now. So why would a wish upon a demon's heart save you?

I've wished on every evil heart I've plundered for this war to end.

I've prayed to Jupiter, the king of the gods, and all the deities above, but nothing can save us now. Not after all the blood we've spilled. Mortal and demon alike.

The demigods are on the brink of extinction. We've pushed the demons too far this time, and now, only a marriage in peace between the two species will bring an end to this senseless war—a deal suggested by the Demon King, of course, whom I assume will be choosing one of his high lords or dukes as a suitable groom.

I was a little surprised that the demons would be the first to offer a peace agreement. Given that they're malicious and wicked, down to their core. Every demigod knows this. The house mother told us to never, *ever*, under any circumstances, trust a demon.

The wicked creatures were sent to Faultore by Pluto, god of the underworld, himself. Perhaps it's because the gods despise their grim brother Pluto and that their demigods naturally fight with Pluto's demons. At least that's one of the assumptions.

It wasn't shocking to any of us that King Borlin, ruler of Alzhor's demigods, announced that he wasn't willing to sink to his knees without a fight. He would rather have thirty years of war at the expense of the few remaining demigods than agree to an arranged marriage for one of his precious daughters.

I couldn't imagine being one of the princesses and having to marry a demon duke. None of us wanted to let our freedom and dignity go that easily.

I've learned that nothing is effortless. Everything has a cost, magic or not.

In my unfortunate case, it would seem that magic, fate, or a horrid curse is in play.

You see, the prospect of an arranged marriage compared to the slaughter I've endured repeatedly would be like walking through a flower garden.

How many times have I died at *his* hand?

I lay my hands together over my jewel-encrusted sword, blood dripping from my brow, and kneel on the disrupted gravel of my burning kingdom once more.

The thought of watching the royal family's heads being severed before my eyes again makes my stomach churn.

I lift my chin to the near seven-foot-tall knight before me.

His ivory armor is bathed in the light of the crimson moon. He lowers his sword to my throat. It *tinks* against the neck guard—something he does every time without fail before ending me. It has become a bell of death to my ears.

The Blood Knight has killed me in twenty time loops—a cruel curse that I've found myself trapped in.

For some reason, my life keeps resetting to exactly one week before his raid on my kingdom. *No, a wish on a demon's heart doesn't save you*, I wish I could scold the house mother. I've wished for every death after the third loop to be my last. And yet I continue to wake and face the fall of my kingdom like clockwork.

A punishment worse than death. One I rightfully deserve.

The Blood Knight is a merciless demon. I cannot defeat him no matter what I try. No techniques I spent countless hours learning. No high-end swords that I had made from the bones of dragons and the blood of unicorns.

Absolutely nothing.

He comes on the night of the war god's moon without fail—at the exact moment the sun dips beneath the mountains behind Alzhor's walls.

Without hesitation or a drop of pity, the Blood Knight always finds me and kills me. Four times it was my head being severed from my body, six times he pierced my heart with his sword, twice he snapped my neck like it was nothing more than a stick.

But in each loop, his gold-stained armor was the last thing I saw before dying.

So what's one more death?

I firm my resolve and strike his heel with my blade, thinking if I can get him on the ground, he'll be easier to slay. He doesn't budge from my attack. My eyes widen as he lifts his arm, and with one hard thrust, he pierces his sword straight through my chest armor.

Blood spurts from my lips as my head is thrown back with the force of his blow. My helmet falls and topples to the ground. Silvery-white strands of my hair wisp around me, and for the first time, I catch a glimpse of the Blood Knight's eyes as he watches me fall.

They are an inferno of golden amber. Heartless flames. For a second, I think I see a glimmer of emotion flash through them, but my mind doesn't linger on the thought as darkness clouds my vision. Then the tide of black waves consumes me whole.

— —— —

I sit straight up in my cot and stare down at my hands. *Again.* To what end will this loop continue resetting? My gaze shifts to the calendar on the far wall of the knights' wing. It's exactly one week before the demons come to take over Alzhor. The mirror beside the calendar reflects my weary lavender eyes.

My silver hair spills over my shoulders and makes my olive skin look rich in contrast. The gold blood in my veins makes my complexion practically glow even though I feel like death.

Korin raises a brow at me from her cot beside me. The sun has just risen, and slivers of light streak across the gray stone walls of this practical dungeon we sleep in. Vines of ivy grow along the windowsills, thanks to the knights who are descendants of Ceres, the goddess of agriculture. The presence of a child of Ceres alone springs life to any dwelling that is unlikely to have it.

Most of the demigods are uncertain of who our parents are until we start to show signs of our gifts. Many never develop their signs though.

I wish that was the case for me.

"What's wrong, Alira?" Korin asks sleepily as she rubs her eyes. I glance over at her, trying not to grin at the messy brown locks of hair strewn over her face.

I breathe out slowly and press my palm to the fading ache in my chest. *Gods, he didn't hold anything back that time, did he?* I muse grumpily. At least he kills swiftly. Not once have I suffered too much from his death blow.

"Nothing, just a bad dream," I say routinely. It works every time I'm sent back to restart the week. The first few times, I tried to tell her that I'd somehow jumped back in time, and she reported me to the healers for insanity. They kept me locked up until the night the Blood Knight came. Long story short, I learned the hard way that no one would believe me.

Korin nods with a drowsy smile before turning into her sheets and almost immediately resuming to snore. Ignorance really is bliss, I suppose. They have no idea what's coming our way. I press my lips together and narrow my eyes as I take a deep breath, memorizing the scent of the mossy stones and my slumbering comrades.

I decided in the days leading up to my last death loop that if I failed to protect my kingdom again, I would abandon it and live for myself this time. Who's to say if I will survive or not? At least I'll have a fraction of peace. I want to do something besides fight and train to no avail. What's the point of all these time resets if I have to watch all my friends die before being slain myself? Nothing I do saves any of them. There are too many demons and not enough of us.

I can't do it anymore.

My pillowcase is heavy with bread, small jars of honey, and dried meats. I secure my sword to my side but leave the rest of my armor behind. It would be suspicious for anyone outside the kingdom to be wearing a full suit of imperial-grade plates, so the sword and black leathers will have to do. It will be easier to explain that I found these things on a corpse if I get stopped and questioned by a guard about them.

My thin pale blue cloak is the last thing I secure around my neck before giving the knights' quarters a final look over.

The men and women in the royal guard are the only people who've cared for me for most of my life. I'm not just betraying my kingdom, I'm betraying them. I firm my hands at my sides and force myself to turn away from their sleeping forms.

I've watched each of them die so many times. I can't experience it again.

Perhaps leaving will alter their fate, I think blissfully. I close my eyes and pray, even though it's been decades since anyone has heard so much as a whisper from the deities who created us.

The gods abandoned us long ago. It won't be long before the final frontier of the deities is gone for good. We're outnumbered a hundred to one. I huff at the thought. If the mortals and demons want a world without gods, then let them have it. See who answers when the plague comes again to rot the world like it once did centuries ago.

The stables are dark, and the only sound is that of the horses occasionally stomping their hooves over the cobblestones and hay, huffing as I pass.

"Venrey," I whisper for my chestnut mare. She trots over obediently and stares at me like she knows I'm up to no good. "You're not going to like the journey we have ahead of us." I pat her neck before getting the saddle strapped.

The air is brisk tonight, making chills move across my arms. I shiver as I lead Venrey by the reins out of the stable. I don't have time to ride around the perimeter of the city, so going straight through the courtyard of the royal gardens will be necessary. I won't be hidden like I want to be, but this is the quickest way. I wince, passing the empty flower beds. When

I was a child, I remember Alzhor being a much prettier place. Much has changed since the war began thirty years ago.

I hold my breath as we make our way across. Venrey's hooves seem ten times louder than they've ever been before, making my teeth clench tighter with each step. I dare to look back when we reach the end of the courtyard and thankfully don't see any lights on in the windows. A grin spreads over my lips.

I should've run away sooner. If I knew it was this easy, I would've. Although I think part of me still had hope we could win the war.

But you can only die so many times before all your hope is stolen away.

I ride the rest of the way out of the cold, winter-fallen kingdom, keeping my hood up in case any early birds are awake. The evening guards don't bat an eye at me since I'm disguised as a civilian. Thankfully, many of our townsfolk work in the surrounding villages and fields at odd hours. By the time Venrey steps into the open meadow outside the silver gates, we're at a gallop.

Tall, dry grass rimmed in frost bends as the wind blows. Alzhor never gets more than a dusting of snow, but still, my cloak isn't nearly thick enough for this time of winter. I only need to make it into the forest of Florum before I'm in the clear to start a fire. So I ignore the icy throb that runs through my limbs and tighten my grasp around Venrey's reins.

I finally dismount after we've ventured deep into the woods and allow a relieved breath to exit my lungs.

Florum is a forest made of the thickest trees in all of Faultore, making it damn near impossible to build a fire unless you bring wood from elsewhere. The height of the branches creates zero visibility, making it safe to have a fire without fear of being spotted by enemies.

The canopy is so dense that it's almost pitch black in here. If not for the glowing toadstools and luminescent vines that drape along the branches, it'd be impossible to navigate the forest without alternate sources of light.

It would've been nice if I had an ability like the children of Apollo, god of the sun. They can light small areas as if they themselves are lanterns.

Most demigods fear these woods. They believe this land to be cursed, but I've snuck off and explored here since I was eleven, and I've only encountered one living thing in all that time. A demon child, maybe a few years older than I was at the time. He was the first demon I met, and I regret our brief time together terribly. He was kind to me, but the four dead demigods that were found that night in Florum ignited the war between our kingdoms. Two demon corpses were found that night as well.

No one ever found the boy's body after that night, but I saw his dull eyes, his impaled heart.

He was dead, and no amount of weeping or praying brought him back.

My hands clench at my sides as I force the memories from my mind. I think of him often, wondering if his fate would've been different if I hadn't stumbled upon him that night.

Since then, Florum has been a hollow forest, filled with only shadows and gloom. The house mother always said the earth of this forest clings to things that happen within it. *"The spirits of the forest remember much more than we credit them for."* Sometimes I think fear is the only curse there ever really was here.

A curse to keep the forest untouched and quiet, as it is. I don't mind curses like that—the ones that protect things. Much unlike the one I've fallen under.

Even Venrey pulls nervously at the reins, trying to urge me to turn back. I'm tempted to release her so she can return home, but I need a horse if I want to get distance from the attack that's coming, and she's better off with me unless she wants to face the battle in one week's time.

The luminescent plants indicate when night has fallen, as they will dim much like the sun until they barely offer any light. It's almost pitch black beneath the trees by the time I find my usual campsite and finally get a fire going.

I've been storing wood in a hollowed trunk for years now, using this place as a reprieve during my short days off from duty, but I can never seem to locate it quickly. It's easy to let your mind believe that the trees move in here. Playing tricks on weary travelers, manipulating things they shouldn't.

That thought makes a cold shiver run down my spine. The last thing I need are moving trees.

Venrey neighs and flashes me with wild eyes as I return with another pile of wood. I straighten and give her a stern look.

"Would you stop—" My mouth snaps shut immediately as I notice a masculine figure sitting by the campfire.

My hand is on the hilt of my sword in the next second, but before I can withdraw it, a voice as smooth and haunting as a rainstorm says calmly, "I'm no threat to you. Why don't you share a bowl of soup with me since I'm borrowing your fire?" He doesn't even look over his shoulder at me. *He's perceptive.*

I raise a brow at Venrey, and if horses could raise brows, I'd swear she was giving one back. *Who is this man?* He bears no weapon and doesn't have an ominous air about him, so he doesn't pose any immediate harm to me. His attention is solely set on the cauldron he's stirring.

Slowly, I push my sword back into its scabbard and walk carefully around the campfire so I can see who's found me. Is it a demigod? Did someone in the knights' wing see me leaving last night? They wouldn't think to look for me here of all places, would they? I worry my lower lip.

The man wears a bulky, black cloak and matching leather pants. Each sleeve is lined with golden embroidery that dips and swirls into elegant arches and arrows. The gloves match in color and style, sharing the gilded thread with an emblem of some sort printed over his knuckles in plated gold. A royal merchant, maybe? At least he isn't wearing a suit of armor, so I know he's not a knight in our army or the demons' for that matter. I let out a relieved sigh.

I move to stand on the opposite side of him, watching carefully as he pulls the pot off the fire and stirs something inside. His hood hides his face, allowing me only a glimpse of his chin. *How long was I collecting wood for him to have enough time to make an entire meal?* I scold myself, quickly shaking the thought before he notices me studying him closely.

He glances up.

My heart stops the moment his smile curls at the ends of his lips. Eyes as golden as the sun meet mine. His hair is as dark as a starless night. Tendrils of his ebony hair fall over his forehead and barely reach his eyes. His jawline is sharp and defined—on his left side, a red scar curves along his cheekbone. The olive tone of his skin matches mine, perhaps a hint darker. He must be from the northern mountains, likely a demigod or perhaps a human. I'd know more if I could see his ears.

Anything I had on the tip of my tongue vanishes. I'm left staring at him like I've just seen one of the gods themselves in the flesh.

His grin grows at my delayed response, and fangs appear just over his bottom lip. My eyes widen, and I instinctively reach for my sword again.

He is no god.

He's a demon.

Only a select few of the demons are known to drink the blood of demigods. And it is said that they are to be feared the most. Many of the stories have been lost through history—it's been decades if not centuries since there has been a report of a blood-drinking demon. Honestly, we believed that they were extinct, what with their food supply dwindling and all.

He takes in my expression slowly. His smile loses a bit of its warmth at my hostile glare before he lets out a low chuckle.

"I'm only here to have a meal. No need to wear yourself out going through scenarios in your head," he says with a laugh before completely dismissing me as a threat altogether. My cheeks warm at the insult.

"You're a *demon*." My voice trembles despite my best efforts.

I've killed hundreds of them. To the extent that I can no longer sleep peacefully at night. So why do I fear him? He caught me off guard, but that can't be why. I reassess him, focusing on the thick muscles that cord down his neck and forearms. He's nearly as tall as I am sitting down. A chill rolls through my bones. He's stronger than any of his kind I've faced in battle.

Every living being on Faultore has essence that they release naturally. Our soul essence, as we call it in Alzhor. When trained properly, anyone, even demons, can sense another being's soul essence. And this demon's essence is overbearing. He's dangerous. It's a gut feeling that makes my palms clammy.

"And you are a demigod. Do you not eat food?" His condescending tone puts a tick in my jaw.

"What is your name, demon?" I demand, loosening the grip on my sword, though I haven't decided yet whether I'm going to sit down and converse civilly with him.

"Kalel, and yours?"

Kalel. What an odd name for a demon.

"Alira."

His eyes flick my way as he studies my face for a few moments; they remain soft as he waves to the spot across the campfire from him, motioning for me to take a seat. I narrow my eyes but hesitantly sit down.

Kalel carefully pours soup into a bowl and offers it to me. I shake my head. I wasn't born yesterday—I'd be a fool to accept anything from him.

"Suit yourself." He shrugs, taking the bowl for himself and sipping on it. The delighted hum that rolls from his chest makes mine warm. It's known as the comfort call, something that male demons do to express assurance of safety.

I've never heard a comfort call before. As a knight's apprentice, I was taught that the demons rarely make such sounds outside their villages. They only do it to calm their own. Though a few demigods have heard it once or twice, and they described it as a warm hug, a pull from within to trust them.

Of course, they also said that if you're close enough to feel the magic of it, the demon will kill you the moment your guard is down.

I couldn't care less if my day starts over again. I'd only wake up back inside the barracks, and it's not like I'll get a chance to speak with a demon like this again. The only ones I've met have been shielded by plates of armor and helmets that conceal their faces. I didn't expect them to be…so much like us.

My toes dig into the soles of my boots.

What is he playing at? Why is he trying to lure me into a sense of comfort? I firm my lips together.

"What are you doing all the way out here anyway?" I ask as I pull my knees up to my chest, staring at him from across the fire suspiciously.

Kalel takes another sip before answering me. "I could ask you the same question."

Keeping his cards close.

"Come on."

He smirks at my curiosity and sets down the bowl. "All right, all right. No need for the dagger eyes, little godling. I'm an apothecary, and I'm searching for a species of toadstool for a medicine I'm developing. This forest is old, and I recall it having a wealth of them."

My brows rise. That's not the answer I was expecting at all.

"Oh." Suddenly I feel rude for being so hostile, but I'm a knight and our nations are at war, so being skeptical is sort of ingrained in me. The king would be mortified if he learned that I didn't kill this man on the spot.

Fuck the king. I'm done doing what's wrong just because I'm told to. For once I want to listen to my heart. "What kind of medicine? You act like you've been here before, even though this is holy territory," I push. He knows as well as I do that he shouldn't be anywhere near here.

Now that I study him closer, there's something familiar about him, but I can't quite place it.

Kalel grins and leans back on his palms, legs sprawled out. *He's certainly getting comfortable.*

"That's restricted information, I'm afraid. Your turn, Alira. Why are you here? Isn't this forest off-limits for the demigods?"

My focus is entirely set on the veins that protrude from his neck and the corded muscles that trail down to his collarbones.

I deflate. An apothecary is harmless, and my time will reset in a week regardless, I'm sure. The truth to him would be nothing, right?

"Well, if I'm being honest, I'm running away."

His brow arches and a look of concern replaces his smile. "From *what*, exactly?"

"From my duties as a knight." I toss a stick into the fire, and the embers dance as it's swiftly engulfed.

Kalel sits up straight and crosses his legs, seeming put off by my decision. "You're a knight? Why are you running from your kingdom?" His tone dips toward the edge of suspicion. Demons hold loyalty as the highest honor. They despise deserters.

I can't exactly just come out and say, "*A terrible attack is coming one week from today, and the kingdom of Alzhor will crumble at the hands of your cruel Blood Knight.*" That sounds utterly delirious.

"I guess I've just grown tired of the senseless killing."

Not a lie—not the whole truth.

Kalel's fingers twitch, but he gives me a weak grin. "Well, that's good to hear, but what if your king sends his men to come looking for you? What then? Won't they hang you for abandoning your duties?" He sounds more curious than worried, like he doesn't entirely believe me. I wonder if he's trying to learn about me as much as I am trying to learn about him.

I stare off into the dark underbrush, listening to the whispers that thread through the twisted roots, and nod slowly. "Yes, but it would be better than the fate I've been dealt." *To die forever at one man's hand.*

A breeze rolls through and sets a chill into my bones. I should've at least grabbed my winter cloak. I didn't think that the weather would be colder in the east than it was in the kingdom. Kalel doesn't miss the shiver that runs through me. He slowly rises.

I move to stand as well, reaching for my blade, but he lifts his hand. "Stay put, you're freezing." I hesitate, watching closely as he walks around me and drops his cloak over my shoulders. It's much heavier than I could've imagined and draws a soft gasp from my lips.

My eyes widen and I lift my chin to him, taking in how much taller and broader he is up close as he circles back to his spot across the fire.

I'm consumed by the scent of earth and crisp leaves—alderwood. His scent. The extra layer instantly adds warmth back to my body. It must be made from a fire dragon's hide, nothing in Faultore can compare to it. In Alzhor, this cloak is worth a small fortune. Dragons don't roam our territory; they haven't for centuries. Not since devilstones and dire wolves were still a problem, and the gods hadn't yet abandoned us. Dragons stick to the path leading toward the underworld. Some believe they guard the Gates of Mortem, but there's never been a soul to confirm the idea. No one dares to go near the gates to the underworld. Not even demons.

My eyes narrow at Kalel. *So how did an apothecary get their hands on one?* And to hand it over so easily to a demigod too? It doesn't add up. Who is he really?

"Aren't you cold?" I ask, staring at his long-sleeved shirt. Suspenders are strapped around his shoulders. One leather belt stretches across his chest with a black metallic buckle at the center.

He shakes his head. "No. I'm a demon. Most of our species

don't get cold at all. The thick clothes are more or less for appearances only."

My lips press together thoughtfully. That's something we've never learned about them. Is that why they aren't suffering in the winter pursuit on our kingdom the way King Borlin assumed they would? How ignorant of us. There is so much our kingdoms don't know about each other, yet we slaughter one another so readily. It's disgusting. It's pitiful how I've come to be much more thoughtful after all the bloodshed. Weariness grows wisdom in guilty souls.

"You're a knight… Let me ask you this, Alira. Did you fight in Thornhall?" His voice turns colder with the question.

I flinch at the sound of the village's name. Thornhall was the first demon village that the demigods sieged after a false treaty was signed. A trick—something the gods are notorious for, and we demigods don't stray far from our parents. King Borlin wanted their guard to be down. He knew they would take the treaty seriously while he plotted their demise. A truly horrible act.

We killed every man, woman, and child. If they were a demon, they were marked for death in Thornhall. It still haunts my dreams. I hear the screams of terror clearly whenever the world around me falls silent. It happened a month before my one-week loop began, so thankfully I'm not forced to relive it repeatedly. If I did, I would've tried to stop the massacre.

I should've refused to participate in the first place, but

I didn't. I followed orders blindly. And that decision has tormented my every waking moment since. Part of me believes what happened in Thornhall is the reason for my curse, but if it's true, then why am I the only one being punished?

"No. I didn't." The lie tastes sour.

A grim expression passes over Kalel's face, like he can sense that I'm lying. My nerves ignite, and I look down at the fire. I know how devastating that attack was to the demons. It was enough to spark the siege we're currently under. Our ruination.

"My mother was killed that night."

A small gasp escapes me. Dread crashes into my chest and freezes my entire body. My words are weak, and I hope he can't hear the guilt they're drowned in. "I'm so sorry."

He nods slowly, staring into the flames. A darkness that wasn't there a moment ago clouds his features as he shifts his gaze to me. "I am too."

Silence stretches between us, and it is only interrupted by my stomach growling. The sound brings him out of his thoughts. He chuckles softly before pouring another bowl of soup and handing it to me. A small dimple forms on the left corner of his mouth, but it does nothing to hide the sadness in his gaze. His eyes linger on my long silver hair.

He's kind.

A very long time ago, I once knew a demon to be kind. But we were children then. I'm sure he must've grown into a ferocious man who killed many demigods, just as I've grown to slay demons.

This time I take the bowl and offer a smile in return. "Thank you."

"I wish you well on your grand escape, Alira, but may I offer you some advice?" Kalel slowly stands to leave. I realize he doesn't have a horse tied up nearby, and I wonder how long it will take him to go back to...wherever it is he's come from.

"I'm listening," I say in a light tone, cupping the bowl with my hands and absorbing the warmth.

His expression relaxes and his lovely smile vanishes. He stares at me for a long while, considering his words.

"No one can outrun their fate."

My brows knit at his grim tone. If only he knew how horrifying those words are for my situation. "So you would believe that I'm just doomed?"

He turns to leave, walking steadily away and into the dark. "Maybe you're looking at it the wrong way. Try something new. I doubt you've tried *everything*," he says.

I stand, willing my legs not to follow after him.

"You couldn't possibly know what I've tried."

Kalel laughs and replies, "No, I couldn't, but you don't seem all that daring. What does your heart yearn for most? I'm sure you'll find that the gods will hear your wishes. You are a demigod after all. They'll likely be listening."

He doesn't know they abandoned us long ago?

My hands are clasped tightly around the cloak he dropped over my shoulders. I watch him walk away, and only after his form has vanished into the gloomy forest do I force myself to sit back down.

Venrey stomps on the ground and whinnies her disapproval of the uninvited visitor. I glance over at my horse and let out a tired sigh.

"Where did *he* come from?"

I sleep terribly and with one eye open practically the entire night. Half wishing he will come back and speak with me more and half wishing I never see him again.

His words revisit me more than once in my fitful rest, and by the time I'm awake, I decide to head back to Alzhor.

There's one more thing I can try besides abandoning my kingdom. If it fails, the worst that could happen is the time loop resetting.

If it succeeds, my life will be miserable, but I'll get to live past this horrible week.

"*You don't seem all that daring*," I mock him with a low voice, then blow out a breath. If only he could see what I'm going to do because of his unwarranted advice.

I pray that the gods will hear me and alter my fate.

Even if I'm about to do something I really don't want to do.

CHAPTER 2

ALIRA

"King Borlin, it's an honor. Thank you for agreeing to meet with me today on such short notice." I hold my right hand over my heart as I bow to the king. The cold metal of my armor burns against my palm.

The king looks ten years older than he should. His dark hair has streaks of gray, and the bags beneath his eyes are heavy. A direct result of the demise he's caused his kingdom and the overwhelming stress that must come with it, one would think.

It was his malicious plan to trick the demons into that treaty, followed by the worst slaughter Faultore has ever known, and it brought upon us a wrath greater than any of us could have fathomed. Thornhall was his attempt at getting the demons to lower their defenses around Devicit, the Kingdom of Chaos. Devicit is all but a memory now to the remaining demigods who once visited. Not a soul outside the city knows where the kingdom is located or where it could've gone. It has all but disappeared. An *entire* kingdom.

It's unknown how they managed to veil it. Only arcane power can be behind it—a lot of it.

No one craves that knowledge more than King Borlin, but his sad attempt to get them to let their guard down and expose the location of their kingdom has proven disastrous.

Perhaps the gods truly have forsaken us…and for good reason.

My hope falters at the thought. But if the gods have turned their heads away from us completely, then why am I stuck in a loop? There must be a reason for it. One god must be observing and tugging on the strings of fate to prevent this blood-ridden path we've found ourselves on.

"What is it, Alira?" he asks sullenly as he looks over the papers on his large oak desk.

King Borlin hasn't bothered to glance up at me once. He's fretting over the army formations reported from the western front. The demons' numbers continue to swell as they merge their forces and armies from every one of their fellow kingdoms across the country.

I've relived it twenty times. No matter how many times he reviews the map, we don't stand a chance against them.

"The demons only ask for a demigod bride for peace to be brought between our kingdoms. I know it has been alluded to that the bride must be of royal blood, but I would like to offer myself as the bride to be sent to them," I say confidently, even though my stomach is curling into itself and sweat begins to collect along my spine.

That gets his attention.

The king snaps his head up and stares at me for a few terrible moments before blinking and composing himself. "Why would they take a knight in place of a princess?" His tone isn't completely shutting my offer down, so I take courage in that alone.

"Because I believe they want this war to end as much as we do."

King Borlin's eyes narrow, the dark brown of them nearing black in his dim-lit study. Walnut-brown bookshelves line the back wall, filled with old books and rolled up scrolls. "I need something to entice them. They won't take a knight…not after what I did." He reaches for his crystal glass and downs what remains of his bourbon. At least he is ashamed, though it's a bit late.

I swallow. I had hoped that it wouldn't come to me sharing the deity gift that runs through my veins. I've kept it secret for several years now. It seems it was all for naught.

"My king, there is one more thing—" I pause and take a deep breath. "I believe I am a daughter to the goddess of fertility, Venus." I say the words so quietly that I worry he didn't hear me, but when my gaze meets his, there's no doubt that he did.

The king's jaw is parted, and shock moves through his eyes.

"Are you certain?" he asks, disbelief cumbersome in his tone.

I slowly nod. "I've been having heat cycles for over a decade now."

The sign of a daughter to Venus.

The first time the heat came, I had no idea what was even happening. My stomach cramped horribly. I felt sick and feverish the entire week. I was in so much pain that I couldn't even train with the other apprentices. It didn't take me long to figure out what was happening. The curse of Venus had come, and I knew I couldn't tell a soul about it.

Venus rarely had offspring, at least not for a few centuries now. The demigods have never had successful reproduction rates, but for the last fifty years, they have been declining rapidly. It's why we're outnumbered ten to one to the demons. They have no complications reproducing.

An heir of Venus is known to possess the rarest demigod blood, above royalty even, for the sole fact that she could conceive offspring easily. Which is precisely why I haven't spoken of this to anyone, not even to Korin.

The king's face pales. He looks down at the maps and strategy reports strewn over his desk. The black candles he'd lit are already down to the base and bleed wax over the old oakwood.

"You know what you're offering them, don't you? They are demons after all. It's not a stretch to think that they plan on breeding you," he says with a wealth of sorrow.

If only he was this kind, defeated king when the first treaty was signed. Perhaps it never would've come to this. I force the thoughts away.

Anxiety curls in my stomach, making me feel sick.

"Yes, I'm fully aware, King Borlin. If it's for my kingdom—for peace—I will happily go." I choke down the knot in my throat and hold my chin high. "It would be my honor."

He's quiet for many seconds, so long that I begin to fear he will refuse my offer, but he surprises me with a weary smile and relief settling into his features.

"Thank the gods for you, Alira. I will send the offer by dove in the morning."

The dove was sent, as promised, at the break of dawn.

Then we waited.

And waited.

I worried that one of the demon's messenger hawks captured the dove and killed it. I dwelled on the possibility that the message would never get through to their king. I worried that the dove would arrive safely, and the demons would refuse the peace offering.

Most of all, I fretted that they would happily accept the deal and be on their way to our kingdom by nightfall to collect me.

But three days passed, and we heard nothing.

I've spent those days wisely, studying the demons and their land as much as I could. There isn't much in our libraries about them, besides how awful and cruel they are. Some books even go as far as to say they will eat any creature that is not their own. I know that the information in here can't all be accurate because I met Kalel. He was kind and calm. Not at all what I was taught they were. He was like any demigod. Had it not been for his fangs, I doubt I would've even known what he truly was.

As knights, we only see the demons on the battlefields. We've never bothered trying to speak with them out there. Of course, hindsight is bittersweet. My hands clench as I think of what happened in Thornhall.

I should have done something.

I shake the somber thoughts from my head and continue reading.

One source of material I find that is relatively helpful explains the different types of demons there are and the abilities they hold. They are much like the demigods when it comes to strength and abilities. The lineage of their parents determines the gifts they possess. Some can shroud themselves in darkness. Others can tear men apart with their hands alone. While the more dangerous ones survive on the holy blood of deities. *Devourers.* The demigods hardly quench their thirst, but they do require our blood to survive. There were always very few of them, but they were known to all. Any commander of the Devicitian army has always been a devourer.

Kalel might be a devourer. I suppose other demons could have fangs though. He was eating normal food when we met in the woods, but there's nothing in our books that says a devourer can't consume other things too.

The Blood Knight is a devourer. That, I'm certain of. The accounts of many demigods that have narrowly evaded him shared that it was only because the Blood Knight was trying to bite them that they were able to escape his blade.

I firm my lips into a flat line when I think of that knight. He's recognized to be one of the last devourers. His ability is unknown. Some say that his curse is to paralyze his prey with his gaze alone. Others say he is a thousand years old and immortal by the blood of the gods he steals from us.

I know rumors can't be fully trusted, but it's frightening to even imagine it.

Is it too ambitious to hope that I never cross paths with him again?

I slam the book shut.

It isn't until the fourth day after the dove took the letter that we finally receive a response.

On the day the demons are set to raid our kingdom.

A black hawk, as large as a cat, perches itself on King Borlin's windowpane—left open wide, allowing the fresh winter air to freeze my nerves as the awful news is read to me.

"They accept our offer."

The king's words bring me relief and horror at the same time. A cold pit sinks into my stomach and puts a chill into my bones.

That was all it took? This entire time? It seems too easy after all the bloodshed I've endured.

I let my eyes find the mirror at King Borlin's back and look at myself. My silver hair is tied back into a tight, high ponytail that reaches my mid-back, and my purple eyes are filled with misery.

My life is over. Sworn to the demons and the man they'll choose as my husband—well, assuming that I can make it past the day I've died on for almost half a year. But if it means that the war will end, then...it's worth it.

It has to be.

I nod rigidly. "Will the Demon King send a high lord to collect me?" I ask and try to keep my expression as neutral as possible.

King Borlin's brows pinch together. "Yes, you will be marrying his favored royal knight, Duke Lornhelm."

Why does he make it sound like this guy is the worst of the dukes?

"A royal knight?" I echo and let my gaze drift toward the open window. The hawk stares at me intently, like it's been sent to study me to ensure this isn't another trick. I don't blame them for being careful. I'd do the same. I didn't expect the duke to also be a favored knight, the likelihood of us getting along just plummeted.

"Yes, and he will be here this evening with his army to collect you."

Oh gods. My heart dashes a beat, and I take one staggered step back. That's not enough time to say my goodbyes. It's already almost sundown.

The king stands and walks steadily across the tiles until he is before me. Then he lowers to his knee. *What is he doing?* I quickly look at the knights standing guard around the room, and they look just as perplexed as I feel.

"My king, *please stand*," I say gently as I offer him my hand to help him up.

He takes my hand but remains on his knee. "Alira, you've saved Alzhor and the remaining demigods with your sacrifice. You will be hailed as a hero for the rest of time," he proclaims.

He makes it sound like I'm going to die and never be seen again. It makes my stomach curl. Is the duke really that awful? I worry my lower lip and try my best to keep the fear at bay.

"Tonight, we will send you off with the song of the gods."

He finally stands, and I can breathe again. "Go collect what little you have in the barracks. Say your farewells. I will prepare a witness to travel with you to Devicit in order to verify the wedding takes place."

"Yes, my king." I dip my head to him respectfully. The song of the gods has not been sung for years. The last time I heard it was as a child. *Please let them hear our plea for peace,* I pray.

The walk down to the barracks is hazy, my mind overflooded with the reality that this is happening. Well, presuming that I actually live through this night. If I wake up tomorrow, then fate truly has been altered, and I'll finally be able to live again.

As a demon's wife.

CHAPTER 3
ALIRA

Korin shakes out the last bedsheet before laying it flat on the table to fold the edges together. It's her week for laundry duty. It has been since my loop started, so I have no clue who's turn it is next, but I'm glad that it was my week off from all chores around the barracks.

"Are you okay?" Korin sets the folded sheet in the storage hamper. "Because you look like you've just seen a demon running through the castle," she jests with a slight smirk. Her expression quickly deflates into worry when she sees the dread only grow heavier on my face. "Oh gods, did you actually see one?"

I shake my head. "No, but I need to tell you something."

Korin sits with her legs crossed on the opposite side of my bed as I explain the peace deal to her and what will happen in a few short hours.

"You're giving yourself to them as a bride? But we can win, Alira! You don't need to do this." Angry tears well in her eyes. I understand her belief in the demigods' abilities to thwart the demons, but she doesn't know how wrong she is.

I've seen every outcome of the battle that takes place tonight. In every single one, we all die.

I press my lips together as I set my hand on hers. "Korin, we won't win. This is the only way to have peace between the kingdoms. I'm honored to take this role." I wish I sounded as confident as my words are.

Her expression twists with pain. "There's no way I can talk you out of this, is there?"

"I'm afraid not," I murmur sadly.

She sits with the information for a moment. "I'll see you again someday though, right?"

"I hope so." I give her a reassuring smile that doesn't meet my eyes.

She swipes her sleeve across her face before shifting off the bed and retrieving a necklace from her nightstand. Korin extends her hand out to me.

I stand and offer my palm. She cups the bottom of my hand and places the jewelry with a burdensome weight pulling her mouth into a frown.

"Always keep it close. I'll be with you," she mutters softly.

I clutch the silver heart-shaped pendant and wrap my arms over her shoulders in a tight embrace. "Thank you, Korin."

The chapel bells ring, indicating that the sun is setting in five minutes. In the past, it was used to signal the departure of the sun god and to send our prayers and thanks to him for another day. Now we just use it as a way to keep track of patrol changes.

I set to packing anything that might be of use to me. It doesn't take long, because I don't have much. Being an orphan who grew up to become a knight isn't exactly a life that comes with luxuries or belongings for that matter.

I don't even have a last name. None of the orphaned demigods do.

I sheathe the dagger that I've carried with me since I could walk. It's the only gift my mother ever left for me, according to the house mother. From what I can tell, there are no enhancements to the blade, but the gods certainly aren't known for being forthcoming.

I have no formal clothes to wear besides my armor, so I find the cleanest set of long-sleeved leathers and pants I have and tug them on before getting into my armor.

I tuck my helmet beneath my arm, frowning as I take one last look at my bed. It wasn't much, but it was all I ever had. My fellow knights were all I'd ever known.

Korin walks silently beside me as we return to the inner

castle. She's wearing the beige prayer robes adorned with gold beads and slips of red around the cowl. As is everyone else in our kingdom who is not positioned at a post right now, ordered by the king. He really does intend to send me off properly with the song of the gods. I huff at the thought. Why stick to our old ways now? The gods won't hear us. They never have before. I glance at the walls, memorizing them in case the demons decide to lock me up in a dark chamber for the rest of my long life.

The old paintings are of the deities. Some depict peaceful settings of them interacting with humans and demigods, while others show their violent nature. The wrath they so carelessly inflicted upon the mortals and demons just for existing.

Statues made of ivory marble line the curved walls that lead into the foyer. I keep my eyes from trailing to Venus. She's no mother to me. I'm only a discarded object to her, but if being her heir will bring peace to the last of the demigods and the merciless demons, then so be it.

I will accept my fate.

Korin grabs my hand tightly and offers a wounded grin that tells me she's as heartbroken as I am about this. She's like a sister to me. The only person who's shown me an ounce of empathy and care throughout my life.

"You'll be okay. I know we'll meet again." She throws her arms over my shoulders and hugs me tightly.

I shut my eyes and hug her just as desperately. "I hope

so," I murmur, and pray that she can't hear the dismay in my tone. Because I doubt I'll ever be returning, and I don't want her to see what becomes of me even if we do get the chance to meet again.

She slowly releases me, tears rolling down her cheeks. "Best of luck, Alira." I place the helmet over my head as I watch her leave to join the rest of the off-duty knights waiting along the balconies for the send-off.

I keep my eyes to the ground as I stand beside the king and his personal guards at the bottom of the steps leading into the front doors of the castle. King Borlin notices the necklace around my neck and narrows his eyes. I flinch as he reaches for it and brushes his thumb slowly over the pendant. "A gift you'll be keeping with you, I hope?" he asks and keeps his thumb over the pendant for a second longer before moving away. I nod and press my lips together in a sad smile. How odd of the king to notice such a simple necklace as this.

We wait.

Golden-brown leaves drag across the ground with the cold winter breeze. Snow will fall soon, perhaps later tonight even, which will make traveling across the wastelands more unbearable. I stifle the miserable groan that attempts to leave my lips.

King Borlin stiffens at my side. I don't need to look up to know why, but I do anyway.

My stomach curls into itself at the sight of the army walking straight through our gates. Their armor as white as snow, tinted gold in some areas with the blood of our own. Demigods are coveted by all for our gilded blood, but to us it is just that, our life force.

The demon at the head of the army is wearing a crimson cape, half of which is pulled over one of his shoulders and affixed to his neck guard with a medallion. The back is splayed out behind him like a wave of blood. It's stark against everything around him. Of all the demons, he alone stands out. Even the air around him is ominous.

It's him.

The Blood Knight.

Chills erupt over my skin, and I have to force my eyes back down to my feet. *Why is* he *here?*

My fellow demigods must be experiencing the same dread, because other than the approaching army's clanking armor, it's deathly silent. I secure my hand on the hilt of my sword. One can never be too trusting of the demons. There's still a chance they could be after the king's head for what he did.

No one so much as whispers. My nerves dance with anxiety up until the distinct scent of smoke and crisp alderwood washes over my senses and the loud metal clanking of armor comes to a halt. The Blood Knight dismounts from the largest black stallion I've ever seen. It whinnies as my eyes scour over the beast.

Gods, even the horses from Devicit are enormous.

Then the Blood Knight approaches us on foot. Every cell

in my body ignites as if his presence alone is enough to be my undoing.

The demons behind him are shadowed by his size, even though every single one of them is taller than me. His ivory helmet is sharp and smoothed at every angle. The jaw latch is held together with a gilded bolt on each side, and a gold metal wreath halos his head. If I didn't know better, I would think he was one of the gods himself.

My eyes lower to the crystal sword sheathed at his side. I know its power all too well. The sword of the Blood Knight can cut through the bones of a forest spirit—a creature all metal blades are useless against. It certainly had no trouble slaying me time and time again.

I clench my hands into tight fists and try to keep my fear in check. Some say demons can smell fear like wolves do prey.

King Borlin extends his hand to the knight as a gesture of goodwill, but the knight only turns his head to me. The muscles in my jaw flex. *Don't look at him. He doesn't know who you are*, I reassure myself. I'm the only one who remembers the time loops.

"*You.*" The Blood Knight's voice is cold, and it draws a gasp from the king's guards that he'd ignore the hand of royalty and speak with a knight such as me instead. "I've watched you slaughter many of my comrades, little godling. I watched you rain ruin upon the innocent villagers of Thornhall, burn cottages and forests to the ground, take and take and take...

Now you will know what it is to suffer at my hand. I swear to you it will be far worse than a vile being such as yourself can fathom." His voice is thunderous as he lowers to my level.

My stomach falls into a pit of despair as I fight the urge to unsheathe the sword at my hip to protect myself from him. His voice alone is as frigid as ice and makes every hair on the back of my neck stand. Any hope I had of a swift death is cast to the wayside.

This was a stupid idea, maybe I should try going for his weapon and get him to kill me. Then I can start the loop over and not endure whatever it is he's promising.

No, I chide myself. Peace is my goal. The protection of my friends and the people of my kingdom.

End the senseless war.

It takes everything in me to lower my chin and not respond to him. That only seems to make him angrier. He's about to reach out and grab me by the shoulder, but King Borlin clears his throat.

"Duke Lornhelm, do you accept the daughter of Venus as a peace offering between our kingdoms?" the king asks with a booming voice for all to hear. Civilians have already begun to crowd the side streets, and many more peer from their windows.

Wait, Duke Lornhelm?

My eyes slowly drag over the Blood Knight. *He's* the duke? My heart falters, and I have to steady my knees to remain standing upright.

The knight bides his time, taking in the king's words, almost as if he's considering turning down the accepted agreement and slaying us all here and now. But then he finally lets out a long, weary sigh as he clutches his armored hands at his sides tightly.

"Yes, King Borlin of Alzhor. I accept the offering and will send our king's declaration of peace between kingdoms upon our safe arrival into Devicit. Any pursuers will be slaughtered, but we will allow your witness to travel with us as you requested." He says the last part with skepticism in his tone. I don't blame him for being careful, not after what the king did last time.

King Borlin nods and extends his hand once more.

The knight doesn't move for a few seconds. Then he carefully lifts his helmet and sets it under his arm before extending the other to shake the king's hand.

Time all but stops, and my heart twists on its axis.

How have I never seen the Blood Knight's face in all the times he's slain me?

A breeze gusts through us and blows onyx strands of hair over his forehead. His brows are prominent and dark, a stark contrast to his fiery amber eyes. They look like the jewels the royal family wears. Ears pointed and pierced with four rings of gold. The cut of his jaw is striking. A scar that looks like a series of *x*'s runs up his left cheek groove, and his straight nose is just as sharp as someone I met only a week ago.

Kalel?

My lips part, but no words come to me. His eyes narrow with thought as he continues to converse with the king. My ears only pick up on the deep muffling of his voice. *He told me he was an apothecary.* Bile rises in my throat at the revelation that I sat and had a meal with the harbinger of death. If I'd known he was the commander *and* duke of Devicit, I would've killed him on the spot.

Well, I would've tried to.

Part of me hopes he won't remember me from the forest, but another part of me hopes that he will. Would he take a sliver of mercy on me, knowing that I'm not as evil as he makes me sound? Or maybe I am evil and this is divine punishment.

How can a demon as merciless as him be so handsome and lovely? Demigods are the only beings to hold such beauty. Never a demon. It's all I've ever known to be true.

I thought as much when I first met him, but there's something about the way his pupils are dilated out and the heaviness to his breath that rattles me now. Was he really the one to kill me in each of my loops? The thought is unsettling.

"The deal is complete. You have safe passage to the edge of the holy lands. May the sparrows be with you." King Borlin says the latter for me. The grimness set in his jaw hits deep into my bones.

It has been years since I've heard anyone mention the sparrows. We stopped saying it when they too abandoned us.

The little birds use to protect us with their warnings and bring us food while on the battlefield. They became a symbol of hope for us. A phrase to wish someone good luck.

May the sparrows be with you. A small smile pulls at the corners of my lips. Perhaps they will return one day. Once peace has been restored to us.

Kalel shifts his attention back to me. His presence is so daunting that it makes my stomach churn. "I need to verify that she truly is a daughter of Venus first. Please escort us to a private room, King Borlin."

My lips part, and an audible gasp escapes the king's mouth.

"How do you verify such a thing?" The king sounds skeptical, borderline mortified.

Kalel doesn't let his hollow eyes leave me. I half wonder if he can see my face beneath the helmet, but the lack of shock that he's expressed proves that he doesn't. Surely, he'd be as surprised to see me as I am him, right?

"There is a mark of fertility on the maidens born of Venus. How else would anyone know?" Kalel has an arrogant, impatient tone.

I have a mark? My throat bobs. *I* didn't even know that.

It's not exactly surprising. The demigods training to be knights don't get a heavy education. That's for the scholars or high royals. But it seems that even the king didn't know this.

Why don't we know more about Venus? I press my lips together at the oddness of it.

King Borlin gnashes his teeth and lifts his brows at Kalel's rudeness but only motions his open hand for us to follow his right-hand guard, Hans. He's the guard that the king decided to send as the witness to the marriage in Devicit. Apparently, he's only allowed to travel with the captive demigods that the demons currently have in an enclosed cart. They will be freed once the marriage commences.

I trail behind Hans while Kalel walks mere inches behind me. It makes my blood run cold with him so close to me and out of sight. All I can remember is the cruelness of his blade. Over and over again. It's completely opposite to the kindness that we shared in Florum Forest. *Gods, I don't want to take off my helmet.*

We're led to one of the kingdom's guest rooms on the first level. It's a small, simple room that is normally used for royal guests when they need to freshen up before dinners or meetings.

I step in first, taking in the room with wide eyes. It's the first time I've seen it myself. The walls are adorned in molding that wraps around large paintings. The room's aesthetic is warm-toned and dimly lit with wall sconces. A single cream-colored bed is set in the center of the room, the frame made of a wide, dark oakwood with curtains on the ends.

It's quite lovely and takes me by surprise. Compared to where I've been sleeping, this room is fit for a king.

I don't have long to gawk as Kalel steps in behind me and

shuts the door. He drags his gloved hand down his jaw like he's utterly sick of me already. He's made it perfectly clear that there's nothing more he desires than to kill me.

"Remove your helmet and trousers, you may keep your undergarments on," he says gruffly. A thick vein runs up the side of his neck, catching my attention.

My helmet? A rush of dread beats through my veins.

"Don't keep me waiting, I'm already holding myself back from just killing you, little godling," he says louder, and it makes me tremble.

I quickly unlatch my armor below the waist and tug down my trousers as he commanded. He refuses to look at me, and it makes me feel only a smidge better. Maybe he won't look at my face.

"Helmet too."

I swallow and carefully take my helmet off. My silver hair slips over my shoulders. It's easily the longest few seconds of my life. I feel completely exposed to the world with no armor between my skin and him.

He's going to recognize me...and I don't know why that matters to me so much. If only I didn't meet him in the forest last week. Why was he even there, in that specific spot? A place that should only have meaning to me.

I set the helmet on the bed and sit down on the edge.

Kalel's eyes are still focused on the paintings of gods when he lets out a deep breath and drags his hand through his dark hair with reluctance. I don't think he wants to do this either.

My lower lip is trapped between my teeth as I wait for him to look at me.

"What is your na—" He cuts himself off as he finally turns and stares at me. He takes me in, jaw slacking and eyes widening with recognition.

For a moment, his amber eyes aren't cold and hard like they were a second ago. His facade breaks, and the torment in his features is evident. A pained frown that tells me what he has in store for me truly is as terrible as he said and that perhaps he wishes it was any other demigod but me sitting here before him.

Wishful thinking.

He wastes no time blinking away the shock and resuming his cold expression.

"Alira." He says my name without a hint of the kind demon I met several days ago.

"Kalel." I echo his callous front.

His eyes dull as he approaches me and lowers to his knees. His alderwood scent washes over me. I can't help but notice how soft his hair looks this close. My pulse leaps as his cold hands brush the tender skin of my inner thighs.

Please find the mark quickly. I swallow the knot in my throat.

Contrary to his expression and intimidating appearance,

he touches me with gentle hands. Searching respectfully and stopping once he spots it.

"It's here," he says so quietly that it almost sounds like disappointment. "You really are the daughter of Venus."

My heart hammers in my chest. I was sure of it, but hearing it confirmed only makes it more real. I let my eyes move down to where his thumb is set to the notch of my thigh that leads to my core. He's an inch away from my center. I silently thank the gods that he let me keep my undergarments on.

Kalel keeps his hand on me for a moment longer before retreating without another word. He stares at me coldly. "Get dressed. We're leaving immediately."

I do as he says and quickly redress. He moves to open the door but stops abruptly before turning the knob.

Kalel's amber eyes find me over his shoulder, and the softness in them flickers as the muscles in his jaw feather.

"I wish it wasn't you, little godling."

His words travel through me as we exit the castle.

I don't hear the song of the gods and hymns for safe passage as my kingdom sends me off with the army of demons. I don't hear them thanking me for sacrificing myself for them.

I only agonize in the fear that Kalel's words instilled in my heart.

CHAPTER 4

ALIRA

Once we reach the edge of the kingdom's gates, Kalel finally whistles for his horse. One of his soldiers guides the black stallion to us. He made me walk through the streets beside him so that every demigod could watch as their king surrendered to the demons. There would be no tricks this time—he's ensuring it.

"Hop on," Kalel orders mundanely.

I assess the horse. It's far too tall for me to climb up, but I try anyway. My hands snag on the horse's saddle as I attempt to jump and pull myself up. I fail miserably. Armor is exceedingly heavy, and this horse is enormous.

The second my ass hits the ground, a roar of laughter rolls through the army, and a hot blush races over my cheeks.

I force myself back to my feet quickly and prepare to try again when Kalel's hands come around my waist and he hoists me up. It's more like him tossing a bag of flour carelessly though.

Kalel jumps up behind me and secures a strong arm around my center. My cheeks flush at how tightly he holds me against his chest. Every fiber of my being is begging to get away from him, but I don't dare do anything that might make him more displeased than he already is.

He sets a slow pace for the rest of his forces as we ride toward the demon's camp. It's a few miles over the ridge lining the kingdom. The sun set an hour ago, and the deep chill of the night has already begun to invade my bones.

Once the camp is in view, he signals to his second-in-command and pulls his horse over to a tent farther away from the rest. My stomach drops. No amount of shivering or cold air burning my nose takes my mind off the dread of this situation.

Kalel dismounts, then offers me his hand with a cold expression. I take it carefully and hop down from the giant horse's back. He nods toward the tent, watching me with wariness and disdain in his gaze.

I wrap my arms around my body and do as he says, heading into the tent. It's empty, for the most part. Only a small pallet bed in one corner and a makeshift desk of crates with letters, newspapers, and maps neatly piled on top. I'm guessing they only set it up for the night.

Kalel enters behind me a few minutes later and ties the flaps together. He hasn't spoken once since we started the ride here, so it startles me when he finally talks. "All that is left is for you to make the sacred oath, and then you may rest."

My throat is tight with dread. The sacred oath leaves a mark on the bonded, and it requires a high degree of soul essence to perform. *I'll be out for days.* I clench my hands at my sides. It's taxing on our bodies—it puts demigods into a deep slumber after. I've never personally performed one, so there's no telling how long I'll be asleep. It's different for everyone depending on their parents and amount of soul essence.

The sacred oath is a power all beings with holy blood hold to make with another willing party. It's used when trust needs to be established. Both individuals must have the desire for the bond, or it won't work. It will tie his life to mine, so he can trust me not to try to kill him. If I die, he'll be fine, but I can't hurt him.

I wasn't expecting him to request an oath. It gives me a breath of hope that I might actually survive until tomorrow, finally breaking the time loop I've been trapped in.

Does he think I'll actually try to kill him in his sleep? The darkness in his gaze suggests as much.

"We don't have all night," he grunts passively.

I clear my throat. "I bind my heart to you, Duke Lornhelm."

As the words leave my lips, a bright light from the holy pact shines between us. Surprise consumes me as an immense amount of power is siphoned from my chest. My skin burns at the center of my collarbones, and the flinch Kalel gives as he looks down at his concealed chest tells me he feels it too. The person receiving the sacred oath gets a mark of faith matching that of the granter.

The light fades, and as it does, my vision goes with it.

– —— –

Low, deep murmuring stirs me awake.

My head is spinning, and my body aches from head to toe. I groan as I try to sit up but fail. Did I pass out? Where am I?

I open my eyes slowly, lids heavy with exhaustion. I'm in a spacious tent, the fabric of which is dressed in the crimson and beige colors of the Devicitian Kingdom. Their ribbons and propaganda hang from the metal framing.

I don't recall seeing these before I lost consciousness. How long has it been?

I let my hands drift down my body, over my breasts and stomach, then my thighs. *I'm still alive.* Excitement draws a loose smile to my lips.

The pain doesn't keep me from sitting up this time. I wince, and my hand instinctively lifts to my sternum where the oath mark lies. A loose-fitting canvas shirt hangs past my waist and dips down to my collarbones. My armor and clothes from Alzhor are nowhere to be found. Who undressed me?

Although I suppose being dressed by strangers is the last thing I should be concerned about. I press my palm to my forehead and try to quell the pounding headache that relentlessly pulses.

"You're awake."

My spine stiffens at the sound of Kalel's voice.

Turning to look behind me, I find Kalel sitting relaxed in a chair. He's no longer wearing his war armor, and somehow, he's still equally as intimidating now that I know what he truly is. *Apothecary, my ass.* I want to call him out on lying, but I keep my mouth shut.

His hair is swept to the side, a strand falling over his forehead perfectly. His cold golden eyes observe me with an equal amount of curiosity to what I find myself experiencing for him.

The black long-sleeved shirt he wears is half unbuttoned, revealing the lovely olive tone of his muscular chest. I'm convinced this man is a god, one of deceit and suffering, but a god nonetheless. How else could one explain away this demon's beauty? His near-seven-foot stature. The oath mark is brandished on his sternum like it is mine, a golden circle with a single gilded line vertically cutting through it.

He tilts his head, and my attention catches on his pointed

ears. Four gilded loop earrings hang from them, making him look like a true duke.

He notices my awe and bares fangs that dip below his top lip. I wouldn't exactly call it a smirk, maybe a warning to remind me that he loathes me.

I turn my face away from him, bringing my focus down to the rest of my body. A gold ring that looks like a small crown has been placed over my ring finger. My hair covers most of my chest, silver and white locks curl in big waves naturally down to my waist. I've been washed in a scent that matches Kalel's.

"Why do I smell like you?" I sound as mortified as I feel. "Where are my clothes?"

Kalel doesn't blink. "Unless you want to be torn to shreds by the demons outside this tent and the ones when we reach Devicit, then you will carry my scent. Demigods smell like death and rot. We can detect the odor of all those you've slain, and, Alira, my little godling, you smell worse than a fresh graveyard. I'll need to scent you frequently to get the tarnish off your skin and to make sure everyone knows you belong to me."

I flinch. I didn't know that was something that stayed with us... I also wasn't aware that demons had such a strong sense of smell. *What else can they smell?* My chest twists with worry.

"*Scent* me?" My voice is mortified.

Kalel grins. "Yes, I prefer it while you sleep. You don't struggle at all."

Oh my gods, what did he do? I blink away the fear that moves through my chest. "How long was I asleep?"

He shifts in his chair. "One day. We are moving out to return to Devicit tomorrow." His voice remains even, although there's a heavy hatred in his gaze. Whatever version of him I met in Florum is not the version I get to converse with now. It puts a weight on my heart, because I liked him. I changed my path because of him.

"Look at me, Alira."

I shift in the bed of blankets I'm sitting in like a pet and face him. My expression absent of emotion.

His lips curve, clearly pleased that I'm obeying him so easily. I don't wish to fight my fate, and struggling will only make matters worse. If this is penance for what I did in Thornhall, then so be it. I'm so tired of fighting.

"Come here."

My knees tremble as I force myself to stand, gritting my teeth against the pain that claws at my insides. Placing the sacred oath took a toll on my body. I've never used so much soul essence at once before. His brows perk up with satisfaction at my inability to conceal my discomfort.

I stand on uneasy legs before him.

"Pity, you look as if you're in a great deal of pain." He unbuttons his shirt more until he's revealing bruises he has from a recent battle. "Care to tell me why the royal family would have you serving as a knight?"

I don't respond, because I don't know what he means. *What, because I'm a daughter of Venus?* He reads my expression just fine.

"You're a demigod from one of the highest bloodlines. Why have they treated you this way?" He taps his finger on the armrest of his chair like I'm testing his patience.

I shake my head. "Well, it's not like I told anyone until I had to." I rub my arm nervously and avoid looking at his face. "I would've been sold off to a royal family the moment I came of age."

His brows twitch, but he keeps his expression vexed. He stands and leans in closer to me, curling a lock of my silver hair with his finger. "You know, you really are such a pretty little thing for being so vile. Far more broken and ignorant than I thought you'd be. Tell me, have you heard of me?"

Broken? My brows knit with disagreement. He has no idea what I've been through.

"Of course I've heard of you. You are the most revered knight in all of Faultore." I fist my hands at my sides. It feels unfair that I've known him far longer. Perhaps it's why I'm so pliant to him. I know what the end of his sword would do to me. "You are the Blood Knight." All the demigods this man has killed and taken prisoner, likely to feast on, and here I am as his soon-to-be bride. How could I *not* know who he is?

"That's right, and you're the knight that led the raid on Thornhall." He pauses before looking at me like I've let him down. I certainly feel like I have. I've regretted that day since the moment I led my troops down into the valley and chased down fleeing families. His voice shakes me back to the present. "Why didn't you tell me who you really were when we met that night?" Kalel lets his hand brush across the top of my shoulder, making me shudder.

"Why didn't *I* tell you? You told me you were an *apothecary*. And why did I have to tell you if you could just smell it on me anyway?" I scowl at him as he appraises my lips.

He glowers at my tone and shakes his head. "I wasn't lying to you. I am an apothecary." He pauses to consider his words before lifting his eyes back to mine. "I knew you were there but not that you led it. Not until I saw your armor." His gaze narrows with anger.

My lips press firmly into a line, and I choose to ignore his latter remark. "An apothecary when you aren't cutting heads off?"

A flicker of emotion passes through his eyes before he hardens them. "You lied about being in Thornhall. I saw you with my own two eyes in your ebony armor. It was practically red by the time I arrived, and you were already out of reach." His fists clench, and the muscles in his jaw feather. "I wish I had arrived five minutes sooner. Then you'd be dead and none of this would be happening."

My heart dips at his harsh words. I bite my lower lip to keep the swell of emotions in control.

"I *never* wanted to be there." My admittance sounds pathetic. It doesn't change the fact of what I did. I know that.

"But you were," Kalel says coldly. I only nod with a trembling lip.

He looks down at me, and I have to force my gaze to meet his. He towers above me, making it uncomfortable to lock eyes with him. He runs his freezing hand down my neck. Goose bumps prickle across my arms, and my jaw flexes.

His silence is something I'm going to have to get used to. I clear my throat and ask, "Why am I marrying you out of all the high dukes? You loathe demigods more than any of your kind. I'll happily switch to someone else."

Someone who won't fantasize about killing me every other second.

"It wasn't up to me, if that's what you're assuming, but it serves a purpose." He leans forward and lets his mouth touch the skin behind my ear as if he actually enjoys the way I smell. He fists a handful of hair as he tilts my head back gently. "Do you know why they call me the Blood Knight?"

His lips coast down my throat, drawing an unsteady breath from my lungs. "I've only heard rumors as to why."

He dips down and presses his lips on my collarbone. Those sharp teeth of his graze my skin, causing me to inhale sharply. Chills race across my skin, and my knees threaten to buckle on me.

"They call me the Blood Knight because I do not have my

own to live off of. As you can see"—he steps back and motions to his stomach, where bruises are all but black underneath his skin—"I bleed darkness, cold and unsustaining, unlike yours."

My lips tremble despite my best efforts to keep them still. Demons are truly terrifying. It's one thing to read about a devourer in an old tome compared to seeing it in person. "And what exactly are you, Kalel?" I already know. But I want to hear him say it anyway.

His cruel grin is as frigid as his hands.

"Partaker of demigods—a devourer."

My heart beats with terror. Is that why he keeps so many half-god prisoners? I thought he was using them as hostages in Devicit, but now I'm unsure. Are we only food to them? Our blood is sacred; it is a mortal sin to drink it. Only a demon could survive such a violation of the holy laws set by Jupiter.

"Monster," I mutter with a heavy glare, tears welling in my eyes.

"You aren't wrong. Devourers' appetites are insatiable, and it's the reason why the demigods rose together to slaughter all demons in the first place," he murmurs as he draws his tongue over his lip, a deep hunger moving through his expression.

Perhaps he really is the last one.

His icy gaze trails down my chest and back to my throat.

"Are you ready to do what it takes to be the bride of the Blood Knight, Alira?" I'm not sure why he's asking, he's already promised to make me suffer. He knows I will do whatever it takes.

"If it's what will stop the war...then yes."

His frown seems genuine. "If it will stop the war, or if it will keep *you* alive? Don't think that I've forgotten your reason for being in Florum Forest that day. You were going to abandon your kingdom. Why did you go back?"

I hate how well he can see through me. "I went back because of what you said." He raises a brow as if he can't remember. "That I didn't try everything to change my fate."

I'm not going to flat out say *it worked because I'm still here.* He could never fully understand.

"Did my advice help?" he asks in a low, condescending voice as he closes the space between us.

"In a way."

I'm still alive, aren't I?

He dips his head until his lips are brushing against my ear. Stroking his tongue up the side of my neck, breath hot against my skin. I shudder and am horrified at the heat that warms my lower abdomen from his touch.

"Good," he whispers before burying his teeth in the flesh of my neck. My entire body slackens at the intrusion, and a small whimper escapes my lips. He catches me around the waist, holding me close to his chest as we sink to the ground together.

My eyes trace the roof of the tent, wide and unfamiliar with the sensation of anything feeding from my veins. It burns like hellfire ravaging through my bloodstream and spreading like venom. The pain is unbearable. I can't hold back the small sounds of misery that slip each time he takes a deep pull.

He's consuming me.

He seems to relish in those small sounds of suffering, taking deeper, longer gulps of my gilded blood until it's difficult to keep my eyes open.

Kalel withdraws his fangs slowly, and even that hurts. I hazily place my palm on my neck and blink slowly at the tenderness of it. I feel drunk—on the cusp of passing out.

"It shouldn't hurt as bad next time. The venom from my bite should help you build immunity to the pain." He almost sounds apologetic. I could be imagining things though, considering I can't even lift my head.

"It w-wasn't so bad." My voice wavers as the hand I had pressed against my neck goes limp and falls to the ground. He looks at me with a callous expression, firming his jaw.

He stands and returns to his desk. "Get some rest. We have a long way to go to get back to Devicit, and it's the dead of winter through the wastelands, so you'll need your strength."

I remain where I am in the blankets on the floor, unmoving, staring at the tent's ceiling and thinking of places far away from here. A weak smile returns to my lips with one hopeful thought.

I outlived the cursed day.

CHAPTER 5

ALIRA

Birds fly across the orange and pink morning sky. Free and without concern for the bustling campsite below them.

I pull the blanket I've been given in lieu of a coat around my shoulders tightly as I sit by the small fire in front of Kalel's tent, mulling over how cruel it was to take my leathers and armor. They discarded them like they weren't the last part of my home I could take with me. Instead, I'm wearing a thin, tattered black sweater. It's an upgrade from the canvas shirt, but I'm still not happy about it. Part of me believes that it's to shame what I am, another part believes that it's to make it harder for me to escape with weather this severe.

No one could survive this cold with only a thin sweater and without proper boots.

Several of Kalel's guards are standing around me to ensure I don't try anything while the rest of camp is packing up and getting ready to travel back to Devicitian territory. The only reason I'm not in shackles is because I'm Kalel's bride, and he knows how easy it would be to hunt me down.

They know I volunteered to be here, right? I set my glare to the men standing above me. Why do they think I'd try to leave, knowing what I signed up for?

"What's wrong with her? She's awfully calm, don't you think?" one of them asks another.

"Demigods don't have emotions, dumbass," the other replies, and they chuckle among themselves. *Funny.* They say the same things we do about them. A frown tugs on my lips, and I stare into the campfire flames.

My entire body still aches from the essence required to place the sacred oath, but my neck throbs worst of all. I rub the bite mark and hope that he's right and it doesn't cause as much pain next time.

A Devicitian healer made a trip to Kalel's tent late in the evening, healing the wound a little before I fell asleep. Kalel was stern on him only being able to heal me enough so that I could rest. *Wouldn't want me to be too comfortable, would he?* I glower at the memory. I caught a small glimpse of the healer, just enough to know he was beautiful like

Kalel, only with fawn hair and gentle eyes that took me in with sympathy.

It's so strange—how alike they are to the demigods, that is.

I take a deep breath and trace the embers that flicker out of the campfire and into the cold air. Someone sits on the log next to me, but I don't pay them any attention.

"Are you really the knight that led the attack on Thornhall?" a soft voice asks me, not of violation but pure curiosity.

I turn and find a lovely young woman sitting beside me. She's dressed in light gray Devicitian armor, her helmet is tucked beneath her arm. Her eyes are red like rubies, and she has golden scales where her hairline fades into waves of rich brown locks, falling past her shoulders. A demon of the sea.

When I don't respond, she smiles bleakly with pity. Her eyes linger around my neck where Kalel bit me.

"So you are… War is an awful thing, isn't it?" She speaks sincerely. I stare at her, trying to figure out if she's attempting to bait me into something.

The demons claim that it is the half-gods that have no emotions, but my entire life I've learned nothing except how ruthless they are to all but their own.

"Your king is a terribly cruel man," she mutters, looking across the campsite at Kalel as he orders his men around. They pack tents onto carts behind ebony horses two times the size of the ones we have in Alzhor.

Kalel's cold amber eyes shift toward us. I quickly avert my

gaze. He has thoroughly instilled fear inside me. From all the times he's killed me so effortlessly down to the blood he stole from me last night. The pain his fangs promise is unlike any blade, and I don't want to know what they would feel like if he was angry.

The woman seems to notice my dread.

"You would've been better off dead," she sighs and gently moves her hand over mine. I flinch at the warmth of it. I'm already so familiar with the cold, bloodless hands of Kalel that I almost want to clutch onto her. "You shouldn't have revealed that you're the daughter of Venus." Her voice is tender and sown with sorrow.

I raise my eyes to hers, defiance burning inside my chest. She has no idea what I've been through. None of them do. I've exhausted all options, and yet revealing what I really am is the worst thing to them? Laughable.

"My life is a small price to pay in exchange for ending the war between our kingdoms," I say with a tight frown.

Concern threads through her eyes as she considers me. "You're telling me that you aren't worried at all about the horrors King Achill will rain upon the surrounding nations once he has holy blood in his forces? You don't think he'll go after your beloved kingdom eventually?" Her eyes lower. I can't tell if she's actually worried or just throwing questions I hadn't thought of yet out there.

"Kalel doesn't seem too keen on breeding with me, so I'd

say we're spared from that reality," I say with no confidence at all. He loathes me, I can't imagine him wanting to… I swallow and shut my eyes at the lewd thoughts of him ravaging my body. It's disturbing how every muscle in my stomach reacts to those images that flash through my mind. He's so much bigger than me. His large fingers going inside would—*gods, stop.* I shake my head.

Her eyes only grow wider as she studies me, then they fill with pity before she forces a sad smile. "I'm Tessa, by the way, one of Kalel's lieutenants, so don't be afraid to let me know if you need anything."

I don't like the way she refused to comment on what I said. Does that mean she knows something and isn't telling me? Well, of course, I guess that's a given. Why would she share anything with me? I'm basically his prisoner. Blood bag, more accurately.

I don't trust her. *Never trust a demon.* That's rule one, but of all of them, I prefer her presence over any of the others.

"How should I address you?" I ask, lowering my eyes back to the smoldering fire that's being put out with heavy snowflakes. It's going to take time to get to know their ways of life and social standings. I should at least try to make a genuine effort.

"Lieutenant or just Tessa is fine." She doesn't wait for me to respond before standing and moving to the far end of camp. I observe silently as she helps Kalel order the knights to prepare their horses for travel and to put out campfires. I remain sitting, cold and shivering under this godsforsaken blanket, until everything is demolished and packed up.

Kalel approaches me with unreadable eyes. He appears irritated to be stuck with me. He's dressed in his full suit of armor, minus the helmet. My eyes catch on his pointed ears again. I'm not sure I'll ever get used to being this close to a demon. Especially one that bites.

"You're with me," he says, implying that he's ready to go.

I stand with the blanket still wrapped around my shoulders since I haven't been given anything else. I'm too proud to ask for anything warmer, especially since he had already given me that dragon pelt cloak in the woods. I wish I had brought it back to the kingdom so I had the chance to bring it with me, but I knew if anyone saw the rare cloak, they'd ask questions. Which is why I left it in a hollow tree by my campsite in Florum. Although I'm not sure Kalel would've let me keep it even if I somehow had managed to bring it with me.

Gods know he enjoys watching me suffer.

I would do immeasurable things to not be me.

Kalel leads me to his tall black stallion at the head of the group. He mounts it easily, throwing his leg gracefully over the side and sitting stoically astride the beast. He stares down at me indifferently for a few moments but offers me his hand when he decides there's no way I can attempt to climb this horse again, especially with a blanket wrapped around me like a shawl.

I take his cold, calloused hand, and he lifts me up as though I weigh nothing. His arms wrap around my waist as he takes the reins and whistles for his army to follow. I've never felt so small in my entire life, physically and spiritually. I was pretty out of my mind the other day with everything that was unraveling, but today my head is clear. And I fear I've made a horrible mistake. Maybe I should've tried testing my chances more on the battlefield with him.

— —— –

My ass hurts before midday.

I've ridden plenty of horses, but not for extended periods of time without proper gear, and having a wall of metal and muscle at my back doesn't help at all.

Riding horses is a complicated way of travel, especially in winter and with unfamiliar company. I shiver beneath the blanket as the cold northern winds flow through the fabric. Kalel has already sighed heavily several times at my reaction to the frigid temperatures. How could he possibly understand what it's like to be cold when he's incapable of feeling it? Demons rarely have vulnerabilities to temperature, according to him. I scowl at the winter wastelands ahead and try to stop shivering to no avail.

His body is like a block of ice at my back, offering no warmth or comfort.

"Tessa," he calls to his lieutenant. She reins her horse to his side in a matter of moments. "Let's take a break to feed the horses and the troops." She nods and whistles in a strange tune that the others seem to understand means to take a break.

Kalel doesn't stop though. His horse keeps heading straight, adjacent with the forest wall to our right until he locates a small red flag hanging from a long outward-stretched branch. He pulls on the reins, and the horse turns into the forest, following a frozen path made of stones to a small cottage tucked away in the woods.

It's modest. The walls are made of gray cobblestones. Hibernating vines cling to the sides of the exterior, framing the old, scuffed-up windows. The roof is made with two foot-thick hay slabs, and a small stone chimney juts out on the left side.

Kalel dismounts and plucks me from the saddle without a word. I keep my eyes lowered as he opens the cottage and steps inside. When I don't immediately follow him, he lets out a long, exasperated breath and runs his hand down his jaw. The darkness in his gaze doesn't falter as he watches me shiver beneath the blanket.

"*Come*," he demands.

I concede and step carefully into the cottage. It's dark and musky. The smell of an abandoned home—stale. I stand in the center of the small room and take it in. It's made up of only a kitchenette, small dining area, a fireplace, and a mussed bed in the corner. From the dust and cobwebs that cling to the surfaces, I'd bet that it's been a long time since someone's lived here. Likely flushed out from the war.

We're completely alone. Why did we stray from the group? My heart sinks with all the thoughts running through my mind.

Kalel lights the fireplace with some matches he pulled from his satchel, then orders me to sit on the floor in front of it.

I do as he says and pull my legs close to my body. My muscles are frail from a combination of essence exhaustion, my reluctance to eat, and being drained of blood. To top it off, I'm freezing too, but it's better than starting over another time loop.

I stare into the flames as Kalel rustles around the cottage collecting things. There's not much to look through, only a few cabinets in the tiny kitchen and some dressers in the far corner.

At least the warmth from the flames is already seeping into me and thawing my bones. I let my eyes flutter closed.

What happens if I die now? Do I reset again? Or is this it? I'm no curse expert, but whatever the gods have planned must be going the way they finally want. Otherwise, I don't think I'd be here.

Why me though? I sullen as I open my eyes and watch the flames dance.

Kalel reaches down and steals the blanket away from me.

I don't complain or raise my chin to look at him. I only hold my arms closer and try to absorb as much warmth as I can. A few moments pass before a heavier fur blanket falls over my shoulders. My eyes widen, and I glance up at him. He doesn't meet my gaze, instead he sets a pot he must've filled with water over the fire.

Is he…cooking? I observe as the revered Blood Knight, in his full suit of Devicitian armor, pulls a small bag of dried toadstools from his satchel and drops an assortment of them into the pot. He adds a few drops of oil and half a bottle of some sort of glittering purple liquid.

"You really are an apothecary, aren't you?" I offer him a small grin, only because it seemed so unlikely that he was honest with me that day. He's honest, I'll give him that.

He sits back on his haunches and gives me a side glance once he's done adding all the ingredients. "I told you I was, didn't I? This soup will help keep you warm for the remainder of the day. Foxflick and Barbosi are essence-rich and will replenish your energy." He actually talks to me like he's not ready to take his sword to my throat. He sounds gloomier and more lost in his thoughts than anything else.

My chest warms at the idea of him making me food just as much as it shifts with unease. He could poison me as easily as he could swing that sword. Or maybe he simply wanted to prove me wrong and show off his academic side. When it's just us, I can picture him so clearly as a man who prefers studying nature and the rules of the world. How did he become a knight of all things? Why not a full-time apothecary?

The thoughts bring sorrowful memories of things I didn't pursue either. I hate reminiscing on the past and lost opportunities. I am what I am. *I'm a knight.*

Neither of us speak for many moments. The crackling of the fire fills the emptiness of the cottage and our hearts.

When he finally talks, my shoulders tighten at the deepness of his voice. "Why don't you seem more upset about your situation, Alira?" Kalel asks, sounding genuinely curious.

I let my head rest on my shoulder as I look at him, studying the contours of his cheekbones. My body finally begins to warm, making me relax a bit more. "Should I cry instead?" I mutter mundanely. He only stares at me. Something stirs inside my chest at the idea of him watching me this closely. Cataloging my features as I'm doing to him. "It's better than dying, isn't it? You led your army to slaughter us all. I'm only a sacrifice. Many have suffered worse fates." My cryptic words hold more meaning than he could ever know. He'd probably love to know that he's successfully killed me many times.

He chuckles. "You would know better than most how ugly death is."

My eyes flash open, and I lift my head.

His brow raises slightly, intrigued at my reaction. "You've certainly ended enough lives to know," he says slowly, letting his attention fall back to the soup and stirring it. He pours a cup and hands it to me.

I take it without question and sip on the warm liquid. It tastes like herbal tea. It's delightfully pleasant. I close my eyes and drink the whole cup.

Kalel grunts. "I could've poisoned that, and it would've gone unnoticed. You didn't even check it. You're just gulping it down like you're starving. Have you not eaten anything yet today?"

The cup makes a sharp sound as I set it down on the stone hearth. I wipe my mouth with my sleeve and side-eye him. "If you wanted to kill me, you would've made it a public ordeal," I mutter. I haven't eaten much for a few days either. He's been keener on paying attention to that matter. I wonder if Tessa has been keeping him updated. It's hard to have an appetite when I know I'm only being fed because he needs me to be healthy if he plans on consuming my blood.

What I eat, he eats. *Ugh.*

"*Monster*," I curse under my breath. He flinches at my words.

He's so easy to upset it's almost ridiculous.

"Oh, little godling, you're right about that. I am a monster. Your worst nightmare. I'd kill you in your sleep if I wanted. I'd kill you while fucking your brains out if I so pleased." My cheeks flush, and I'm mortified at how his tone makes my thighs warm.

I glare at him and throw the blanket off my shoulders, making to stand and walk back outside. "Fuck you."

He catches my wrist and drags me down into his lap. "You need to warm up so we can be on our way. We aren't stopping again," he growls. "And I need to scent you again before we leave. You reek." He can say those words with as much volition as he wants, but it doesn't change the way that he buries his nose in the crook of my neck like he can't get enough of the way I smell.

I wriggle in his arms, but he leaves no slack. I don't want him to know how his hot tongue running up my throat puts a deep ache in my core. I've already begun to feel feverish around him. My heat cycle is bound to be in full effect soon, and the thought of it coming on when I'm so close to him makes me anxious.

"Stop moving, you'll only make this take longer."

My lower abdomen warms, and my undergarments are already wet from his foul mouth. *Please, if there are any gods left, don't let him know how my body lusts for him.*

Kalel stills, hands clamped down on my waist and thigh. He inhales hesitantly.

Oh. This is bad.

CHAPTER 6
KALEL

Do. Not. Fuck. The. Godling, I chide myself as her sweet scent nearly knocks me over.

She's so delicate in my arms, even when she struggles against my hold. I close my eyes and try to will away the blood flow that's been redirected to my cock, but the bulge inevitably grows under her ass, and she gasps when she feels it. Her scent thickens with excitement for it.

No. I'm not going to fuck her. I clench my jaw and bite down on my lower lip with the last remnants of my restraint. Well, maybe if I just don't knot her, it would be okay, wouldn't it?

Fuck.

I hate her so much, is that why I want to rut into her so badly? I want to make her scream in pain, but I'm not allowed to hurt her. Fucking her isn't hurting her, but it would fulfill that dark need I have building inside me. King Achill would have my head if he knew I bruised her precious little knees from knotting her before the ceremony.

As I'm hashing out my internal conflict over her, she starts grinding her hips over my crotch. The breath leaves my lungs and my throat dries. All my control goes to the wayside.

She whimpers out in pain and clutches her stomach.

Is she? No, please tell me she isn't going into heat. My cheeks warm, and the veins in my hands are protruding.

I tamp down my monstrous urges and let my teeth sink into her neck instead. It's either feed and bring her body back to normal levels with my venom, or I'll end up breeding her in here for fucking hours.

She cries out as I suck down her golden blood. It tastes like the sweetest of apples. Rich with life and nectar. How can something as vile as her taste so ethereal?

I groan over her throat and readjust my grip on her. She's limp now, and the scent is finally fading. Alira lets out a relieved sigh—she must find me utterly repulsive. I wish she was as horrendous on the outside as she is on the inside. The lull in my rage and vengeance for her when she lifted her helmet pisses me off to no end.

I can't despise her less just because she's the most enchanting creature I've ever laid my eyes on, but the curve of her pouting lips begs to differ. The sorrow in her eyes is tangible, like violets dipped in salted tears. I crave her to no end.

Her blood spills down my lip and trickles over her breast. I release her neck and stroke my tongue over her soft flesh. She sucks in a breath and lets it out when I don't lick her chest more.

Fuck.

I want to bite her breast and flick her nipple with my tongue—make her whimper and writhe in my arms like a helpless little thing. I like that she's so weak to me. It makes the urge to fill her with my come overwhelming. I want her to suffer, but why do I also want her to see me? I want her to find comfort in my arms as much as I wish to bring tears to her weary eyes.

She will endure my pain, no matter how I yearn to comfort her. I've sworn to it.

Pluto almighty, let me bring her punishment no matter what spells her beauty casts upon me.

CHAPTER 7

ALIRA

Kalel wipes his lips and lets me go. My body is definitely warmed up now. I try to ignore the fact that I just had a flare-up and was grinding my hips on his cock like some lovesick succubus.

I just thank the gods that he doesn't bring any attention to it. I put it out of my mind as I rub my throat and wince at the slight pain that flashes at the touch. It will likely bruise.

Kalel's brows crease at the motion. "You make me out to be such a brutal man, you know that?"

"Brutal *demon*, and aren't you? You've spoken so much about how terrible I am. But what about you? The deaths on your hands outnumber mine, twenty to one," I grumble. Not that he'd understand my jab.

I expect him to get mad at my comment, but he remains silent, staring into the fire.

I've seen firsthand how he fights. How he *kills*. So why does the melancholy I find in his gaze make my heart ache so much? Perhaps it's because together we carry the weight of many souls. No one comes out of war unscathed.

Kalel remains silent for a long time before he slowly mutters, "I'd like to think I'm more than what I am on the battlefield." His voice is smooth and placid. A dark strand of hair falls over his forehead as he gives me a sidelong glance. "Are you only a knight? With the hundreds of lives at the end of your blade?"

It's been so long since I've actually been to the demon's territory, what with the loop I've been trapped in, but his words land in a place inside my heart I thought I killed long ago.

"Yes. I know nothing else." I tell him what I think he wants to hear.

He shakes his head slowly as he stands and moves to my back. My spine straightens as his thighs wrap around me on either side. His cold lips meet my shoulder, making my chest lurch. At least the fire is warm; I try to focus on the flames. They cast out the chill that had set into my bones—another kiss, this time on my neck.

I prepare myself for the sting of his fangs once more, but it doesn't come. Instead, I'm surprised by the weight of his chin on my shoulder.

"Are you warming?" he asks. The cruel edge his usual tone carries has lightened.

"Yes."

He remains behind me, holding me, relaxed with his chin on my shoulder. I don't bother telling him that his body offers no warmth. I'm sure he's aware of that fact.

Demons that don't feel the deep cold of the world, they'd never be able to warm others. It's almost sad if I think about it too long. He's rare among his kind too. I'm sure he had a lonely upbringing. I can relate to that—never really belonging somewhere entirely.

"What will happen once we reach Devicit?" I ask in a mere whisper.

He rolls his face so that his cheek is now pressed to my shoulder. I can feel his gaze. "There will be a peace agreement issued once we arrive safely, then the war ends. That's it. Then you will live in my mansion for the remainder of your days. Although you'll hear the demon-folk call it Lornhelm Palace."

A palace? Demons are oddly similar to the mortals in the way their societies are formed. If that's true, then they must have grand gardens and architecture. Balls and extravagant events.

Sometimes I wish the demigods would indulge in things like that. To enjoy a little of life. Most things in Alzhor are mundane and gray now. Although I've been told by the elders that there was a past when our kingdom flourished with all the societal niceties. A tale as old as time, everything was dulled when the gods left us. Even more so when the demigods' numbers dwindled.

I turn and look at Kalel. His hair is as dark as night—the fire's glow is absorbed into the shadows of it. And yet his eyes flicker like embers lost in the dead of winter.

"And then what? Will I be your prisoner until I die?" I imagine being locked in a dark room for the remainder of my life.

He brushes his hand through my hair, the silver luminescent strands reflecting the warm light of the fire. I try not to flinch at his touch, but his eyes catch the movement, narrowing before he pulls away. "That depends on you, little godling. If you try to escape, I'll have to place wards to keep you from leaving the kingdom, but I'd prefer not to do that."

"I'm free to roam the *kingdom*?" I raise a brow.

He nods. "You're not my prisoner, Alira. You are going to be my wife. Even if we don't like one another, I will respect your status as my equal." His voice lingers like smoke and moves through my chest. I didn't think he was capable of kindness. Not after realizing who and what I really am.

"Will we be expected to..." *Breed.* I can't even finish saying the words. He shifts uncomfortably at my back, knowing exactly what I'm asking.

"Yes, it's the only reason the king approved the peace offering. It's why you put yourself up as a sacrifice, is it not?" he says mundanely, but he sounds as displeased with the circumstances as I feel.

I shrink into myself more and let the numbness in my mind take over. He doesn't say any more either. He just breathes in a soothing rhythm.

We stay by the fire until the trembling in my limbs finally ceases. Kalel throws a bucket of water on the fire and tosses me the fur blanket. Then we're heading back to the group and resuming the horrid trek across the wastelands. The snow falls heavier now, making visibility extremely low.

By the time the sun sets, I'm frozen to the core again and my back aches. But my mind is the weariest of all, thinking about my future and if I'm willing to endure a life of retribution.

As soon as Kalel's tent is set up, I groggily go to the pile of blankets on the ground and collapse into the nest. I find a small fragment of solace in it—it reminds me of hiding when I was a child. The knights would often look for me and find me on the floor curled up in blankets. Someplace warm and hidden away from the world. The nostalgia of it soothes me.

Kalel's elite knights stand at the tent's entrance, speaking in low whispers until Kalel finally enters the tent, retiring for the night and dismissing them. I overheard them talking about their commander visiting the captive demigods and making sure they are accounted for properly. It doesn't sound like they get nearly as much leniency as I do, but I hold on to the idea that they will be freed after the ceremony takes place.

I watch him carefully as he moves about the tent. His hair is perfectly smoothed to the side, and his golden eyes remain empty as he looks through the reports on his desk for several minutes. When he finishes the first batch, he glances my way. It's dark in this corner of the tent, and I'm peering at him through slitted eyes, so I don't think he realizes I'm also observing him. He pauses for a few beats before returning to his pages.

There are a thousand thoughts in those burdened eyes. I find myself longing to know what they are. Why does he look so weary and melancholic all the time? Why doesn't he smile as easily as he did in Florum?

He spends the better part of half an hour reviewing his reports before stretching his arms over his head and standing. My hands curl into the blankets as he approaches me and kneels at my side.

This is the one part I don't think I'll ever get used to.

I slowly sit up and tilt my head for him, gathering my hair to one side so it's out of his way, assuming he wants to feed. He only had a few sips earlier today, so I'm sure that's what he wants.

He hesitates this time and is slower to bring his mouth to my flesh.

The bite doesn't hurt like it did earlier. I hardly notice the penetration this time, though he's also not being as brutal as he was in the cottage. A wave of exhaustion rolls through me, and a whimper flees my lips. He wraps his hand gently under my neck and guides me down to the blankets so I fall backward.

I can hear each draw of blood he takes from my neck. Each savored gulp as his Adam's apple bobs. My eyes fight to remain open as my blood is drained.

Kalel finishes, stroking his tongue over the wound until it's clean, then releases me.

I drowsily crawl into my blanket nest and curl into its comfort. My heavy eyes stay pinned on him when he doesn't leave right away.

"I need to scent you, I promise I'll be quick." He guides me into his lap, pressing a kiss on the side of my throat before stroking his tongue over it a few times. A rumbling purr rolls from his chest as he continues to lick me.

It's much more intimate this time. I writhe in his hold as my body instinctively responds to it. Heat pools in my lower stomach, and an ache throbs for him. *Gods.* Not again.

I swallow the anxiety building in my throat and try to ignore the way my muscles relax in submission to him.

Kalel notices and lets out a low growl as he moves to my wrists. He presses kisses on each before lapping at them with his tongue. My cheeks burn. I want to bury my face in the sheets, but all I can do is watch as this handsome demon marks his scent on me.

He licks his lips when he's finished and slowly stands.

"Are those the only spots?" I ask in a heady voice, hoping he can't see the blush across my cheeks.

His eyes widen, and he flexes his jaw. "No, but for now it's good enough. We'll need to build up to the rest when we get closer to Devicit. We will have more time to be...acquainted that way. Otherwise, the demon-folk will be more prone to try to kill you," he says in a gravelly tone.

I offer a nod and settle back into the sheets. He gets comfortable in his bed, licking his lips like he wants to keep feeding from me or scenting me.

We watch one another carefully, distrustfully. Borderline lustfully.

A demigod lusting for a demon. Gods, I must've fallen into madness.

CHAPTER 8

ALIRA

It's still dark when I'm woken by sharp, uneven breaths. Pained gasps and groans. I sit up instantly, alarmed. It sounds like someone's been badly hurt.

The tent is dark and cold. The *ticking* of snow against the tarp brings me into my surroundings. I'm still not used to waking up away from the barracks in Alzhor.

My eyes adjust in a few moments, and I realize the distressed sounds are coming from Kalel. Has he been wounded? I rise from my bedding and approach him carefully.

"Kalel?" I whisper, hesitant on getting too close to him.

He snaps his head in my direction, those sharp teeth

flashing at me. "Stay back, Alira," he rasps. His eyes are feverish, and another roll of pain has him clenching fistfuls of his sheets and exhaling heady breaths.

I freeze, something visceral hitting my nervous system and making my core flutter. I watch the rise and fall of his chest, the painful way his veins are protruding from his neck that make his eyes narrow as he tries to stay in control. *This is the same way I get when I'm in heat.* My chest tightens at the thought.

Is he in his heat cycle right now? Do demons have heat cycles?

Oh gods.

"What's wrong?" I ask again, trying to keep my panic contained.

He sits up, grinding his teeth and shaking the sweat clinging to his forehead as he bites out, "*Nothing*. Go back to sleep, godling."

My brows knit together. "I can't sleep with you making all this noise."

He groans and lets his body fall back into the sheets. His breaths are heavy, and he kicks the blankets to the floor as if they are burning his skin.

"Are you…in heat?" I ask awkwardly, cheeks on fire.

His eyes fill with horror, and he looks away sharply. "I won't tell you again, little godling. Go. To. Bed." Kalel's voice is gruff and on edge. Like he's on the verge of losing his self-control.

I don't listen to him. Maybe it's because I know what it feels like firsthand. It's agony, especially if you don't *deal* with it. It's almost like he's never experienced a heat before, because he's not handling this one well at all.

I take a step closer, realizing it was a mistake a second too late.

Kalel lunges at me, pinning my arms to the ground and breathing heavily over me. His eyes are filled with anguish, and sweat beads down his forehead. My eyes trace over his bared fangs.

"Alira, run. I don't think I can keep myself back much longer," he growls, forcing himself off and clutching his head like voices are shouting at him.

What do I do? I want to help him. He's in agony right now, and I can't explain the way that his groans are causing me heartache. Each one digging into my chest more and tugging at my sympathy for him.

"Let me help you," I whisper, reaching for his arm and trying to give him comfort.

Kalel jerks away from me and shoves my chest back. My shoulders hit the ground, and his hands are slamming on either side of my head in the next breath. "I don't want your fucking help. Leave!" he shouts an inch from my face. My eyes widen, and I stare at him with fear racing through my blood. His eyes narrow with disdain. "I want to destroy everything about you. I loathe every part of you. Why is it that I must be punished to be with a filthy creature such as yourself? You want me to fucking tear you open? You want me to fuck you raw until you can't walk straight?" His eyes are feral. Drool spills from his lip as he thirsts for hurting me.

My body trembles. Terror has never moved through me the way it does in this moment. Kalel pounds his fist against the ground again, and it sends a shiver straight up my spine.

"I won't tell you again. Get out, or I'll hurt you in ways that I've longed for. Ways that you'll never recover from," he threatens with a sinister snarl. Kalel's breaths are ragged, and his expression is hard, but there's so much agony in his amber eyes. It takes the sting out of his words. I still feel them, but they come from a place inside him that is bruised—a wound that has long since festered into rage.

I force my jaw to stop trembling and stare into his cruel gaze. My heart hammers in my chest, and I can't look away from his torn expression. He's in so much turmoil right now. Leaving him like this would be harsh. Even if he hates me. Even if it makes me hate him just the same.

I take a grounding breath and slowly lift my hand to his face. His hair is wet with sweat, and he's trembling like I am. Kalel's eyes are hooded by dark lashes as he gazes down at me, stunned by my soft touch after his outrage.

You don't scare me.

"If hurting me will soothe the pain that wreaks havoc in you, then hurt me, Kalel. You'll find there's not much left inside me that can be broken." My voice gets lost somewhere between us as his control fractures and he drops to his elbows so our noses are touching.

"How bold of you to assume I feel anything," he whispers against my lips. His alderwood scent slips into me like an intoxicating drug.

I shudder at the touch but hold his gaze steadily. "One has little to assume when your weary eyes give you away." His eyes rake over me, filled with desire and hunger.

"You foolish flower." Kalel leans into me more, pressing that taut body against mine as he strokes his tongue up the side of my neck. Tasting me. His cock is already hard and throbbing against my thigh. "You make me crazy, you know that?"

I let out a small gasp as he lifts my thin sweater and hooks a finger around the waistband of my pants. He pulls them off easily and stares down at my underwear for a beat. Kalel glances at me before moving the fabric to the side, clenching his jaw tightly and turning his head like he can't bear to think about what he's about to do.

He lowers his hand to my center and presses two fingers inside me. I firm my lips to stifle the moan that tries to escape as he stretches my core.

He groans and pushes his fingers all the way up to his knuckles. Kalel's head lowers to mine, lips against the shell of my ear. "I won't knot you. I only need enough relief to make this go away. I despise you, little godling. I hate everything that you've made me do." He removes his hand, soaking wet with my arousal for him. Then he lines up his engorged cock, and with one brutal thrust, he fills me up completely.

I wasn't prepared for his girth. The sudden intrusion and stretch tears a scream from my throat. Kalel's hand comes down hard over my mouth as he ruts into me hard and fast. My insides are being rearranged.

"You made me a monster. *I* hate you. I *hate* you. I hate *you*." He stares down into my watery eyes as he thrusts his hips into me like I'm nothing more than a rag doll. His face is contorted with hatred, but his eyes are filled with so much misery it hurts.

I wrap my arms around his neck and pull him down so our chests are pressed together. His cold heart beats erratically against mine, and his breaths stutter.

"I would take your suffering if I could." His hand falls away from my lips as I hug him tightly. He allows it for a moment, then seems to remember himself and pulls away.

Kalel's arms are veiny as he stares down at me. Furious tears fall from his tormented eyes and pelt my face. I catch myself admiring how beautiful he is when he lets his emotions bleed into the night. How he alone is a somber song only the nightingales know.

Kalel resumes his ruthless thrusts. His hand returns to my lips, keeping all my cries and screams muffled.

I hate me too, I try to tell him with my gaze, but only streams of tears fall from each of my temples. His jaw flexes, and he looks away sharply.

He pumps his hips into me a few more times before cussing and abruptly withdrawing from me. He pulls his pants back up, snags his coat, and storms out of the tent. My body feels broken and empty. My mind feels fractured like glass from our encounter.

I carefully rise, feeling bruised everywhere but especially at my core. He was merciless and rough just as he said he would be. I'm glad for it. It makes it easier to see him as the devil he is. It hurt, but at least it looks like it took the pain away from him.

I collapse in my nest. Thinking of death and how it would ease the suffering I've brought everyone in this world. Yet even death itself evades me.

He hates me.

I can't stop thinking about the way he looked at me with such loathing. The thoughts remain in my head until dawn.

Sleep eludes me, and Kalel doesn't return to the tent until the sun is hitting the tarp. The Devicitian knights are bustling around outside and preparing to leave.

I let the last few restful moments go and sit up to see if he's feeling better. His hair is smoothed back into perfection like it normally is, but his eyes still have that wild look.

"Here, wear these." He tosses a bundle of clothes at me. I unravel them and find a cream-colored, thicker long-sleeved garment, winter-grade pants, and a fire fox cloak. A frown pulls at my lips at his kind gesture, but I'm not about to decline it. The cold allows no mercy, and after yesterday's horrendous trek, I don't think I'd make it without the extra warmth today.

Is he just going to pretend last night didn't happen? I wonder as I lift the cloak to admire its quality.

A small necklace falls onto my lap. It's the one Korin gave me—I thought they'd thrown it away with my other belongings. I raise a brow and look up at Kalel. He's watching me closely and takes a deep breath when our eyes connect before forcing his gaze to the ground.

"I had it fit with a warding charm," he says gruffly, refusing to look at me.

My brows pull closer together. *He kept it for me.* I clutch the necklace, the only thing I have left of Alzhor, and try to make it look like it doesn't mean as much to me as it does.

I've heard of the warding charms demons can use, but I don't know what exactly they do. Demons are much more into wards and spells than demigods. Though the only ones used were tracing spells. We once used to heavily rely on prayers, but look at where that got us.

Kalel's cheeks are starting to turn red. "Having to scent you is causing my heat cycle to flare up." He covers his mouth as he says it, looking like he's about to be sick. I know our kinds find each other repulsive, but last night I thought Kalel was the most beautiful creature I've laid eyes on. He must feel differently...and for some reason that hits me in the gut. "You need to wear it to prevent any more"—he clears his throat—"mishaps."

My eyes widen as I finally understand.

"Oh. I didn't know that was something demons were affected by. I didn't even know you experienced them. Why is it happening? Have you had a heat before?" My eyes travel to his hands. There are bite marks on them, and they look like they belong to him. Was he trying desperately to stop himself last night? My thighs ache with the memory of his ruthless thrusts.

His eyes narrow with annoyance. "Haven't you been educated in scenting and heat cycles?"

I lift a shoulder and let it fall. "No, I'm the only daughter of Venus in Alzhor. Demigods don't get heats like I do. I'm the outcast in the bunch."

He opens his mouth a few times like he wants to say something, but he can't get the words to come out. Finally, he says quieter, "I shouldn't have to explain this to you." Kalel drags a heavy hand through his hair and sighs. "The scenting I did last night is something only partnered demons do with one another, so the act of it increases our natural instincts. I'm not one to be intimate with others, so this is highly unusual for me. And no, I haven't had a heat before." He turns his back to me.

"Kalel, I have frequent heats, and I know how painful they

can be. It's okay if you need to do it again." My voice wavers, and I try not to dwell on the way his shoulders tense. I focus my attention on the tips of his ears and how red they turn.

He drags a hand down his jaw with discomfort as he shifts to face me. "I'm sorry if I…if I frightened you last night." His eyes soften as he stares at the ground. Then he hardens his gaze. "I'll make sure to have our healer visit you before we leave."

The ride is different today.

Kalel's presence is more defeated and heavier with his silence. Now that I'm not shivering the entire day, I'm able to admire the cold landscape and the slow march of the horses.

There isn't a single sign of life amidst the snow. The wastelands truly are a desolate place. Normally, the mortals linger in these areas, waiting in the thick underbrush to ambush travelers or take out entire groups for goods and food. I doubt we'll need to worry with an army this big though.

The healer made quick work of me this morning, and I've been relieved all day that I didn't have to ride a horse with soreness.

We set up camp along a cliffside tonight. The northern winds are intense, but the steep rock face keeps the frigid air off us for the most part.

It's the first day that I don't feel entirely drained from the ride, so I decide to sit by the campfire and listen in on some of the knights as they share stories of their families. The longer I sit here, the more burdensome the guilt of what I've done becomes.

They're talking about their loved ones just as demigods do. A frown forms across my lips. I rise just as they're serving bowls of beef stew. It smells good, but I lost my appetite thinking about the demons I've slain that were just like these knights. Or their innocent family members that never should've been involved in the war in the first place.

The snow crunches beneath my boots as I trudge to the edge of the cliffside and look out over the expanse of the wastelands. Now that the storm has cleared, I can see over the entire valley we crossed today. Jagged rocks break from the ground and extend toward the sky. Patches of forest cover each end of the valley, going as far as the eye can see.

I jolt when I hear footsteps. I conclude that it must be Kalel, so I let my shoulders relax and continue looking over the landscape solemnly.

Two hands slam down onto my shoulders and shove me to the ground. The snow is easily a foot deep, and it instantly pushes up into my shirt. The cold stings my skin, muddling my senses as I turn to face my attacker. My heart drops.

There's more than one.

It's a group of angry soldiers, still dressed in their armor. Three of them surround me, with a fourth on his way up the slope.

"You killed my cousin, you witch," one of them snarls at me, unsheathing his sword. My heart skips a beat. I'm unarmed and defenseless.

The others glare at me with hatred.

"You killed my fiancé."

"My childhood home was burned down by your soldiers."

They berate me with their grievances as they circle around me like wolves. "I'm your duke's betrothed. Don't you want this godsforsaken war to end?" I shout, gnashing my teeth together and shaking my head with frustration.

The broad-shouldered demon closest to me cackles. The hair on the back of my neck rises as I prepare to fight for my life.

"You think we want peace? *Now* of all times, when we finally had you abominations cornered? All it would've taken was a single breath, and we would finally be rid of the demigods for good." His grip adjusts on his hilt, and I move just in time as he swings his sword at me.

Of course their kingdom would be divided on the matter of peace. Especially considering the tricks we played.

Thornhall. My heart aches for the loved ones I stole from them.

"I don't want to hurt any of you." My voice gets stolen from me as a sword is swung across my shoulder blades. A pained scream is torn from my lips as I'm thrown down into the snow again.

Panic races through my veins, and my heart pounds loudly

in my ears. They're on top of me swiftly, like wolves to sheep, covering my mouth so I can't scream again.

I try to remain calm, breathing steadily and taking long, slow breaths through my nose. My shoulders are hot and wet, but I can't feel the pain yet. The adrenaline coursing through my body is similar to what I experienced each time Kalel killed me.

Am I going to die?

What will happen to me if I kill them? I don't know what Kalel will do as punishment. He wouldn't believe me, that I'm sure of. I swallow slowly and take in the rage that floods through the demons' eyes.

"Hand me your devilstone," the one keeping me pinned to the ground snaps at his comrade. A small black rock that resembles coal is passed over my head.

Devilstone? How do they have one of those? Horror races across my expression. I thought they were all destroyed in the raid Apollo led five centuries ago.

Demigods' flesh burns when touched by the stones. Gods all but turn to ash if they get too close, which is why they were obliterated. It was too great a weapon against the deities. Well, we thought they were all destroyed. Clearly not though.

Have they dug up more in the underworld?

A cry bubbles up from my throat as the soldier holds the devilstone close to my face. He sneers at my reaction.

"So it's true then. Demigods can be hurt by the stones." He

barely touches my neck with it, and a deep burning sensation spreads.

I scream, but it's muffled by another knight's hand. "Amazing," he mutters emptily as he stares down at my neck. I try thrashing from their hold but get nowhere.

"Don't worry, I won't damage your pretty face. But if you think we're going to sit idly by while filth like you is mated to our noble duke, then you're deranged."

His words don't make sense to me until he scoots down, sitting on my legs as he lifts my shirt. My blood turns cold. He's going to use the stone on my reproductive organs.

I try to tell them to stop, but the words are muffled by the gloved hand.

I don't have a choice.

My heart lurches as I close my eyes and let my deity ability seep into the air. The hand covering my mouth vanishes as well as the weight of the knight on my legs. The devilstone drops to the snow beside me.

I slowly sit up, staring emptily with tear-stained eyes at the four flowers that are lying atop the snow. It's always the same. They always turn into blush-colored cherry blossoms. I can only use it against foes who've touched me. Once contact is made and our soul essences have met, I can turn them into flowers. What I would've given to have had the chance to do this to the Blood Knight before the time loops.

Now, I no longer know him as the Blood Knight.

He's just Kalel, Duke Lornhelm, my betrothed.

"That must be another gift from your mother." His dull voice startles me.

I whirl, finding Kalel leaning against a tree with his arms crossed and a bored look on his face. He was here the whole time and just watched them attack me?

My cheeks flush with rage. I stagger to my feet and shudder from the chill that's set into my bones already.

"Well, thank the gods you were here to help," I say scathingly. "At least I don't have to try to convince you why I had to kill them."

His expression remains hard pressed. "Don't expect me to ever save you, little godling. I'm not here to be your babysitter."

My jaw ticks. "I didn't need to be saved, asshole. But your knights would still be alive if you had intervened. Their deaths are on you." I fist my hands at my sides and head back to camp. The trembling is bone deep; I need to get out of these clothes as soon as possible. My shoulder throbs painfully as gilded blood seeps into my shirt.

Kalel's footsteps aren't far behind me.

Is he serious right now?

"Can you give me one godsforsaken moment to myself?" I growl, furrowing my brows as our tent comes into view. It's still bright out and I haven't eaten yet today, but I don't want to see anyone for the rest of the evening. Kalel included.

He ignores me and continues to follow me into the tent anyway.

The warmer air instantly hits me, offering a little relief. I spare a quick, reluctant glance at Kalel before peeling my soaked sweater off. He's sitting on the edge of his bed, watching me with mild interest.

The sweater makes a wet, plopping sound as it hits the tarp floor cover. My bare breasts are exposed, the assault of air making my nipples harden. I try not to look at Kalel, but his gaze burns into my skin. My eyes flick nervously to his, and I find a softened expression as he looks over my chest.

Heat spreads through my core at the tenderness in his gaze and the flex in his jaw. *Traitorous body.* I grit my teeth as I let my pants fall to the ground. I'm about to crawl into my nest of blankets when Kalel breaks the silence.

"Where did you get that?"

I know exactly what he's talking about. The long scar down my left side, just over my ribs. My hand unconsciously lifts to the spot, fingertips brushing gently over the old wound. The first injury I received after becoming a knight. I'd grown careless out on the battlefield. Korin had my flank, but I was naive to the viciousness of the demons. Some can indeed still swing a sword even with their heads lopped off.

Kalel doesn't get to have that part of me though. There are some things that should stay locked away. We aren't necessarily close by any means.

When I don't respond and another cold shiver runs through me, he relents with a deep breath and sighs. Kalel rummages through a crate near his bedside. "Come here, little godling."

I wrap my arms around my body and fight the bone-deep trembling. I take him in, sitting leisurely with his legs spread wide and slacked. My feet stop once I'm a foot away from him. The coldness has returned to his eyes.

"Turn around." He sounds as tired as I feel. I do as he says, and he pops the lid to something and smears some ointment over the cut on my back. I cringe at the sharp pain, but it quickly fades. A relieved breath escapes my lips. "There. This will seal your wound until Mav or his apprentice can see you."

Mav is their main healer, and I've seen him around camp. The apprentice must be the attractive one with fawn hair and brown eyes that healed me in passing this morning.

I turn and face Kalel. "Thanks," I say wearily, ready to just go to bed, but I know that's not how this night will go.

Kalel frowns before offering me his hand. Every time he holds me, he gets this pained expression, like he's forcing himself to touch me. "*I hate you.*" His words echo in my head like a dull blade. He made that clear while he was tearing up my insides.

Am I that appalling to him? I shouldn't care how he feels about it, but it still makes me self-conscious.

I set my hand in his. He turns me so my back is facing him, pulling me against his chest. It's cold, just like it always is, yet a fire ignites in my lower abdomen. Are all demons empty of warmth like this, or is it only the devourers?

I clench my jaw and worry my lower lip.

He starts purring, that deep rumbling against my spine is pure bliss. It sends a shiver down every vertebra in my body, and with it comes a pulse of warmth from his skin everywhere he touches me.

A soft, relieved breath escapes my lips, giving him a moment of pause before he tugs the covers off his bed and lies me down on it. The brief moment that we're parted brings all the cold crashing back into me, and the trembling returns.

"Bear with me," he says tightly, avoiding eye contact as he pulls his long-sleeved shirt off and tosses it to the floor. His broad chest is on display, revealing all his scars, sacred oath mark, muscles, and veins. I lick my lips and suppress another cold wave that makes my teeth chatter. My eyes linger on the scar over his chest that matches the one on his cheek. *It must be from the same fight.*

Kalel lies behind me, covering us with a blanket that carries his alderwood scent. His arms wrap back around me, and he pulls our bodies flush together again. His comforting purr resumes, and once more, I'm consumed by the heat that pours from him. He must be using his essence to do it. It's a type of transferal to easily share heat that we learned in chivalry training.

It's much warmer now. I refuse to admit how much I'm enjoying it. How his deep comfort call makes my core ache and twist to be filled. Is he experiencing it too? My legs fidget, accidentally tangling with his.

"Stop moving so much," he growls, his hot breath coasting over the back of my neck. He hooks his legs around mine to keep them still, but it only angles my body, jutting my ass against his crotch.

I go deathly still. His cock is stiff and pressed against my backside. I think of last night and how rough he was with me. How upset he was about all of it happening.

Our breaths are the only sound that permeates the tent besides the soft sound of snowflakes *tick*ing against the tarp.

This wouldn't be so uncomfortable if our circumstances were different.

I shut my eyes and try to focus on the warmth he's offering me. His hands are fisted, and the only place his arm touches me is around my rib cage, keeping me tucked close. Perhaps in a different life we would be two lovely mortals, not damaged and covered in the blood of our enemies. Not beastly and corrupt.

"You didn't have to warm me up." I sound ungrateful, but really, I'm soaking in every ounce of it. The only discomfort are the cramps that are beginning to flare up in my abdomen.

I do my best to ignore them. Will the charm he gave me be enough to keep my scent from reaching him? I hope so. I swallow the dread.

"I'm not doing it out of the goodness of my heart. The king

would have my head if you were found to have fallen ill from being poorly looked after," he says coldly.

"You should let him cut off your head."

He chuckles at my snide remark, the sound of his amusement drawing a smile to my lips. "I would if I didn't have a kingdom depending on me. I'd choose death over being stuck with you any day."

"*Ouch,*" I murmur sarcastically.

"Do you blame me? Wouldn't you do the same?" he chides.

I think on it for a few moments, then shake my head. "No, I wouldn't. I actually don't mind you, Kalel." The admittance feels like a forbidden secret to share.

His muscles stiffen. I long to see what expression he's making, but I don't dare to move.

"Why?" His voice has a pained twinge to it.

"Because you're making sure I'm punished for my sins. You take care of your troops. You put your kingdom before anything—no matter what. I was trying to desert mine, remember?" I cling to the blanket, unsure why I'm sharing this with him, but it feels good to get it off my chest.

He's quiet, considering my words maybe, but before he can respond, a throb of pain tears through my abdomen. I curl into myself, pulling my knees up to my chest and whimpering at the ebbing muscles.

Gods, why did Venus have to be my mother?

Kalel flinches. "What's wrong?" His hands unfurl. He

forces my chin to him and assesses my face. "You're in pain." His voice trails off like he's confused.

Another rack of pain twists my stomach. This time I cry out, and my hands clutch around my abdomen. Tears prickle in my eyes.

Now he seems to understand. He goes deathly still and takes a few staggered breaths.

"*Fuck.*" His tone is graveled, and I can feel his Adam's apple bob as he pulls me closer, trying to uncurl me from the fetal position.

"No. It hurts." I barely get the words out. It feels like a sword has impaled me. The ache only grows, and the need to be filled becomes unbearable.

Kalel hesitates, not knowing what to do, but he softens his voice. "Alira, let me help. I had Nikolai teach me some healing tricks last night that will soothe the pain."

Nikolai? Is that the healer's apprentice? The blood drains from my face. *Oh gods, he learned tricks to "soothe" my heat pain from him?*

He tries once more to bring my back straight against his chest. I groan at the ache but let him move me this time. I'd do anything for this feeling to go away.

It hurts... It feels like he's killing me all over again.

"You need to let go," he whispers as he moves my hand away. I clutch the blanket desperately. Another strong cramp rolls through me, and I choke on my breath.

"Shh, it's okay." He starts purring again and splays his palm over my abdomen.

If it didn't feel like someone was tearing out my uterus, I'd be bothered by the intimacy of this, but it feels like I'm losing my mind more by the second.

I grit my teeth, preparing for the next wave of pain, but Kalel digs his fingertips into me enough to make me jolt. A second later, heat is directly inserted to my core—now I'm certain it's essence sharing. The pain lessens considerably. My muscles instantly relax, and I only now notice how sweaty and out of breath I am.

Kalel nuzzles into my neck. I'm assuming instinctively and not as a show of adoration, but it makes my heart flutter all the same. "Better?" he asks, sounding a little out of breath himself. He massages my abdomen, and a small whimper escapes my lips from the relief.

"Yes," I whisper, shutting my eyes and letting my mind catch up. The more lucid I become, the more I wish I wasn't. Kalel's erection is massive. It has grown out of his pants and is reaching halfway up my back. Neither of us have shirts on, and I can feel the wet beads of his precum dotting my spine.

Oh. My. Gods.

CHAPTER 9

ALIRA

The ache starts to return. How could it not with something as filling as he is up against my back, waiting for me?

Pretend you don't notice, I advise myself and try to focus on how good his palm feels as he kneads my stomach. It's euphoric and oddly erotic, as if he's preparing for a breeding session.

My blood goes cold at the thought of that.

Kalel's breathing is erratic, but he manages to say calmly, "Did you eat anything today? I didn't see you around the campsites during lunch or dinner. You can't keep skipping meals, Alira, you're already so thin." His lips coast the ridge of my shoulder and send shivers rolling through my entire body.

"I wasn't hungry," I say softly.

"I can't feed if you don't. So I need you to eat something, okay?"

My lips flatten. "I usually don't eat much during travel, especially when my heat is off and on. I get too nauseous on horseback."

He only sighs and mutters, "Needy little godling." But there's no animosity in his tone. His voice is smooth, and the length against my back throbs again. I swallow and try as hard as I can not to grind into it.

Sweat slips down my forehead as he lets his lips move across my shoulder, drawing chills down my spine.

"You can drink my blood, I'm fine. I'll eat in the morning… And I've been meaning to thank you." I slide my hand down so it's on top of his.

He breathes heavy, lips parted, begging to consume me. His hand is still massaging my abdomen. "For?" he murmurs like he can't imagine what I would thank a demon like him for.

"You didn't need to keep my necklace or return it to me, but you did. You didn't need to warm me up either, but you are. Thank you." I desperately want things between us to be less volatile. I don't know if that will ever be possible. And I'm okay with not being close, but the nonstop hatred I could go without.

He gnashes his teeth together so hard that I hear it. A chill crawls up my neck.

"I'm doing this to end the war, *not* for you. I need you in peak health, because my children will have to grow here." His tone is dark as he palms my abdomen for emphasis, and it actually feels good.

My features twist. Why did I like hearing that so much?

"My children will know you as their mother, they will feed from your breasts and fall asleep to your songs. I won't have them believing me to be a monster. I want them to know I am kind. That we ended the horrors and deaths between our kind by creating them." Kalel sounds miserable as he says it.

My chest sinks.

I know he hates this as much as I do, but I'm relieved it's him and not anyone else. His mother was in Thornhall when I raided it, and I doubt that's something he will ever forgive me for.

"I'm sorry, Kalel. You must've had to sacrifice so much for this… Is there a lover waiting for you back in Devicit?" I never thought about it. Maybe because I never had someone waiting for me. The knights in Alzhor were almost all single. We didn't really do relationships like mortals and demons do. Demigods aren't known to…well, love, I guess. We're just naturally not very affectionate. I mean, look at our parents. They never cared to know us.

So why do I long for it? For the warm embraces and the

nights no longer alone. For *his* arms. I don't understand my own feelings. No one has ever taught me how.

He's quiet for some time before murmuring, "No, I find mating and marriage to be an utter waste of time. I'm doing this for my kingdom, for vengeance."

"Why? Don't you crave affection and love? I thought demons were as utterly lovesick for each other as the mortals are."

Kalel doesn't respond, but his fingers curl into my side a bit. I expected as much. He doesn't want to open up just as much as I don't want to.

Deep wounds, I suppose.

He slides his hand from me and nudges my back. "You should try to eat something before bed."

"Okay," I whisper, grabbing the spare set of clothes that I have and slipping into them. A small, cold shudder still lingers in my bones, but I'm warm for the most part.

I turn to face Kalel, he's leaned over with his hands threaded together, elbows on his knees, blanket bundled in his lap. He looks lost in a sea of somber thoughts. "Kalel."

His eyes slowly lift to mine, hollow and empty. Ethereal. Gold blood is smeared over his chest, reminding me that I should visit the healer tonight like he suggested after he applied the ointment earlier.

I clear my throat. "I know you didn't do it for me, but I'm still grateful. Thank you." My lips curl into a weak smile. He stares at me, eyes narrowing, filling with dreary thoughts.

He doesn't respond, but he doesn't say anything cruel either, so I count it as a win.

Small steps, I remind myself.

— —— –

The camp moves slowly. The last tendrils of twilight are already fading into dusk. I frown at the lost time as I head to the meal station. There are only a few knights still out, sitting around the last couple of campfires and speaking in low voices.

Tessa lingers around the meal station, helping the people on food duty get everything packed up. She throws on a smile at the sight of me. "There you are. I was wondering where you've been. Here," she mumbles as she bends down and retrieves a bowl of soup that's been set to the side. Her brows pinch together. "It's cooled down, but you can warm it up over a fire." She nods toward the one closest to Kalel's tent.

I gratefully take the bowl even though I'm not hungry. With a forced smile, I murmur, "Thank you for thinking of me."

Tessa shakes her head and waves me off. "It's part of my duties to make sure you're properly cared for. Are you okay? I saw you and the commander walking back into camp. A few knights aren't accounted for, so I sort of put two and two together." Her voice lowers as she says the latter.

The cold inches its way back into my chest. Is she going to

try to attack me when I admit that I killed them? "Um..." I try to think of something to say, but she shakes her head with a grim smile.

"I know how angry some of our knights are with the way the war panned out. We anticipated that some of them might try to ambush you. Don't worry about it, Kalel will brief us in the morning about it. Go enjoy your meal." She brushes her hair from her face and leaves a grease mark on her cheek. I admire how hard she works, even helping with the food rations.

I give her a small nod and take the meal back to the fire. The bowls are made of metal, so I note that I'll have to be careful once it's warmed up.

I sit as close as I can and let my hands soak in the radiating heat. *What a fucking day.* Kalel still needs to feed, and then I can finally get some rest. What will our days look like once we reach Devicit? I'll have an abundance of time on my hands, since I'll no longer be a knight.

What did I use to do for fun? I close my eyes and think. Beautiful dresses and ball dances flicker into my memory. A sad smile stretches across my lips. That's right, when I was a young godling, I dreamed of becoming a dressmaker. A silly dream, especially for an orphan who was already being submitted to the knight faction for an apprenticeship. But once upon a time, a demon told me I could be whatever I wanted when I grew up.

I wanted dances, princes, lovely dresses with wine and

royalty. Things that I only read about in the house mother's fairy-tale books. Growing up taught me that I didn't know anything about reality. Because all I have are scars, a betrothal to a villain, and curses.

A frown tugs at my lips as I watch the embers smolder like my past self.

That hopeful girl is dead. I buried her to survive this war. Now I only have grief, penance, and guilt.

Someone sits on a log adjacent to me and brings me out of my thoughts. I assume it's Tessa at first, but when I look up, I'm met with the softest brown eyes I've ever seen. A demon with fawn hair and pale skin. He has small goat-like horns and one of the kindest smiles. He's handsome and dressed like Tessa with armor and leathers, so I'm guessing he is probably one of Kalel's top knights. Though that doesn't quite seem right, he looks familiar. His mussed hair and charming smile throw me off, or perhaps it's my weary mind.

"You look like you've had an absolutely abhorrent day," he says, cracking a wide grin and quirking a brow like it's funny. I'm so tired that maybe it is funny, but I can't seem to tell anymore.

My eyes shift to him as I sarcastically say, "What gave it away? My ratted hair or my dying complexion?"

He stifles a laugh. "Actually, it was the long frown." He reaches out and gently taps my lips. I flinch at his playful demeanor toward me. After the day I've had, it's honestly welcome.

I grunt and let my eyes fall back to the bowl over the fire. The contents are steaming now, so it's probably warm enough. I use my sleeves to grab the edges of the bowl and quickly move it to the flat rock in my lap that I plan on using as a makeshift table.

"You also look like you really don't want to eat that," he throws in. I grin at him. *I like this demon.*

"No one is holding a knife to your throat and making you keep me company."

"Ah, but you're wrong. I've been meaning to check in with you. My name is Nikolai. I believe I quickly healed you this morning, though I was in a hurry and didn't really get to exchange formalities with you. I'm the healer's apprentice, so naturally they assigned me to practice on you," he says cheerfully. I can't tell if the latter is meant to be an insult or not, but he seems genuine enough, so I keep the loose grin.

Oh, now I remember him. He was wearing the apprentice's cloak earlier. A matching taupe color to his mentor, Mav.

"A healer? That must be a difficult practice to learn." I take a reluctant sip of the soup and force it down. It tastes amazing, salty and thick with vegetables, beef, and broth, but I have little appetite for it.

Nikolai nods, smiling like he's reminiscing on his early training days. "It's taken me twenty years just to become an apprentice. Difficult is an understatement." He chuckles, the sound is light and inviting. I find myself smiling easily with him and relaxing my shoulders. I hadn't even realized how tense they were.

"Twenty years? How old are you? You look so young," I tease. I know demons can live as long as demigods, some probably longer. There may even be a few that are immortal like the gods.

"I'm ninety-two. My bloodline stops aging at the age of twenty-five, so we all look young. My parents *and* grandparents could be my siblings," he says with amusement. "How about you, Alira? I'm fascinated with the demigods. I've always wanted to pick their brains about their ways of life and all the gritty details, but as I'm sure you know, most are willing to cut off their tongues rather than speak with a demon." His soft features grow grim as he says the latter.

I wonder what they do with the stolen demigods. None have returned home. Does Kalel consume them until they breathe their last breaths? Part of me doesn't want to know. But learning their fate will be inevitable, I fear.

"I'm not surprised. We're raised to know better than to open up to demons." The hope in Nikolai's eyes falters. "But I'm betrothed to a demon now, so I'm not sure those rules apply to me anymore." I wink, and Nikolai lights up again. "I'm thirty-eight, demigods typically stop aging around thirty. We can live a few centuries, but with the war, there aren't many older half-gods left."

His eyes grow wide. "Wow, you're only thirty-eight? You're

just five years younger than the commander. He's barely even begun the long life ahead of him."

I lean forward with interest and take another sip of the savory soup. "Really? How long does a devourer live? We actually don't know much about the demons either," I admit sheepishly.

Nikolai's eyes sparkle with eagerness. "This is amazing. I've wanted to learn about you for so long, and to find out you know so little about us as well is truly astounding."

"Astounding? I don't know if I would go that far."

He eagerly nods. "We always thought the demigods were superior beings to us. I mean, Neptune almighty, you *are* half-gods. It never dawned on me—or anyone, I think—that you were just as in the dark as we are."

I take another small sip before setting the bowl down, my stomach isn't pleased that I consumed even a tiny amount of it.

"Devourers are one of the few breeds of demon that are immortal. As I'm sure you're aware, they can eat normal food, but they require the blood of demigods to survive. Well, there's a reason it has to be deity blood." He shuffles his feet uncomfortably, glancing toward Kalel's tent to make sure he's not coming out. "They siphon life from those they feed on. Demigods are the only creatures that cannot be depleted due to the gods' blood in your veins."

Kalel is immortal. For some reason, that makes my heart ache, yet I do not understand why.

"Well, we aren't immortal. At least not anymore. Our lifespans are around three hundred years if our parents are strong deities. Very few of us reach immortality. It can only be bestowed on us if we prove ourselves to Jupiter as being worthy, but the gods have forsaken us and have left us to slowly disappear."

His expression darkens. "That's awfully bleak."

I lift a shoulder and drop it before grabbing the bowl and offering the remaining contents to Nikolai, since he's been gawking at it. "Care to finish it?"

He nods greedily with a large smile. "Gods, I was hoping you'd offer. The rations are always smaller on the way home from battle. I keep telling King Achill that we need to increase the stock we bring. Are you sure you're not hungry?"

I shake my head. "I'm fine. Just promise me you'll tell Kalel I ate the whole bowl if he asks."

Nikolai's brows pinch with concern, but he nods. "All right, but I'm making sure that you eat breakfast in the morning." He extends his hand to me. I lift a brow. What is he doing? "You don't know what a handshake is?" he says disbelievingly.

My lips flatten. "No."

Nikolai laughs and reaches for my hand. I jolt at the motion and freeze when he grips it tightly, shaking it up and down a few times. His brown eyes flicker, and his cheeks flush red at the contact. He studies my face like he's seeing me differently.

"It means: deal. The mortals do this all the time. We picked up on it years ago." He slowly lets go of my hand.

"Demons are strange," I mutter with a grin. Tessa and Nikolai give me a sliver of hope for my new life. Maybe I won't have to do this alone after all.

The tent is dark when I return.

Kalel is sitting at his desk, writing a note before sealing it into the canister on his hawk's leg. It's the same one from King Borlin's study the day we received the news that they agreed to take me as an offering.

Kalel's eyes lift to mine. He waits a moment, staring at me with that unreadable gaze before standing and moving past me to release the bird from the tent.

"Did you eat?" He assesses me like he won't believe me either way.

"Yes, Tessa saved some for me."

Kalel grunts and moves to the edge of his bed, offering his hand to me. I go to him and sit on his left side. He gently moves my hair from my neck and leans in close. Inhaling deeply over my scent glands before stroking his tongue across my skin, lighting every inch of where he touches me on fire. My hands curl into the sheets as his fangs brush down the side of my neck until he finds the spot he likes. His teeth enter my bloodstream.

The muscles in my back shut down, he was ready for it though, with his hand wrapped around my lower spine. The venom in his bite that causes the sudden relaxed state isn't so bad now that I'm used to it. A slightly unsettling thought, because if he ever truly wanted to kill me, it'd be easy for him to.

The bite feels more like a small discomfort. I listen to the sound of him feasting from me. He seems hungrier today, his pulls are fervent and his grip is tight on my back.

"*Mhm,*" he growls, the sound hitting me like an axe to the chest. His teeth sink in farther, pulling a cry from my lips.

"*Ow*, that hurts." I gasp as he readjusts his hold on me, moving a heavy hand to my thigh and squeezing hard. My pulse leaps with adrenaline, and he must taste it, because he pauses before quickly releasing me.

His breaths are staggered. Those golden eyes are filled with shock for a second before he blinks it away and drags his sleeve over his bloody face. He's never been this messy with it before. Was he really that hungry? Fear trickles through me. I lift my hand and press it to my throat hesitantly. The gash is much larger than usual. Gold liquid stains my sleeve.

"Go to bed," he snaps, turning his back to me and running his hand through his hair.

"What was that?" I ask with a trembling voice. Is he losing control of his hunger? What happens if he lets go? Gods, I don't want to even think about it.

His shoulders tense. "I said go to bed, little godling."

CHAPTER 10

ALIRA

The wind dies down as we reach the border between Devicit and Alzhor. An entire week of travel through the grueling cold wears down your soul. Although I'm not sure many places can be more dreadful than the valley of the Fallen Ridge.

Blood was spilled on these grounds from both armies—the red-and-gold-imbued ground discloses as much.

Kalel's army seems glum as we pass through. Their eyes linger on the broken flag stakes that were driven into the ground during the battle.

It still looks so fresh. Frozen in time until spring will thaw it.

I remember our leading general telling us about this particular battle in a war briefing six months ago. Our forces held this border for a few weeks, but we were no match for the sheer number of demons. Part of me thinks that King Borlin was holding out in hopes that the gods would refute the spilling of so much deity blood, but they stayed silent. They never came. Many of our knights lost what little hope they had left when their prayers were left unanswered.

This was one of the few battles that King Borlin did not send me on. I was to remain in our kingdom and protect the castle in case of a secret raid.

My shoulders slump at the weight of death that hangs in the air here.

It's rumored that deity blood will stain the land it is spilt on. In small instances of death, it goes unnoticed, but this is something entirely different. I've never felt so sick to my stomach before. The horses trample beautiful, wilted flowers as we pass through. Peonies.

Tessa pulls her horse close to ours. "Kalel, we should stay at the battlefront camp until the coming storm passes."

Kalel considers her briefly and then curtly nods.

He really doesn't speak much, especially while on horseback. Which is a small blessing I genuinely appreciate. The rides are long, but at least I get to remain in my mind prison for most of the day.

The horses walk across the bloodied field until we reach

the opposite end on Devicitian territory, finally crossing the border of the holy lands.

Strange, though, there are no bodies of demigods left behind like I had expected there to be. There wasn't time for King Borlin to retrieve his fallen army, not when the demons had already run them out. So where are their bodies?

Kalel halts his horse as shouting erupts from the back of the line. A pulse of fear shoots through the air—sticky like pine sap on the tongue. It's a signature fear scent of the demons, and to say that it puts horror into your chest like quick rot is an understatement.

It's the kind of scent you experience once and never forget. Their essence lashes out like a solar flare, striking every living being in a perimeter to let them know that something awful is coming. It's a scent I associate with killing them. Their fear hits your very soul, and you can never forget it.

Kalel lets out a growl of distress that slips into my veins. "Tessa, keep an eye on her," he snaps, leaving me atop his horse and taking off toward the back of the group to see what the commotion is.

Tessa eyes me like she actually thinks I might run away. Which, in any other predicament, I most certainly would. But Kalel is the only saving grace my kingdom has left. Where do they honestly think I'd go?

Kalel's horse stomps his hoof and starts nodding his head like he wants to buck me off his back.

"Whoa, it's okay," I murmur as I slide off the tall black stallion and pat his neck to soothe him. The horse grunts and tilts his head away from me like he can't stand the idea of me touching him without Kalel nearby. I purse my lips at the creature's ambivalence toward me. "What's going on back there?"

"I'm not sure." Her eyes linger over the heads of the knights as they continue to move toward the back to help. "The horse is responding to the fear scent, but he's also just a grumpy beast. You're lucky he even tolerates your presence. He kicked Princess Helen off when she tried to acquaint herself with him." She smiles at the memory, making me think she doesn't like the princess very much.

"I didn't know the Demon King had a daughter," I mutter as I move a few steps farther from the horse. Just in case he tries kicking me.

Tessa hops down beside me. "Not a daughter—it's his sister. She was after Kalel's heart for a few years, but he wasn't interested in her. He's never been particularly interested in anyone." She says the last part with an odd tone.

I stare at her with tired eyes, not too interested in Kalel's admirers.

"Helen shouldn't be a problem, but you should know she's no stranger to having people murdered." At least Tessa is thoughtful enough to warn me.

It's not the first time I've heard of royalty using their assassins for personal gain.

I nod. "Thanks for the heads-up. Anything else I should know?"

Tessa shakes her head. "Kalel will tell you everything there is, I'm sure. I shouldn't have even mentioned Helen, please don't bring it up to him." She looks away toward the destroyed fields.

"Did you fight here, Lieutenant?" I ask, shifting the subject to something other than Kalel. He seems to be the topic of everything, and I'm eager to learn more about the others around me instead.

The golden scales tracing her hairline shimmer with a warm hue for only a moment as her eyes soften on the distant trees with sorrow. "I did."

The shouting from the back of the line increases and draws our attention back to the knights below. What on earth is—

No.

Dire wolves.

The knights have dispersed and are trying to chase away huge creatures that crash into the groups of horses and try breaking carriages apart. Specifically, the one carrying the demigod captives.

The demigods kept as leverage escape from the caged wagons the wolves pushed over and disperse rapidly. Some make it to the tree line quickly, and others fight for their lives against the beasts. Fresh blood quickly curls in the winter air. I search frantically for Hans, the attendant King Borlin appointed to join us to confirm our vows once we reach Devicit.

I don't find him among the torn-up demigods. A small reprieve, but my stomach curls at the carnage that has unfolded in a matter of moments.

My heart leaps into my throat, and my hand instinctively shoots to my side to grab my sword. But it's not there, I forgot they took it away from me on the first day.

I can't be weaponless out here. Not with dire wolves. I'm practically a beacon for them. They can smell demigod blood from miles away. It's sweet to them, like nectar of eternal honey. We eradicated them in our territory long ago, but I didn't know they still lived in Devicitian forests. Why are all beasts of this world after our holy blood? I bury my teeth in my lower lip.

Kalel shouts as he impales a dire wolf in the back before it can catch a small-framed demigod. It whirls on the commander furiously. The beast is at least three times his size, and his crystal sword seems to have barely inflicted any damage at all.

"Dire wolves?" Tessa mutters in disbelief, arming herself before she's about to charge down to the field to help. She stops on her right foot and glances back at me. Her eyes quickly find my empty hands. "*Gods*," she curses, reluctantly unsheathing her dagger with one sharp jerk of her arm. "Do *not* make me regret giving you this."

Tessa shoves the blade into my hands. I blink at her, shocked but grateful.

She doesn't bother waiting for a *thank you*. She sprints off down the field and rushes to help the few remaining demigods left. They're cowering behind Kalel and his four strongest knights.

My jaw slacks. It's unheard of to hold off an entire pack of dire wolves when demigod blood has been spilt. They will pursue it to no end—a hunger so deep that they are willing to die to quench it.

Kalel's eyes flick to mine, hard-set and narrowed with fury and confusion for the dire wolves' appearance. It occurs to me just as I feel the vibration of the ground behind me that the demons might not know about the lure the beasts have to our golden veins. That the aftermath of the battle here may have drawn them from the deepest parts of the forest.

Kalel's gaze widens, and he lets out a piercing shout before teeth clamp down around my entire chest.

One thought rings through my mind. Perhaps through the universe.

A prayer, but not to the cruel gods.

Please don't let me die, Kalel.

CHAPTER 11
KALEL

The forest spirit, an enormous white dire wolf that controls the pack, buries her teeth in Alira.

I never anticipated how cold the blood in my veins could run. But watching her lovely, silver hair quickly drown in gold makes every chamber of my heart turn to ice.

A sound escapes my throat. One I've never made before.

"Alira!" My voice sounds muffled as my pulse roars through my ears—all I can hear is Tessa and Nikolai shouting behind me as I run to her. I think they're trying to make me stop, to let her die instead of risking myself.

It's not even a question for me. I can't let her die.

Not just that I can't, I *won't*. It's like a calling through my very soul. A plea. Then I hear her voice. Clear as morning dew. *Please don't let me die, Kalel.*

My heart twists, and a surge of power thrums through my bones.

Did she just pray to me? All sense flees my mind. The only thing I care about is saving my little godling.

My grip tightens on the sword as I let my legs falter and slide to get beneath the white beast. As I pass below, time stalls and beads down like slow rain. The wolf's eyes are a flurry of burning red coals, filled with hatred for everything that has dared step foot into her forest.

The pit grows in my stomach as my gaze reaches Alira, limp in the wolf's jaw. Her chin is tilted to the sky—throat smeared with the color of the sun.

The moment is a millisecond at most.

My blade finds the throat of the spirit. She cries out in agony as I quickly roll to the side to evade the collapsing beast.

"Alira!" I shout, tossing my sword into the dirt and setting to pry the wolf's jaw open by force. Her bloodshot eyes track my movements.

An unsettling voice rolls through every bone in my body. Chills race across my skin and bring me pause. *"Kalel, why have you come to my forest with such a feast only to stop us from feeding? Pluto will punish you for hurting my pack."* The dire wolf speaks through telepathy—an ability I've only known the old forest spirits to have.

"You cannot have this one. I will leave the others to their fates, but you cannot have her." My voice is graveled.

The old spirit searches my gaze, finding only an unwavering expression. She laughs—a raspy, haunting sound. *"Very well. But I suggest you leave my forest at sunrise. I will kill every single one of you if you remain after tomorrow's twilight."* She releases Alira, her body soaked in drool and blood. I bury my teeth in my lower lip, instantly tasting iron. *"If it were anyone but you, Kalel, I would've taken out the entire army,"* she warns.

I gather Alira into my arms and stand, feeling the weight of her limp body against my chest. I offer a nod of respect to the ancient creature before quickly turning and rushing to Nikolai. Mav is somewhere in the back of the group, trying to save as many knights as he can.

"Alira, I'm here… You can't die on me. Not now," I whisper, desperately holding her closer.

CHAPTER 12

ALIRA

A rich scent of alderwood stirs me awake. My lashes flutter against the warm light cast from the lanterns—too bright and arresting to fully open my eyes. My body feels frozen and aches terribly. A cold I've never known wraps me in its embrace, as if the hounds of the underworld are lingering nearby to collect my soul.

"Kalel, she's awake." It's Tessa's soft voice. She moves to my side and leans over me until her head is in my line of vision. I gaze at her for a few moments before shutting my heavy eyes.

"I'll send for you if I need you, thank you, Tess."

She hesitates but leaves shortly after. I wince at the light again, it's still too bright to look at Kalel. I drape my forearm over my eyes; the relief is instant.

His thumb brushes over my cheek, surprisingly warm. *That* gets my eyes to open. I squint to see him.

He's sitting beside me, and by the grim expression on his face, I'm assuming something awful has happened. His ebony hair is messy and covers his forehead. He's dressed in his evening attire, so it must still be early morning.

What happened? How did I get here when the last thing I remember is… My hand flies to my chest, where I vividly remember a piercing pain and teeth burrowing into my flesh.

How am I alive right now?

I sit up slowly, expecting pain, but I feel better than I have in days.

"You look like you are feeling well," Kalel says indifferently, but something about his tone is off from his usual broodiness.

"What did you do?" My hand rises to my chest once more, fingers meeting a shirt, not bandages. I feel everywhere I know I was injured and find nothing, not even a scar. I'm completely healed, but I should be dead from those wounds. That dire wolf had me in her mouth, for gods' sake.

Kalel looks exhausted. Has he been by my side the entire time I was resting? He mulls over his thoughts before lifting his eyes to mine. "I gave you my blood. It healed you, but you cannot be so reckless, little godling. Unless you truly wish to die."

My stomach curls. "Your blood healed me?" I search his eyes and find only truth. But that doesn't explain why he's warm to me now. My brows knit at the thought.

"It only works once," he says darkly as he drags his hand down his face like he's done something terrible. Something he's unsure about. "Alira"—he clears his throat—"we need to discuss what happened to the captive demigods tonight."

I stare at him, unsure what he means, until the memory of demigods running for their lives resurfaces in my mind. "Were you able to save them?" I ask quietly, dreading how few may have survived. Surely at least a few though, right?

He leans back and runs his fingers through his hair with a distressed pinch to his brow.

The longer he remains silent, staring at me with cold eyes, the more confident I am that no one survived the attack.

"A handful succeeded in escaping. I bargained with the dire wolf to let them have claim to any demigod left in their forest in order to save you." His tone is thick with dread. He thinks I won't take this well, and he's right.

An ache rises in my chest again. Why must so many of my kingdom's people die? King Borlin will be furious and unlikely to believe that we were attacked by dire wolves. He'll think Kalel killed them.

"You're lying," I seethe, pushing his shoulder back and glaring at him.

"I have no reason to lie to you." His eyes are even, and the bleak expression on his face is convincing. Why would he let them all perish like this? Even *I* know that this could be enough to reignite the war.

Fuming, I stand and walk straight to the tent's entrance. Kalel's up and blocking my way in the blink of an eye. "I need to search for survivors." I fist my hands at my sides. They can't all be dead—without them, this might as well have been all for nothing. I need to at least find Hans.

"You will be torn to shreds, Alira." His impassive face drives the rage deeper into my heart.

"You idiot." I shove his shoulders. He takes a single step back and raises his brows in annoyance. "If we lose them all to the wolves, King Borlin will ride to war. He won't believe any reason you give him if there's no one to send back home as agreed upon."

I try turning to leave again, but he grabs my wrist tightly and growls.

"Let the foolish king sentence the last of his demigods to death then. We outnumber them hundreds of times over." His words are sharp and cut into me. He must see the pain in my eyes, because he grits his teeth and furrows his brows.

My arm falls to my side as he releases my wrist.

Kalel takes a long breath. "I'm sorry, little godling, I shouldn't have—"

I don't wait for him to finish whatever it is he has to say. I dart through the tent flaps. Kalel curses under his breath, but

I'm already sprinting through the field toward the forest line where I saw many of the demigods escape to.

My bare feet traverse the ground quickly, and with a still mind and healed body, I move over the frozen ground with ease. The heavy footsteps behind me let me know that Kalel's not far behind.

"Stay at camp. I'll get her!" he snaps at his guards. I'm guessing they tried to join in chasing me.

I leap nimbly over the prickly brush that lines the forest and enter the thick wall of trees soundlessly. It's dark already, so it's difficult to see clearly, but the underbrush is pressed down where many feet have trampled over it. I follow the trail.

The ferocious sounds of Kalel trampling through the forest after me send urgency through my veins. *Gods, he could learn to be a bit more light-footed.*

I dash through the brush, ignoring the thorned branches that whip at my face as I carelessly maneuver in the dark, looking for any sign of surviving demigods.

"Little godling, you're testing my patience," he snarls from a few long strides away. I ignore him, pushing through the woods, deeper into the forest, until—

My feet, stinging from the brush and rocks, stop on a dime as I burst into a small opening in the thicket. Frost-covered leaves have been pressed down in the center, as if a struggle took place. Blades of grass are smothered in gilded blood. My hands fly to my nose as the scent of slain demigods hits me—the metallic smell curls in the back of my throat.

I sink to my knees and fist my hands in the frozen foliage.

Kalel approaches, his footsteps slowing.

As I stare at the blood-smeared grass, it becomes apparent to me that *this* is what my kingdom and many others will have to face if the war does not end—hunted down by beasts in the forest and demons taking over our territories.

Is this truly the fate of Faultore?

I lower my head and let the tears fall to the frozen earth. They trickle to the ground, and an ache in my heart spreads to my throat and lungs, coaxing me to make guttural sounds.

I swallow down the pain.

Kalel stands behind me like a ghost as he watches my misery unfold. He wanted me to suffer, didn't he? This is what he was after all this time, he said so himself. He wants revenge for everything the demigods have done. What *I* have done… And I don't blame him. Is this enough suffering for him? He probably enjoys the way I'm breaking at this moment.

I raise my head, a blank expression remaining on my features and tears still streaming down my cheeks as I turn to glance at him from over my shoulder.

His amber eyes flicker in the dim light. I expected him to be smiling at my despair or pissed off for making him chase me out here, but his face is as empty as my own.

"You even cry with no emotions, like a stone kissed with rain," he says flatly as his eyes shift reluctantly over to the gilded grass before snapping back to me.

We stare at one another for a moment that feels stretched into many.

Then he offers me his hand.

I don't take it, instead I look away, back to the grass where wolves spilled divine blood.

"Alira. *Please* don't make me drag you back. We need to leave the forest before we anger the spirits further." Kalel's tone is bitter and weary.

What's the point of staying now? Would he kill me if I ran?

A heavy hand weighs down my shoulder, making the breath in my lungs stall. I look up at him—Kalel's gaze is far from warm. "Whatever you are feeling, if demigods can even feel, is nothing in comparison to what you did in Thornhall." His grip tightens on my shoulder, and he hoists me up with his other hand hooked around my waist.

Guilt tears into my chest.

I shoulder out of his hold and fall to my hands and knees on the matted-down grass. Kalel pins me with a death glare. "*Don't*," he warns.

"Don't what? You can't stop me from searching for them." I hang my head and fist the broken strands of grass.

"Want to bet on that? They are all dead, Alira. All of them!" he growls sharply, raising his voice and making me flinch. My emotions are like a beast losing control inside me, welling up and about to erupt. Screaming and bleeding. I want it to stop.

He reaches for my arm again, and this time I slap him across the face. His head jerks from the strike. Kalel's eyes widen, and he stares at me hollowly. The shock quickly fades and is replaced with fury.

"Don't touch me again!" I scream, tears spilling down my cheeks with rage. I turn and make to run farther into the forest. There has to be just one who survived the attack.

Kalel laughs. It's a bloodcurdling laugh that makes chills crawl up my spine. "Little godling, I've been patient with you, but you're stoking a fire you can't put out." He catches my ankle with his foot and sends me to the ground, not allowing any time for me to stand before he's on top of me and pinning me to the ground.

His icy stare settles into a hostile grin. My stomach sinks as he pushes me into the grass bed and lowers to his knees over me. His hands are heavy against my wrists as he sets his thigh between mine, forcing my legs to part.

"I am a high duke, and you will not strike me again. I don't think you understand how much I loathe you. If you keep this up—" He pauses at the hopelessness in my expression, I think.

My lips kick up in a combative, self-sabotaging grin. "What? You'll do *what*? Kill me? I've dealt with worse things, *high duke*." My tone is scathing.

"It seems my saving you wasn't enough to earn your respect.

As I thought, demigods are heartless things. You only learn through pain and misery."

He brings his face to mine. His straight nose presses into my cheek, and a dark strand of his hair falls over my forehead. Kalel releases one of my wrists and runs the pad of his thumb over my bottom lip. A starved look flickers through his eyes.

"I find it amusing that you think you're able to disrespect me. But I've grown tired of it." His thumb lifts from my lip, but his gaze lingers there. "Will you continue to disobey me?"

My heart thrums in my chest with emotions ranging from despair to fury. "I will, you devil."

His brows pull lower, and a cruel smile reveals his sharp teeth. "Call me devil again, and you will discover how evil I can truly be." His composure is slipping. The usual calm and smooth voice is growing ragged and sharp.

Drawing in a shaky breath, I smile nervously. "All of you are devils."

His grip on my wrist tightens, making me wince at the pressure. Kalel grins maniacally, and his eyes widen with anger. Pushing a man to his wits' end is the best way to see his hidden cards.

I wish I hadn't pushed so hard.

"You're a stubborn *masochist* of a godling." He cackles wildly and pulls my wrist up to his lips. "I think you enjoy suffering at my hand, and who am I to deny your wishes, wife? I promised you pain, didn't I? I'm a demon. A monster.

A devil. I'm tired of pretending I'm not," he says bitterly, but there's an edge of hurt in his tone. I don't look too much into it because his fangs sink deep into my wrist. I clench my teeth hard to stop the pained cry from bubbling up my throat.

He hasn't bitten my wrist before, and it hurts worse than any other place on my body where he's sunk those demonic teeth into. There isn't enough flesh there, so his fangs graze against my tendons and bones. I shake my head, and a whimper slips out as I struggle beneath him.

He holds me down firmly, watching me intently as I wriggle in pain. Gilded blood spills from the corner of his lips and down my forearm. He sucks my blood savagely, letting me know just how "gentle" his prior bites have been. He allows it to be messy and is careless with his teeth.

Another cry wrenches out from my throat as I thrash to shake him off me, but he holds me securely. His body weight presses me down, and his eyes are filled with anguish and loathing. He's waiting for me to beg him to stop.

I won't. I refuse.

I've been trained to resist worse torture.

His teeth burrow deeper, much farther than I thought they could.

He doesn't want to just make me suffer; he wants to break me, mentally, spiritually. The screams and tears that follow his vicious bite distill my very soul. He drinks until I'm sobbing and limp beneath him—hardly holding on to my senses. Only one thought reverberates through my mind.

He is as cruel as they say—as soulless as demons come.

Kalel slowly removes his fangs from my wrist and drops my arm. My entire body trembles with the aftershocks of the pain. Sobs stunt my breath and sound more like whimpers from a fatally wounded animal than those of a person. My head feels heavier than it's ever been. It's tilted to the side, and I can't find the will to move.

Everything is so limp. Everything is burning.

Kalel sits back on his haunches. The callousness in his eyes has faded, and the expression on his face looks more like self-loathing than anything else. The red hue that lingers around his eyes makes him appear weary. A broken man.

His lips are smeared in gold. "Why don't you ever try to turn me into one of your flowers like you did to the men who attacked you? Why do you let me..." He grits his teeth and shakes his head, staring at the ground with a torn frown.

Because I deserve the things you're doing to me. I deserve to be punished... Because I don't want to get rid of you. Words I can't find the will to give voice to.

He hesitates before looking at me, swallowing his emotions and hardening his glower. "What is my name, godling?" he demands.

My chest seizes, warranting me to answer before he can inflict a bite like that again.

"K-Kalel."

"Repeat it *louder*. Kalel, what?"

"Kal...Kalel Lornhelm," I cry, covering my face with both hands and ignoring the blood that spills from my wrist onto my face and hair.

"*Louder*!" he yells, slamming his hands on the ground to either side of my head. The sheer venom in his voice triggers me, lighting up the adrenaline through my bloodstream.

I sit up quickly, my silver hair lashing with the momentum. His eyes widen as I scream in his face. "Your fucking name is Kalel Lornhelm!"

My breaths are hard and shaky as we stay nose to nose. Hot tears still stain my cheeks as his shocked expression fades into a flat, angry stare, but my jaw tightens with my outburst.

He leans forward, making my body still. "Don't call me a devil *ever* again," he rasps. His breath is hot against my neck.

I don't respond, I just swallow the fear that's nestled itself inside my throat.

Kalel pulls back and assesses my features. He doesn't look satisfied with my silence. "You want to kill me, don't you?"

My head shoots up, and our eyes meet.

Yes, there is nothing in all of Faultore that I'd like more than that. But as the thought flutters through my mind, I picture Kalel dead, lying in a field of darkness, and it sends dread through my bones.

"No...I don't."

His hostile eyes temper, searching mine like he genuinely didn't expect me to say that. He lowers his head after a few moments.

"Fuck," he says, shaking his head and threading his fingers through his hair roughly. His lips press together, and he gives me a look full of turmoil. A suffering man who only knows how to make others suffer. "I never wanted to be this." He grinds his jaw and lowers his head between his knees.

I tremble, holding my wrist delicately and wincing with each throb that rolls through me.

There's a desire deep inside me that yearns to understand Kalel more, but we come from two entirely different worlds. I don't know how I'm supposed to even comprehend how he came to be the demon he is today.

"I never wanted to hurt anyone," he says quietly. His eyes lock on his hands, muddied with my blood.

"I didn't either." He looks up at me, sadness blooming in his gaze. "And I hate what I became, Kalel. I can't take any of the things I did back, and no one gets to return." I lean forward and lift my hand to his face. He pulls his head back a little, like he might retreat from my touch. "If I have to spend every single day of my life repenting for who I used to be, then that's the price I'll pay."

I close the gap and softly rest my palm against his reddened cheek.

"I'm sorry I hit you."

He holds firm to his callous expression, but after a few moments, he lets his gaze drop to my wrist. "You don't remember, do you?" he asks with a broken smile.

My brows pinch together. "Remember what?"

A snap in the woods gets his attention. He stares into the darkness with golden eyes that practically glow. I try to turn around to look too, but a dizzy spell from the blood loss makes me topple against him.

I try to move away, but Kalel wraps an arm around my waist and pulls me close. *What was that sound?* My breaths grow staggered, and it feels like I'm going to pass out. I blink away the drowsy spell.

Something is coming. Something big.

My heart drops.

The large white dire wolf that bit me earlier steps out from the underbrush. *The forest spirit.* Her fur is tipped in metallic gold with deity blood. Chills erupt across my arms. I mindlessly wrap them around Kalel, his breath stuttering as I do, but his reaction to me curling into him is the last of my concerns right now.

The wolf's eyes are pinned on me with hunger.

Then a haunting voice fills every crevice of the forest, or perhaps it's only in my head, but it sounds like it's coming from the trees themselves. *"Feeding in my forest? Do you wish to invoke the wrath of the wolves?"*

I tremble against my best efforts. I'm so drained of energy

from Kalel's punishment that I'm completely defenseless right now.

A low growl rumbles from Kalel's chest. "We were just leaving." He doesn't let his grip on me lessen as he slowly stands, picks me up, and carries me, cradled in his arms against his chest. Kalel walks backward, not showing his back to the beast until we are out of its sight.

Kalel's heart pounds wildly against me. It makes my heart follow suit, wild with the fear that the dire wolf instills in us. He turns forward and walks steadily once we are in the clear. We remain dead silent until he breaks through the forest wall. The air instantly feels colder against my skin without the shelter of the trees.

The camp is quiet, and many of Kalel's knights are standing guard, waiting for our return. I meet several of their gazes as Kalel struts by them. I feel so ridiculous being carried by him like this, like some damsel in distress. They look pissed that I made their commander chase after me through the forest.

Kalel steps into our tent and sets me down on the blankets. He moves to his desk and brings back a white cloth, giving me an uneasy look before reaching for my wrist. I don't try to stop him. He wraps his fingers gently around my arm and inspects the wound.

My heavy eyes are almost closed when he strokes his tongue over my palm. He moves to my wrist and licks my wound clean. I watch through hooded eyes, taking in each caressing stroke and gentle press of his lips. One would think he was trying to convey a million small apologies in these adoring gestures.

"I'm not a cruel man, you know," he confesses with his lips against my skin. "I just… I can't…"

My heart twists at his loss for words. I study the scar on his left cheek. "What don't I remember, Kalel?"

He smooths his thumb over the bandage as he finishes wrapping my wrist, then looks at me. "If you don't remember, it's not important." He's avoiding the question. What have I forgotten? He presses my sternum with two fingers and pushes me backward until I lie down in my blankets. "I need to scent your other areas now. We're getting closer to the kingdom."

I swallow thickly, ashamed of the excitement that races through me after he was so cruel. I want to be angry, but part of me feels so much empathy for him that I can't find it in my heart to hold resentment.

Kalel bends and lifts my shirt to the bottom of my breasts. He inhales at my ribs, and it makes my back arch at his closeness. His presence alone does ruinous things to me. Electricity shoots through my body, and my core painfully twists. Kalel flinches and lifts his head, staring down at me with pinched brows.

Oh gods, please not now.

"*Ow,*" I whimper, clutching my abdomen and curling into the fetal position.

Kalel curses under his breath, dragging his hand down his jaw.

The need to have him inside me is unbearable. The ache is so strong that even though we just had a scuffle in the woods, I'm ready to beg him for any sort of relief. *I refuse.* My teeth sink into my lower lip. *But gods, do I want him.*

"Alira." Kalel whispers my name like it alone is causing him misery. His eyes flick down to my squirming thighs, his tongue swiping out and sucking in his bottom lip like he's ready to eat more of me.

Another whimper escapes my lips, and I clutch the blankets tightly. "It hurts so bad," I cry. It's never been this intense before. It's the worst aching, empty feeling. I need him inside me. It feels like I'll die if I don't get relief.

Kalel flexes his jaw and swallows thickly as he moves to my legs, pulling them toward him so that I'm no longer in the fetal position, and spreads my thighs apart. My core is so wet that it's already seeping through my pants.

"Neptune, have mercy," he mutters, sounding weaker than I've ever heard him. "Little godling, this is my fault...so I'll make it right." His voice is heady and dripping with lust. My back arches, and I only manage to respond with another pleading whimper.

My heart beats faster as he hooks his fingers around my waistband and pulls my pants down to my knees.

He hesitates as he brings his hands to my hips, fisting my

underwear in his palms. Kalel's skin is hot against mine. A rush of excitement moves through my veins.

Gods, what is happening to me?

I shouldn't be attracted to him. I shouldn't, and yet here I am, soaking wet for him and growing more feral each moment he's not filling me. The air has shifted between us. He's not consumed with rage and hate like he was when he fucked me before.

This time, he looks completely bewitched.

"Please, Kalel," I beg shamelessly.

His amber eyes flick back up to mine, a different kind of hunger flashing over them. Pleasure pulses through my entire body. With my underwear fisted in his hands, he pulls them down to my knees and lowers his head to my slit. His breath is hot against my pussy as he spreads me out. My cheeks burn with embarrassment. We hardly even know one another and here he is, about to devour me.

I cover my face with my forearm.

He growls and digs his fingers into my waist, drawing a gasp from my lips that quickly evolves into a moan as his long tongue dips into me before stroking up my center. "I have to scent you anyway, so don't assume I'm being generous," he murmurs over my clit, his breath warm against my sensitive flesh.

My head instinctively snaps up to look at him.

I wish I hadn't, because he's licking his lips and staring at me like a predator eating prey. Dark locks of hair are strewn over his forehead. He's devastatingly handsome when it's disheveled like this. I have half a mind to touch the strands, but I restrain myself from doing so. I can't just forget what he did to me in the forest. My wrist aches just thinking about it.

For a moment, I think Kalel's going to let up and leave me unsatisfied as a heartless punishment, but he moves to my clit, circling his tongue around it gently before sucking it into his mouth. A sharp cry is pulled from my lips, and I fist the blankets so I don't clamp my hands onto his head like I really want to.

Then two fingers enter me, spreading me open and curling up until he finds my sensitive spot. My head falls back into the sheets at the pleasure of being filled by his hand. It feels so fucking good as he pumps those long fingers inside me and swirls his tongue over my clit.

My moans fill the tent. I have no idea how loud I'm being. I can't focus on anything right now except how he's building me closer and closer to my orgasm. My hips lightly buck against his hand. *It's not enough.* I need more. More.

Kalel seems to pick up on my needy whimpers as he withdraws his fingers and moves his mouth down to my entrance. His eyes find mine as he shoves his tongue deep inside me. The tips of his fangs brush against my core—I don't know if they draw blood or not, and I don't care. All I know is he's devouring me and fucking me with his tongue.

I lose my resolve. I fist his hair tightly and try not to squeeze his head with my thighs. He doesn't seem to mind at all. In fact, a deep moan rumbles from his chest, and his stare floods with lust.

That look pushes me over the edge, making me come so hard that my hips move with each wave of pleasure. Kalel holds me tightly, lapping up my juices and continuing to stroke his tongue through my slit until I'm clean.

I breathe heavily, releasing his hair with horror now that my wits have returned to me. Kalel follows my motion, moving up my body, pushing my shirt up and pressing kisses against my stomach and ribs before he pauses at my breasts.

"This isn't me showing you affection. I'm marking you further, it should help hide your scent from the dire wolves while we finish passing through their lands tomorrow." His tone is stern, but his gaze has a tender edge to it.

I bury my teeth in my lower lip as he takes one of my breasts into his mouth and sucks on it. A moan escapes through my gritted teeth as I wriggle beneath him.

He groans and palms my other breast, massaging it until my core is starting to ache for him again. I want his dick inside me. Just as I think it, something hard, thick, and long brushes up against my thigh. My breathing stalls.

Kalel lets his hips come down on me, pressing his length into my leg.

Gods—how did he fit inside me the first time? It was so rough and quick that I barely remember much of it.

He moves to the other breast, sucking and licking it before sitting up. I'm wet from my pussy to my breasts because of him, and he gazes down at me like a finished meal, sucking in his lower lip like he's savoring me.

"At least you taste divine, little godling." Kalel stands to go to his desk. "You'll have plenty of restless nights when we get to Devicit. Rest now while you have the chance."

CHAPTER 13

ALIRA

The snow started falling around midnight. We've set up camp just outside the forest, beyond the dire wolves' domain. It took half the day alone to make it out of that valley, but Kalel was driven to keep his word and have his army out of Fallen Ridge. The forest spirit made it clear that it would kill anyone left on its land by twilight. At least Kalel cares about his knights.

Several demons were slain in the fight yesterday; many more were injured. The men are tired and weak, with only one healer and his apprentice. Kalel can't afford for sickness to break out among the troops. So we settle in for the night.

Tessa sits beside me around a campfire—a few other knights sit across from us. No one bothers me, which is nice. Either they're too afraid of Kalel to mess with his pet, or they respect him explicitly. Something tells me it's the first option.

"Hey, are you hungry?" Tessa offers gently.

I'm sure everyone in a hundred-yard radius of the tent last night heard us moaning. Possibly even my screams from the forest when he bit my wrist. *Ugh.* I try to keep the blush from my cheeks, but I can feel the warmth race across them anyway.

Tessa's been keeping close to my side today. She seems to have picked up on my diminished mental and physical state.

I nod weakly, keeping my eyes on the ground. Something inside me changed last night. I'm broken. Kalel saw to making sure that I was a shell of myself before he made me come in his mouth, and his tactic worked because I feel utterly helpless.

He's cruel in everything he does. I want to hate him. I want to resent the way he made me writhe in pleasure last night after the way he hurt me, and yet I've been yearning for him to hold me all day. My eyes constantly trace to him when he isn't looking. I want to see more of him. More than just the dark, grim parts. Who is he really when he isn't around me?

Why did he answer my prayer and save me? A weight burdens my chest.

My wrist aches, making my eyes narrow in pain, shifting my thoughts. Mav has yet to make his check-in with me, and

I won't ask for him sooner. He's tending to those who were injured by the dire wolves. Nikolai will probably pop in soon anyway, so I can wait. It's odd though, the other bites haven't festered the way this one has. My holy blood should've healed the small wound by now. I worry my lower lip.

Tessa hands me a chunk of bread and soup. I take a few bites of the warm, buttery loaf. She sighs and sets her hand on my knee. My body jolts instinctively at the contact.

A frown pulls at her lips. It's unsuitable for a demon to look so concerned for a demigod like me.

"Are you okay?" Tessa's ruby eyes lift to mine, and after a moment, I shrug. Her frown deepens. "Did he hurt you? We heard you screaming from the woods." She clenches her hands over her knees as if recalling the sounds makes her uncomfortable.

"Isn't that what he promised? Isn't that what all of you want? My suffering is none of your concern," I say, my voice raspy, before sipping another spoonful of soup. I know she means well, but I'm tired and bitter. Untrusting.

She lowers her head and seems troubled by my response. We finish eating in silence. I try to remain as small and unseen as I can until another demon sits on the other side of me.

Tessa greets him respectfully, but I am reluctant to look up.

"Alira, can you follow me to the tent?" His voice is soft and free of disdain. *Nikolai.* I lift my gaze and consider him.

He wears similar black healer robes as Mav does today. I

wonder if word got to him about what happened last night or if he heard it too. *Gods.* My cheeks flush with embarrassment. His medium-length fawn hair is swept to the side, and the kindness from our first meeting hasn't left his brown eyes.

I nod and stand up to follow him back to the tent. Tessa's brows are still pinched with concern for me, but she trails us silently and stands guard at the entrance.

Nikolai patiently waits as I grab a chair and sit in the center of the room, where most of the natural light leaks in.

"I wanted to make sure I got to you as soon as time allowed. I heard you last night, and I want to make sure you're not in pain," he explains as he sets down the bag he brought in with him. I can't help but find comfort in the worry that accompanies his tone.

Nikolai waits as I roll my sleeve up. I watch his face turn to horror.

"Oh...Alira," he stammers, seeming to be at a loss for words. I glance down at my wrist and see why. The wound has festered like a snake bite would for a mortal. My entire forearm is bruised purple, and black veins sprawl out like branches from the two dark gold puncture holes on my wrist.

Nikolai kneels and gently takes my hand. His brows are pulled together with anguish, and his eyes flick up to me, then back to my wound like he wants to say many things that he can't find the words for. *His kindness will only earn him misery one day.* I let out a breath but smile weakly.

"It's okay. You don't need to say anything to comfort me, Nikolai. Please continue."

His mouth is pressed into a thin line. "This may sting a bit. *Shit.* He knows better than to bite the wrist. It always festers like this on extremities. Usually, he only uses it for interrogations," he mutters as he raises his hands, a warm glow of magic brightening the space around them.

My eyes widen with awe. I've always admired healers' abilities. Their magic is arcane and passed through their elders. The healers are the demons we have the most research on. For whatever reason, King Borlin found them to be closer to demigods because of their restorative powers. He's always had a keen interest in their abilities. I heard that once, many centuries ago, some even lived in Alzhor.

Nikolai utters a few words I don't understand beneath his breath, and a sharp pain spreads through my arm. I hiss and shut my eyes against the assault.

"I know. I'm sorry, Alira. Just a bit longer." He slides his hand down my arm. I open my eyes in time to watch all the bruising lift from my flesh and into his palm. He flicks his hand behind him, and black liquid hits the ground.

What is that? I stare in horror at the black bubbling ooze and shiver at the thought. The throbbing pain is gone, and my wrist looks perfect again.

"Right as rain." Nikolai grins up at me. His eyes give away the strain his healing magic takes on him.

I'm overwhelmed with gratitude. I wrap my arms around his shoulders, and he gasps with surprise before patting me gently.

"Thank you for your kindness, Nikolai." I'm certain that at some point, he's had to help Mav heal many of the knights who've been horribly injured at my hands. Perhaps he even bore witness to the aftermath of Thornhall. It must be hard for them to let me live among them, let alone keep me from being in pain when Kalel left me in that state on purpose.

Nikolai chuckles lightly and stands to pull away from the hug. "It's no trouble at all. I was just surprised that a demigod threw her arms around my shoulders." He laughs in a relieved way. "Feel free to find me should you need healing again, okay? You shouldn't be left to suffer like that." His eyes linger on my wrist before he forces a small smile.

"I will. Thank you."

He nods and stands to leave the tent, stopping at the flap and turning to look back at me. "Can I ask you something, Alira?" His voice is more serious than before. I blink at him with a pressed frown, dreading his question if it makes him look this upset. "What is it like now that you've had to be so close to us—to the demons? Do you still hate us?" His expression is filled with sorrow.

I consider him before forcing down the knot in my throat. *No.* Of course not. They are far from the monsters I was raised to believe they were.

"No, I don't," I whisper. My jaw trembles with emotion, but I don't understand why. Maybe it's the genuine concern in his tone or the despair in his eyes.

He offers a weary grin before turning and leaving without another word.

— —— –

The snow stops falling midafternoon, and I overhear Tessa giving orders to the knights that tomorrow we will resume our trek toward the kingdom.

I inhale the cold air as I walk through camp. Tessa trots beside me and talks freely about the next few days of travel and how excited she is to return to her home. She has an ill brother who awaits her return—she's the sole provider for him and his young daughter. Life in their kingdom must be complicated right now with all the supplies and money going straight to their army. She shares that the mother of her brother's child died in the attack on Thornhall.

I stop walking and face her. "Were you there that day?" The battles are a blur to me—I don't remember many of the demons' faces. But in Thornhall, they were mainly villagers, and they were running away. I couldn't see their faces. Is that why it felt so impersonal? It's horrendous what we did, and it rots the very core of my soul.

Tessa's cheeks and ears are red from the frigid air. She takes a moment to look over the gray landscape before giving me a sad smile. "Would it matter if I was?" She kicks some snow with her boot and lets a short laugh out. "I know *you* fought there. Their blood lingers on you." Her voice is low, but she shakes the thoughts and gives me a blank expression. "We're passing through Thornhall tomorrow, you know."

My blood freezes.

I don't know how to respond to that. Her grief is tangible.

My house mother always told us, *"Demons are wretched creatures born to destroy the very world we live in. They lie, steal, and murder everything in their paths."* But we were the only ones who did any of those things. I would even say we were the ones who felt nothing.

Tessa's kindness wears on my weary mind.

We continue walking without another word.

The tents stretch out far into the valley. Lanterns start to light the field with a warm glow as the sun sets over the distant tree line.

"Tessa."

My spine straightens as Kalel's voice rings through my ears. My heart beats faster from both the pain and pleasure he invoked in me last night.

She gives me a worried look before leaving my side to speak with him. They talk in low voices, so I don't bother trying to eavesdrop. I continue to stare out in the direction of Thornhall until Kalel approaches me alone.

I ignore him, and after a few agonizing minutes, he breaks the silence.

"Nikolai visited you?"

I nod and keep the indifference smoothed over my features. I can't even bring my eyes to meet his.

"Let me see your arm." He holds out his gloved hand. I hesitantly extend my wrist to him. He doesn't miss the fear in my slow response. "I won't hurt you, Alira."

But you have. I narrow my eyes at the ground.

He pushes up my coat sleeve, examines my arm for good measure, and then gently lets it fall to my side.

"We are passing through Thornhall tomorrow," he starts.

I flex my jaw with discomfort. "I know."

Kalel side glances at me. "Our kingdom, a few days after."

"Is there a chance your king will want to kill me and continue with the war?" I ask in an empty tone.

He shifts and stares out into the misty forest. "What would you do if he ordered it?" He makes it sound like a test.

I let out a short breath. "I'd want you to do it. At least I know you kill swiftly." His brow quirks. "I've heard as much," I add. We never met in battle before the time loops. If we had, he would've killed me long ago.

"You have my word. It will be by my sword or no one's, little godling."

I find Nikolai slumped up against a tree, warming his feet by the fire as several other demons share stories over dinner. He grins and welcomes me with ease.

I don't know why I feel so comfortable around him. Maybe it's because he looks the most like a demigod, with little features that would point to him being a demon. But I think it has more to do with his contagious smile. It's too kind and inviting. Not in a way that draws doubt but in a way that tells me he harbors pain from his past and yearns for a person to take solace in. A twin flame.

I relate to that.

"Alira, there you are. Here, have a mug of ale!" Nikolai already has an extra one, like he's been waiting for me this entire time. He thrusts it into my hands. I take it and give him an awkward smile.

"Ale?"

His jaw drops open, and he gawks at me. "Demigods don't have ale? *No.* What do you drink for fun then?" He sounds utterly mortified.

I take a sip of the bitter liquid and wrinkle my nose at the alcohol sting. "Oh, we have wine."

That earns me a savage eye roll. "Gods and their fucking wine."

"It's much smoother than this." I lift the iron mug, spilling a little. Tessa plops down on my other side with a laugh. Her breath is heavy with alcohol.

"Nikolai, is this godling giving you trouble?" she jests, nudging her elbow into my side and making me scowl. "Oh, come on, you're always so serious. Let loose. Have some fun while you can." She lifts her mug and takes a few gulps.

She's already plenty drunk, but Nikolai hands her another. "Cheers!" they say together with wry grins, looking pointedly at me. I relent and clink my mug with theirs, then down the entire thing, only feeling the burn after it's all gone.

My cheeks instantly flush warm, and a loose smile lifts the corners of my lips.

"Strong, isn't it?" Nikolai smiles, chuckling as he pats me on the back. Tessa laughs and bumps her shoulder into me again. I take them both in, feeling a sense of belonging and happiness. They're embracing me like I'm one of their own. Like they can forgive me for what I've done.

No. I can't let them make me vulnerable. They're definitely trying to get my guard down, but for what? I try to blink past the spell that the alcohol has cast on me. But no matter how hard I try, only giddiness and good feelings fill me.

Kalel stalks past us. The light from the fire illuminates the side of his face as he glances at us, takes us in, *glowers*, then struts across the camp to sit with his close circle of knights. The ones that are always so serious they practically compete with his level of cruelness. I only know one's name because he's usually guarding our tent. Gabriel.

Gods.

I don't know if it's just because the alcohol makes me bold, but as I lean against Tessa, I ask, "Why are Kalel and his elite knights so uptight? The war is done. Someone tell him to loosen his corset." My eyes are heavy and a sarcastic smile pulls at my lips.

Nikolai's expression drops, and he shares an uneasy look with Tessa before setting his hand on my shoulder. "Alira, you must remember that some of us lost more than others. Some of us lost everything to the demigods." His tone is filled with warning.

As if Kalel can hear us, his eyes flick back to me, catching all three of us staring at him. I'm compelled to look away, but something keeps me from doing that. I hold his heavy gaze. "Kalel is a good person. He's just damaged in ways that cannot be mended overnight. Or over years, for that matter," Nikolai whispers.

I force my eyes away from Kalel's and meet Nikolai's soft gaze. "His mother was in Thornhall," I murmur, not disrespectfully but as a fact.

Nikolai bristles at the mention of Kalel's mother, eyes flashing to Tessa. She sighs beside me. "Yes, and unfortunately, her death scent lingers around you. Not directly, so at least you didn't kill her yourself, but you were close enough that it stains you. His mother, Rene, was all that Kalel had left in this world," Tessa mutters sadly. My eyes shift back to

Kalel in the distance, he's speaking with his men, a tired frown weighing on his jaw.

It's hard to picture him as someone who can be gentle with others. As someone who cares, like his friends paint him in my imagination. He was once a boy who loved his mother. He was once not filled with this deep-seated hate.

I picture him younger, wondering why the world revealed how dark and callous it is to him to make him this way.

"What about his father?" I pry, focusing back on Tessa.

She purses her lips and considers my question. "You know, I actually don't remember hearing about him. I think it was always just Kalel and his mother. Nik?" She tilts her head to see Nikolai on the other side of me.

He shrugs. "I've never heard him speak of his father, not once."

I open my mouth to ask more questions, but the knights around our campfire stand and beckon the three of us to follow.

"Come on, you'll love this." Nikolai throws back the last of his drink before dropping the mug to the ground and hooking arms with me. His scent is sharp, like bark and leather. I grin as he tugs me along. Tessa trots to keep up with us.

We pass Kalel's campfire, and they watch with heavy glares as we do. Kalel's is the only one whose gaze is filled more with curiosity than hatred. A small reprieve that is quickly dashed when he stands to follow us.

"*Shit*, walk faster." My tone has an edge to it. I attempt to drag Nikolai behind me, but he's dense with muscle. I barely get two steps ahead before he's reeling me back in tightly to his side.

"Don't worry, he never participates. He never watches either. I'm sure he just wants to keep an eye on you." Nikolai sounds so nonchalant about it.

"*Delightful.*" I force a tight smile, and it gets a chuckle out of the apprentice. "What are they doing anyway?" My attention lingers around the demons as they build a large bonfire at the end of camp, far away from any tents.

Tessa snags my hand with hers and squeezes tightly. "The send-off for those who died last night. It's a dance and a fire so big that the gods must take them to the underworld. No soul left behind to wander, lost in the forest." She nods to the tree line where the wolves are likely still watching us.

Just thinking about them makes me shiver.

They do all this for their dead? It's a warm sentiment that brings an ache to my heart. King Borlin lights a torch and lists the names of only the top knights who don't make it back.

Some say that long ago, he used to hold prayer circles and a proper send-off, but after the gods abandoned us, his faith went with them. A few centuries without tradition and ceremonies has left our kingdom void of spiritual festivities like this.

"Is that why everyone is drinking ale tonight?" I look

around and see a pleasant smile on every demon's face, save for Kalel and his elites.

Nikolai nods. "It's imbued with a potion to make everyone's spirit high, even if they are mourning. A send-off is meant to be a celebration." He eyes me dubiously as he explains it. "Demigods don't practice send-offs?"

I sheepishly shake my head. I mean, we literally have the blood of the gods in our veins, and yet we seem to be the furthest away from them.

How did it come to such dark times?

Nikolai pats my back and pulls me in close against his chest. My cheeks flush at his closeness. "It's all right, you'll learn tonight," he says with a bright grin.

My teeth dig into my lower lip with anxiety as I watch the great fire spark to life. Cheers erupt from everyone. Half of the knights remain standing and watching while the rest start to clap and dance around the fire. Their boots pounding on the ground like war drums, and their voices calling for the souls to gather.

It's a sound so enchanting that I become entranced. The embers flick from splitting wood and fill the dark sky with ascending bright sparks.

"Okay, watch one round and then join in!" Tessa says as she grabs hold of Nikolai's arm. He winks at me before letting go and trotting into the dancing circle with her.

The hymn the demons sing is sad and filled with longing,

but it grows happier and more uplifting as they call their fallen friends home. Chills spread over my arms as the sound works its way through my bones and into my own soul.

Nikolai's voice is lovely, carrying over the rest. His eyes catch mine as he loops back for another round. He waves for me to join. I hesitate. This isn't my place, but demigods died last night too. I should be a part of this for them.

I take the leap and merge into the bodies of dancing, singing demons. Nikolai catches me, his warm hands meeting mine and offering me a charming grin. "For a second, I thought you wouldn't even try!" he shouts. It's so loud in the crowd that I barely hear him.

"Your voice is enthralling," I say loudly, but he doesn't hear me, so he dips in close, letting his ear brush against my lips. My heart leaps in my chest at the contact. I repeat what I said, and he pulls back, smiling, *really* smiling like he appreciates it more than I thought he would.

"I can sing any creature to wealth or ruin. It's my ability. So count your blessings that I like you, Alira." He winks at me again. My cheeks warm, and a giddy smile that I'm sure is more alcohol than not has me shadowing his movements and dancing among the demons.

It's intoxicating. A feeling so strong and overwhelming that I lose myself to the song and the orange glow of the fire. My gaze drops down from the sky and lands directly on *him*.

Kalel.

He must've just spotted me, because his eyes fill with rage and he bares his teeth with what I'm guessing is a shout of fury.

Nikolai sees it too. His features flash with worry, and he glances down at me with horror. "I'm sorry." I read his lips, because his voice is too low to hear the words.

My chest sinks, and as I turn around to look back at Kalel, I'm met with his broad chest. I tilt my chin up and find his amber eyes lit with hellfire.

CHAPTER 14

ALIRA

Kalel's grip around my wrist is firm, and he practically drags me behind him. The blood drains from my face as he leads me away from the bonfire and into the dark corner of camp.

He hasn't said a single word to me this entire time.

When his tent is in view, I jerk my arm from his hold. He whirls on me, teeth gritted together tightly.

"What's your fucking problem?!" I snap, leveling him with a lethal glare. I credit the charmed ale for my bravery tonight.

Kalel's eyes are empty. He's the most frightening when he's

like this. There's no telling what he'll do when he gets that blank look.

"*My* problem?" He says it with a sarcastic laugh, his fangs showing from his manic smile. "My fucking problem?" he shouts. It makes me shake, but I hold firm, fisting my hands at my sides and staring up at him defiantly.

"That's what I asked you."

Kalel works his jaw, veins protruding from his neck. "How dare you participate in *our* ritual." His voice is lower now yet no less horrifying.

My lips press together. "Nikolai said I—"

"How *dare* you, when you… You're the reason so many of my knights are dead." He swallows the rest of the words he wants to say. *The reason his mother is dead.*

A knot forms in my throat. "Kalel, I'm sorry. I wasn't thinking."

His eyes are unwavering and cold. "No. You weren't. You never do," he bites out and sharply looks away from me.

"Don't act like it was all me. Nikolai and Tessa—"

He cuts me off again, pushing me back with his chest. "They were baiting you. They knew I'd get pissed off at their silly joke. *Stupid* little godling."

My eyes widen. They were baiting me? Is that why Nikolai said he was sorry? My cheeks warm with the ale and the heat of their antics. I doubt it was meant to be malicious. My eyes trail back up to the dancing, and I catch Tessa and Nikolai watching, big grins on their faces before they laugh at my scowl.

They're worse than the knights in Alzhor. I hold back the smile that threatens to pull at my lips, because Kalel certainly doesn't find any part of this to be entertaining.

He didn't miss them laughing either. After a moment, he lets out a long sigh. "Let's just get some rest for the night. We have a long day ahead of us tomorrow." Kalel drags a weary hand down his neck before letting it fall to his side.

We're a few feet from our tent when a small orange orb forms in the distance, uncomfortably close to the forest line where the dire wolves dwell. At first, I think it's a torch from one of the patrolling knights, but the light is too soft and moves oddly through the field.

My chest flutters. *A will-o'-the-wisp?* I've heard tales of them and how they flourish out here in the Eastern plains, leading souls to their doom or salvation. Either way, it's usually to enlighten their chosen traveler. At least that's what I've read. I've never actually seen one before though. A strange magnetic pull from within beckons me to follow it. *What strange magic.* Ever since entering Devicit territory, we've been met with many magical forces. Both horrifying and enchanting.

The warmth of the pull makes it feel right to follow the wisp.

I take a step toward it. Kalel's hand snaps down to mine and brings me to a halt.

"Ignore it," he states flatly.

Gods, of course he wants me to ignore it. "It might be important." I tug against his hold, but his hand is firmly connected to mine.

"Oh, it certainly is, but no good ever comes from the wisps. They always guide you toward something bad. Always bringing you there too late to do anything about it." He walks steadily. I can only see the back of his head. He sounds remorseful when he speaks about the wisps. *What's that about?*

"You speak from experience?" I stop resisting his pull and walk alongside him. His grip loosens, but he doesn't release my hand. I try not to focus on how warm it is.

He side-eyes me and grunts. "Twice, actually." He keeps it brief.

I squeeze his hand, and it makes his back straighten a bit. "But did they lead you to something consequential?" My tone is barely above pleading. "I want to know."

If there's even a chance that it might explain the time loop I was trapped in, I have to follow it.

Kalel stops and faces me. "No." His eyes flick untrustingly up toward the wisp, still waiting at the edge of the forest for us.

"What if it's for you and not me?" The question makes his brows pull together. *Got him.*

He works his jaw and groans. "Fine, but we stay like this." He lifts my hand for emphasis. "Will-o'-the-wisps are powerful beings. There's no telling what will happen once we start following it."

I nod nervously.

We get within ten feet of the wisp before it flickers—happily almost. Then it goes out completely, drawing a gasp from me before it pops back up farther into the forest. Moss and creaking branches make the night seem more sinister than it originally was. A dreadful feeling replaces the warmth that the wisp initially gave me.

Kalel lightly tugs my hand. "We cannot go back now, once you follow it, you must see it through to the end." He nods behind us.

I glance over my shoulder and flinch at the darkness at our backs. No field, bonfire in the distance, or smoky scent in the air from camp. Only shadows and ominous pines. A chill crawls up my neck.

"Where is it taking us?" I whisper, uneasy now that the magic in the forest seems to breathe.

Kalel walks slowly, minding where he steps as if he's anticipating traps or creatures below. I follow his lead and stay vigilant.

"It could be somewhere now. Somewhere yesterday. A glimpse of tomorrow. It depends on the strength of the wisp and who sent it." His voice is gravelly. I focus on his warm hand wrapped around mine. I don't want to know what happens if we let go.

I wasn't aware that wisps could transcend time, giving us small glimpses into ripples that only gods should know. "Wait—did you say *who sent it*?"

Kalel nods. "They don't just appear randomly, little godling. *Mercy*, what do they teach you half-gods in Alzhor? Do you know nothing of the world you live in?" His brows pinch together, and he gives me a pitiful, sarcastic look.

"Can you skip the part where you make me feel dumb and just tell me?" I glower at him.

That gets him to crack a grin. It takes me by surprise, and I find myself memorizing the way his fangs barely hang over his lower lip when he smirks like this.

"It could be a god that has sent it, or sometimes forest spirits, like that of the dire wolf. Although I doubt this wisp was sent by her." He comes to a stop as the wisp vanishes completely, leaving us in the dark, eerie forest.

I fall silent and listen to our surroundings, where not even a squirrel stirs in the underbrush. Kalel's hand tightens around mine.

I inhale sharply and look up at him. "Now what?" I whisper.

He stays quiet for a few seconds before shaking his head. "I've never had one disappear without showing me the message it wanted to convey."

That doesn't sound good at all. I swallow the nerves building in my stomach.

"Could it be here, in the dark of the wood?" I glance at our feet, something sticky is covering the forest floor.

Kalel lets go of my hand and bends at the knee to inspect the substance like I am. A metallic sting hits the back of my throat, making my eyes flash wide.

"*Blood*," we both say simultaneously.

The underbrush reaches our eyes, and as the word leaves our lips, something races through the ferns. Loud, fear-filled steps that thunder on the ground as if they are fleeing danger.

I'm standing to chase after them before Kalel can stop me. I hear him mutter a curse as we trample through the dark.

I can barely see the figure of a smaller male. Perhaps a young human. He's fast, breathing heavily, and with a bit of a pained whimper. *He's hurt.*

"Alira, wait!" Kalel calls out, seeming farther away in the forest than he was a moment ago. Fear strikes me as I cast a look over my shoulder for him. He should be right behind me, but there are only shadows. The wisp wants us apart, but why? I worry my lower lip and continue following the boy.

I'll have to do this alone.

CHAPTER 15

ALIRA

With a few more strides, we break free from the dense forest and are let out into a vast, almost turquoise-lit field of sweet grass. The wind makes it look like waves, rolling and dipping like an ocean.

The boy falls to his knees and lets out a blood-chilling scream. I slow, tensing up at the harrowing sound. It's pain. It's agony. It's…loss.

The moonlight trickles through the field as the clouds move by. The boy has pointed ears and dark hair that's matted down with liquid. He's hunched over and fisting the ground, sobbing.

His voice sounds hauntingly familiar.

I move slowly to the side until I can see the side of his face. There's a long gash on his left cheek that's been freshly sealed. Blood is dried along his jaw and chest.

My heart stutters. *Kalel?*

Who did this to him? I assumed he got that scar as an adult in battle, but he's only a boy. My chest aches with sorrow, and I have the urge to comfort him.

"Alira. The path you walk will only bring misery to all." A voice moves through the grass blades and slips into my veins. Echoing behind me. A breath as cold as a winter's breeze coasts over my shoulder and forces a shudder across my skin.

I turn quickly but find no one behind me.

"A demigod mixing blood with a demon? Preposterous."

This time the voice is coming from where the boy is on his knees. I whirl, finding a tall figure cloaked in a shimmering beige robe that meets their feet. A wreath of gilded leaves crowns their head.

A deity? Chills crawl up my arms and make me swallow hard.

I blink a few times to ensure this is real—that I am speaking to one of the gods right now. Although I cannot tell which one it is. King Borlin tore down most of the pictures in the castle after we were abandoned to our gruesome fate. The statues were left, but they lack the fine details of the immortal beings.

The god grins at my confused expression. "I am Mercury, messenger of the gods." He *tsks* and shakes his head with pity. "And, Alira, you foolish godling, you've got one hell of a warning." His hair is sandy brown, glittery with specks of gold in each strand.

I swallow, wary that after all these years of silence, they only now send a messenger. What have I done that's so bad compared to King Borlin's actions? I'm saving what's left of the kingdom and saving myself from that awful time loop. My eyes flick to the ghost of young Kalel.

Mercury laughs. "Don't worry about him. He's only a memory. A vision I want you to see." He speaks in a riddle-like voice. Mercury's bubbly demeanor makes me uncomfortable. It's like a fake smile that people give you when they are actually burying daggers in your back.

"A memory?" I mumble, staring at the boy.

His face is smeared with black blood, and I hardly recognize him. He lifts his head up to the sky with heartbreak. "Why do the gods hate us so? What have we done that's so unforgivable? Why do they despise us just for existing?" he cries to the stars.

The misery is palpable. I watch as vengeance sows roots deep into his heart. Those watery eyes narrow with rage, and his sobbing halts, transitioning to gritted teeth.

Mercury's hand is heavy on my shoulder as he leans against

me, murmuring close against my ear, "The message is from Jupiter himself, godling. If you marry this demon, there will be no happily ever after for you. Not for anyone."

"Why?" My voice is low. I can't tear my gaze away from the hatred that grows across Kalel's expression. What did we do to him? My chest falls, heavy with grief on his behalf.

"Alira, do you really believe a demon, *this* demon, could ever truly love a demigod? Look at what the poor thing has been through. He is a merciless man. One who only knows how to take. He *will* kill you. He was born to kill all half-gods. It's been written in the stars, and this is your only warning." Mercury's words weigh my shoulders down and make my stomach curl with dread.

Kalel can be cruel and untrusting of me, but I've seen how devoted he is to his kingdom. I know he's kind. Sure, maybe we will never love one another, but my heart is already yearning to be closer to his. I can't deny that I have a longing for his eyes to gaze upon me.

I lift my chin and glare at the god. "That's not who Kalel is."

Mercury's lips curl into a cruel, handsome grin. "Then you do not know Kalel. He was made from the very ashes of the underworld."

I'd be lying if I said the god's words didn't put doubt into my heart.

"What will you do, daughter of Venus? With this warning

from the gods, my job is done." He slips by me and moves beside the boy. Mercury's robe fades into a shroud of smoke, announcing his departure.

"Wait! Mercury, please hear my plea. Are the gods responsible for my time loop curse?" I shout.

Mercury lets his head fall back as he cackles at me. "It is a peculiar curse, isn't it? Powerful. Only a deity can cast one like that, I would think." He taps his lip mockingly.

I bite back my rage. "What happened to make Kalel like this?" I ask, my tone a little too pleading.

Mercury only winks at me before disappearing altogether.

The vision goes with him, and I'm back in the forest, standing alone against the night itself. Only my labored breaths fill the underbrush. *Only a deity.* So I was right, it was a god that placed the curse on me. But why? My brows pinch, and I clutch my hand over my heart.

The ferns rustle loudly, and Kalel runs out a second later, flinching when he spots me.

"There you are. What happened?" he asks with a heavy frown that makes his scar chisel his cheekbone. I can't help but stare there, knowing he was so young when he got it. He stops a breath away, too close yet too far. I want to hug him and console him like I wanted to for his younger self.

My chest caves, seeing him after the vision Mercury showed me. How could someone as lovely as Kalel have a bad fate? How could the gods believe that the peace agreement won't change mine?

Kalel must notice the sorrow in my eyes as my gaze burns into his scar.

He takes one step back, worry flashing across his features.

"What did the wisp show you?" he asks coldly as a guarded look falls over his features.

My fingers curl into the edges of the cloak. I don't want to lie to him, so I tell him the truth. "You."

His brows lower, casting shadows in his eyes. "Me? You'll need to be more specific, little godling."

I swallow nervously. "I followed you as you ran through the forest and collapsed in a field. You had…" I lift my hand to trace my finger over his scar, but he catches my wrist, and a fractured expression sweeps over him.

"You saw what happened?" His voice is darker than his gaze, both making me feel sick to my stomach.

I shake my head. "I only saw you in the field, cursing the demigods for hating the demons." That seems to put him at ease a little. He lets go and turns, stalking back toward camp without another word, his shoulders slumped.

My mouth opens more than once to ask him what really happened, but I can't seem to bring myself to ask. An unsettling fog follows close behind us, making me nervous enough not to bring it up again.

CHAPTER 16
KALEL

Thornhall was a beautiful village, tucked away in a valley between two mountain ranges, that never should've seen the horrors of war. Yet here we are.

I stare at the desolate buildings and take in the hum of silence that fills the air here.

The attack took place at night, and the village was so small that the demigods didn't even bother using fire to destroy the homes to draw the villagers out. They just killed everything in them instead. Now it's an empty land, the gardens unharvested, the livestock and anything that ever lived here dead.

My feet guide me to a familiar door. I stop and grind my

jaw. Her blood still stains the front steps of my childhood home. *Mom.*

Tessa sets her hand on my shoulder, offering me a brief look of sympathy before ordering the rest of the fleet to follow behind her. I'm grateful for the moment alone with my thoughts.

Heavy are the memories of the ones we leave behind. I cannot rid myself of the guilt for not being here in time.

Hooves and boots beat down against the cobblestones until there's only silence behind me, but I know Nikolai is lingering nearby. My oldest friend. I was shocked when he volunteered to join my army as Mav's apprentice. He's never been one for the battlefield.

I let out a long sigh. "I was going to move her into my palace the week after the attack." My fingers glide nostalgically down the doorframe where my mother marked my height over the years. Thornhall will always be my home.

Nikolai grunts. "We should've moved the villagers out when the war line neared the border. But none of us could have predicted this would happen, Kalel. Not you, nor the king." He steps up beside me and leans against the old red bricks.

"You're wrong, Nik. I should have seen through King Borlin's tricks. I was the one who accepted his peace agreement." My jaw flexes, and I have to tamp down the urge to punch a wall.

Nikolai gives me a consoling look. "Is that why you agreed to marry the demigod? As punishment unto yourself? You know, she has a good heart. I've used my sight on her a few times already, and she's clear. No motives other than to survive."

I give him a weary look. *Of course, she only wants to survive.*

He runs his hand through his hair. "She's messing with even *my* mind. She's not like the other half-gods I've interrogated. Alira's guilt is eating her alive. It's so strong that I have remnants attaching to me." Nikolai clutches his hand over his chest and gives me a pitiful expression. "You know, I actually think she might even like you—"

"*Stop*," I snap. A long silence stretches between us. Nikolai shifts on his boots and shakes his head.

I set my gaze on the ground. A sense of shame always lingers with me after I ask Nikolai to use his sight into others' heads. I know it's a strenuous gift to use—even if he can't read direct thoughts, he gets an overall picture of one's predicament and what their intentions are.

It's a gift that can harm his own mind if he isn't careful, but these are trying times. We cannot afford another slip-up like Thornhall.

"You think I'm marrying her as punishment to myself?" I whisper, and the word brings me a bit of solace. I scoff. "Yes, you could consider it a self-imposed punishment, but it is also a message to all demigods. They cherish the daughters of

Venus more than any others. And now she belongs to me." I meet Nikolai's gaze. He doesn't look completely on board with my plan still. He's had reservations about it since we received that letter with King Borlin's offer to save his kingdom. But now, after he's met her, I can see in his eyes that he's already growing fond of her. It makes my chest twist with an ugly emotion. *I hate the way he looks at her.*

Nikolai chuckles uneasily. "All right, but could you be more gentle with her? No more wrist biting, you know how painful it is." His tone hardens, and he gives me a rigid look.

I'm not in the mood for him telling me what to do. I lift a brow and glower. "What? Don't tell me you care about her."

Nikolai's expression gives nothing away. "I'm not saying I care, but she's not the monster you're making her out to be." He fidgets uncomfortably. His eyes trail up the hill our army is marching up, and his gaze softens the moment they land on her. On *my* little godling.

I face him, fisting the cowl of his cloak and shoving him up against the wall. "Her beauty clouds your judgment, my friend. I still plan on spilling her blood on this land as penance to the dead—or have you forgotten what *she* has done? What that…monster has taken from us?" I press him against the wall once more before exhaling an irritated breath and stalking away.

Everything is on fire inside my chest. My mind is fuzzy with rage and vengeance.

"Will it make you feel better?" Nikolai murmurs. I stop, fisting my hands and casting him a glare over my shoulder. His expression is filled with only misery, long sleepless nights that perhaps neither of us will ever escape. "Will it bring anyone back?"

I force my head back forward and march ahead, leaving his words and wisdom to fall behind me. I can't let anything take this moment from me. *Nothing.*

Tessa holds the attention of our army as they wait up along the slope. Alira sits on my horse at Tessa's side, staring off, down at the village that she helped destroy.

Forgive me, Mom. I know you didn't want me to become this man. I send her a prayer and hope somewhere, somehow, she can hear me.

CHAPTER 17

ALIRA

This once-enchanting valley has turned a muddled gray. It's as if the very life has been siphoned from the soil. Upon first glance, one would think it's only a sleeping village, but I can recall the bloodshed as if it were yesterday.

I watch as Kalel and Nikolai stride to the top of the hill where we await them. My eyes follow Kalel. Hurt has been threading through my chest since last night, seeing his past self collapse in that field disturbed some old trauma in my heart. He was deeply wounded, emotionally and physically. Those are the moments that shape us the most, aren't they?

The pain. Suffering. You can't truly relate to something unless you experience it for yourself.

Tessa hasn't spoken much since we arrived. Everyone has a dark air about them here, but there's a grim expression she keeps giving me that makes me worried. Not to mention the way the troops are stationed, waiting below like they are expecting a sacrifice. They stare up at us with anticipation in their gazes.

I firm my trembling hands beneath my cloak. *Kalel wouldn't kill me*, I tell myself, shaking Mercury's warning from my thoughts.

"Dismount your horse, little godling," Kalel growls as he approaches. The clouds are heavy behind him. Dark and promising a freezing rain.

Kalel's been in a particularly bad mood since last night. Whatever happened to him in that vision haunts him more than he's willing to admit. And passing through Thornhall today seems to have only made it worse.

I do as he says and swallow my pride as he stares down at me with callous eyes. Nikolai moves to my other side and leans in to whisper, "Be strong, Alira. I'm right here to heal you, so fear not. I've got you, lovely goddess."

My stomach drops. "That's not as reassuring as you think it is."

Nikolai sees the fear in my gaze. He weaves his fingers with mine. "You'll be fine, and I'm sorry about luring you into the dance last night. I was only trying to get on Kalel's nerves. Perhaps even to see if he'd join in the send-off for once." He offers me a sincere grin.

It's impossible to stay mad at someone like Nikolai. He has that innocent smile and flicker in his gaze that only makes his charm more endearing.

"I'll forgive you if you tell me what he's going to do." I let my eyes shift to the back of Kalel's head. The gilded cuff earrings even seem dull in this death valley.

Nikolai groans as he pulls his hand down his jaw, contemplating whether he should tell me. "He's going to completely drain you of your blood as penance to the innocent souls lost in this village. It will pay their fare into the underworld if they weren't able to make it through the Gates of Mortem."

Every muscle in my body halts, and I give him a horrified look. "*What?* But I'll die." My fight-or-flight response kicks in, and my heart thrums loudly in my ears.

I need to run.

Nikolai senses my urge to flee and tightens his hold on my hand. "No, you won't. You are a demigod. I've seen it firsthand, unfortunately, and I can attest that you cannot die from Kalel's bloodletting. It's not like being wounded on the field. His poison keeps the host alive, and you go into a state of rest for a few days while your body recovers."

My face pales. "That's a terrible ability to have. A never-ending source of food?" I feel sick just thinking about it. All the demigods that were captured over the years... We assumed that they were all killed, but now I fear that Kalel has been using them only as cattle. "Will it hurt?" I murmur so quietly that it's more for myself.

Kalel hears me and turns, glancing over his shoulder. "Only in the ways that matter. Come." He offers me his hand like the wicked man he is.

What is that supposed to mean? I reluctantly take Kalel's hand and let go of Nikolai's.

"Have faith, Alira." Nikolai whispers his encouragement, staring at me longingly as we part ways. It earns him a low growl from Kalel, but the healer's apprentice doesn't seem to care what his commander thinks.

Kalel guides me to the ridge of the hill, where his army looks up at us from below. Their eyes are all filled with remorse, hatred, and eagerness for what Kalel is about to do.

Mercury's words ring through my head ominously. *"He was born to kill all half-gods."* I don't want to believe his foretelling, but it's hard not to find a sliver of truth in it when Kalel can be so heartless.

Kalel doesn't bother looking at me before he addresses his army below.

"This is what the demigods have done to us. Look around and take heed. They tricked us, lied to us, *killed us* after agreeing to peace. The demigods only surrendered once we cornered them in their kingdom. Only once we invaded and eradicated what little forces they had left." Kalel's voice rings through the valley below, cutting even the cold drizzle that has begun to fall like tears from the sky. The troops are perched on their horses, watching their leader intently on top of the hill.

"They begged for mercy, but we made sure to show them none. And finally...*finally* they gave up. We will take the offering of their holiest of blood," Kalel says coldly as he wraps his hand around my waist and pulls me to be in front of him. "I will take this godling's blood and give it back to the earth so that our lost ones may find peace. Then, when we return to Devicit, I will breed her and defile her holy womb. The gods will then know true fury—despair for the wicked things they've created within us. I intend to have all our suffering paid in full."

The breeze on this gray hill moves through me, shifting my hair and chilling me down to the core. A shiver travels down my back. Shame fills me, because I'm okay with all the penance if it's Kalel who reaps it. I don't know why I feel so indebted to him. Perhaps because of the prayer he answered. Or maybe it's his burdened soul that I connect with so much.

If it saves the kingdom of demigods, I alone will suffer for them. I've made peace with that.

"Our mercy died with Thornhall," he shouts, and a roar of cheers from the knights below echoes through my ears as Kalel buries his fangs in my neck.

My limbs fail me, but Kalel is already supporting my body

with a steady arm around my hip and another gripping my chin tightly. The cheering doesn't stop, and neither do the savage pulls of blood he takes. Each gulp is audible and messy—gold spills down the side of my neck and trickles to the ground.

A whimper escapes my parted lips as my vision starts to blur. I must be close to losing consciousness, but as I'm thinking it, a surge of adrenaline rushes through every vein in my body, giving me strength to writhe in his hold. He doubles down, lifting me up completely in his arms and sinking his teeth in deeper. A choked cry escapes me.

"*No*. Stop," I whimper. "It hurts."

Struggling becomes harder, and the feeling of everything fades until I can no longer feel his lips on my skin or the press of his fingertips against my arms and legs. A bone-deep cold enters my veins—a kiss of death.

My lashes flutter shut, and my head drops back against his forearm, hanging with my throat exposed. The last gulp he takes from my artery feels like a tight cord being cut.

Everything halts at once, as if the world has ceased to exist entirely.

— —— —

The air stings my nose, making my eyes fly open. I'm staring up directly at Kalel. He's dressed in his white armor with a maroon single-shoulder cape; gold beads wrap around his chest plate, keeping it in place. Formal Devicitian attire for a knight. His armor is freshly shined, revealing the lovely beige swirl designs. The sky behind him is filled with dark clouds—the color of bruises. Warm splashes of orange bloom here and there across the horizon where the sun is already setting.

How much time has passed?

I blink slowly and try to sit up. I realize we're moving, and I'm seated in Kalel's lap, resting against his chest as he holds the horse's reins.

His amber eyes flick down to mine. A bolt of cold moves through me, and I can't help the trembling that follows. There aren't many things I fear in this life or the next. But Kalel has become one of them. *He truly did drain me of all my blood.*

His eyes darken before looking back ahead without saying a word to me. I want to ask him where we are and how long I've been asleep, but I decide to wait until Tessa or Nikolai comes to check on me.

Is this my life now? Being consumed with fear every time my husband looks at me? *Gods, what have I done?*

After a few minutes, I feel strong enough to sit up. I try to straddle the horse so I'm not burdening Kalel anymore. But he presses his hand against me, making me lean into him.

"You need to rest more, little godling. You've only been asleep for three days. Most demigods take four or five days to recoup after the bloodletting," he says gently. He looks defeated in the way he stares longingly at me. If I didn't know any better, I would say that he feels guilty about it. I've never seen him look so melancholic. The dark circles under his eyes must be from sleepless nights. Did he worry about me? Did Nikolai stay by my side as he promised? My mind is heavy with the thoughts.

I ignore his advice and struggle to sit up again. He lets me straighten in the seat this time, but dizziness falls over me, making me slump into him again.

A rumbling, soothing purr rolls from his chest. I hate how warm and inviting it is, but I greedily lean into it. My hands rest over his wrists, and I can't help but notice how small my frame is compared to his. The sleeves of my cloak are gilded with my blood. I'm guessing they ran out of spare clothing for me.

"Where are we?" I rub my eyes, trying to brush the drowsiness away to no avail.

"We are approaching the gates to the Devicitian Kingdom." He secures his arm around me like he's worried we're about to be attacked. My brows quirk, there's nothing out here except black molten rock and a thick fog or mist that's curling around the cliff's edges. We must be close to the eastern coast cliffs.

"Commander! On the west side, three Vorntails banking and circling back to us," Tessa shouts from somewhere off to our left.

"Four Skelihearts on the bridge!" Gabriel, one of Kalel's elite knights, calls from ahead.

"Full charge ahead until we reach the gates. Don't stop for

anything, is that clear?" Kalel orders his knights. They let out a battle cry from all around us. It's then that I realize we're positioned in the center of the fleet.

We're thrust forward, hundreds of hooves pound against stone in a split second. The wind bites at my face. Everything is happening so fast, and the visibility is too low to see much.

"Hold on to me," Kalel growls in a low voice, unsheathing his sword and lifting it into the darkening sky. The blade reacts to him, thrumming with bright light before pulsing a strong magical wave of power that casts away all the fog surrounding us.

Instantly, I can see the hundreds of knights, racing on horseback toward an enormous bridge. A wall of sharp black rocks juts up around the entire kingdom on the other side of the steep drop-offs. It's as if we are racing on ebony ice, shiny and slick like glass. I've never seen such a lifeless land before. I've never even heard of a place like this in our tomes that describe Faultore.

I'm so taken aback by the landscape and the battle cry of knights that I overlook movement to our left. My eyes snap in that direction when a flash of red whirls through the sky.

The blood drains from my face as three giant creatures swoop through the air, diving down toward the knights. *What in the name of the gods are those?* My eyes are dry from not blinking as I watch the creatures take out ten men at a time with a single swipe of their tails.

Shouting and chaos unfold, but those who aren't caught in the beasts' radius remain charging straight ahead as ordered.

Wait, those are… "D-dragons?" I stammer, my voice nothing short of a rasp, torn from disuse.

"Yes, and they are here for you." Kalel keeps his eyes ahead, clearly not worried about the big, red-scaled dragons that are tearing up the left side of his fleet.

Tessa. Isn't she over there? I desperately search for her but can't find her anywhere. Wait, did he say that the dragons are here for *me*?

"Why would they be here for me?" I ask, searching the other side of the group for Tessa or Nikolai.

"I'm assuming because the gods don't want this union, and they will do whatever it takes to put a stop to it. We will be safe once we reach the city. The veil protects Devicit, even from the dragons."

Why would the gods send such abhorrent creatures after us? It makes no sense. First the wisp, now dragons? I reach for the necklace Korin gave me and clutch it tightly.

Screams erupt from ahead, banishing all thoughts from my mind and forcing my attention to the bridge. Four black dragons with skeleton markings on their scales blow turquoise fire over the stone, destroying everything and everyone who'd already made it to the bridge.

"Shit!" Kalel yells and urges his horse to go faster. "Stay clear of the bridge!" he relays to his knights, and they all shout their battle cries, moving away from the dragons' reach and staying nearby Kalel's horse, ready to push through the last of the trek to the gates.

My breath curls in my lungs as we ride straight toward the dragons. Their eyes are as red as the blood that spills over the lip of the bridge from slain men. Fire crackles on both sides of the bridge beneath their feet.

Kalel brings his horse to a slow trot. He lifts me by my waist and tosses me as gently as he can off to the side. I miraculously land on my feet before crumpling down to my knees from the weakness in my limbs.

"Kalel! What are you doing?" I cry out after him. He ignores me and lifts his sword to the magical beasts.

They regard him but quickly look past his blade and focus on me. The dragons move as a unit, blowing fire at Kalel from all angles. My heart leaps into my throat as I think I'm about to watch him be burned alive, but the fire deflects easily in a wide circumference around Kalel with one swing of his sword.

The dragons don't seem fazed by it or him at all. They fly past Kalel and straight toward me. Kalel whirls, and the look that races across his face is nothing short of doom. He thinks they're going to kill me.

Oh gods.

I fist my hands against the rubble. This is it for me.

Hands come down on my shoulders and pull me close. My eyes widen, and I look up at Nikolai. He's embracing me and shouting something, but my heart beats so loudly, and the sound of the roaring dragons mixed with my terror is all I can hear. A noise so piercing that the pebbles along the bridge tremble at the vibrations.

The dragons land on the stones pillaring the bridge, hanging on the sides and peering up with their long necks. Their eyes alone are as large as a knight.

Nikolai pushes me behind him as he unsheathes his sword. "Get ready to run!" he shouts over his shoulder at me. One lashes out and hooks Nikolai's ankle with its tail. It drags him viciously across the stones and opens its mouth to either breathe fire or eat him.

No!

"Stop!" I cry out, lifting my hand out to Nikolai desperately.

All four dragons freeze and take me in. Dust twists violently in the air between us. The one holding Nikolai studies me for a few moments, red eyes moving over my features as if it wants to make sure I won't change my mind. It growls and releases him, dropping him on the ground like a sack of rocks. Nikolai scrambles to his feet and collapses beside me, pulling me in close again. His entire body trembles around mine.

Did they just listen to me?

Kalel runs toward us, sword in hand and a flash of horror pulling at his eyes. The knights behind us try to move in closer, but the dragons climb fully onto the bridge and land, blocking the fleet from getting too close.

Kalel makes it to us and faces the dragons. He's breathing heavily and seems as confused as we are.

"Why did they listen to me?" My voice hardly breaks over the sound of the winds blowing through the canyon below. I can't bear to look over the edge, we're so high up that it makes me nauseous at the idea of even glancing over.

Nikolai shakes his head, eyes wide and staring at the dragons with shock.

"Perhaps I was wrong, and the gods didn't send them," Kalel starts, not letting his eyes off them. "Maybe it was you being in the state of neither living nor dead that summoned them."

"But that makes no sense. Why would they do that?" I say in disbelief.

I manage to stand with Nikolai allowing me to lean against him. His leg is bleeding, and his forehead has a terrible cut, but other than that, he looks unharmed. *Thank the gods.*

"I've never even seen a dragon before." The beasts stand calmly, watching me like they wish to converse. *They aren't going to hurt me.* But I have no clue as to why.

I stagger toward the largest one. Its skull face markings are beautiful, a creature so morbid, yet it has such thoughtful eyes. Nikolai stops and I move closer alone.

"*Alira,*" Nikolai warns with a hiss.

I nearly fall as I step up to the beast, but a strong arm hooks around my waist. I glance up at Kalel. He flinches like he doesn't know why he caught me and forces his attention to the dragon.

"I've never seen them this tame." He reaches his hand up in offering to the dragon.

"Are they common in these parts?" I narrow my eyes at them. They seem uncertain of Kalel, but with him holding me gently, they remain calm.

The large creature blows warm air from its nostrils over us and lowers its head to Kalel's hand. He tightens his hold on my side as he touches its snout.

"Yes, we've lost many of our kind to them. They've never acted systematically like this though. We received a message by hawk yesterday that warned us of unnatural activity from them… I assumed the gods were angry. I could never fathom that they'd be here to ensure you were all right." Kalel lets his gaze shift to mine. His hair is disheveled from the chaos, and yet he still looks as ethereal as ever.

If it's true that they came to protect me, then I could easily have them take me back to Alzhor. I could have them protect the demigods from the demons. Change the tide of war.

I can go home.

It's a tempting realization.

But is that what I really want? More death when we've finally reached peace? And now I don't even know where "home" truly is. I don't belong in Alzhor. I don't belong in the city of demons either. Where do broken souls have left to go?

Kalel must have the same train of thought, because his eyes darken as he waits for me to say something. I fist my hands at my sides.

I can't believe I'm doing this.

"Please leave, and do not harm any more demons. They are…my friends," I say carefully as I extend my hand to the dragon. It nudges my palm, then slowly blinks at me as if it's saying it understands.

Nikolai's breath of surprise behind us is all I hear before the dragon lifts its head to the sky and calls to the others. The sound vibrates the ground again and makes my footing unstable. The four on the bridge tilt to the sides to fall into the canyon below, opening their wings and flying away as if they never had business being here in the first place.

The three red dragons at the rear, west side of the troops follow suit and fly south.

Kalel takes a few seconds to take in what just unfolded before turning and looking at me, then his eyes lift to the rest of the fleet behind me. I glance over my shoulder.

Every head is focused solely on me. Shocked. Hopeful. Some are even envious.

Nikolai grins and motions his hands toward me in a grand gesture.

"Alira, peace bringer and a dragon tamer!"

The explosion of cheers from hundreds of knights sends chills up my spine. I take them in with awe as they cheer for me. I never thought I'd see the day when demons would be smiling at me and cheering. Just a handful of days ago, some of them were trying to kill me. I look at Kalel to see how he feels about his army's sudden approval of me.

Kalel's expression is considerate, still untrusting, but he doesn't look at me with as much hatred as he did a few days ago.

"Let's go home," he says under his breath and sweeps me off my feet, carrying me back to his horse to ride into the lost kingdom of Devicit.

CHAPTER 18

ALIRA

The ebony metal gates close behind us with a heavy thud. They are thick enough to keep even dragons from breaking through. How long have the demons been surviving in such extreme environments like this? Did they go this far just to be away from the demigods? A place where even the deities themselves wouldn't venture?

I'm not entirely sure where we are, but the Gates to Mortem cannot be far. The sharp black rocks in this terrain are only located near the underworld. A place no god, half or not, should venture. It is said that the dragons dwell near Mortem to guard the gates as well. I'm not sure what they're trying to keep locked up down there. Or perhaps they are warding off anything from getting inside. It's a mystery to the demigods, no book I've read in our libraries has ever mentioned Mortem.

Is that why they came? My lips press together. The gods are up to something.

We step through a bubble-like wall, shimmering and glinting with hints of rainbows when caught by the last rays of sunlight. The air sweetens the second we cross, hitting the back of my lungs like blossoms in summer.

I knew that Devicit was warded with old magic, but I didn't expect the inside of the veil to have enough power to create a completely different terrain from the outside. I've read about concealing wards, but nothing I read went into such detail. I doubt anyone in Alzhor would believe it.

This is how they've hidden the kingdom, I muse, looking around with awe.

The kingdom is lush with greenery, and the temperature is considerably warmer. A forest stretches between the gates and the inner city. A loose smile draws up the corners of my weary lips. The sky is shimmery with the magic that keeps this place hidden. It's beautiful, and as the sun sets, the glittering veil mimics the galaxy far above.

We pass cottages along the main path. The lights are on, and as Kalel's army passes, street lanterns turn on, and the civilians exit their homes eagerly to welcome their knights home. Some of the fleet breaks off in the outer clusters of houses, returning to their loved ones, I assume.

The castle finally comes into view with several palaces surrounding it. The palaces are smaller and must be where all the dukes reside. I can't help but wonder which is Kalel's. My eyes light up at the magnificence of this kingdom. The streets are made from crystal cobblestones, and they light up as the hooves of the horses meet them. Every intersection and storefront is adorned with signs, greenery, and lanterns above every arched doorway.

It's like stepping foot into a completely different world from the one I've known.

Alzhor is mundane and gray, even in the summers. The streets are void of plants and life—only stones and carriages with a few white marble statues. Envy prickles in my chest as I ponder what it would have been like to grow up in a kingdom like this. Are there many orphans here? There are so many things I want to learn.

Kalel guides us to an enormous city square where a water fountain sits at the center. Illuminated liquid spills from the top, a bright blue substance that appears fresher than any mountain stream or potion I've ever seen. I let my eyes wander and drink everything in as Kalel orders Tessa and Gabriel to handle dismissing the knights and getting the horses taken care of. Nikolai lingers behind us, casting uncertain looks around the square like he's preparing for something terrible.

Many demons spill out of doorways to pubs and from streets leading into the square. Their eyes flash almost instantly at me. *Oh, that's why Nikolai is on edge.*

It's not hard to tell a demigod apart from the group. I'm the only one with silvery-white hair and gawking eyes that trace every inch of the city. Kalel seems anxious and nods at Tessa. "We'll regroup tomorrow. I'm taking her to my palace."

Tessa firmly places her fist over her heart and nods. Then her eyes shift to mine, and she gives me a warm smile. I return it and hope that I'll see her tomorrow. I've already grown so accustomed to traveling with her and Nikolai, this is all new territory for me, and it makes me uneasy.

I'm conscious of the growing number of demons that fill the square and how their glares burrow into my skin like fire. They probably hate my kingdom as much as Kalel's knights do, and I don't blame them.

My head turns, and I catch eyes with Nikolai. He nods and grins. "I'll be at the palace shortly, don't worry, lovely goddess." I take a breath of relief and smile before Kalel urges his horse forward.

Kalel throws my hood over my head and mutters, "Keep your head down. We don't need more attention on you."

I do as he says and keep my chin lowered, even though I want to look at everything. This kingdom has so much to offer.

"Does Nikolai live in your palace?" I ask to stave off the silence that falls over us as we turn down a quiet, dark alley.

Kalel grips the reins tighter. "For now, he will. He's assigned as your personal healer." It's obvious that he's not happy about the arrangements. I thought he was fond of Nikolai.

"Healing for what? Are you still going to torture me? Haven't you had your fill?" My tone is flat. I'm tired and could use a good four days away from him. I scoot forward a bit so my ass isn't rubbing against his crotch.

Kalel chuckles darkly and pulls me back against him. "Little godling, I promised you a lifetime of suffering. If I must endure it, so will you. Besides that, no demon has mated a half-god before. Wouldn't you rather have his assistance through it?"

My stomach twists. Gods, I don't want to even think that far ahead. Would Nikolai help me get an elixir to prevent pregnancy for a few months? I ponder the thought and decide I'll risk asking him when we're alone. Kalel doesn't say anything more and seems content with my silence.

By the time we reach Kalel's palace, I can no longer keep my head down. I'm too curious to see where the infamous Blood Knight lives.

The moment I see the brilliant estate, my lips part, and a small breath escapes me. The entire palace is built out of marble and white stone. Spires reach far into the sky, and each tower has a handful of lancet windows. The palace is three stories high, with balconies on multiple rooms with double doors that welcome anyone who looks upon them.

This place is enchanted—more ethereal than anything the demigods have ever built. I've never seen a palace as lavish as this. Surely, he has a library here, maybe the demon-folk have books on time loop curses or more information on the lore of gods that we didn't have in Alzhor. If I set my mind to figuring out more about the time loop, maybe I'll be able to survive here. The mind is powerful. You can escape any reality if you keep busy enough.

Kalel slows his horse to a trot as we enter the front gardens. Rows upon rows of flowers, pillars, and shrubs. Birds sing their evening songs as the palace attendants smile brightly at the return of their duke.

The peonies are in full bloom. They look so untouched that for a moment, I question if they are truly real. My heart leaps at the scent of flowers and earth.

It smells like somewhere that could be my home. A warm, welcoming sense cradles me. I don't understand it, but a small smile pulls at my lips all the same.

"Is this truly where you live?" I say without a thought as I continue to take everything in. It's the most beautiful place I've ever seen.

"Is it so surprising, little godling?" he comments back, though there's no bite to his tone like there usually is. It oddly sounds like amusement, and I'm tempted to turn and see the look on his face for myself.

It is surprising to me, because we were taught that demons

lived like beasts. Like one would think a creature from the underworld would. Uncivilized and like monsters.

The fracture in my heart grows. Why do the demigods believe these things to be true? It makes no sense. Did a half-god lie centuries ago, and it was taken as truth? Did the gods teach us falsely? A frown grows across my lips as I consider the possibilities of what went wrong in the past.

A young male greets us at the stable and takes Kalel's horse. The attendant spares me a curious look before leading the steed away to care for it.

Kalel nods at me to follow him through a back door instead of the main palace entrance. I'm guessing because he's tired and doesn't feel like being greeted by his entire staff, or perhaps because he's ashamed to have a demigod bride.

Either way, I'm grateful for our shared level of weariness.

The narrow staircase Kalel takes us up has old portraits on the walls. Crown moldings extend throughout the entire passage. I remind myself to look closer at the portraits later when I'm not so weak.

I feel like I could sleep for days, even just having woken up from a three-day slumber.

We make it to the third floor and finally stop at a gilded door that must be worth more than the amount of money I've made in my entire servitude to the Alzhor Kingdom. These must be his chambers. My pulse quickens as we stand side by side.

Kalel opens the door and motions for me to go inside.

I hesitate.

"Little godling, I'm too tired to argue with you. You're sleeping with me in my chambers. You will be my wife soon, remember?" He sets his hand on the small of my back and softly nudges me in. I swallow the unease in my throat and step through.

The room is enormous, big enough for six king-size beds. Walnut-colored wardrobes line the wall that leads into the bathroom, and deep-red drapes hang from the vaulted ceilings. A double lancet door lets out onto a balcony with a bistro set and potted plants.

I hold my breath and walk to the center of the room, looking up at the ceiling that is adorned with paintings and gold.

"This is—" I don't even have the words for what this is. It's beyond lovely. Tears prickle my eyes, yet I'm not sure why. Emotions I don't fully understand cloud my mind.

Kalel's eyes are heavy, but he offers a weak grin. "It's more than you ever thought of us lowly demons, isn't it?" His expression is hollow, but more sorrow lives there than vengeance. More pain than disdain.

Guilt is a burdensome thing. It rots my insides and makes me sick for what I thought of them…and for what I did in servitude to Alzhor.

"What did you think when you laid eyes on Alzhor?" I watch him as he crosses the room to his nightstand.

He pauses for a moment. "Comatose, almost like a place lost in time." His amber eyes flick back to me.

My lips press together. He's not wrong.

Kalel unbuttons his shirt and lets it fall to the ground before walking past me. "You may do as you please, but don't leave the room," he says as he steps into the bathroom and shuts the door. The water runs for his bath, and I don't move until I hear him sink into the water and sigh as the hot water surely soothes his muscles.

I'm the only monster in this kingdom, I think as I look around once more, shrinking into myself and wishing our fates could be rewritten.

I grab the extra throw blanket on top of his bed and slip out onto the balcony. The night is a bit chilly but relatively warm compared to outside the veil. I'm still in awe at the magic that the veil adds to the kingdom. I wrap myself in the thin blanket and curl against the stone railing, letting my eyes slowly close to the sound of somber nightingales and the ache in my chest.

CHAPTER 19

Kalel

I leave the towel over my head as I exit the bathroom. When I don't initially see her in my chambers, a bolt of panic surges through me. Did she leave? I look over to the balcony and find her bundled up on the ground with a blanket wrapped around her shoulders.

My muscles relax, and I stare at her form for a moment. *Of course she chooses to sleep out there like a masochist.* I grin, drowsily amused with her.

I step outside quietly. She doesn't stir, so I assume she's sleeping. I crouch beside her and gaze down at her face. The little godling's hair is like starlight, lashes as dark as raven's blood. She's the most beautiful creature to have ever walked these halls.

I reach out and let my fingertips brush delicately across her forehead, sweeping away strands of hair. Warmth and a curling sensation in my stomach frequently accompany her presence. As much as I want to hate her, she's slowly thawing my resolve. I long to hold her. To tell her of her beauty and how it haunts my every thought.

I cannot allow myself to care for someone like her though. Not when she's taken so much from me. I bite into my lower lip, tasting the bitterness of my blood.

But...

She could've fled tonight. She could've used the dragons to destroy all of us out there. I saw the thought flash through her eyes. Then I watched as she quickly discarded it.

She chose to stay. She chose me. And for some reason, that dug a knife into my heart.

Does she truly wish to make this peace agreement work? If King Borlin learns that the dragons aided her, he will surely go back on his word and try to eradicate us again. To him, we have no place here in Faultore. What would be next? Taking over the mortals and their land too? It's enough to make me sick.

Nik was right, she is different.

I ponder these thoughts as I gaze down at her soft lips and worried expression as dreams cloud her mind. She's unlike anyone I've ever met.

Perhaps…she is not as evil as I believed her to be.

What a strange godling.

I scoop my hands under her and carry her back inside. She blinks groggily up at me before closing her eyes and burying her face in my chest.

That draws a torn grin to my lips. *Foolish girl.* She shouldn't trust me so thoughtlessly.

I toss back the covers on my bed and set her down. I have to work to get the throw blanket out of her grasp, but she eventually lets it go. I grab the nightgown that my maids set in here for her arrival and carefully undress her before slipping the dress over her. She mumbles and shifts in the bed.

With a moment to finally breathe without hundreds of my soldiers around, I bow my head and drag my hand down my face. I put on a strong appearance for everyone, but I'm only a man, and I'm far from holding my shit together.

I'm so close to breaking. To caving in to this ruinous yearning that pulls at my heart to let everything go that isn't her.

I shut my eyes. *I need to hold it together.*

Thank gods we are back in Devicit. It's been over a year since I've slept in this bed. I didn't plan on having a bride to bring back and share it with, but I'd be lying if I said I haven't grown fond of having her near. Her soft breaths are like a song that fills where silence used to lie heavily beside me.

It's odd how you don't realize the loneliness in your soul until you meet someone who stubbornly plants it there.

I let the towel on my head fall to the floor before slipping into the sheets and pulling her close against my body until her back meets my chest. I'm too hungry to sleep. I haven't fed in three days, since the bloodletting.

Sometimes I hate what I am. It's not like I ever wanted to be a demon that has to feast on blood to survive, but I made my peace with this part of myself long ago.

My hand smooths over her back until I reach the top of her shirt. I pull it down to her shoulder so her flesh is exposed to me and let my lips coast across her skin. She writhes in my hold as she stirs more.

I sink my teeth into her shoulder. A soft whimper escapes her, and she stops fighting against it. I drink from her, savoring her sweet, gilded blood with each swallow. Feeding is always intimate with her. It has never been like this with anyone else, but it is with her. I hold her closer, shutting my eyes as I gorge myself and feel her warmth against my chest.

It's the closest feeling to contentment I've ever had—the nearest I've allowed another person to get to me.

Her hand moves over mine, gently brushing her thumb over my scarred knuckles. I flinch, realizing that my hands are trembling. Is she trying to soothe me?

An empty ache hits deep in my gut. I'm still hungry, but

if I keep holding her like this, I don't know how long I can hold myself back.

Why do I yearn for her so deeply?

Gods help me.

CHAPTER 20

ALIRA

Kalel pulls his hand away like he's going to retreat from me.

He was shaking. I don't know what battle he's fighting in his mind or if he's weak from hunger. Either way, I catch his hand before he can withdraw completely.

"It's okay," I whisper, holding his hand over my chest. When I'm sure he won't move it, I let go and lift my arm to his head, stroking his hair back a few times while he hesitantly continues to drink from me.

He doesn't lean into it right away, but with the third brush through his hair, Kalel lets his body relax into me, and the stiffness leaves his arms. This is how I imagine lovers embrace one another. How affection should feel in the dark hours of the night.

After a few more gulps, he removes his teeth from me, licking the bite marks and pressing his lips to them. I'm too tired to try and wriggle away from him while he scents me. I just close my eyes and let him drag his tongue up the side of my neck, telling myself repeatedly that I don't enjoy it.

But I do, and there's no hiding it.

"Alira," he whispers, begging my eyes open.

"Hm?" I mumble sleepily.

Kalel shifts under the blanket, pushing me onto my back and moving on top of me. His palms are pressed heavily into the bed on either side of my head. My eyes widen a little because he has me in a vulnerable position but also because of the look on his handsome face. It's too dark to tell if his cheeks are red, but his eyes are filled with heady thoughts.

"Why did you tell the dragons to leave?" he asks. It's the softest he's spoken to me, brows pinched with doubt.

Would he believe me even if I told him the truth? He's been so sure that I'm nothing more than a monster, and he isn't wrong. I wouldn't blame him if he didn't trust me.

"Because they were hurting your men." I lift my hand slowly to his cheek. He stiffens at the contact but doesn't pull away. "Because I didn't want them to hurt you."

His eyes dip to my lips before lifting to my eyes once more.

"You could have destroyed my entire army with the four dragons alone. Why didn't you take the chance? I saw the realization spark in you the moment it crossed your mind." His voice darkens and he puts more weight down on my hips.

I wince at the pressure.

"Kalel, I want to be here. I want this peace agreement as much as you do." I plead with my eyes for him to believe me. Now that the demons know I'm a weapon, they could decide to get rid of me, for nothing more than to keep the dragons untamable.

Dark locks of his hair halo his face as he gazes down upon me. I could stare into the fiery embers of his soul all night. This hurt, tame side of him is lulling. Enamoring.

He considers my words but doesn't reply. Instead, he lowers to my chest, working my shirt up until my breasts are exposed.

I know he's only scent-marking me, but it's so intimate and sensual that I can't help but whimper and rub my thighs together as he licks my breast and sucks down on it.

He lets out a long breath, sliding an arm beneath my lower back and pulling my core into his crotch. The air hitches in my lungs as I feel how hard he is beneath the thin pants. *Gods help me.*

Kalel moves to my other breast, lapping at my sensitive flesh and sucking until I'm melting in his arms. I run my fingers down the corded muscles of his arms, admiring how fit his torso is. He's twice as big as me, and he's being so gentle tonight that my heart twists.

He presses a final kiss to my breast before sitting up and staring at me. "We are in the kingdom now, little godling. The demons will be more dangerous here, eager to kill you if they get the chance. I need to make sure they understand that if they try anything with you, they are also crossing me."

My core is soaking wet. *Fuck.*

Kalel's eyes narrow and his jaw flexes as he glances down at my thighs. He swallows and licks his lips. "Spread your legs." His voice is gravelly.

I suck in my lower lip and do as he says, letting my legs fall to either side of me.

His hands go to his waist, and he pulls down his pants. My heart drops into my stomach.

Kalel's cock is huge. I can see it clearly now with the moonlight shining in. It has the same anatomy as a demigod's except… Wait. My brows quirk, and my tongue swipes over my lips to wet them.

"Um…what is that?" I look at the bulbous part at the base of his shaft. I recall feeling it when he fucked me in his tent, but I didn't see it like I am now; I only felt it hitting my entrance as he thrust his dick into me.

He grins at me, one that shows off his fangs and makes my center weep. "You've never seen a knot? Oh, little godling, you don't know what you've signed up for." He chuckles as he pushes my nightdress up and removes my underwear.

A knot? Why do demons have knots? My cheeks flush with

heat, and I have to bite my lower lip to keep the shameless curiosity from my face.

Kalel tosses my underwear to the floor and lies back down behind me. He rolls me over on my side and brings my back to his chest again, but this time he guides his thick cock between my thighs and bucks his hips lightly. His dick rubs against my slit, coating himself in my slickness.

He moans in my ear and lowers his hand to my clit, circling it in small motions that have my hips bucking against him.

"*Fuck*," he rasps, burying his lips in the crook of my neck.

"Are you going to knot me?" I take a deep breath. I'm not sure why I want it so desperately, but it's like my body is telling me that he's made for me. That he will fit so snug in my pussy.

"No. I'm not going to claim you completely yet. This is an exchange of scents. I will be in you and your scent on me." He barely gets the words out without moaning.

My thighs instinctively squeeze together at the pleasure from the friction where his dick rubs me. Every time his tip glides over my clit, it makes my back arch into him more. My orgasm is building quickly. My eyes loll to the back of my head with each thrust.

"Does my little pet like having her slit fucked?" he groans against the back of my head, inhaling the scent of my hair, and I swear as he does, his dick throbs and hardens a bit more.

I've never felt so good in my entire life. It's like he's put a spell on me, and every part of him that touches me is on fire.

Kalel abruptly stops and lifts my top leg, hooking it with his arm. A gasp escapes me with the sudden rush of cold air. He aligns the tip of his cock with my center and slowly pushes his cock inside me. He spreads me open and lightly bucks so just the tip is fucking me.

My head falls back on his shoulder, and my breaths hitch with each thrust. He takes his time inching in farther. I bite down on my lower lip to keep myself from screaming. He's being so gentle this time that I can feel everything. Every stretch and movement is driving me crazy.

His hand glides down my stomach, and he presses over my lower abdomen to add pressure where my belly has already expanded to take him in. I watch as he rubs himself through me, and a deep rumble escapes his chest and instills deep into mine.

"Divine gods, what were they thinking when they created you?" he murmurs into my shoulder as the tip of his dick kisses my cervix, over and over, stirring me into a drunken, pleasured state. I barely hear his words, half wondering if I heard him correctly.

He hooks his other hand around my throat and tilts my jaw up. Kalel takes my ear between his lips and bites down enough to make me wriggle. He moans and holds his knot up against my entrance, not quite pushing it inside but edging that line and making me nervous. *There's no way he can fit that thing inside me.* My pulse leaps into my throat, and I let out a staggered breath.

"I'm going to mark every part of this womb. Every part of you belongs to me, little godling."

Wait. *Mark?* Is he going to come inside me? A gasp escapes me. "I'll get pregnant if you come inside me!" I cry out, fisting the sheets at how full he's filling me with his engorged cock. I can't keep my orgasm from exploding with his last few hard thrusts. I come on his cock, hips trembling and lips parted.

He moans as I come on him, then his hand tightens around my throat, and he stills completely. Every muscle in his body is motionless except his dick. It throbs in my deepest parts, pulsing, releasing so much hot come inside me that I whimper at the pressure building in my abdomen.

"Don't move. Our releases are longer than demigods'," he growls over my neck in a possessive way that makes my core tighten around him. He groans, and another hot wave of come spills into me.

I'm going to get pregnant. Tears start to spill down my cheeks. I knew what I was signing up for, but I didn't think it'd happen so quickly and like this.

Kalel strokes his tongue up the nape of my neck and murmurs, "Stop crying, Alira. You won't get pregnant. You have to knot with a demon in order to conceive. Even then, you are a demigod. It might not even be possible for us to have children. It's never been done before, so cease your weeping."

Is that true? The tightly coiled anxiety in my chest uncurls a bit. A relieved sigh leaves me, and I relax more into his arms.

"Thank gods." I don't think anything of it when I say it, but Kalel flinches like he's been wounded.

"Are you so relieved that you won't have a filthy demon's child yet?" His voice has hardened back up, and he withdraws from me. More liquid than I thought possible for a male to produce leaks from my center.

"That's not what I said." I sit up to look at him, but he's already up and securing his pants back around his waist.

"You didn't need to." His eyes are dull and filled with anger. "I'll be in the other suite. Tessa and Nikolai will be here in the morning to collect you." He storms out of the chambers and slams the door behind him, the sound making me flinch.

Did I…hurt his feelings? I look down between my legs and frown at the mess we made. I'm tired, but not "sleep in Kalel's come" tired.

The bathroom is larger than I thought it would be. Vaulted ceilings and stone finishes from the sinks to the steps that lead to the built-in bath. It's more like a hot spring than a bathroom.

After figuring out their faucets, I let the hot water run until the square stone tub is filled, and then I find some soaps and salts to make the water smell like fresh blossoms.

No matter how long I bathe and try to find some peace in my thoughts, I can't. All I can think about is Kalel. The way he touched me and how hurt he looked when he left. He hates the demigods so much, more than I ever despised the demons. But I don't think he hates me, even if he wants to. Is that why he always has that anguished look on his face?

That thought brings a hopeful smile to my lips.

I hope for more nights where he holds me, and I can run my fingers through his hair.

— —— —

"Kill her."

My eyes flash open at the strange voice, and the next thing I know, a dagger is thrust into my shoulder, pinning me to the mattress. Adrenaline rushes through my body and spikes my pulse.

I'm being attacked.

My training kicks in, and I tear the dagger from my shoulder, lashing out at my attacker. I cut into someone's flesh, but it's still too dark to see clearly.

They stumble and fall to the ground. In the next second, all the candles are lit at once, and Kalel is kicking and shouting at the door, attempting to get inside. Three people are standing in the room. Two men and one woman. I slashed the shorter, younger male across the chest. He's writhing in pain on the floor and bleeding profusely.

I don't recognize any of them, so I doubt they are a part of Kalel's army, but it's clear that I'm not welcome here. So much for Kalel's scenting being enough of a warning to keep them away.

"She cut me!" the young male screams.

The woman glares at me and unsheathes her sword. "Demigods *will* be extinct. If you think we're going to let you survive and marry Duke Lornhelm, then you're fucking insane!" She charges at me.

I chuck the dagger at her, striking true, straight through the center of her neck. Her eyes widen, and she chokes on her blood. She falls to the side of the bed before slipping to the ground. The clatter of her sword rattles on the ground just as Kalel bursts through the door. He takes me in briefly to make sure I'm okay, then he looks at the two remaining intruders.

"How dare you," Kalel says as he unsheathes his sword. "How *dare* you try and kill what's mine."

"Wait, Sir Lornhelm, we were only trying to free you from this fate!" the wounded male shouts, eyes teary.

The other one nods. "We can all kill her, right here. Right now. Let us get rid of her for you—" Kalel cuts him in half before he can finish his sentence.

The wounded intruder only has time to let out a sharp cry before Kalel swings his arm sharply and lops the man's head off. His body follows the heavy *thunk* of the head landing on the ground.

Kalel breathes heavily, his eyes are weary and have dark marks beneath them. He curses under his breath. "I shouldn't have left you alone." He lets his eyes meet mine before he focuses back on my shoulder wound. "I'll get Nikolai."

"No, I'm fine. There's no need to wake him. He can check me in the morning." I rise and make my way to the bathroom. My reflection is unsettling. The white nightgown is drenched in golden blood. Sections of my silver hair are sticky and cling to my neck.

Great, this won't come out for a while. I frown at my hair.

Kalel lingers by the doorframe, leaning against the wood with his arms crossed. "Are you sure you don't need him now?"

I roll my eyes and slip out of the ruined gown. I ignore that he's staring at my naked body and check my wound to make sure I don't need Nikolai. "Yes. He needs his rest too, and it's not so bad. It's already sealing up." At least our holy blood heals us at a quickened pace.

I'll need another bath though. I make my way over to the tub and start it again. Kalel's presence starts to wear on my patience, so I give him an annoyed look. "Don't you need to report them as deceased or something?" The edge to my voice is lost as I take in how he's looking at me.

There's a well of guilt in his eyes and more conflict than I've ever seen in another's gaze.

"Just get in the tub," he says with a tight jaw. Kalel kneels beside me and rolls up his sleeves. When I don't move right away, he tilts his head to the bath. "Get in, or I will set you in there myself."

I huff and shed my nightgown. "You're one of those guys, huh?"

He gives me a quizzical look. "A gentleman?"

I laugh. "No, I didn't even think that word was in your vocabulary. You're one of those people who does things out of guilt to try and make up for something."

Kalel glowers as I lower myself into the tub and let out a sigh. The water quickly turns metallic gold. His eyes soften just as fast.

"So what if I am? I'm not some heartless fiend." He grabs one of the apothecary bottles from the side table and pours the liquid into the water.

I smile at the humor in his tone and the uneasy way his eyes lift to mine a few times before dipping his hand into the water and gently rubbing his thumb over the wound on my shoulder. I wince at the dull pain, though it's nothing like it was a few minutes ago.

"This concoction should heal you enough to relieve the pain." Kalel slumps against the steps leading to the tub and rests his head on his forearm as he lets his hand rest in the water.

"So you *can* make more than just soup, Apothecary?" I tease, and it's worth the amused look he throws my way.

"I told you that I make medicine."

We look at each other for a few moments. It's a rare moment that we aren't glaring at each other. Our eyes are only filled with curiosity for one another.

"Why did you become a knight, Kalel? Clearly you are suited for your potions."

He doesn't emotionally pull away like I was afraid he would; instead, he blinks slowly and rubs the back of his head. "My life took a different path. I still get to have my potions, and I wouldn't change my decision. Not for anything," he says softly. "What about you? Tell me what you wanted to be. Surely it wasn't a knight." He sounds so sure, a nostalgic grin tugs at the corner of his lips.

I smile and think of my past.

"I wanted to be a dressmaker. I would change my decision if I could." I move to the center of the bath so I can see him clearly. "I would go back and make sure I chased that dream until I had it. Until I was dancing at balls and wearing the finest dresses known in Faultore. Of course, we don't have many balls in Alzhor anymore, but I would've left and run to the mortal kingdoms if I had too."

His expression is solemn. "Why didn't you?"

My smile fades. "Orphans in Faultore are assigned roles. I was placed in the knights' faction, and the rest is history. I was silly to dream of a role that didn't exist in my kingdom." I lift a shoulder and drop it nonchalantly.

Kalel dips a finger into the gilded water and pops it in his mouth. "I'd like to see you in those dresses you once dreamed of." His gaze burns into me.

I wasn't expecting him to say that. My heart stutters, and I have to clear my throat before changing the subject. "Were you really in Florum Forest that day just to collect mushrooms?" I ask, bringing the gentle air between us to a mild chill.

His jaw flexes. "No."

"You were scoping out the kingdom, weren't you?"

Kalel nods. "That, but I was visiting that place because I played there often as a child. Even I was foolish and too hopeful, once upon a time…" he says with a voice that suggests the memory is tainted.

I sink lower into the water until my chin is touching the surface. "Why were you so far from home?" It makes me think of the demon I found there when I was eight. The one I watched die.

He did have some similar features to Kalel, but he died. I watched him die.

Kalel smiles. It's a sad one, tugging wearily with longing. Regretful in the fluid curve of his lips.

"I was scouting with my uncles. It was the same year that the war started. Mere months before everything collapsed and the trade routes were shut down. We were on the hunt for the wild Griffon's flower. It was said to only be found in Florum Forest, and my uncle Dakre needed it for his potion. He was teaching me everything I needed to know regarding becoming an apothecary like him. We knew it would be a dangerous trek through the forest that night. We went farther than we normally did, and somehow, I got separated from them."

Kalel stares into the water as he twirls his finger around my floating hair.

That's strange… I remember finding the demon curled up and crying against a tree. He was lost and needed help. He was cold. I will never forget the way he looked up at me when I set my coat over his shoulders. Those big amber eyes were scared of me.

Amber eyes.

My gaze shifts up to Kalel's. He watches me with deep sorrow, eyes like fire. My attention is brought back to the scar on his cheek. The boy from the vision Mercury sent looked a little similar, but it was too hard to tell with all the blood.

No. I saw the boy die.

How could he…

Tears form in my eyes. "What happened to you?" My voice is low with dread. I think I know how this story ends, and it isn't good.

Kalel lifts his head from his arm, and he stares at me. Wordless. Scrutinizing me. *I may have a blurry memory of that night, but he seems to remember everything.*

"A godling found me. Hair as silver as yours. Beautiful, I had thought, but I didn't know how foolish the children of the gods could be." His eyes hold mine fiercely, making it hard to draw breath. "I thought she was helping me when she guided me back to her kingdom. I thought that because I was accompanied by her… I don't know what I thought.

That the demigods would help a lost demon child? Was that so unfathomable?"

"Kalel...you are the boy I set my jacket on?"

His face is empty of emotion. "How could you forget? I even placed my jacket on your shoulders, and yet you still didn't remember."

My heart clenches painfully, and I shake my head. "I saw you die. I thought the boy I met that night had perished. How are you alive?" Tears stream down my cheeks.

His eyes harden, and he glances down, gritting his teeth on words I know he wants to say but won't.

Kalel. If we met all those years ago...why tell me now? A frown tugs at my lips, and my heart sinks like a stone.

I sit up and draw my knees to my chest uncomfortably. This is the part that I never truly received the whole truth on. But with the vision Mercury gave me, it's not hard to guess what happened. Chills spread over my arms, and tears stream down my cheeks.

Kalel's expression remains impassive. He has no tears left to shed. Not for this world nor me. Not when I took everything from him.

He reaches his hand to my face and slowly wipes away my tears as he says coldly, "But we both know the demigods didn't help me that night, isn't that right, Alira?" My jaw trembles and more tears spill over my cheeks. "They marched me back into that forest and used me as bait to lure my uncles in."

"*What*?" I gasp, my voice a mere whisper.

As he says the words, I relive the screams I heard that night. I couldn't see much from the bushes where I was hiding, but I knew something awful was happening. Something that was my fault. By the time I was able to sneak farther into the forest, it was already too late. The boy was dead—I wept for him. I remember the dull eyes that watched me. I prayed to the gods who abandoned us. I prayed that they would have mercy on him.

"They cut both of my palms, and the scent of my blood drew them in. I tried to scream for them to leave me, but they were enraged by the betrayal of the demigods. They attacked first, freeing me and telling me to run. To run and not look back."

He pauses. The moment of silence is like a drop of water on a glassy lake. Sadness ripples through me and has no limit to the depths it reaches. Kalel brings his thumb back to his mouth and licks my tears from the pad of it.

I don't want to hear the rest. I war with my guilt.

I was only a child, but I should've helped him somehow. I should've done *something*.

A broken, heartrending smile breaks across his face. "I ran. I was so filled with terror that I couldn't think of anything except my own fear. I didn't try to help them. I didn't even think about it. I just...ran—" He swallows thickly. "I heard Dakre scream first. Then, moments later, it was Collik.

The forest was dark, but I heard them coming for me. They wouldn't even let a child escape." He starts laughing, because what else can he do, telling such a horrific tale?

"Kalel," I whisper, moving my hand to set it on top of his at the stone's edge. He flinches away from me, turning those sad, broken eyes back to me.

"I didn't know what I was to the rest of the world before the moment they cut me down, but I knew after they drew my blood. I knew as the god of the underworld appeared like shadows spun from the stars."

Pluto saved him? The god of the underworld hasn't been spotted in centuries. Why did he show up at that moment?

Kalel's scar has a deeper hue to it in the dim light of the bathroom. The very air has a melancholic weight that burdens my shoulders.

He grins, but it's far from happy. "Turns out not all the gods have abandoned this world. Not completely anyway. Pluto killed the four demigods with a mere sweep of his hand, taking their souls like pebbles to the ocean."

We sit in silence for several heavy seconds. "But, Kalel, I saw you. I grieved over your body. There was no god. No demigods that were found near your body. Their bodies were located at the edge of Florum Forest."

He watches me distrustfully. "Your mouth is full of lies. I never saw you that night after they took me away."

Maybe Pluto came to Kalel in his journey to the

underworld, and that's why he doesn't remember me finding him... I mean, he was dead. A chill runs up my arms. It was my first brush with death.

So Pluto is the one who killed the Alzhorian knights that were found in the forest. A harrowing pain spreads through my bones. Those knights were the last spark of the war. The demigods blamed the demons for a foul attack and were furious that they were even in our territory.

"I was disappointed you didn't remember me in Florum. I knew it was you. I had waited for such a long time to see you again." Kalel's voice slips into my veins and freezes my blood.

I was the reason that Kalel's mom was slain.

I was the reason the last match was struck, igniting the war.

CHAPTER 21

ALIRA

Kalel remembered me.

I suck in my lower lip and try looking away to hide the heavy tears that fall. He catches my chin and tilts my jaw toward him, forcing me to look into his eyes. His arm is in the water and getting wet, but he doesn't seem to care.

"Why do you cry?" he asks, bringing his lips close to mine. "Is it because you know you're the root cause of all my suffering? Of all my pain?"

"Kalel…I was only trying to help you. I didn't know they were going to do that." A sob breaks from my chest. "Please. Please forgive me."

His eyes are empty. "Forgiveness?" He leans forward and kisses me softly before releasing my chin, standing and staring down at me. "Perhaps in another life I could have forgiven you. Perhaps even cared for you. But my heart is dead, little godling, it died the night you found me in that forest."

Kalel takes a deep breath before he firms his resolve and leaves the bathroom, calling out before he exits the chambers, "Nikolai will be here to attend to you shortly." The door clicks behind him.

And I break into a million pieces.

Nikolai heals what little imperfections remain from the injury quickly. "Gods, one day without an injury to heal on you is all I ask," he grumbles in a light tone and shoots me a playful grin, but I can't bring myself to smile. My eyes are red and feel heavy.

He lets out a defeated sigh. "You know, my dad used to tell me that the best things come after having bad luck." I look up at him as he grabs a comb from the nightstand and kneels before me. Those honey-brown eyes warm as he brushes my damp hair. He looks at me like I'm a precious jewel, like I've never taken from him, when I know that's not true.

"I know many who have terrible luck and still never had anything good happen to them." My tone is sour. I can't stop thinking of Kalel. All I want to do right now is talk to him. There's so much I want to tell him. I want him to know that I thought of him often too.

Nikolai chuckles, steadily gliding the brush through my silver hair. "My dad also told me that if you focus on only the bad things, you'll miss every opportunity that comes your way."

"Like what?"

He shifts his focus from my hair to my eyes. "For example, I suffered when Thornhall fell, and I'm not saying that it didn't hurt or make me want to turn vengeful, because it definitely did. But I saw the chance to aid Kalel's forces and took it. I saw the opportunity to talk to the captive half-god and see if she was truly evil and filled with malice. And you weren't. You were oddly like me. I was able to make a new friend and meet someone I never thought I would. I was able to aid in bringing peace to our lands. A future with harmony." He hums and closes his eyes with a smile. "That's the best future I can picture, don't you agree?"

Nikolai is the kind of man who could fill your head with a thousand dreams. The best kind of person someone like me could ask for.

I nod. "That's the future I want too."

He grins. "I know," he says a little too surely. Nikolai stands and grabs the bags of clothes he brought in with him. "Which is why you need to start looking for the good things. No matter how small. We can start with the fact that Tessa ran all over the kingdom this morning to get this dress for you. So you're not allowed to cry on it, okay?" He holds up a cloth bag that must have a dress in it. I give him a quizzical look. "For your wedding this evening, Alira."

I stare at him blankly. *This evening?*

It seems awfully cruel that this entire time, all I wanted was to escape the time loop and to save the demigods. Selfishly, I think the only thing I wanted to do was to live. So why does it have to be me who marries the Blood Knight? Why not an innocent demigod princess? Or a lovely maiden with unstained hands, unlike mine… *Why did it have to be me?*

The one girl who is the cause of all his suffering.

He must have been hurting so much this entire time.

My lips press together tightly. The worst of his scars were my fault. Is this why the gods punished me? Why I was slain twenty times at his hands?

"What did I just say?" Nikolai takes the bag away from me and sets it on the bed.

"I'm sorry, I just…" More tears well in my eyes and crash to the ground.

He sits next to me and pulls me into a tight hug. My eyes snap open, and a breath escapes as Nikolai embraces me. "It's not your fault. None of this is your fault. Fate has a way of stringing us along sometimes, but you must trust your path," he murmurs as he caresses the back of my head with his hand.

"Apologies for invading your thoughts," he adds, not seeming sorry at all.

He's a mind reader? I didn't know that demons had them. Mind readers are few and far between in Alzhor. I can't find the energy to be upset with him when he's so kind to me though.

I sink to my knees on the floor and melt into his arms. Nikolai's minty-bark scent invades my senses, bringing that calm, tender feeling that always accompanies him.

"It *is* my fault. I…I wish I had never found him that day."

I pull back and lift my face to look into Nikolai's eyes. Gentle, understanding pools of honey greet me. His gaze shifts to my lips for a moment before he lowers his head and shuts his eyes, setting his forehead against mine.

"Alira, what if you hadn't found him that night, would it have led to his death? What if it led to yours? We can't know everything, nor can we alter the past." His eyes open, and my chest aches with the way he looks at me. Like I'm both something he wishes to save and care for and an already lost cause.

I steady my heart.

Change the subject. I shake my head and blink a few times. He's right, there's nothing I can do, and I need to make the best of it.

I try to clear my throat. "What time is the ceremony?"

Nikolai kisses away the last of my tears and smiles down at me. My eyes widen at the sentiment. "At twilight. After the ceremony is complete, you will meet our king, and then the celebration will begin." He hooks an arm under my legs and hoists me back up to the bed effortlessly.

I fist the sheets. "Celebration?" My tone is skeptical, wondering if this is another one of his tricks like the bonfire.

Nikolai lifts his hands innocently. "No tricks. The grand balls that are thrown for dukes are some of the most prestigious events. It's all anyone talks about around here." He takes the dress out of the bag, and my jaw drops. It's the loveliest shade of pink—like a pastel painting of cherry blossoms. It glitters as if it's gifted with magic, and perhaps it is. A simple pink dress, yet it's the most beautiful article of clothing I've ever seen.

Tessa enters the room as I reach for the dress. Her smile is as mischievous as Nikolai's.

Twenty minutes later, I'm fitted into the dress with my hair curled halfway down my back. A blossom crown is placed over my head, and Tessa nods approvingly as she crosses her arms. Nikolai stares at me with desire. I try my best not to pay attention to his wanton gaze.

"You are the only demigod who could steal a demon's heart," he murmurs, running his fingers through my curls so they collect more natural waves.

I offer a mild grin. "No hearts will be stolen. Especially not from Kalel."

Tessa shrugs. "It's not like he's the only demon with eyes,

Alira." I lift a brow at her in the mirror. She tilts her head back and laughs. "Oh, you didn't know? Just because you're marrying the duke doesn't mean a prince or other high lord can't take you from him if they so desire. It's common that a higher power takes another's bride as their own. Our practices here are a little different than yours, I'm sure."

My throat tightens. "What?" That wouldn't happen, would it? My eyes shift to Nikolai, and he only looks at the floor to avoid answering.

"Don't worry though, I'm sure Kalel, of all the dukes, wouldn't do that. He seems to be fond of you." She tries to comfort me.

Yeah, you don't know our history though. I flatten my lips and stare at the woman in the mirror I don't recognize. I've lost weight, and even with all the beautiful things I'm wearing, I look weary and out of place.

"He would be a fool to let anyone take you away from him," Nikolai reassures me.

I offer him a small smile. "I hope you're right." My tone is defeated.

Nikolai's expression flattens, but his brows shoot up with a thought. "Oh gods, I forgot to tell you about the Krinsle."

That doesn't sound good.

"The *what*?"

CHAPTER 22

KALEL

King Achill tilts his wineglass boredly as I enter his study. His appointed royal guard is flipping through a tome on one of the chaise lounges, offering me a brief once-over before looking back to the book in his hands.

"Duke Lornhelm, I was relieved to hear that you and your army returned to our kingdom safely last night." The king's words are formal, but they hold no weight or genuineness in his tone.

Achill has envied me since we were children. Even the wealthiest and most powerful people will loathe those who can find a fraction of happiness in nothing. I was happy with what little my mother could afford us. I enjoyed training to be an apothecary and then a knight. Achill watched from his tower and would sneak out to practice with me from time to time.

I'm only the most revered knight because he sends me out on every battle, hoping I'll perish. Nikolai informed me of this a few years ago after he'd used his sight on the king. Because what better way to inspire Devicit's army than that of the demon who came back from death?

One of my biggest regrets is telling Achill what happened that day in Florum Forest.

I narrow my gaze, thinking about it. Recounting the past with Alira damn near tore my heart from my chest. Her lavender eyes and all the misery that rolled over her expression were enough to bury a man. Did she really see me that night after the attack? I blink away the thoughts before I get lost in them.

I nod and flatten my lips. "Thank you, King Achill. I am happy to be back in my palace."

The king stands, leaving his glass of wine on the oak desk. "Do you have the demigod in your possession?" he asks, eyes narrowing with disdain. Although I doubt he'll have that look for long. He's a man of vanity, I'm certain he will be smitten with her the moment he sees how beautiful she is, and that thought infuriates me to no end.

I don't want anyone to look at her except me. I've already caught Nikolai watching her in a daze several times. *She's mine.* Even if I can't bear the thought of loving her, she belongs to me.

"Yes, the godling is at my palace."

He grunts his disapproval. "I can't believe it's come to this. Are you sure this is the path you want to take, old friend?" He sets his hand on my shoulder—the weight of it is as heavy as his gaze. I firm my lips and give him a tight nod. "Your sacrifice in marrying that half-god will be rewarded, Kalel."

It certainly felt like a sacrifice after I realized that the girl who found me in the forest that day was the same one who aided in destroying my childhood village. I knew it was her when we met in the forest two weeks ago. I could never forget such starlit hair, nor her floral eyes.

We were only children when she tried to help me. She couldn't have known what would happen to my uncles or me, but the hatred that was born in my heart that day can never be completely washed away. It's who I am now, and nothing can change that.

I can't get her out of my head. The way she carries her heart on her sleeve. The way the little godling's eyes go soft when she looks at me like I'm something more than I am. Like I won't destroy every last spark of hope in her soul.

Guilt is a heavy burden to shoulder, but I can't change what's already been done.

CHAPTER 23

ALIRA

My stomach is in knots as Tessa and Nikolai extend their hands to me. We exit the carriage in front of the enormous chapel. The clouds have already blocked out most of the sunset, but the warm sconces lining the exterior of the beige stone building light it up magnificently.

I take in the sharp points of each spire and the lancet windows beneath them. The doors are made from twin ebony wood. Symbols are scrawled on them, but I'm too jittery to focus on them to decipher what they are.

"Loosen up, you'll pass out if you lock your knees while standing up there," Nikolai scolds.

"How long do weddings last for demons?" I ask, darting a look between the two nervously.

Tessa has a smug grin and shrugs. "It's usually pretty short, but I doubt it's anything like what the demigods do for marriage."

"What do you mean?" I hastily ask as we reach the doors. She only winks at me before music spills out of the chapel and the doors swing open.

I inhale like it will be my last breath. Hundreds of demons turn to face us. They're all standing with solemn faces, as if this were a funeral and not a wedding.

At least we're all on the same page. I shrink into myself and stare straight ahead. Waiting beneath the altar, made of a clear crystal stone that bounces orange and purple hues, is Kalel.

My eyes widen at the sight of him. His hair has been tamed, and he wears a gilded wreath atop his head—a tradition many mortals use to celebrate the gods and to show their social standing. Gold necklaces drop down Kalel's chest and cross over the white robe that only covers half of his chest. My eyes linger on his exposed muscles, the sinewy bronze of his skin that dances in the flickering lights of the candles above. His shoulder and forearm leather plates are gilded as well, tying every piece of his attire together perfectly.

He's the kind of handsome that demands time to slow.

His eyes catch mine. He looks tired and not enthusiastic to see me. Nonetheless, he takes me in, letting his gaze move from my lips to my chest, down to my feet, before forcing his attention toward the altar instead. The muscle in his jaw tenses, and I swallow nervously.

I know we are two souls who aren't meant to be tethered to one another, but an ache settles in my heart at his reluctance to even look at me. Something from deep within my soul yearns to be with him, even if the gods revolt at our coming together.

"It's all you from here," Nikolai murmurs, giving me a little nudge to walk ahead.

I swallow and cast him a worried look. He smiles reassuringly.

I straighten and start walking down the long aisle, startled when a choir begins singing a haunting hymn. Their voices are chilling, some deep and low and a few with high-pitched voices that make your heart twist. The arches in the ceiling rise at least three stories high and carry the sound divinely.

The demons whisper as I pass by them. I try my best not to listen, but their words reach me anyway.

"Dirty half-god."

"Murderer."

"She should be hanged along with her kingdom."

My fingers intertwine over my abdomen, and I try to remain as composed as I can. *This is what you chose*, I remind myself, desperate to hold on to the hope that my life here won't be as terrible as I fear it will.

I stop at the altar and hesitantly look up at Kalel. He's

impassive to my presence. His only acknowledgment of me is the slight tick in his jaw as he grits his teeth.

My heart skips a few beats as a very tall, very slender figure approaches us from the head of the building. This must be the Krinsle that Nikolai told me about before we left the room. He kept it brief, but the Krinsle is one of the oldest demons in Devicit, with an ancient sort of power that has found its use in the chapels.

The demon is at least eight feet tall, draped in bloodred robes that trail on the marble floor behind it. Its hood is pulled up, and I can only make out two white dots for eyes. Chills run down my spine, and a shudder moves through my entire body. Nothing Nikolai said to describe this demon could've prepared me for the darkness that rolls from its shoulders.

"In all the centuries that I've walked in Devicit, I've never borne witness to the union of a devourer and one of holy blood." The creature's scratchy voice curls and bends through the room like a curse. My palms are clammy, and it takes everything I have just to remain standing here and not bolt for the door.

The Krinsle extends its long, charcoal-like hand to Kalel. The fingers are practically bones, and the nails are overgrown and sharp.

Kalel takes the Krinsle's hand, then looks at me. I flinch, not sure what I'm supposed to do, so I just stare into Kalel's eyes and hope that he'll signal me.

"Duke Kalel Lornhelm, I will bind you to this half-god if you so wish it." That awful, haunting voice slithers through the room once more. No matter how long I look at the Krinsle, all I can see are the two dots for eyes. Perhaps it does not have a true face. Somehow, that's even more disturbing.

"I wish it." Kalel's tone is steady and sure. His eyes bore into me, hurt still flickering there.

The Krinsle makes a clicking sound, almost like a clock that's been spun backward. Then it extends a hand to me. It looks cold and like it will suck the life from me if I touch it.

I force my breaths to be smooth as I reach for its hand. Kalel holds his breath and tightens his fists at his sides.

"I won't let her filthy blood contaminate our beloved Duke Lornhelm's heirs!" a woman cries out. Her voice rings from behind me, and an audible gasp moves through the entire chapel as she tears my head back by fisting my hair. A cold stone is pressed to my neck, and in that split second, a pain like fire bolts through my arteries and brings me to my knees.

My vision clouds, and all I can hear are the hammering breaths that escape me as I lift my trembling hand to my neck. Ash residue is left on my fingers. Only a devilstone can inflict this damage to the flesh of a demigod.

Another devilstone? Where are they coming from?

It feels as though time has slowed, because as I force my head up to flee from the demon trying to kill me, I'm faced with Kalel. His hand is buried inside the woman's chest.

Horror drowns out all sound in the room. The woman's face is mortified, but she can't mumble words as he rips her heart out in one fluid movement. She collapses on the ground beside me, twitching as her blood flees her flesh in a large pool of red.

I lean back on my elbows and inch myself away from Kalel. He takes notice and stares down at me. Her heart in his hand, his amber eyes glowing like fire.

"Would anyone else like to try to stop this union?" he asks in a lethal voice. He doesn't let his eyes lift from me, assessing the wound on my neck that still throbs. He drags his tongue over the woman's heart, tasting her blood before crushing it in his hand and dropping it.

The room is silent.

"Then let us continue." Kalel reaches down and hooks his hand around my waist, hoisting me up and supporting my weight against him.

I grit my teeth and force my thoughts away from the pain. *Let's just get this over with.*

The Krinsle offers me its hand once more. This time, I don't hesitate to take it. I want to get out of this chapel as quickly as possible.

A magical pulse spreads through my hand at its touch. It's a soft and gentle magic. Not malicious like one might assume from the Krinsle's fearsome appearance.

It tilts its head at me. "*Hmm.* You are a strange half-god.

Alira, daughter of Venus, I will bind you to this devourer if you so wish it."

Kalel's grip tightens over my waist like he's about to be stabbed in the chest.

I swallow thickly and shut my eyes. Of all fates I've lived, this one I hope to keep. My eyes open and land on Kalel.

"I wish it." My resolve is sure.

There can be no other path for me. And as much as Kalel despises me, I can't help the emotions that swell in my chest whenever I'm near him. When he touches me, I feel like I'll melt in his hands.

The Krinsle's eyes arch as if it is smiling. "So be it. The devourer and the half-god are bound by this kiss." The Krinsle touches its thumb to Kalel's lower lip, leaving a black smudge of ash down the center. Then it does the same to me.

Kalel turns to face me. His earthy scent wraps around me and settles into my bones as I stare into his eyes. I want to tell him how sorry I am that everything has unfolded this way. Sorry that he has to marry the person he loathes most in this world. But as he lifts his bloodstained hand to my chin and tilts it up, I find a yearning burning in him. I find that it burns in me too.

Kalel's lips press against mine.

It's without a doubt a kiss the gods will wage a war over, but how is it that his kiss breathes life into me like I've never known? As if all the air before this has been bitter. His hand moves up my jawline and threads through my hair as he deepens the kiss. There isn't a hint of hatred. Only whispers of our hearts—truths we have not yet shared.

For a moment, I forget that we're in front of hundreds of demons. Kalel seems to remember himself and slowly pulls away. His brows knit as he holds his face close to mine for a second longer than he should, studying my features and sucking in his bottom lip as if to savor the taste of me.

I swallow and lick my lips anxiously.

The Krinsle announces, "Kingdom of Devicit. I give you your new duchess, Alira Lornhelm."

CHAPTER 24

ALIRA

The next hour is a blur of meeting the high lords that Kalel is acquainted with, accepting their congratulations on the Lornhelm name, along with the disapproving looks they cast me before heading to the banquet.

I've never felt so insignificant in my entire life. It's evident that I'm worthless to them.

A mirror along the far wall reflects the disarray of my appearance. My hair is mussed, and demon blood smears the side of my face where Kalel brushed my cheek. A burnt, ashy mark is left behind on my neck where the devilstone touched me. Pain still thrums lightly through my veins, but my body is slowly healing.

As Kalel speaks with an older couple, I look over my shoulder and spot the Krinsle watching me. I spare a glance at Kalel; he's deep in conversation, so I leave his side to speak with the demon that bound us.

It is still just as intimidating as before, but the magic I felt from the demon beckons me to believe that it can be trusted.

"Half-god, I was hoping you would come and speak with me." It crouches down so I don't have to angle my head up to look at it.

I offer a weak smile. "You don't loathe me? I wouldn't blame you if you did," I murmur, gazing down at the woman who tried to kill me with a devilstone. It's still clutched tightly in her hand. The worry blooms in my chest once more. *Where are all these new stones showing up from?*

The Krinsle follows the path of my vision and takes the stone from the woman. It holds the rock up to the light and inspects it carefully. "I have no reason to dislike you, Alira. I am a tired, old demon who will return to the underworld soon. There are centuries of wars that have come before you and likely more to follow long after." Its voice isn't as eerie now that it isn't filling the room with it. The white dots beneath the hood shift to me as it crushes the stone in its palm. Dust as fine as sand filters through its fingers and trickles to the floor. "You are different from the other half-gods."

My brows pinch together. "Different how?"

It stares at me for an uncomfortable stretch of time as it considers its words.

"Alira, we are departing for the banquet," Kalel calls to me, extending his hand for me to come to him. I smile again at the Krinsle before turning to leave.

It wraps its long hand around my wrist, stopping me dead in my tracks. I shudder and look over my shoulder at it.

"The gods watch you closer than the others. Be careful." The Krinsle mutters its warning before letting me go.

The Krinsle's warning puts ice into my veins. Mercury has already warned me too. What will the deities do to me now that I've married Kalel?

It bothers me through the carriage ride to the banquet and further into the celebratory supper.

"Must you look so miserable?" Kalel sighs, and it brings me from my thoughts.

I sit straighter and plaster a fake smile on. The banquet hall is bustling with gossip. It's not the jovial type either. It's clear that hardly anyone in attendance is happy about the marriage.

"I'm not miserable." I take a sip of my wine. I catch my reflection in the glass and am relieved that Nikolai was able to fully heal the burn on my neck before we arrived here. He is a saint for bringing maids to redo my hair and wipe the blood from my face too.

I quickly find him in the crowd, speaking with a group of royal knights and laughing before his eyes flick to me. I offer a smile at his warm gaze before returning my attention to my husband.

Kalel takes a few long swigs from his cup. *Is he drunk?* I blink at him, shocked that he would allow himself to be this intoxicated when around his peers. He's usually so put together and in control. Everything he does is always with purpose.

"Come on, I'm your monstrous husband now, you can be honest," he grumbles as he sets his cup down, throwing me what I think he intends to be a scathing look, but it's heated and filled with a craving to give in to his desires. His cheeks are flushed, and his fangs dig into his lower lip.

He hasn't had any of my blood yet today, so he might be hungry.

Great. Hangry *and* drunk.

I turn my head and look away from him. He's trying to toy with me, and I'm not in the mood.

Kalel wraps his hand around my jaw and guides my head until I'm looking at him again. "Tell me how much you loathe me. Tell me I'm nothing more than demon scum to you. A monster."

My mouth firms. Is that what he thinks?

I set my hand on his cheek gently. The motion makes his eyes widen with anguish. "Kalel, I've never loathed you. You were never a monster. It was me all along. Not you," I whisper, and for some reason, my eyes linger on his mouth. My tongue swipes over my lower lip, remembering the taste of his kiss.

Kalel jerks from my touch and focuses back on the banquet. He flexes his jaw a few times as he gulps down the remainder of his wine.

Tessa leans in from behind us and whispers, "The ball is set to begin in an hour. King Achill will see you both now—he will be waiting for you in the library." Kalel grunts and dismisses her. She gives me a concerned look about his drunken state, and all I can muster is an appreciative nod for her notifying us.

"Let's go then." Kalel stands on uneven legs, wrapping his hand around my wrist and dragging me behind him as we exit the banquet hall. The sound of all the chatter and music fades out as he takes me down a few corridors.

My eyes travel along the walls and ceilings. Beautiful white stone pillars and arched ceiling frames lined with ivy and old paintings.

The dream-like walk is abruptly stopped when Kalel pulls me off into a dark hall. He pushes my chest up against a wall, gliding his hands up both my wrists and pinning them above my head. He grips them beneath one hand and uses the other to move my hair to the side, exposing my neck.

I inhale and try to move my hips forward so that my ass isn't jutted out into his crotch, but he holds me firmly in place. Kalel's cold lips coast across my skin, sending heat straight to my core. *Gods, I hate that he does this to me.* I hate how badly I want him when I shouldn't. But he's my husband now, so is it so wrong to want him inside me? I want him to scent my womb with his come again so everyone knows I'm his.

He opens his mouth and lingers as if he's about to sink his fangs into me. I brace for the pierce of his teeth, but it doesn't come. Instead, his hold on my wrists loosens, and he sways a little before setting his forehead on my shoulder. The weight of his thoughts is so heavy.

"Are you…okay?" I whisper, but it feels like my voice carries through the ceiling.

Kalel shifts, leaning more of his weight onto me, and rests his cheek against my bare shoulder. A half sigh escapes his lips, and he threads his fingers through my hair once more. "No. I suppose I'm not, little godling."

I'm not sure what to say, but my heart weeps alongside his.

"Me neither." I let my hand slide down his arm until my palm smooths over his face. I slowly turn so my back is against the wall and I'm facing him.

Kalel's eyes are hooded by his lashes, reluctant to look at me. It's strange how soft and vulnerable he truly is when no one is around to see. I like him most in these fragile moments. When he really lets me see him without his safeguards. I can't imagine the pressures that come with having a household name belonging to a duke. The things he's witnessed in war. The cruelty he's experienced at a young age.

The vengeance that festers inside him like a cancer.

"I'm sorry it had to be me, Kalel. If I could go back in time and change it…" My voice breaks. Why did the time loop lead to this? Wouldn't it have been better if it ended with him slaying me?

"I looked for you." His voice is broken and wavers. His amber eyes search mine. "I came back to Florum because I was looking for you." He chokes out the words, and they hit my heart like an arrow.

My lower lip trembles. "You what?" I whisper.

He gives me a sad smile, one that could grind me into dust. "I never stopped thinking about you."

CHAPTER 25

KALEL

Thirty years ago

My feet are blistered from walking for hours in circles. I swear I've walked in one direction, but the trees are tricking me. Seeming to move almost, always bringing me back to the same location.

Exhausted, I finally sit down and lean against the largest pine. The bark is covered in moss and glowing toadstools.

I know magic is less common in the holy lands, but I can't help but feel like the Florum Forest spirits are trying to tell me that this is where I should be. Why else would I keep ending up here? My mom always said that it's good to listen to the spirits when they are loud. It could be a god playing a trick or an important slight of fate.

Perhaps they are helping my uncles find me.

Hours pass, and my hope starts to dwindle. *My uncles will find me soon*, I tell myself. It's going to be fine. It has to be.

A branch snaps, drawing my attention up. I'm expecting to see Dakre or Collik, but instead, there is only a small demigod girl. Her hair is long and kissed with moonlight. Lavender eyes that seem to glow just as the toadstools in this grim forest do.

I'm struck by her ethereal appearance. She looks only a few years younger than I am. Yet there are eons of time locked within her gaze.

My mom told me never to trust a demigod. She said to run if I ever spotted one, especially when our kingdoms are this close to war, but I don't see anything wrong with this godling.

The girl studies me in the same way I study her. Her brows pinch together distrustfully before she takes in my weary state. Her eyes lower to my blistered, bleeding feet. Sympathy replaces her hesitation.

"Are you okay?" she asks, approaching me and lowering to get a closer look at my face.

My cheeks warm. "I'm fine," I lie. Tears are already building in my eyes. When I try to blink them away, a few fall. I'm embarrassed and don't want her to think I'm crying because I'm scared. It's because I'm no longer alone.

"It's okay. I'll take care of you." She sets her coat over my shoulders before wrapping her arms around me and hugging me tightly. My eyes widen, and my heart lurches. A demigod embracing a demon? She treats me like an equal. Slowly, my arms wrap around her in return. Warmth fills my chest, and I soak in the comfort she gives.

"I got separated from my uncles." I rub the last of the tears from my eyes.

She sits back and frowns. "Lost? Oh no." Her brows wrinkle together, and she thinks for a moment before her eyes light up with an idea. "You can come back to my home with me, and we'll get help. The house mother always knows what to do." She stands confidently. I smile and nod hopefully.

We start the long walk together toward Alzhor. She holds my hand like she'll never let me go, and I find myself hoping that she won't.

"What is a *house mother*?" I ask, thinking that it's weird she would refer to her mom in that way. But we know so little about the demigods, maybe that's normal for them.

The girl just shrugs. "Most of us are orphans in Alzhor. The gods have no interest in us, and mortal parents leave their half-god children at the steps of our kingdom to be raised with our own."

I cast her a sidelong glance. "Seriously?"

She nods, quirking a brow at me. "Is it not the same for

demon-folk?" She seems genuinely curious, and I can't help but grin.

"No. Most of us have families." My voice is filled with melancholy. I'm one of the only ones in Thornhall who doesn't have a father. Mom refuses to say who he is or what happened to him.

The girl weaves her hand with mine. The motion makes me flinch, and my eyes snap down to hers. She gives me an understanding look, not bringing any attention to the truth of what lies between my words. I grip her hand tighter.

We walk for a long time, but the time goes quickly. She never tells me her name and nor do I, but she tells me many other things. How she likes to sneak out from the orphanage to get away from the other kids. She dreams of becoming a dressmaker someday. She tells me of a bright future she sees for herself.

The longer I listen, the more I realize that we aren't so different. Demons. Demigods. Even the mortals. What would it take for us to get along?

I know my mom doesn't think I listen in on her conversations, but I hear her talking to my uncles almost every night, fearing the start of a war between Devicit and Alzhor. There's tension between the territories, but I don't feel any of the hatred that the adults seem to have for one another.

I don't understand it.

But it doesn't take long to grasp.

It doesn't take long for me to understand what hatred does to a soul. It consumes your organs, twists them into coals, and sets your heart on fire.

The little godling's house mother is a cruel woman. She's already lashing out at the girl for being out late before she notices me. Then chaos spills. "*A demon! A demon within the gates!*" they shout.

I see the way they push the silver-haired godling to the ground like she's nothing. As they drag me away, I hear her scream and cry. She doesn't understand why they are doing this either. Why they hate and fear me so much when I have done nothing wrong.

The demigods beat me senseless before tying me up and bringing me back to the forest. They throw me to the rubble with my hands slashed. My blood seeps into the moss of Florum Forest's floor. I let out a harrowing cry as pain ebbs into me. I curse them and beg. "Why are you doing this? We are just looking for the Griffon's flower, I swear! Why are you doing this?" I scream, thrashing as hard as I can against their bindings.

"Shut up, you filthy demon. We're going to kill you out here and leave your bones for the forest to consume," one knight says, malice rolling from his ebony armor. Words so cold that I feel them impale my heart.

Why? Why? What did I do?

They kick my chest and send me face-first to the ground.

My cheeks burn with cuts and bruises from their fists. My heart races, beating faster and harder than it ever has before. "Dakre! Collik!" I scream, stumbling and trying desperately to get away from the half-gods lifting their swords to kill me. "*Help me*!"

The ground trembles as power rattles through the woods. Collik is bent at my side in the next moment. His ruby eyes are wild and filled with fear, yet when he speaks, he forces a calm voice. "Kalel, we need you to run. *Run* and don't look back, no matter what you hear. Go home and don't wait for us. Do you understand me?" he orders sternly.

My eyes are focused on Dakre behind him, who's fighting off the four demigods alone. We were out here to collect flowers, not fight. We have no armor. No swords. Dakre's head swings our way, his blond hair smeared in his blood. Yet he still grants me a warm, reassuring smile. He can't fool me like he did when I was younger.

We don't have a chance against them.

"*Kalel.*" My eyes are forced back to Collik at his chilling tone. His expression is grave, and sadness looms in his eyes. He cuts my bindings, hoists me to my feet, and shoves my back. "Run!"

I run. I run like the hounds of Mortem are chasing after me. No matter how much my feet sting and bleed and the branches whip at my cheeks, I run as fast as I can.

I don't stop.

Not when I hear the fighting stop.

Nor when I hear the demigods chasing after me.

I look back for a split second when I hear them right at my heels. Tears fall from my eyes as I take in the four half-gods covered in my uncles' blood. The one closest to me swings his sword at my heel and cuts it.

I let out a bloodcurdling scream as my body crashes to the ground. I roll a few times before trying to get back up and continue running. But another demigod has his blade drawn and swings it at my face. I dodge only in the nick of time. The blade cuts open my left cheek. My heart is racing so fast that I hardly feel it; I just know that it's bad, blood gushes from my face and my lips won't close properly.

Another sword impales my heart, jerking my body back and pinning me to the earth. My sight trembles on the thick metal that pierces my chest. I don't feel pain, I only feel warmth spreading across my back and a heavy sleep trying to pull me under.

I'm going to die. My eyes trace the dark leaves of Florum's canopy, watching as small orbs of light shift through the branches, whispering almost. Tears trickle down my cheeks, and my breaths slow until it's too burdensome to sip in even one more ounce of air.

Then everything crawls to a stop.

The knights linger around me, staring at my body. Murmuring about me being dead. *I'm not dead. Am I?*

A wall of shadow lifts from the ground before me, expelling a deity from nothing more than black smoke and embers. His form is entirely concealed in a dark robe with the hood pulled up.

The demigods gasp. "God of the underworld?" one says with horror.

The god lifts his hand and waves it once over the four knights. Their eyes go from frightened to dull in a matter of seconds. As if this cloaked deity has stolen their very souls with the simple motion of his hand.

He turns and glances over his shoulder at me, revealing eyes the color of pomegranates. For a moment, I worry he might take my soul too, but he only stares at me for a handful of moments, expressionless.

"Whether you wake is not decided by either of us. But fear not, a prayer is all it takes." His voice is cold like water over stone.

The god extends his hand to me and brushes his thumb over the cut across my cheek and does the same over my heart before looking away and disappearing altogether. My eyes grow weary and flutter closed.

The next thing I know, I'm lying in the forest, alone, birds chirping somewhere far away in the tree boughs.

What just happened? I lift my hand to my cheek and my eyes widen. The gash has been sealed, only minor grooves that feel like *x*'s remain where the flesh was reconnected. It's the same with my chest.

The second of surprise passes and panic rolls back into me. *I need to get out of Alzhorian territory.* My legs carry me until I'm finally breaking free of the forest. The moment I come out of the dark trees, I collapse to my knees in a turquoise field of sweet grass.

The reeds are welcoming, and a cold breeze lifts locks of my hair as if begging me to look up at the sky.

The tears stream from my eyes, but something broke inside me tonight. Something in my soul has rotted down to the core.

Half-gods are evil.

I swear to kill them all. Every last one of them, except the silver-haired girl who tried to help me. I stare down at my hand that she held so gently and with care.

But did she lead me to Alzhor on purpose? Did she know we'd be killed in Florum?

I didn't expect to think of her much after that day. But as time passed, she plagued my thoughts more and more. When I turned twenty-four, an insatiable urge to return to Florum sparked inside me. It wasn't just an urge. It was a calling, as if the fabric of my soul was woven with her thread.

I had to be close to her. I needed to meet her again.

It took everything in me to resist going. *What is her name?* I wondered. Did she grow up to be the dressmaker she dreamed of becoming? I longed to speak with her, to see her beautiful starlit hair. She held every last hope I had left for the demigods.

I trained for years to become a knight. It took even longer to become a duke after successfully rising in the ranks to commander and fending off many attacks.

Until the horrid day a wisp showed up inside my tent and beckoned me to follow it. I was hesitant at first. Will-o'-the-wisps could be bad omens, but for me, on the front lines, it seemed imperative that I know what the orb was sent to show me. I didn't know who sent it. I only knew that it took great power to do so. It couldn't be for nothing.

I followed it to my horse, and with a pit in my stomach, I mounted my steed. The wisp darted to the top of the far hill that Thornhall was just on the other side of.

No.

I turned to shout for my army to prepare to ride to the top of the slope, but everything behind me had vanished. *I have to finish the vision before it lets me go.* I dismounted and charged ahead alone the rest of the way, tripping a few times in my disarray.

When I reached the top, I was transported into my mother's home. She was cooking a meal and humming a soft tune. My breaths were staggered, and the blood in my veins chilled. *Why is the wisp showing me this?*

"Mom?" I called out to her. The moment the word left my

lips, her front door was kicked down, and knights of Alzhor rushed in.

"What are you doing?" she screamed, fighting against them as they tried to drag her outside.

"Mom!" I shouted, trying to cut through the knights with my sword, but it went right through them. "No. No!" I continued to swing my blade at them to no avail as they reached the doorway.

"You will pay for this. You will pay!" my mother cried. One knight shoved her to the front steps, and another lifted his sword.

Every piece of me shattered as I watched the knight's blade cut through my mom. The second her body collapsed, I was thrown into darkness.

My knees gave out on me, and my hands hit the ground.

"Why are you showing me this?!" I yelled, tears spilled down my jaw, and a hatred so deep burned in my stomach.

The wisp formed before me.

I lifted my head and pleaded, "Please. Tell me this has not yet happened."

It glowed brighter before disappearing, and in its place was a knight. I stared at the armor, confused at first, but then I understood. This was the knight who led the attack or *would* lead it.

I must hurry.

My fingers curled into my palms, and I stood.

Just like that, I was back atop my horse, just at the base of the slope. *Tell me, gods, that it is not too late.*

I called for my elite knights to ride with me to Thornhall to ensure it wasn't in danger.

The moment we rose above the top of the hill, the last screams hit us.

The screams and the stench of blood.

I'll kill them all. I'll rid this world of the demigods once and for all.

I led my troops down to the village, but as we descended, I watched as a knight in ebony armor with a white dragon-bone sword atop the far hill raised their blade to the sky and guided all their paladins out of the valley.

That's the knight who led this attack. The one from my vision. I memorized everything about their armor. Their scent of death. It was one I would never forget.

We were too late.

I swore I would find this half-god and kill them along with the entire kingdom of Alzhor. They made me into something I never wanted to become.

They put hate into my heart.

So I put a curse of my own on that knight, with the help of the only god who ever cared to help the demon-folk.

Pluto only grinned at my request. He shook his head but granted it.

Gods and their games.

I swore to destroy Alzhor, but I needed to find the lovely girl first and save her from the fate I would bring to her kingdom. If she felt the same beckoning call within her to find me, I knew I would find her.

CHAPTER 26

ALIRA

He came back to Florum for me? I stare into Kalel's weary eyes. They break me more with each moment that sifts through us.

"You were supposed to become a dressmaker. Remember?" He chuckles sadly.

Tears prickle my eyes.

"I was going to spare you from the fate of your kingdom for your kindness. But when I smelled the deaths on you in Florum, I knew you were there in Thornhall that day. I couldn't bring myself to kill you, because I wasn't sure what part you played in the attack." He pauses and brushes his thumb over my cheek. "But then we got the letter. Something in my bones told me to accept it. So I agreed to marry this mysterious daughter of Venus. I saw your armor, and I knew you were the knight I sought. I knew what you had done, and I was prepared to burn the kingdom to the ground after killing you in the guest room..." He clamps his mouth shut like he wants to say more on that specifically, but he doesn't.

My heart races with the truth. My jaw trembles as if I'm freezing to death.

"Then that helmet came off, and it was *you*." He runs his hand through his hair, making it disheveled. "Why did it have to be you?" he murmurs, heartbreak cumbersome in his tone.

Is that why he looked surprised in the last loop he killed me in? I saw his eyes and the emotion that flickered through him when he saw my silver hair. My chest curls. I wish many things could be different.

"I'm sorry it's me, Kalel." I let the tears fall from my chin.

His eyes soften, and he slides a hand behind my neck, leaning down until our foreheads are pressed together. "All I ever truly wanted was you...and the guilt of that is ruining me, little godling." Kalel kisses me, curling his fingers into my hair as he does.

We slowly part. He stares down at me, leaving me dazed. Breathless.

He wants me? My brows knit, and a warmth coils inside my chest. He must feel this tether we have to one another, as

I do. Perhaps we were always promised to one another. The gods' doing. So why did Mercury tell me to leave? What games are they playing with our hearts?

Kalel remains mere inches from me, studying my features for a few seconds longer before he straightens. Recomposed, for the most part. It's hard to tell if he's still affected by the wine or not, but I doubt the blush across his cheeks right now is from the alcohol.

I shift off the wall and pat the wrinkles from my dress. *Get it together,* I chide myself and take a deep breath.

Kalel drags his hand down his jaw and offers me a defeated look as his eyes move up and down my body. "Sorry, I'm not sure what came over me." We start back down the hall toward the library.

He probably didn't mean to share that much with me. But I'm glad he did. I glance up at his fretful eyes. "You aren't the only one ruined by guilt," I admit with a forlorn smile.

Kalel looks at me for a few moments before he lets his expression smooth into a relaxed state. A lovely grin pulls the corners of his lips up as he looks ahead.

We walk in silence for a minute. It's not uncomfortable. Just a bit melancholic, like the air between us is charged with our weary thoughts.

"So tell me about your king." I try to change the subject and lighten the mood.

Kalel lets out a relieved breath. "King Achill is the youngest king Devicit has ever had. He's not as wise as they come, but he is generous. He wanted to spare your kingdom, so you should thank him for that."

I nod thoughtfully.

We rise two floors before reaching the king's private library. Two imperial knights stand posted on either side of the door and nod as we pass them. Kalel doesn't offer his usual greeting to them. I assume it's because he's still a bit inhibited and is in a foul mood.

The library features a wine cellar located on the right-hand side. A dark walnut desk is placed in the center, with a glass bottle of bourbon on one corner and maps and official papers scattered around the midpoint.

"I was wondering when you would finally arrive," a male demon says as he steps away from the enormous lancet windows.

He must be the king. It's evident by the crooked onyx crown that sits on his head and the haughty black feathered robe that trails behind him. His ears are pointed like Kalel's, but his hair is ashy like mine. A silver that has warmer hues, like frosted pampas grass. His eyes are a deep cerulean blue that pierce through the room.

He looks at me and every cell in my body freezes instinctively. Unlike King Borlin, the demons choose their king because of their inherited powers. King Achill is not only a royal figure, but he is also the strongest demon in Devicit. I can feel it just from entering the room.

I divert my attention to the ground and try to stick close to Kalel's side.

King Achill chuckles as he steps down to his desk and pours himself a cup of bourbon. He doesn't let his eyes stray from me as he tilts the cup back.

"So you are the daughter of Venus." He smiles charmingly as he approaches me. "Much prettier than I thought you'd be. I didn't know demigods could be this attractive." The king sets his icy fingers on my jaw, tilting my head each way and assessing every angle of my face before moving behind me and letting his hand brush through my hair. Kalel shoots him a death glare.

"I'd prefer if you didn't intimidate my wife," Kalel says bitterly. My heart beats faster when Kalel looks at me and that tortured expression returns to his face.

"I'm only verifying that she's of high quality. And I'm afraid she is. Kalel, my friend, you'll need to make sure you keep her safely tucked away in your palace. We all saw how my poor sister tried to slay her during your ceremony. There are likely more people willing to risk their lives to rid our kingdom of a half-god. Or even steal her away from you."

Wait. What?

"Your sister?" I mumble, brows knitting as I look from Kalel to the king. Wouldn't that make her a princess? Please tell me Kalel didn't…

"Yes, Kalel killed one of only three princesses today. But

our law states that it is permitted to slay any person if they are trying to harm a bride to a favored duke." King Achill smiles, not bothered at all by the fate of his sister. *Cold.*

King Borlin would've executed anyone who dared to hurt one of his daughters. I think Borlin would likely do it for much less, considering his track record.

"I wanted to welcome you to Devicit personally. We certainly expect great things from the two of you. And I heard you were even a knight in Alzhor?" I nod. "Well, you won't need to worry about fighting wars any longer, Alira. Your only role now will be to bear Kalel's children."

My stomach twists with rage. I try to keep the anger from my expression, but King Achill sees it nonetheless and takes my jaw in his hand, forcing my eyes to look up at his.

"Perhaps some of mine as well. I did not expect you to be so lovely. And what's this I hear about you having control over the dragons?" He speaks over my lips, coldly, as if I belong to him.

Kalel growls, "It hasn't been confirmed." But the look in the king's eyes tells me he heard a very different account of events. *Gods, I was worried about that.*

"Imagine a royal heir who can control the beasts." King Achill looks at me with greed in his gaze.

A pit forms in my heart. *This is the path I chose*, I remind myself repeatedly, but the tears still prickle in my eyes. I hate that I cry when I'm pissed off, and I can't hurt the asshole causing it.

"Oh, there's no need to be sad. You will be treated like a queen. You will want for nothing. What demigod gets to say as much?" He presses a kiss to my cheek that carries the scent of bourbon and books.

Kalel's glare is like a knife.

"I won't be sharing her."

King Achill stops in front of his desk, shoulders stiffening. He waits a dreadful second before turning and casting a frigid look at Kalel. Something in the air grows heavy between them, and it makes sweat bead down my spine. But then the king slowly grins, and the energy breaks.

"Of course, old friend. Perhaps a few years down the line, after you have a child or two, or if you should die in battle. I'll take care of her."

Kalel is quick to reply. "I will not die in battle."

Another awkward and tense moment passes.

King Achill grits his teeth and looks at me with a cold fire burning in his eyes. "Well, we'd better get down to the ball. We certainly don't want to be late. You'll save the king the last dance, won't you, sweetheart?" He lifts my hand and presses a kiss to the back of it.

I smile uncertainly and mutter, "Yes, of course, my king. And thank you for sparing my kingdom." I make sure to follow Kalel's advice on thanking him.

King Achill's eyes light up and flick an intrigued look at

Kalel. "The night won't wait for us. Kalel, go dance with your enchanting bride."

Kalel watches the king with hesitation but offers me his hand like a gentleman. I cast one final look over my shoulder at the intimidating king. He swirls his glass of bourbon slowly, staring at us as we exit. I would hate to discover what that man plots. The darkness in his eyes is enough to make me shudder.

I hope he wasn't serious about the last dance.

"I don't know any of the songs your kingdom will play or the steps," I whisper to Kalel as he guides me out of the private library.

Kalel dips down and presses his lips to mine, pushing his tongue inside my mouth and surprising me. He wipes his thumb over my lips and grins. "*Scenting*, not affection. And just follow my lead, little godling."

"What about the kiss in the hallway?" I blurt out before thinking it over.

Kalel's eyes widen. "A drunken kiss," he insists, clearing his throat and sharply looking away. I don't know if he's aware that his ears turn red when he's flustered. I smile to myself.

Though the way he's holding my hand right now feels a lot like affection to me.

CHAPTER 27

ALIRA

As we step into the ballroom, music lifts the unease that the king instilled in me.

I hadn't realized that we'd be entering from a grand staircase, but gasps roll through the ballroom as we stop at the top of the second-floor landing. Even the musicians have a hiccup in their song from the distraction. Large glass containers are filled with peonies, glittering gold water in the base that makes the room feel welcoming.

My heart seizes and my feet stop moving.

Kalel goes down a step ahead of me and turns to face me. His eyes are warm and endearing for once. I wonder if he has nerves in front of this many people like I do. *Wouldn't that be something?*

"Don't let any of them unnerve you. This is by far the least dangerous thing I've seen you do." He brushes the stray hairs from my face.

I nervously smile. "You say that now, but you haven't seen me dance yet, Duke Lornhelm."

He blinks at my use of his formal name. A wicked grin that reveals his fangs flashes at me, then he resumes escorting me down the stairs. Every head is turned up in our direction, and I quickly spot Nikolai and Tessa near the back. They are dressed formally, appearing fit to be royalty themselves.

Half the crowd looks up at us in awe, while the other half have disgusted frowns and hateful glares directed toward me. I hold my chin high and walk with a steady stride. We reach the center of the floor, and everyone gives us a wide berth of space.

Kalel makes a low bow, his knee almost touching the floor as he lowers his head to me. My cheeks warm as he comes out of the bow, offering me his hand. I slowly place mine over his palm, and he stands tall, pulling me gently into him until our chests meet. My eyes widen as I gaze up at him. I didn't know that dancing could be this intimate.

Sure, I've watched a few balls in Alzhor, but it was long before the war. I never danced with the royals or partook in the celebrations. I once longed to be the girl in the beautiful dress, dancing with the handsome prince.

Although I'll take the broody demon any day over a prince.

Kalel leads, moving slow and with purpose. I follow his strides, and after a few songs, I think I have a handle on the movement of it. The music stutters and turns more jovial, signaling the rest of the attendees that they can now join in the dancing. They swarm to the floor and begin moving like lovesick doves with their partners.

The ballroom turns into an ocean of song, a movement of joy and peace.

Kalel doesn't let go of me as we sway and spin. He holds me close and lets his hands move along my waist when the music demands it. Each time his eyes lower to mine, I find myself falling deeper into his pull, until it feels like his gravity will never let me go.

The song ends, and we come to a stop, staring at one another in awe. Everyone else in the room is worlds away. I only see him, and a warmth moves deeper into my heart.

He blinks, seeming to come out of his own trance. "Let's take a break, you look like you could use it," Kalel murmurs as I inhale laboriously to catch my breath. The room has grown terribly hot.

"What about the king? I thought he—"

Kalel cuts me off. "We'll be back before the last dance." He sounds annoyed that I'd even bring him up, but I'm just trying not to get my head lopped off for pissing off the king.

Before Kalel can guide me away, he's approached by Gabriel with a grim look pressed onto his face. Kalel leans in and listens to him for a moment before looking back at me and frowning.

"I'll be five minutes. Tessa is across the ballroom, don't stray from her side." He gives me a stern look before following Gabriel. Kalel's one-shoulder robe billows behind him and makes him look like a king.

He'd be a better king than Achill, of that I'm certain, I muse.

As I turn to make my way across the floor to Tessa, I bump into a flat chest.

"Oh, my apologies—" I start before looking up and realizing it's Nikolai. I'm met with his gentle smile and curious eyes. He looks clean-cut in his formal attire and with his hair styled for once. His jacket is a deep maroon with gold accents, bringing out his naturally warm, earthy tones.

"My lady," he says as he bows and offers me his hand. "Care to dance?"

I return his smile and set my hand in his. "I was hoping I'd get to see you again tonight." He and Tessa are the only two people I feel safe around. It's not exactly easy being in a sea of angry demon-folk.

"I'm honored." He dips his head and moves into position for the next song that begins. It's slower, more timeless than the others. Nikolai moves elegantly. He's as fluid as his voice was the night of the bonfire send-off.

"How are you good at everything you do?" I chuckle as he spins me and offers a daring grin.

He shrugs. "I'm ninety-two, remember? I've had a long time to learn many different things. I was even the librarian when I was in my fifties."

My eyes light up. "There's a public library?" Thank gods, the king's private one isn't the only place to find a book here.

His eyes narrow with his grin. "Yes, eager to learn something in particular?"

I swallow my anxiety. If there's anyone here I can trust, it's Nikolai.

"I want to learn about curses." He furrows his brows at me. "How to break them," I clarify.

Nikolai's smile fades, and he leans in close to whisper in my ear. "You must be careful speaking of curses here, Alira. But I know a few books that might help you." He pulls away and glances over my shoulder. "I think our time has come to an end. Thank you for the dance." He bows.

I flinch and look behind me. Kalel is marching over here with a ruthless set to his brow. My attention falls back to Nikolai. "I'll see you tomorrow." I squeeze his hands, more for self-reassurance than anything.

Nikolai nods and quickly turns to leave.

Kalel stops beside me and gives me a disappointed look. "You're terrible at doing as I say."

I huff as he grabs my wrist and tugs me outside. "Nikolai is just as safe as Tessa," I shoot back.

He stops at the stairs that lead down to the garden below and faces me. "I don't like the way he looks at you. So no, I wouldn't say he's as safe as Tessa," he grumbles.

My eyes widen. Is he...jealous?

I clear my throat. "What did Gabriel have to report that was so urgent?"

Kalel presses his lips into a thin line. "You're no longer a knight. You are my wife, and you won't be hearing of military matters."

I glower at him, but he ignores it and nods toward the stairs. I reluctantly follow.

We walk into the gardens. To say they are far more extravagant than anything Alzhor has would be an understatement. The flowers have a rich scent that floods my senses, leaving a soft smile on my face as the cold night greets us. That sense of belonging fills me once more, and I take it in.

"This garden is beautiful. I can't believe how many flowers there are. I didn't know demons had green thumbs," I chide him.

Kalel gives me a confused look. "Only the sea dwellers have green thumbs, and even then, it's very select species—"

"Pffft!"

His eyes narrow, and a large smile curls his lips. "Ah, I see. It's a jest." He bats my nose with the tip of his finger playfully. "Do you like flowers?" Kalel stares at them with an empty gaze, like he's only now seeing them as something beautiful.

I lift my shoulders and intertwine my fingers together behind my back as we stroll beneath the moon and through the hedges that look as if they can go on forever.

"Of course I do. They remind me that gentle, delicate things hold so much power over us." I let my gaze lift to his.

Kalel tilts his head. "How so?"

"Because they make me smile. They welcome us home. Brighten any landscape and remind us that life is all around us. Don't you feel better when you smile?" He nods. "Exactly."

"Would you be happier if I planted more flowers around my palace?"

It's a bit sad because I don't even have to lie. "No. Your palace is already so beautiful, Kalel. This is the happiest I've been in a long, *long* time," I admit sheepishly.

He looks down at me with melancholy tugging at his frown. "You weren't happy in Alzhor?"

I shake my head, feeling guilty for even speaking these words. I pray no gods hear me, but I know they will. The Krinsle told me that they watch me closer than most. What did it mean by that? I'll need to speak with it again soon to pick its mind.

"You know how, when you are in constant, deep pain, you get used to it? You don't realize how much misery you were in until the pain is gone. I didn't realize how miserable I was until I left."

I bring my hands in front of me and stare down at them.

They still look smeared in the blood of demons to my weary eyes.

"I never wanted to become a merciless knight. But somewhere along the way, I lost that sense of right and wrong. I'm so sorry, Kalel. I'm—"

Oof. I walk straight into his back. I rub my nose as I back up and lift my chin. He's looking down at me with sympathetic eyes.

"Let's not talk about the past. Maybe another night, but tonight we should try to be happy. It's *our* day after all." He smiles sadly at me before he continues up the path. I follow silently, listening to the hum of the garden insects.

We come upon a marbled tower, pillared with columns that look as if they've been built for the gods. Kalel takes us to the top balcony, three stories up. It overlooks the gardens and the palace. My lungs fill with the sweet floral air, and a weightlessness I've never known sinks into my chest.

Kalel takes a seat on the stone bench and motions for me to sit on his lap. I assume he's hungry from the long day without my blood.

It's so quiet here. I could close my eyes and never desire to leave this place. With the breeze rolling across my skin and Kalel's warm hands, why would I wish to be anywhere else?

"I used to come here when I was a boy." Kalel's voice is low as I settle on his lap. I straddle him so we're facing one another. He wraps his hand around my ass and secures me there so I don't fall backward. "It's the prettiest place in the kingdom, wouldn't you agree? The gardens, the castle, the sad song of swallows and nightingales. I would come here to clear my head. Almost always, I thought of you. For the short time we had together, you marked my heart somehow."

I listen intently, studying every line and groove of his face. His amber eyes shift to mine. He always looks so tired, it breaks my heart—a man with a million thoughts that refuse to leave his mind unburdened.

I thought of him often too, but I believed he was dead. I saw his body, the pierced heart. He *was* dead. It must be Pluto's doing that he was saved. Kalel said he saw the god, and I believe him, because there's no other explanation as to how he's here right now.

Kalel presses his nose to my throat and inhales my scent. I'm self-conscious about it because he told me I smelled repulsive to him when we first met. He strokes his tongue over my skin, drawing a sigh from my lips and relaxing my muscles. I practically melt into his lap, and he lets his chest rumble with the calming purr I've come to yearn for.

The vibrations make my core tremble, and a soft moan escapes me as he slides down the shoulder of my dress. He dots my collarbone with kisses and moves down to my breast. My head tilts back, and I breathe heavily as he sucks on my nipple and grabs my ass.

"You truly are the most ethereal being known to this

world," he whispers against my tender flesh. I shut my eyes and let the pleasure of his scenting me wash away any thoughts. Then his teeth sink into my breast.

My eyes flash open.

At first, I'm scared that I'll be in pain, but it's the opposite. A wave of ecstasy crashes through me and tears a cry from my lips. Kalel groans as he takes deep gulps of my blood.

I weave my fingers through his hair. With each drink he takes, my hips buck lightly of their own volition. *Oh, my gods.* I'm losing my mind to this demon, and I'll gladly fall into madness for him.

He swallows once more before removing his teeth and licking the wound clean of my golden blood. I whimper at the sudden loss of pleasure and slump in his arms. I don't think I'll ever get used to how a devourer's bite affects a demigod's body. It once felt so wrong and violating, but now the sensation is entirely addictive. I want Kalel's lips on every part of my body. I'd give him all my blood until the end of time if I had to. And whether that's the venom in his bite that makes me think this way or the fact that my heart is starting to beg for his adoration, I cannot tell the two apart.

Kalel fixes my dress and looks up at me while licking my taste from his lips. Those eyes are drunk with my blood. Lustful, I'd dare say.

"If I knew I'd be marrying a godling one day, I would've prayed much more," he says sarcastically.

I smile and press a kiss to his lips.

We both flinch.

Did I just…kiss him?

My heart hammers, and I try to move off his lap. "Oh my gods, I don't know what came over me—"

Kalel holds my lower back securely and brings his lips to mine, kissing me fervently. A moan slips from my parted lips, and he follows it, deepening the kiss and consuming me entirely. His hands move to my hips, and he rocks me over his crotch, his cock swollen and throbbing beneath me.

My breaths become shallow, and my core aches to be filled by him. *Not the heat. Not now.* Another painful throb racks through me, and this time I can't help but cry into his heady kisses.

"I'll take care of you, little godling. Your pussy has wept for me long enough," he practically growls over my lips.

Kalel hoists me up and moves aside his robe, easily pushing his undergarment out of the way and freeing his dick. My mouth dries as I take in how big he is, and fear coils in my abdomen at the sight of his bulbous base. His shaft last night was enough to stretch me to my limit. What will the rest of him do to me? And why do I want it so badly?

I suck in my lower lip with lust and worry. Kalel leans into me and kisses my thoughts away. He slowly lowers my pussy onto his cock. He moans when he finds how wet I am for him already.

"*Fuck*, you're ready to be stuffed, aren't you?" He bites my lower lip and pulls on it until I'm chasing his mouth and kissing him deeply as his tip sinks into me.

My center stretches to fit him, and I cry out, letting my forehead fall to his shoulder. "It's too big. I don't think it will fit in this position." My voice is trembling, mostly with aches to be filled.

"You will fit me, little godling, don't you worry," Kalel says with a borderline growl as he turns me around so my back is against his chest. My muscles relax as he purrs again, the vibrations being directly against my spine does something to me. It sends me deeper into his lustful spell.

He holds both my thighs and slowly lowers me onto his dick. I writhe in his hold and moan as he works himself into me.

"Kalel, it's not going to work," I protest as his girth continues to fill me up. My head falls back against his chest, and tears prickle in my eyes.

He tilts his head to mine and licks away my tears, releasing one of my thighs and placing his hand over my clit and rubbing it. "Does it hurt?"

I nod. "A little." But it also feels so fucking amazing.

He sinks a little farther inside me, and my pussy reacts to him, tightening and gripping him like it wants to suck him dry.

Kalel groans and lowers his lips to mine. "Can you handle a little pain for the things you've done?" he says scathingly over my lips. I whimper, nodding.

This is my penance. This is my ruination.

Kalel is my punishment. But I've already grown to care about him deeply. Is that even punishment? Oh, how cruel the gods can be.

"I can handle all the weight of the worlds. Can you handle the pain in your heart, Kalel?" I press my hand to his jaw, guiding his lips to mine, and as we collide, I prepare for what's to come.

His fingers dig into my waist at my comment as I thought they would. He responds by thrusting the remainder of his length into me brutally. His knot smacks my entrance, and his tip is pushing against my cervix.

A scream is wrenched from my lips, covered just in time with his hand. He doesn't give me a second of reprieve before he's rocking his hips and pumping his engorged cock into me. It's aggressive and filled with emotion.

The pain and pleasure mix into a feeling of chaos. My thoughts are swept away, and all I can focus on is the way he ruts into me like he'll never be able to pull away again. The hatred and despair I once felt in his movements have turned into affection and guilty desire.

Kalel forces two fingers inside my mouth, and I bite down on them to keep myself from screaming as he pulls out to the tip and then thrusts his hips ruthlessly back into me, his knot repeatedly edging my entrance and making me moan at the girth of it.

He groans as I bite harder on his fingers. He buries his teeth in my shoulder and drinks my blood greedily as he fucks me in the moonlit garden.

His motion becomes heavier and slower. Kalel pulls his teeth from my flesh, gold liquid spilling on my skin as he chokes out, "I wished it wasn't you, Alira. But I was lying. To myself. To you. I've longed for this. To make you mine forever."

Kalel pushes down on my thighs hard. The fat, thick knot at his base slowly enters me, spreading me and securing itself in my deepest parts. My insides are on fire, and my stomach feels tight.

I weep at the sharp pain and pleasure. They are so similar, and the pressure is so intense that I can no longer differentiate the feeling. "*Wait.* I'm not ready," I cry, looking down at where we're connected and seeing how my stomach already bulges just from taking in his huge knot. He moans and kisses me, bucking his hips until his knot grows bigger. He rubs my clit until the tension is so powerful that I come all over his cock. He consumes my cries with deep kisses. Then his whole body tenses and he stills.

Kalel's cock pulses and hot liquid pours into my pussy, throbbing into my womb and filling me up. I whimper at the pressure that builds in my abdomen. He leans us back so I'm resting on his chest comfortably.

"*Shh.* I know, little godling. You did so well. It will take a while before we can part. You likely won't get pregnant, so don't cry." His voice sounds pained as he presses hot kisses to my forehead. His knot swells more, until I'm convinced it will never come out. His cock continues to throb deep inside me, spilling into my deepest parts and filling me completely. My stomach already looks swollen with his child.

Tears spill from my eyes.

His purring doesn't stop, and it's the only thing that soothes me. Kalel remains quiet, caressing me gently and keeping one hand where his knot is latched inside me, massaging softly.

"I'm a selfish man, you know. The timid boy you met long ago is dead. This is all I am now." His words make my heart twist painfully. Why did the gods do this to us? Why must we suffer so greatly? He never deserved the suffering he was dealt.

"I don't mind who you are now, Kalel," I murmur as I move my hand over his.

He stops massaging over his knot and lets out a defeated sigh. "Yeah?"

I only smile and close my eyes, letting my head lean against his. I wish this moment would last forever.

At least five minutes have passed, and his cock is still slowly releasing his seed inside me. The pain has at least subsided, but my mind is weary, and every muscle in my body is limp with exhaustion.

"You did so well, little godling," he murmurs, smoothing his hand over my stomach. Does he long to have a child with me? My heart warms at the idea of a little demon-godling mix of us.

I don't respond. I don't feel like I am even capable of it. My head rests against his shoulder, and all I can do is keep my eyes open enough to see the rise and fall of his chest.

"Would you like to sleep here tonight? I'm afraid we've been out here for over an hour. The gardens are likely littered with demons trying to have as much fun as we did," he says with a bit of humor in his tone, but I'm too tired to laugh. I'm struggling even to keep my eyes open.

He falls silent and brushes his hand over my head.

"Do gods sleep? I've always wondered. I never believed it fully until witnessing you rest myself. Gods *do* sleep, and I wonder how much that fact scares them. When demons like me have been waiting and watching for our chance to rid this world of them all." Kalel sounds nostalgic on the matter, but his words are ominous.

His knot finally unswells—the sensation relieving my inner walls from the pressure, and they are finally able to relax. Slowly, he pulls himself from me, and I whimper at the sudden emptiness. It feels cold, and the pain lingers.

He wraps me in his arms as I curl into the fetal position. I can't give a moment of thought to how he sees me right now.

I'm broken from today, and yet I've never felt more whole.

Gods, I'm falling in love with a demon.

CHAPTER 28

KALEL

Alira faints in my arms. Her limbs are completely lax, and her soft breaths make my heart ache.

I hold her tightly and rest my head against hers.

"I truly am a monster, and I will do unspeakable acts for the things I want. I really am sorry, Alira," I murmur against her forehead, pressing a kiss there as penance.

I decide to carry her back to my palace. We'll both sleep better in my bed, and she'll wake up more comfortable after the night we've had. She's going to be sore. I make a mental note to have Nik heal her in the morning.

The gardens are surprisingly quiet tonight. After most

weddings, this place is a sex haven. I listen for any whispers or moans but hear nothing. Unease sets into my bones. Something is wrong.

Then it hits me. *We didn't return for the king's last dance.*

Just as the blood drains from my face, I hear his heavy footsteps behind me. My shoulders tense, but I keep my hold on my little godling tight. I turn enough to see him from over my shoulder.

King Achill stands alone, with a mildly irked expression, but I know better than any that the less anger he shows, the more furious he truly is.

His eyes shift down to the sleeping half-god in my arms.

"You thought it was wise to insult me in front of the entire kingdom tonight by leaving before the last dance? With something as important as *this*, Kalel?" He grinds his jaw. "How ignorant of a demon are you?" His voice is as soft as a stream. No one holds their emotions better than Achill. Which lends to the reason he is so terrifying.

"I saw the way you looked at her. I can't let you breed her, my king." I try to sound as respectful as I can, but I wanted to tear his throat out tonight. The scent of his lust for her was maddening. He was going to take her to his chambers tonight, even after everything I've done for him and the kingdom.

He was going to try to take her from me.

My eyes shift down to her face. I could stare upon her for the rest of time. My little godling. *Mine.*

King Achill crosses his arms and smiles, but it's anything but happy. It's a threat.

"Is that why you thought you'd beat me to it? Keep your demigod. But know that your insolence will cost you greatly." He levels me with cruel cerulean eyes.

I bow my head. "I am indebted to you, my generous king." The words taste bitter in my mouth.

He grins. "Yes, you are. Did Gabriel brief you on the movement detected outside the gates? It would seem that her little necklace was charmed by their king with a tracking spell, just like you thought. They couldn't help themselves, could they?" Achill laughs, his eyes darker than I've ever seen them.

"I don't think Alira knew of the spell. She had no response when I took it away. She was happy to have it back, but only because of its sentimental value. Nikolai confirmed it. So I don't want any punishment to fall upon her." I make myself clear. He nods, but it doesn't bring me much comfort.

"Go, rest while you can. I'll send someone for you in the morning. Now that our initial plan has been enacted, we need to move quickly."

His words linger with me long after I return to my palace and tuck Alira into my bed. I step out to the balcony and lean against the guardrail, staring up at the universe of stars with a forlorn frown.

What a mess. What game are the gods playing with us? I

want no part in it. Not when it's our lives that are always at stake.

I close my eyes and tighten my fists.

She could never love me. Not after she realizes what I've done.

My eyes lower to the gardens below, staring upon the flowers she loves so much. If she knew that each of those peonies were once demigods, would she still covet them so? After finding their gilded blood in the stems? After learning that I buried their bones there in the flower beds? How does she think we keep our kingdom warded with such magic?

If she knew I prayed to Pluto to put a loop curse on her that day in Thornhall—that I cursed the knight who led the attack on my mother's home to relive many lives until I was satisfied with killing them repeatedly for punishment—could she forgive me?

I didn't know my precious little godling was the knight I'd slain twenty times. Evil and vengeful as I am, I couldn't willingly kill the only being that has plagued my mind for the last thirty years.

And yet I did. Many, many times.

My memories aren't as clear as the victim of Pluto's loop curse, but I remember her helmet coming off in the last reset. I remember seeing her silver hair and lavender eyes. Is that why I was so eager to convince Achill to accept their deal for peace?

Would she forgive me if she knew that my blood was the

only way to save her and break the curse? At least that's what Pluto told me. He said it was the only way to free the cursed knight.

I couldn't let the loop reset again, not after finally finding her. But if she should die now, it would be for good.

A deep and ruinous pain moves through my chest at that thought. I stare down at the flowers she adores so much.

My foolish half-god.

I return to the bed and stare down at her somberly, brushing my thumb over her cheek gently.

"My mercy died long ago," I whisper to her. As did most of my heart. All that's left of it remains with her. "You should know that I die slowly with each tear you shed. I love you, Alira. I'm sorry for what I am." I shut my eyes and hold her close to my chest. Can she hear my heart? Can she hear how it agonizes for her?

No, she will never love a man like me. Not after what comes next.

Not after vengeance is served.

I will bring Alzhor and every half-god to rubble now that she is out of harm's way.

"I'm sorry for tricking you."

EPILOGUE

PLUTO

The dark water in the pools surrounding my throne reflects a story of sorrow and love. A confession of a demon's sins.

Lounging on my throne, I lean against my fist as I gaze into the pools. A cruel grin lifts the corner of my lips. "Kalel, what a mess you've made for yourself."

I tap my long finger against the stone armrest. If Venus hadn't sent him that wisp to try to stop the attack on Thornhall, her only daughter would've died the first time he had slain her in Alzhor. Venus's wisp showed him a specific knight to put his rage toward. I chuckle at her risky move. To show her daughter to a monster like him, a monster I helped create, was a bold move to say the least.

Was it luck? Or did the goddess have a fate that prophesied a way to keep her daughter alive? Lovely Venus. Her heart is pure. I fear that her empathy rubbed off on me long ago.

My eyes narrow with a wry grin as I move a chess piece across the game board.

I tried to give the silver godling a clue. Every demigod should know that any being cold to their touch is evidence of a curse they've placed on you. Once the curse is lifted, they are warm once more.

Hmm. Although I suppose King Borlin did burn most of their history books. And what with there being so few of them left, how could such a foolish girl know any better? Being assigned as a knight too, she'd never had a chance to learn the way of curses.

Pity.

I *tsk*, enamored with their longing for each other nonetheless. As opposite as they are, their attraction is magnetic. Alluring.

It was by chance that I happened to be watching the night he was slain. An act as terrible as what unfolded that night was enough to garner even Jupiter's eye.

I connected with the pain that flashed in that boy's eyes as he was slain for merely existing. A compulsion tugged on my heart to save him.

But unlike the gods in the sky, I require a prayer from one with holy blood to keep a soul from entering the Gates of Mortem.

So when I watched that young demigod girl weep over his body and cry out to the divine beings who abandoned them, I answered her call.

Once upon a demon's heart, it was done—only written in gilded blood can it be undone.

The story will continue in *Once Written in Gilded Blood.*

READ ON FOR A SNEAK PEEK OF THE NEXT NOVEL IN THIS DUOLOGY, *ONCE WRITTEN IN GILDED BLOOD*

PROLOGUE

VENUS

Once upon a time, there was a goddess, one of love and fertility, whose only desire was to have a daughter. She wasn't particularly fond of her fellow god companions—they were too prideful and cruel for her liking. Which only left her with the mortals below or the demons of Mortem.

Venus was beautiful in both heart and features. Her skin was rich in warm tones; most mortals claimed that when she walked in the sunlight, it looked like she had speckles of gold woven into her being. She left her peers dazed by her long silver hair, serene, narrow eyes, and tall stature. Venus was beloved by all. She attended as many mortal balls and tranquil parties as she could find. Always in hiding, disguised as a maiden so as not to attract too much attention.

Humans feared anything they didn't understand. They were quick to kill creatures that they could not control. And yet they created such beautiful things. Marvelous buildings and statues of the very gods they were so afraid of. Venus couldn't help but linger in their world longer than she should, curious if she could find love and hopeful for a daughter.

Though something that seemed so easy to find for others proved almost impossible for Venus.

She had a few children with a couple of different mortal men. Demigods were to be left on the steps of Alzhor, everyone knew this. And for Venus, she could part with a child every hundred years. They were all male and, as sons of Venus, were beneficial to the demigods' reproductive efforts.

Venus cared for them but still longed for a daughter. She had all but given up until the Fates gave her the news she'd been hoping to hear for centuries.

She had a daughter. Alira, she named her.

Venus stared at Alira's beautiful silver hair for hours, wondering how she could be so perfect, like a star of her own. Venus couldn't let her go—she didn't want to leave her on the steps of Alzhor. But the God of Death, Pluto, warned her that the demigods belonged in Alzhor, and Jupiter would never let her keep her daughter in the heavens.

Venus took his warning to heart and decided to visit the

Fates once more. They were an arcane group of fortune tellers. All-seeing and eternal, always watching, always observing every reality. They were a group of three rather frightening-looking demons. Their skin was a dark gray, and they had little to no hair. They resembled humans who appeared long dead. One covered its mouth, the second covered its eyes, the third its ears.

They showed the goddess the fate of her daughter, the golden blood that would slip from Alira's veins and one excruciating truth: Alira would not live a good life. It would be filled with suffering and her time would be cut short.

The Fates showed Venus the way the demigods would use her daughter for her gift—the gift of Venus. She would be used for her fertility, abused, and treated differently from the rest of the demigods for the rarity of her gift. Her daughter would never live a normal life until the demons slaughtered all of Alzhor.

Seeing the cruel fate that her only daughter would be dealt was the hardest part of Venus's existence. It wasn't fair.

Venus refused this prophecy, for it was too merciless for any creature.

She did not know why she agreed to have the vision offered by the Fates. But she knew there was truth in their vision; something felt different when Alira was born. Her hair was as silver and as shimmery as the stars, her eyes a lovely shade of blue that made her olive skin radiate. She was more god than demigod, a blessing and a curse.

Sadness was born in Venus's heart.

No matter how many times she asked the Fates to show her another version of Alira's life, the result was always the same. Alira died at the hands of demons.

Time and time again.

Venus pleaded with the Fates. For there had to be a way to change it.

"Goddess of Love, you know better than to alter fate. The ripples are dangerous and won't serve your intentions the way that you are hoping they will," they warned her, all three speaking at once, their haunting voices bouncing off the cave walls.

Venus's stomach twisted with guilt as she replied, "I will do anything to change her fate."

They observed her and gave Venus a pitiful shake of their heads.

"Very well, but you will need to follow the actions perfectly. Any misstep will result in tragedy, and there is only one chance for this to work. Are you willing to sacrifice your gift of the flowers?" The Fates pulled down their ancient book from the tallest shelf along the stone wall of their cave—a small corner of Mortem that Pluto allowed Venus to visit.

"Yes." Venus did not hesitate, even though her gift of flowers was precious to her. She'd turned many humans and demons alike into flowers for their crimes against others. She'd also learned the past through them—they held memories from the things they'd used to grow.

The Fates glanced up at Venus with dull, cold eyes, tapping their long fingernails at the bottom of a page in an offbeat. Venus could only imagine that the paper was filled with other hopeful altered prophecies, written by other gods or demigods.

"In gilded blood, it must be done," the Fates' voices carried through the cave and made chills crawl up Venus's arms.

The goddess took the black dagger they handed her and made one firm cut down her palm, gold blossoming from her perfect skin, and there she wrote, even at the cost of others, for her daughter to escape such a cruel fate.

"It is done." The Fates slammed the book shut and grinned in a way that left the goddess worried about what she'd just done. *Jupiter must never find out—he disapproves of anything being tampered with in the world below us.* But she could not turn a blind eye to her daughter. Venus's love for her was unconditional.

The goddess frowned and delicately touched her finger to Alira's cheek. The child was sleeping and unconcerned with the world around her. Venus choked back tears when she set the demigod on the steps of Alzhor's kingdom, placing the sheathed dagger she used for the ceremony on top of Alira's blanket.

"May the sparrows be with you, my sweet Alira."

ACKNOWLEDGMENTS

This story has been living in my head for a few years, and I'm so happy that it's finally in your hands! I can't thank my readers enough for all the support for my books.

I'd like to thank my beta readers, Jay, Kenzie, and Cierra, for being the first to read this story and making it shine!

Thank you to my husband for being my rock. I seriously couldn't get much done without your help with everything else in life.

ABOUT THE AUTHOR

K.M. Moronova is a dark fantasy and romance author. She lives in Montana with her partner, two dogs, and three cats. She loves drinking tea and writing stories with worlds that she can get completely swept into. Her favorite characters are the misunderstood villains.

Website: kmmoronova.com
TikTok: @K.M.Moronova
Facebook: K.M. Moronova
Instagram: @K.M.Moronova
Threads: @K.M.Moronova

NEW BLOOD

TERRY M DUNN

The DANEBURY Series

Dannu's Man
One Man's Honour
A Man of his Time

Published by Daneburyverse books
Printed by book printing UK
Remus House, Coltsfoot Drive,
Peterborough PE2 9BF

ISBN 978-1-9162657-4-5

For **Sandy**, just because...

3,506 BC

1

The village on the brow a few miles beyond the eastern side of the great river, that would eventually in modern times be known as Woolbury hillfort, had been working hard to establish itself. Barely a year previously, Chieftain Parrish of Dane-bre had offered it to the people who now lived there as a site of a new home. Their old village had been all but completely destroyed by a great storm the winter before. No one but Parrish knew the real reason why the destructive weather had punished everyone, but he wasn't saying. After Chieftain Shimon had come to Danebury, leading his depleted villagers and had demanded help by challenging Parrish to combat, and being soundly beaten, an agreement had been reached. Dannu's man, for that is what the people called Parrish when they thought he was out of earshot, had made the surprising suggestion that they try and establish a new home. Surprising because the site for Woolbury, although some seven or eight kilometres distant from Danebury, was still in plain sight of the other. But it was a chance for Chieftain Shimon to try and establish a new home, a safe haven for his remaining people, on top of that hill east of the river.

Unimaginatively, they named their new home after the great flocks of sheep, scattered across the open land between Danebury and where their temporary wiki-ups had been sited against the forest edge. Flocks that they watched whilst they waited for the Chieftain of Dane-bre's decision regarding their future. With 'Olann' being the old Celtic word for wool, their new home was promptly labelled Olann-bre or wool hill. The word would eventually revert through old English into the Anglo-Saxon and then to the modern era. And so Olann-bre would be known in that far distant future as Woolbury.

Chieftain Shimon and his people had laboured in the last few seasons to erect some sort of defence wall and ditch system, and build decent shelters, trying to re-establish themselves as a new, bone-fide village on Dannu's land.

It was a strange situation. Villages were never anywhere near other villages for good reason. Otherwise fighting would ensue, heads would be taken and the stronger force would wipe out the weaker one. So each village kept its distance from all others.

But the unique change that Chieftain Parrish had put in place was that the river that flowed north to south through the valley between the two encampments would be a barrier, a line none would cross without the specific and direct order of the respective Chieftains. This had kept the two potentially warring parties apart. But both Chieftains also knew their people well and, once the threat of imminent death had been removed, Chieftain Shimon's people would sometimes be on their side of the riverbank at the same time as some of those from Danebury would arrive on the other. In direct line of sight and definitely within hailing distance

What had started with the occasional acknowledging nod, and then a furtive wave, had gradually expanded to friendly greetings, cheery hellos and over time a few, mostly between the women, distant friendships had sprung up.

Parrish was quite sure that this would naturally happen when he had set the whole thing up, and he was quietly appreciative of the Neolithic detente that had grown. He also smiled when the occasional gift and useful items began to pass between the different peoples, from one side of the river to the other.

Again, the women of the villages were the instigators of this. They were the usually unseen backbone of the village and the few who were struggling in Woolbury began to receive discrete help from the Danebury ladies. It might only be small food parcels, woollen goods or small pieces of equipment they were lacking. Parrish had no idea, and was not even supposed to know, but liked to try and guess what was passed across the flowing waters. Needles, cutting tools, leather for shoes or straps? Anything that might make the day-to-day running of a village that much easier. Things that the warriors of the village took for granted but in themselves took up precious time to make if they were not already to hand.

Parrish loved the people too for their ingenuity on deriving a simple system for passing packages across an expanse of water some thirty meters wide, deep and quite fast flowing. Simply throwing packages across was a bit hit and miss. It required someone with a good arm and a package that wasn't too heavy, too light or too bulky. After losing several into the water, carried away and down by the flow, a simple but effective idea was born.

A stake was driven into the edge of the riverbank a short way up stream. There was a corresponding stake in the opposite bank. A weighted length of twine, usually of braided or twisted wool was then thrown across from one side to the other. The catcher of the weighted end would then haul it across pulling along the more sturdy rope attached to it. One end of this was secured to said stake, the other end, still on the opposite bank, was tied to a small wooden raft roughly about the size of a pallet. The item or items to be passed across the river were secured to the pallet, usually in leather pouches because sometimes the uneven water flow caused it to capsize. Now loaded with its little cargo, the raft was set afloat and the natural flow of the river would take it briefly downstream until the link line went taut. Then it would sweep almost majestically across the flow in a quite speedy arc and come smartly up against the opposite bank, where someone would be waiting to scoop it up. For return trips the light rope would be thrown back from one post to the other and once the heavier rope was tied off to the opposite side stake, the pallet raft was ready for a return journey. It was simple, almost always worked and it looked somehow serene to Parrish's eyes. Sometimes he would go down to the river, staying back a discrete distance so as not to disrupt the operation, and watch the system in action. He would laugh out loud and clap his hands when some large or slightly unstable package made it safely across. The intense look on the ladies faces as it all happened always cheered him. The first time he had witnessed the deed the ladies there were so intent they had not heard his approach. When that first raft package swooped across the water and was gathered safely into the waiting arms opposite, he clapped and laughed out loud. The unsuspecting women at the river's edge visibly jumped in surprise and on turning to find their Chieftain behind them were horrified at having been found out. They bowed deeply to him. When they straightened back up they found the smile still on his face. He just winked at them all, nodded back then just turned and walked away. The ladies understood this to be a sign of approval, and as Parrish walked off he heard the sudden burst of giggling and chattering amongst those by the river bank.

That'll do, he thought. Yes, that'll do.

But items were still sometimes lost to the river. At best it was just annoying but sometimes it could be soul destroying and heartbreaking if the item or items lost had been difficult or very time consuming to make, or it was something of particular need to its intended recipient.

Yet, his people were resilient and stalwart, so it was a while before Parrish found out about these occasional bad losses.

And then what he had secretly hoped might happen, finally happened. He was called out from his log cabin and found a young lad waiting, perhaps fourteen or so years of age. An almost warrior, as he privately referred to them. Out of the corner of his eye he saw a true warrior, standing discretely off to one side. This was the boy's father, trying discretely to back his son up during his first direct approach to a Chieftain. Parrish pretended not to see him and, smothering a knowing smile, squared up to the youngster.

"Yes?" Just the act of straightening his back and looking down on the lad added a layer of trepidation to the boy. But then he too straightened up. Parrish approved.

"I have come to ask for your permission," he said, then paused. "And some advice." Parrish just raised an eyebrow. After realising that no words were forthcoming, the lad continued. "We ... I have decided it is time I took a wife." Deep breath. "And there is a girl. I have seen her many times and my father and I would like to speak with her father to barter for her."

"And?" asked Parrish, having a good idea what was coming next.

"She ... she is from the village across the river." As he spoke the words he winced in anticipation of a blast of strong words or even a blow. But Parrish did nothing and the boy quickly almost babbled on to get his reasoning out for disobeying the Chieftains 'no mixing' policy. "We think we could do well in trade for her. They are low in people over there and so must be in need of many things ..."

Parrish was just letting the boy go on but nodded and held up a hand for him to stop.

"I believe you may be right, my young friend." The lad sighed in relief. "Also, I think it would be a good thing to bring some new blood in from outside of Dane-bre."

The boy's expression changed to a frown but Parrish just waved away his confusion. He couldn't explain to him, or anyone else, about the benefits of expanding the gene pool but it was the first event that he had really hoped for. And he hoped that in time there might be more like it. Again, without looking directly at the boy's father, he waved the man to join them. The warrior started at the fact that he had been noticed, but moved quickly at his Chieftain's bidding. When he reached his sons side Parrish nodded.

"Can I take it that you have somehow gotten word to this girl's father that you would like to barter, and that because you are here, he is of the same thought?"

"Yes, my Chieftain."

"Then it looks like we should pay this man a visit to agree terms, no?" There was a chorus of two nods. "And then we must exchange goods." He hated referring to a living human being as goods, but that was the way of the people. Also, it did seem to him that the pair had given the whole enterprise some thought so, rather than take charge, he let them expand on their idea. "So, how do we go about this task? How do we get across the big river?" He had to admit he hadn't given it that much thought himself. The river Test was wide, quite fast flowing and too deep to wade. Even a year earlier, when Chieftain Shimon's people had been offered the distant hill opposite, he'd just sent them on their way and paid no attention to how they had crossed the flowing expanse of water.

The warrior kept to himself his surprise that once again his Chieftain, who should know all, had revealed he had no idea about something everyone else in the village took as common knowledge. He just eyed the tall man for a second, and then spoke in even tones.

"Half a day's walk up river there is a narrower place. The flow is faster and it is of some danger, but it can be crossed."

"Well then, it looks like this will take a little longer than I thought." he smiled at the pair before him. "Do what you need to, then meet me at the gate shortly."

They both bowed deeply to him then spun on their heels, and Parrish went back inside his cabin to tell Juli what was going on.

The trio made their way down to the riverside in silence, eyed the wide flowing waters for a moment then set off northwards, upstream. Parrish asked the warrior to let him know when they had reached his crossing point, but other than that there was no talk. Parrish was

Chieftain so it fell to him to speak first if he so chose. The warrior was silently respectful in his presence and the warrior's son simply kept pace beside his father. Parrish doubted much that if they did engage in conversation it would be the most stimulating exchange, so he held his peace and they made their way in a roughly northerly direction, keeping the river close on their right.

It *was* a long way, perhaps three or four kilometres upstream, before the warrior pointed to a place just ahead of them and finally spoke.

"Here, my Chieftain. Not too deep but it is fast flowing. And also, it is not very even underfoot." he added, hoping the words would be taken as they were meant. No insult of ignorance intended, just adding information about the hidden dangers.

"Thank you." Parrish nodded, missing any inference at all. "Good to know." And the smaller man mentally sighed in relief and nodded an acknowledgement.

The river here wasn't really all that much narrower, perhaps twenty or so metres wide, but just as described, it was shallower. Parrish could see the gravelled bottom between the strips of waving weeds beneath the surface of the crystal clear water. There were a few large trout, holding position just above the gravel riverbed with lazy flicks of their tails, but he had no interest in them today. His concern was, that although he could see the bottom, it still looked four or five feet deep in places. A daunting enough crossing for him let alone his two shorter companions. Hmm. This could be a bit dodgy.

"OK." He turned to them. "We are all going to need a sturdy pole." The looks on their faces said, huh? He smiled. "Cut yourselves each a staff at least as big as you are tall. A bit longer wouldn't hurt." There was no argument and they all moved off into the woods, each returning shortly clutching what amounted to over long quarterstaffs.

"Right. Now, when we cross, spread out. Face *up* stream and thrust your pole into the riverbed before you. Use it to feel the river bottom and seek out any trouble. Extra deep spots, that sort of thing. With your feet wide apart you will make what is called a 'tripod'. Move slowly sideways across the river using the pole as a support. Lean into it my friends. It will help you be strong against the flow and so will be safer than just trying to wade blindly across."

The two Neolithic men didn't look too convinced about this untried, at least to them, system but Parrish set off first to demonstrate. He sidled slowly out into the clear, fast flowing water. They watched as he made his way, driving his staff into the river bed, occasionally feeling about for a firm purchase with it then leaning on it before side stepping, then repeating the whole process again. The force of the water, now almost up to his waist was strong, but he appeared outwardly confident and sure of what he was doing. Bolstered by this the two Danebury men followed suit and found, if they were also slow and careful, they felt more in control. It was still a perilous journey. Parrish kept up a constant verbal flow of encouragement, as much against the threat of the dangerous river as for the smaller men. At his words they found that if their next sideways step revealed a previously hidden deep spot, they could retreat and move either up or downstream for a better footing. This was infinitely more preferable to genuinely risking their lives by plunging blindly on and wrong footing in a desperate attempt to cross the river as quickly as possible. Parrish verbally applauded them when he saw this and with his encouragement, the use of their staves and their newly learned crossing technique, the trio slowly crossed safely to the far bank. The looks of triumph on the faces of Parrish's men made him grin widely.

"There you go." He said cheerfully. "Easy when you know how, eh?" He would have liked the pair to have laughed and even taken the mickey, in that old Army way he loved so much, but he knew what was coming instead.

The warrior and his son bowed solemnly to their Chieftain, grateful for being shown a new thing, no doubt passed down to him from Dannu, and now to be passed on to the two warriors by her man. They were truly grateful. Parrish accepted the bows with a somewhat magnanimous nod, casually discarded his stave and turned, setting off back the way they had come, the river still on their right, only this time heading south.

"So, what's the SP?" he said suddenly to the man beside him, the man's son still respectfully a step behind. The frown on the warrior's face said he didn't understand but his Chieftain was not annoyed by that. In fact he smiled. Parrish might not be receiving any Army banter but he could still enjoy dishing some out. He laughed at his fellows confusion then translated.

"What has been arranged when we get near to the village. I am hoping that they at least know that we are coming? I will not be impressed if there is trouble because we have turned up unknown!"

"No, no." The warrior hastened to put his Chieftain's mind at rest. Nor did he like the thinly veiled threat of some kind of 'trouble' if he had failed in his duty to his Chieftain. "Everything is known. Their Chieftain has agreed to the visit and the barter for one of his people."

Parrish nodded his approval.

"I have not done any bartering for a woman." He confessed to his suddenly wide eyed companions. "What is the going rate?"

"I am sorry, my Chieftain ... going ...?"

"What would be expected to trade for a new wife?" he corrected, with a smile.

"It can be many different things." The elder of the two replied, again not outwardly appearing to be surprised at his Chieftains ignorance. "But most likely it will be for goods or tools that the girls owner will be in need of."

Parrish inwardly frowned at the word owner, with its blatant slavery connotations, but that truly distasteful word was unknown here.

"Then I think this bartering today might be very interesting."

"You do?"

"Yes. There are things that someone needs, and there are things that *people* need." And with that he strode on, leaving the two Neolithic men pondering on what exactly the remark meant.

Again silence reigned as the miss-matched trio made their way back towards the area of river between the two hillforts a few kilometres downstream. Parrish automatically became more wary now he was 'technically' on foreign soil and he noticed his companions doing likewise. Although almost within sight of their home village, this was still virgin territory to them since crossing the great river had never been an option to hunting parties before. Also, they knew another village was nearby. Although a pact had been made between the two Chieftains it was not unknown for hunting warrior bands to forget any contrary instructions in the heat of conflict and the chance of trophies! If a band of men spied another it nearly always descended on them and battle commenced immediately. Parrish knew how powerful a Chieftains word was when given, but that did not stop him from being on his guard against an 'accidental' sudden death at the hands of some hot headed warrior whose lust for blood and trophies overcame his usual allegiance to his village chief.

With eyes constantly darting to the dense and virtually virgin forest to their left, being acutely aware that an attack from there would pin them against the edge of the river, they continued. Parrish seemed to be the only one who appeared to notice that it *was* virgin. Considering that Chieftain Shimon's village was only perhaps an hour's walk away, there were no worn pathways, cuts through the undergrowth, deliberately felled trees or in fact *any* signs of recent human passing. He was beginning to realise that Olann-bre might be seriously undermanned.

They followed alongside the never ending, unstoppable flow of the river and eventually emerged from the trees into the open area on the bank adjacent to where those of Danebury came when they sent their little raft parcels across. There were a couple of Danebury women near the bank and they looked surprised to suddenly see their Chieftain on the far side. Even so, they bowed respectfully across the space between them.

Parrish bowed back lightly and took a moment to look back past them, away to the horizon where thin spirals of smoke rose from his village. A good sign. Then he turned his back to the river and looked towards the east and the rising ground that was distantly topped by Woolbury hillfort. Hmm. Not so many fires there.

Word had clearly been sent, for the trio had not gone too far up the intervening slopes when two figures approached.

One was a warrior. Non descript was Parrish's initial thought as he took in the man's standard build and that he walked a pace behind the leading man. This man he recognised as Chieftain Shimon.

They met on a small plateau a hundred metres or so from the river and stopped a few paces apart. Both parties bowed, as per protocol on meeting a Chieftain. Two Chieftains meeting without the threat of immediate combat was unheard of outside the solstice gathering at Avebury, so Parrish took the lead.

"Greetings, Chieftain Shimon. It is good to see you." He took in the slightly haggard look and the stress lines spidering out from around the corners of the man's eyes. The warrior who accompanied him looked much the same.

"Greetings." Shimon said no more.

There was a slightly awkward silence before Parrish picked up the lead again.

"You look tired, my friend. Are you unwell?"

"Never mind my condition." came the gruff reply. "We are here to barter."

"Yes." Parrish's reply was curt then, but he did not display any outward displeasure or annoyance at the lack of respect given. He indicated to the warrior and his son at his side. "There is a wish for the boy here to take a wife, if an agreement can be met."

The warrior accompanying Chieftain Shimon stepped forward at that and opened his mouth to speak, but was silenced before even uttering a sound by Shimon's abruptly raised hand.

"If our terms are met, then and only then is the girl yours." He turned to the boy's father, rather arrogantly dismissing Parrish from the conversation. "We ... This man needs tools." He stated bluntly.

"I have some tools to spare." said the Danebury warrior, hope rising in his voice. This could be an easy trade he was thinking, with little or no inconvenience to himself or his family. Shimon's next words crushed that thought.

"Picks and shovels." He said. "A hand full of each." And he held up his right hand, fingers splayed wide to show he meant five of each.

"That is ... a lot!" said the man beside Parrish, who looked sideways at the warrior and saw his mind working behind the eyes. Wondering how he might meet such an order. No one kept that many picks and shovels at the ready. Antler picks and shoulder blade shovels could only be obtained when a hunt brought back a sizable stag, and of course antlers were only available in the rutting season.

"Also," Shimon continued. "Both hands full of good sized flint felling axe heads!" and he spread out the fingers of his left hand to join the right.

"I ... I have a small number of axe heads." countered the warrior in a faltering voice. "But only one or two."

Parrish knew that his friend the flint knapper made virtually all the large flint tools in Danebury and that each one had been individually bartered for. It was never questioned, his skill was unmatched and the quality and effectiveness of the tools he made was second to none.

"That many are far beyond my ability to give. If you ..."

"Those are my terms!" Shimon stated bluntly.

So much for honest negotiation, thought Parrish sourly. He turned and looked at the pair beside him. The warriors face began to set in resignation and the boy's face fell.

"We will meet your price!" barked Parrish over the sullen silence. "A hand each of picks and shovels, and two hands worth of axe heads." Shimon tried to look him in the eye but Parrish turned away, deliberately turning his back to a Chieftain as an insult, and said quietly to his two companions. "We will do this. I will not have it be said that Dane-bre is not worthy of a hard bargain, so I agree to this. But this girl had better be worth it!" The warrior just nodded dumbly but the boy visibly gulped.

"OK." Parrish turned back to face Shimon and his cohort, who had still not uttered a word. "We will gather up the goods you ask and send them across the river. On the day of the next full moon." He added, giving he and his people just over a week's breathing space to make up the order. "Make sure she is ready."

"The river bank. The day of the full moon." repeated Shimon. "Good. Send over the tools and if they are to my liking, I will have the girl sent in return."

Parrish finally bristled. His eyes hardened noticeably and through almost gritted teeth he said slowly.

"My village tools are more than good enough. If you do not honour this bargain, you will answer to me!"

And with that he spun on his heel and headed back towards the river. His own men could do nothing but fall in behind him. The boy stole a glance back expecting to see the Olann-bre Chieftain furious at the insult but he was just in time to see a satisfied grin on the man's face as he too turned away, patting the shoulder of the father of the girl as he did so.

As they approached the river, now safely out of earshot, the boy's father put a hand on Parrish's forearm, stopping them both in their tracks.

"My Chieftain, I cannot meet those terms. Who would ever hold so many tools at all?"

"Do not worry." The tall man smiled down at him as his son came up alongside them both. "I will speak with the rest of my warriors. I am thinking if that each family donates a single tool we should have enough picks and shovels. It is my old friend the flint knapper who will have the heavy task. That is why I demanded the extra days to get the axe heads made. I am hoping that he will be more pleased that his work is in such need rather than be angry about all the extra work I have agreed he must do."

"But ..."

Parrish just raised his hand, just as Shimon had done, but somehow with benevolence instead of aggression.

"Do not worry. I will see that he receives what he needs in return for the extra effort." Parrish, having already considered how to gather up such a list of items did acknowledge that it was a big order, but not too big for a well run village. "The tools will be gathered in good time."

"Then we are both greatly in your debt." Both his companions bowed deeply.

Parrish turned to them and smiled thinly.

"I can see by your faces that it is a very large price to pay for a girl." At that they nodded. "But I am happy to bring new blood to the village." This brought more uncomprehending frowns from the pair. "But more than that, it is worth it for the information I now have about the condition of Shimon's village and its people."

"How so?" asked the warrior, momentarily forgetting himself and asking a Chieftain to explain himself.

Parrish tapped his finger to the side of his nose, then grinned at the looks of puzzlement then disappointment on this companions faces. They really wanted to perhaps get an insight into their Chieftain's brain and felt like they were going to be denied it.

"All right. I will say what I think." His two follower's eyes widened. A Chieftain explaining was a rare thing. "It has been almost a year ... er ... several seasons since Shimon and his people moved to Olann-bre. Now, we know they are not many, for he lost some of his people to the great storm, yes?" There were two nods of agreement. "So, I see no real pathways leading very far from his village, which means few have walked those paths. If they are low on antler picks and shovels then they cannot have brought many with them and cannot have had much hunting success. I think that also means that they do not have a great many warriors in Olann-bre. And, if they are in great need of good axe heads, I also think that they have no skilled knapper of their own." Slack jawed amazement now hung on the faces of his companions. "Did you not notice how tired they both looked? I think that things are not going well at Olann-bre. Without tools and not enough warriors to use them or to go hunting, it is my belief that Olann-bre is in poor repair." And not just the camp, he added in thought. I suspect the people are struggling too.

The two Danebury men stood, still open mouthed. Such words! It is true then, Dannu's man sees all, and they were at that moment privileged to be witness to it. Unbidden, they both bowed in great respect to their Chieftain.

"Yes, well." Parrish nodded back then squinted over their heads at the woodland alongside their side of the river. The knowing smile dropped from his face.

"Now we have a bit of a hike just to get back home." he growled. "Ah well, onwards and upwards."

His mouth set in a firm line and he led off, back upstream towards the distant crossing point. As the other two fell in alongside, half joking, he said to no one in particular.

"Hope we are home in time for tea."

2

Just as Parrish had surmised, a week later, on the day that heralded the first showing of the full moon, a fair sized gathering had assembled on the banks of the great river. On the Danebury side, Parrish held sway. He stood a few paces back from the water's edge as the warrior and his son who had instigated this unusual exchange secured their precious bundle of goods to the tiny raft, linked with its single rope to the post on the opposite bank a little way upstream.

The raft was less than the size of a pallet and the cluster of antler picks and shoulder blade shovels stuck out over its edges. In the centre, securely lashed in place, was a decent sized leather pouch that held the precious, skilfully knapped axe heads agreed upon. The warrior checked the lashings again. It would be a great loss if the river took the stones, which had required many days work to complete. Especially as the old flint knapper of Dane-bre never slackened or cut any corners on his creations. They were always of the finest quality and much sought after.

All the other spectators of Danebury, many of whom had contributed a tool to the booty and so didn't need any sort of excuse to be there, thought that the price about to be paid was much too high for a single girl. But Parrish had ordered it. And so the raft was being readied.

On the opposite bank stood Chieftain Shimon, the father of the girl being exchanged, the girl herself who was wrapped in a large animal skin, and less than a dozen other people, not all of them warriors.

This helped confirm Parrish's assessment that there was a serious lack of manpower at Woolbury. He understood too that this lack of warriors was being kept quiet lest some other village get wind of it and saw the village as an easy target that could be overwhelmed and then plundered for its goods, women and trophies.

After a silent acknowledgement from the far bank, he turned his attention to the girl, trying to get some sort of gauge of what all this fuss was about. Even at a distance of more than thirty metres away, she seemed quite tall for a Neolithic girl. He guessed at least five feet, even maybe a little more. Because she was clutching the skin tight about her he could also see that she appeared to be narrower in all the right places but verged on what Parrish would call 'sturdy'. She was no beauty, he decided, but from here she looked sound to him. A good addition to Danebury.

The two men by the Danebury side raft looked to their Chieftain and he nodded approval. The pair gently pushed the laden raft/pallet out into the flow. It drifted briefly before being picked up by the flow and carried off downstream. A few moments later the rope linking the raft to the upstream stake on the opposite bank twanged taut as the slack was taken up. At a surprisingly rapid rate, Parrish assumed it was because of the weight, the tethered raft swept out into midstream. It described a splendid arc and swooped in a slightly choppy way across to the far bank, in less than a minute, guessed Parrish. Welcome arms were ready to catch the precious cargo and it was arrested and hauled up onto the far bank in a matter of moments.

"Nice." said Parrish and smiled at his men before turning his gaze back to those on the far bank. While the goods there were unloaded, laid out on the ground and inspected, people upstream were busy hurling the link rope across then securing it to the pivot post on the Danebury side. Now the small raft was ready for its return journey.

Chieftain Shimon and his followers checked the tools and axe heads thoroughly, lingering with glee over the superbly made flint implements and finally the Chieftain looked up, gazed across the thirty metre expanse of open water and nodded in acceptance.

Parrish gave him a thumbs up in return but got no reaction until he returned the nod.

Only then did Chieftain Shimon point to the father of the girl. The man took his cue and led his daughter to the water's edge to stand before the little raft. Without ceremony he whipped away the covering animal skin to reveal her completely naked. It was the way,

Parrish knew, a good Chieftain gave away nothing, but it still did not sit well with him to see a defenceless person so exposed. But that thought was immediately superseded by concern as he saw the girl's father instruct her to lay down on the small raft.

"Hold on," gasped Parrish, "Hold on!" He turned to Klud and said in a horrified tone. "I thought they would accept the tools and send the girl off upstream to the crossing point?"

Klud looked back at his tall friend and explained quietly in blunt terms.

"My friend, once a trade is made, the girl is the property of her new owner. They care not what happens to someone else's property."

"Shit!" Parrish hissed and the pair turned back in time to see the clearly unhappy girl lay face down on the raft. Gripping the sides of it tightly, her chin jutted over its front edge. Her chest and most of her upper torso down as far as her navel lay on the timber, but the entire lower half of her body was trailing in the water.

"Not happy about this." said Parrish to no one in particular. "This is NOT a good idea." And he watched with everyone else as the girl on the precariously small raft was pushed out into the flow. Like its previous crossing, the raft with its oversized, naked cargo slid out and began to drift downstream until the slack on the guide rope ran out. The girl was so much heavier than its previous load and the rope snapped taught with a sharp jerk and it swooped rapidly out towards mid stream along its arc across the river.

The harsh jerk of the tightening tether had an unstabling effect and it started to wobble and oscillate. This was quickly compounded by it being top heavy and the girl, with no idea how to stop it, spread her legs wide, causing the drag on the raft to increase. The weave increased and the clearly terrified girl began to kick with her legs against the unstoppable flow while gripping the edges of the raft as tightly as she could. The combined effect was enough to completely destabilize the whole thing.

Parrish's 'Oh, shit!' exclamation was drowned out by the girls sharp scream as the raft on a rope went completely out of control and almost aggressively tipped her off into the fast flow with a bright white splash.

Suddenly she was gone from sight and there was just the rippling water and the starkly empty raft, automatically recovering itself and continuing on its now serene way across the remaining distance to the near bank.

Everyone except Parrish stood like statues as they watched the girl swallowed up by the waters. Hopping from one foot to the other he hastily pulled off his moccasins, tugged his buckskin shirt off over his head and sprinted along the bank, heading downstream. The warrior father and prospective husband of the vanished girl stood agape, but Klud and Tomps recovered quickly and set off after their Chieftain.

Parrish ran along the bank, his eyes not leaving the flowing water. He saw flashing glimpses of the girls white skin beneath the surface, like the darting of a large fish. Just as he reached the water's edge she breached the surface mid stream with a huge gasp for breath and panicked splashes before going under for a second time. Parrish now had his target and changed his trajectory with his next steps. Angling downstream just ahead of the girls last known position his bare feet hit the bank edge and he launched out over the water, executing a flat racing dive into the rivers flow.

Leading the following charge, Tomps pulled up at the water's edge, Klud but a few steps behind, and they both looked on in amazement as their Chieftain torpedoed beneath the surface for several body lengths before surfacing and breaking into a fast front crawl.

The girl was still submerged but Parrish closed within a few seconds, took a breath and duck dived into the deep. The chalk streams of southern England are, and always have been, crystal clear and Parrish could easily see the girl fifteen feet or so from his position, bowling untidily along the bottom. He reached her in a few powerful strokes, clamped his arms around her and dug his bare feet painfully into the stony bottom of the river bed. With a hard thrust he drove upwards towards the surface with all the power in his legs.

The river at that point was no more than ten feet deep and the pair erupted through the surface. Parrish took a deep gasping breath while the girl managed both a choking inhale and a terrified shriek. While Parrish tried to keep her head above water she began panicking, shrieking with each breath and thrashing against the deadly water.

They submerged briefly again, bringing a sudden surface silence while silent panic writhed beneath it. When they re emerged, Parrish had managed to manoeuvre himself behind her. He clamped his left arm hard across her breasts, pulled her tight to his chest and before she could shriek again he shouted.

"BE STILL!"

The power of his command stopped the girl in her tracks and, taking advantage of the brief lull, he skulled urgently back towards the bank. It was enough. Just as her fear of the water overtook her obedience to a Chieftain, Parrish's feet found purchase on the bottom and he stood up. The girl, still thinking she was out of her depth, twisted in his embrace to face him, wrapped her arms around his neck and clung to his chest as if she never intended to let go. Her eyes were so wide Parrish half expected them to fall right out of her head.

Waist deep in the flow, he slipped his left arm behind her back so it was supporting her shoulders and his right arm slid under her knees. He stood straight and lifted her clear of the water. Taking steady strides, the still stinging soles of his feet feeling every stone he stepped on, he emerged dripping from the water with the naked girl in his arms. Breathing deeply to regain his breath he passed his two friends and faced the rest of the watching people.

The sight stopped all the others in their tracks. Parrish walked back to the group and stopped before the young man who had bartered for the girl.

"Your wife." he grinned.

The youngster just gaped for a moment more then bowed deeply to his Chieftain.

"Are you not going to take her then?" Parrish asked, still grinning. "And after all the trouble I just went too to collect her?" He laughed. No one else did. He set the naked, glistening girl down on her feet and she turned to look up at him.

"No bother now." he said softly to her. "But let's get you covered up, eh?" She just nodded. The look of hero worship was plain on her face before she remembered herself and bowed. "And what is your name then?"

"A ... Anna." she muttered.

"Well, Anna. Welcome to Dane-bre!" He grinned again, took her hand and offered it to her new husband.

"Thank you, my Chieftain." The boy said and took the girl by the elbow.

"No problem." Parrish replied with a casual wave of the arm. "Couldn't just let her die after all that we had paid for her, eh?" He winked at the still stunned girl then turned to look once more across the river to the Woolbury men on the far side. But they had already turned their backs and were busy carrying their new possessions away up towards their distant hillfort. Parrish scowled then. They'd gotten what they wanted so now they clearly didn't give a toss about the girl.

"Are you all right?" asked Tomps as his two friends stepped up beside him.

"Oh yes." He replied somewhat absently. "Just a bit damp."

He looked back along the river to where the little tethered raft bumped and bobbled innocently against the edge of the bank.

That won't do, he thought. That won't do at all.

He laughed suddenly at a distant recollection and with a secret smile turned to his men.

"We are going to need a bigger boat."

3

Parrish knew he had absolutely no civil engineering nous so to his thinking, trying to build a proper bridge spanning thirty meters of open water, plus both approaches, was clearly beyond him. But, he had seen a movie once where there was a scene in which the characters crossed a wide river on what was more or less a giant version of the little raft system used here.

So he decided it would be a good idea to build, with the help of his men, a large raft, capable of carrying at least two people, guided by a heavy rope secured on either bank. And to have that rope pass through some sort of eye or pulleys fixed to the two upstream corners of the raft. Sort of like a ski lift laying on its side. For ease of operation he could raise the eye mounts to waist height by having some sort of balustrade or hand rail affair. Yes, then the operator could pull the whole floating contraption back and forth across the water, eliminating the need for additional guy ropes to keep retrieving the raft from the opposite bank. He smiled as he roughly sketched the whole thing out in his head. Like one of the old Southampton floating bridges, he suddenly realised. Good stuff!

He called Klud and Gant to his cabin the following day. The three sat at his table, while his wife hovered in the background ready with food or water should they need it. It was a planned part of Parrish's process that, by allowing his wife to be discreetly 'in' on the planning, she could later explain it all to the women of Danebury. He knew of their very effective female grapevine. The women would of course do their husbands biddings, but he wanted them to know the reasoning behind it all. His concern over the well being of *all* his villagers was always at the forefront of his mind. He fully understood the benefits of high morale in any organisation, from a simple Neolithic village to a full blown military conflict.

Once he had outlined his idea to the men, with Juli all the while casually listening in the background, Klud immediately asked if the people of Olann-bre would be involved. Parrish shook his head and after more thought considered this a good thing.

"Nah. We will build it. They will have no say in it and then if we choose to use it, bin it or even burn it, then that is our choice alone."

Klud didn't fully understand Parrish's military tactical thoughts but nodded.

Gant sat in considered silence for a while, then simply looked his Chieftain in the eye.

"We will need to make, then braid together a large amount of cord. Leather, wool, bast or some such, to make this long rope. And it will not only have to reach across the river and longer to its tie down points, but it will need to be very strong, so quite thick, I am thinking."

Parrish clapped him on the shoulder and laughed.

"You are a wise man as ever, my friend, and truly in the right of it. Can it be done? And if so, can you get this work started, without of course causing the people to be put out from their own tasks and chores? I will not have my people put to trouble, discomfort or be overworked because of some half baked idea by me."

Neither of the Neolithic men would ever consider an idea by their great Chieftain as 'half baked'. Nor did Gant see his leaders questions as an insult to his organisational skills. He just nodded, a very businesslike look on his face.

Parrish could not conceal another grin and clapped the man on the shoulder.

"Klud is my right hand, but when it comes to sorting things out, I think that you must surely be my left."

Then both men grinned widely and Parrish looked up, throwing a discrete wink at Juli, who had to turn away to hide a smile of her own. Her husband was such a clever man.

*

"The whole shebang has come together quite well." commented Parrish casually to a warrior standing nearby, as everyone took in the sight before them. The baffled warrior did not understand the phrasing or the incomprehensible English word in the middle of the sentence, so he thought it wise just to nod in agreement.

Parrish cared not. He was trying to check out the fruits of his idea with a professional eye, but in truth he just saw a superbly constructed raft linked to a long rope, almost as thick as a girl's wrist, looping out and away from a well driven in post on his side of the river. It rode gently up to the raft and passed through the first of two tree trunk sized newel posts, each with a bored out fist sized guide hole through it about a hands width down from the top. Support bars like splayed out legs kept the posts in position and a thick guide-cum-handrail linked the two posts together, the guide posts being securely fixed to the two upstream corners of the raft.

Once through the second newel guide post eye the rope sagged into the water, disrupting the surface flow, till it emerged on the far side to another post sunk into the far bank. Several people there from Olann-bre looked on in motionless silence.

The raft itself was constructed from two layers of sturdy straight logs. The surface of the top layer had been shaved off to provide a more or less flat standing platform or deck. The lower layer, at right angles to the first, was semi submerged. Everything was securely lashed together and Parrish was pleasantly surprised at how high in the water it sat and how sturdy and businesslike it looked. Almost confidence inspiring, he thought. Almost.

"It is a proper little ferry." he said not quite to himself and walked down to the water's edge to examine it more closely. "Good job everyone."

He smiled broadly at the crowd that had parted for him so he could step right up to the wooden ferry. He offered an appreciative nod to Gant as he passed him. The man said nothing but a hugely satisfying grin split his features and Klud, stood alongside him, patted him warmly on the shoulder. No words needed to be said, but everyone was pleased to have their work appreciated by the Chieftain. A lot of time, effort and materials had gone into the creation of his 'ferry'.

"Good work." He repeated. "Now, we need to see how she goes."

The massed reply to that was silence. A silence that began to grow uneasy as the moments dragged out. A phrase from Parrish's military past came to his mind. Never volunteer for anything! A knowing look briefly crossed his features and he waved his hands down to the gathering before him.

"Woah! Don't all rush at once." No one laughed. "Anyway, I baggsies first go!" Still nothing but blank faces. Parrish laughed at himself, stepped up to the raft and gingerly climbed on. Steadying himself with a hand on the rail he turned and looked again at the small crowd.

"Klud, Tomps. Bear a hand here. Give me a small shove off and we will see how she sails."

The Neolithic warriors stepped up, eyeing the contraption warily.

"You are sure this will work?" Klud questioned his Chieftain. The humour dropped like lead from Parrish's face. Suddenly he was deadly serious.

"Only one way to find out, eh? Now push."

The pair duly pushed and with surprisingly little effort the tethered raft broke free of the bank and slowly began to drift out into the current.

Parrish was acutely aware of all eyes on him as the raft moved steadily out and was almost immediately caught by the flow. It began moving diagonally away down stream, slowly gathering momentum. Then came the moment all the slack was taken up and the guide rope jerked taut. It jarred the raft and Parrish had to hold on to the handrail with both hands to keep his balance. Once it had steadied itself, he switched his grip to the rope at the point between the two guide posts and began to haul on it, intent on pulling the raft along the rope to make its way across the divide. It was not as easy as he had envisaged and with some effort he began to traverse the craft out towards mid stream.

But he had not made it more than eight or ten meters out from the bank when he felt an unexpected give in the ropes tension. Looking down he saw the babbling white water buffeting against the upstream waterline of the raft and only then realised the power and pressure the river was exerting against the tethered raft and through it to the now very taught guide line. Parrish was just on the point of doubting the strength and potential breaking strain of the rope when a much harsher jerk shook the little ferry and it seemed to instantly move away more with the flow. The rope was snatched from his grasp and Parrish almost lost his footing on the suddenly unstable, moving deck beneath him. He instinctively dropped to his knees to prevent himself from being tipped into the water and spun his head to look as a rough, whirring, rasping sound started beside him. The guide rope was running away uncontrolled through the post eyes. In that same instant Parrish saw further upstream that the securing post on the Olann-bre side of the river, which should have been bedded deep in the ground, had pulled out!

The man and his now out of control raft were gathering momentum as they moved away downstream with the flow, increasing in speed to match it, yet it looked as if the unseated post, still attached to the rope end like a huge wooden toggle, seemed to be charging at an even faster speed towards the raft, skipping and splashing white across the rivers surface, leaving foam in its wake. The raft, going now at a good walking pace was being shaken by the singing rope that thrummed loudly through the eye posts and Parrish braced himself as his craft finally ran out of rope, and the wildly thrashing post at its end leapt up out of the water and fetched violently up against the eye post in front of him.

Trying to steady himself against the impact, Parrish tried to lower his centre of gravity as low as he could so as to not be thrown into the water. But he could not get away from his close proximity to the posts. He hoped the loose post would just jam up against the eye post, tethering the raft to the Danebury side bank, pull the raft to a stop and then the whole contraption would swing back to the riverbank. He screwed his eyes shut as the two post clashed together.

With an ear splitting crack the timbers smashed together but, with a savage final jerk the rope pulled straight on through the post hole as the attached toggle post shattered. The rope end snaked through both eyes, the thrashing end narrowly missing Parrish's face, and dropped with a splash into the water, releasing the raft to the mercy of the river. But this went unnoticed. Parrish's kneeling position had unfortunately brought his head level with the height of the handrail and the thrashing post as it shattered against the more sturdy eye post. Parrish was blasted in the face with exploding pieces of timber of all different sizes. One large, violently spinning fragment caught him squarely on the left temple and across the side of his head above his left ear as he tried to turn his head away.

Those on the bank, transfixed by the spectacle, gasped in shock as they witnessed their Chieftain briefly in the centre of this maelstrom of timber splinters. To the background noise of wooden shards splashing into the water around the raft, they watched helplessly as their Chieftain, blood pouring from a sudden wound to the side of his head, tipped slowly back and flopped limply to the floor of the raft, unconscious.

First to react to the stunning scene playing out before them all was Tomps and Klud. As the raft carrying the limp, motionless Parrish headed off downriver in the middle of the flow, the two men broke into a run to catch up with it. Others started to follow but quickly realised that they could do nothing and pulled up from the chase, watching the two warriors continue in pursuit of their fallen, floating friend. They were both soon gone from sight, for although the pair quickly caught up then continued along the riverbank parallel with Parrish and his raft, the flow of the river was relentlessly steady. The raft stubbornly insisted on staying out in mid stream and kept to its pace of what amounted to a fast walk. Klud and Tomps were having to cope with bushes, stands of trees, uneven ground and other obstacles as they travelled along the riverbank, all the while keeping an eye on their unmoving friend. As they moved southwards away from the occupied land around the locale of the hillforts, the untamed, wild natural growths of nature proved to be an ever more difficult obstacle course, hindering and tripping them as they went. Not more than a couple of kilometres of this sequence of fast walk, dodge, stumble, fall, pick yourself up, run to catch up and do it all again was telling on the two men. Klud was first to really start flagging and when a tree root caught him out he fell headlong into a thicket. By the time he had extracted himself and regained his feet, Tomps was out of sight amongst the trees and the floating raft and its unconscious cargo was away in the middle distance. It tore at Klud's heart to give up but he knew he could no longer sustain the relentless pace and it was a private agony for him to abandon the chase, and his friend. He hoped that young Tomps might fare better and rising dejectedly to his feet turned his back on the continuing chase and trudged back towards Dane-bre.

Tomps was in fact just as fatigued and frustrated as Klud. His youth kept him with Parrish for a little longer but even he could not keep a constant, never ending pace across unknown and heavily wooded ground indefinitely, while hoping against hope that the raft would for some reason run aground on one bank or the other. The thing just kept going in mid stream and just did not stop! What happened to Klud finally happen to Tomps and he missed his step in an unseen dip in the scrub covered ground and went sprawling. Chest heaving for breath, sweating and flat on his front, he looked up in dismay to see his good friend, mentor and Chieftain moving further and further away from him. Dead or alive, he knew not.

Where or when he would stop, he knew not. And what happened then, only Dannu knew.

4

When Tomps had returned alone, shaking his head and looking down at the ground, everyone knew. Someone who had managed to coil up the thick rope let it drop from their limp hands and it flopped in a empty, deadening way to the ground beside the river. There was a sort of finality to it and the crowd returned in silence to Danebury.

By the next morning, the sombre mood had penetrated into every last corner of the hillfort. No one had come right out and said it, but the villagers had all accepted that they had lost their great, beloved Chieftain and it felt like the whole village, of its own accord, begun to mourn his passing.

Sad faces with down cast eyes told the tale. Since Parrish had been taken by the great river, the people were stunned, shaking their heads in dismay and going about their daily business and chores as if sleepwalking.

The holy man was acutely aware of the glances cast in his direction as he passed by. The people did not blame him for what had happened, they just could not understand why Dannu had to take back her man in such a way. For no great reason. Not for any gain or glory. Why for him was there no heroic death in battle or some great quest for the honour of the Earth Goddess? He had just drifted away. Carried off back to the mysterious southlands from whence he had come all those seasons before. The little shaman felt the same unhappy confusion, but he could not and would not speak up against his goddess. He was just as sad, shocked and uncomprehending as everyone else.

Well, almost everyone else.

The next morning Klud made his way up to the Chieftains cabin on the highest point inside the hillfort. As ever, he followed protocol and called out the occupants there, even if there was no longer a man of the house.

Juli duly appeared, young Chris in her arms. Her eyes were still red from crying. She bowed to the warrior and waited for the inevitable. But for a few long moments he just stood before her. She was broken hearted but had expected to see Klud the saddest of all. This man had been with Parrish since the very first days when the tall man had come to Danebury. He was his greatest friend. They had been through bloody battles and many great adventures together. Theirs was a special bond. He must be feeling the hurt most keenly, and it was there in his rugged, battered features, but there was a defiance too. The silence began to drag on and Juli, unable to bear what that silence meant, broke the hush, and the proper honour given in deference towards a warrior in that it was he who should speak first. But she had lost her husband and the love of her life. She cared not for any consequences now.

"Great warrior. I know why you have come here. With Parrish gone," she almost choked then, "with Parrish gone, it is likely that you will be next Chieftain. So I will empty the cabin of my things so you can take your rightful place here before nightfall."

Klud allowed her to finish her words, and she saw the anger in him. She had spoken unbidden to a warrior and she now expected punishment. But to her surprise it did not happen. He just braced up and said evenly.

"You shall do nothing." The puzzled look on her face clearly begged for an explanation. He continued. "Everyone else can think what they like. It is true that Parrish, my friend, is missing. But not gone. If he was dead, I would know. I would know! Do not be so quick to give up on him."

There was a moment then, breaking the strictest rule, as Juli looked deep into his eyes for confirmation, she asked. "You are sure?"

There was another silent moment as the pair were locked together in the total commitment and love they had for the same man. Klud didn't even feel the need to answer the question. He simply waved at the building she had just emerged from.

"You will not leave his house and I will not take his place. I never could. Look after it for him until he returns, because I believe he is not dead." And with that he spun on his heel and walked away back down the slope towards the village.

Juli bowed to his receding back and turned to face the cabin. Klud was a brave and honest warrior who spoke true. As she went back inside a small grin was trying very hard to lighten her sad and tear streaked face.

Elsewhere, there were others who were aware of the supposed demise of the Chieftain of Dane-bre. However, they were not in the least bit distraught at his passing. Word had gone straight back to Olann-bre just as quickly, relaying to their Chieftain not just that Parrish had been taken by the great river, but also the demoralizing, abject dejection that had settled like a smothering blanket over the people of Dane-bre.

Chieftain Shimon, still gloating over the great haul of tools he had wheedled out of their so called 'great' Chieftain, rubbed his hands with glee as he saw a possible opportunity for even more gains at the tall mans expense. Even perhaps a fully stocked, well provisioned, functional and successfully run village. One he could see in the distance from his own not so prosperous village.

*

And all the while, a deeply unconscious, badly concussed Parrish drifted away southwards, completely unaware of the shock of his people, their plunging morale and that someone was already planning to usurp his power, influence and even manipulate the dedication his people had for their Chieftain, to his own ends.

The quiet, constant waters of the river Test carried him on. Whether by dumb luck, fortunate fate or the will of Dannu, he was kept safe away from further injury or potential death. The raft stayed mid stream and was now really covering some distance. Even with the constant danger of being tipped off and drowned by hitting an underwater object, either bank or wedging against or even under some outstretched tree limb or a fallen trunk stretching across the flow, he moved steadily on. A good walking pace is around four miles per hour across flat ground. Just in the time from the moment of his accident till the high of the sun, Parrish had unknowingly covered almost ten miles.

The wooded banks of foliage that lined the river were as the tube of a large pipe, funnelling him along and keeping his trajectory straight. The odd wild animal, watering at the bank, saw without knowing the silent piece of flotsam with its unconscious cargo on board, and watched it pass almost serenely by on its way southwards.

All along the way, the virgin land he passed, untouched by the hand of man, showed no inkling that it would, in some fifty five centuries time, be completely transformed. The passing of the ages would invoke many changes. In the far distant future the river Test, now an only slightly meandering solid body of water, would in various places along its length be steered, dammed and redirected into many side streams and tributaries. All this was to create water ponds, fisheries and shallow beds for harvesting edible water plants. Its life supporting properties would enrich either side of the shallow, sloping valley it bisected. In time it would be the reason for the construction of a water mill at the picturesque village of Broughton, a scant few miles south of Stockbridge, itself sitting in the shadow of Danebury hill. Another mill would spring up at the market town of Romsey, bringing it prosperity and expansion.

Its flow would draw the attention of people through the ages, being used in many guises to create wealth and resulting in great properties like Broadlands, a stately home sitting in majesty along the bank of the Test just south of Romsey. And at the end of its journey south, the river would conjoin with its Hampshire basin fellow, the river Itchen.

In its own time there would be a Roman encampment on this juncture. Turning into a settlement, Clausentum would be a stepping stone to the rise of the medieval walled city of Southampton, its culmination into a great port and a staging post to the world. Eventually trading in goods from all four corners of the globe, a vibrant bustling modern metropolis and, in the latter half of the twentieth century, birth place of one Shaun Parrish.

But now, where the two rivers meet, they become the long tongue of tidal water that reaches out to the Solent. And there at its mouth, a barrier to the open sea beyond, lay Vectis. This was the Roman name for a diamond shaped isle, 26 miles from west to east and 16 miles north to south. Isolated from the mainland by the double tides, swirling currents and sandbars of the Solent, the island has stood guard over Southampton water for 10,000 years, since its separation from the mainland at the end of the last ice age. The Isle of Wight.

An island of mystery, superstition and the unknown. Who knew what lay beyond that distant shoreline and on the dark, rising silhouette of land across the waves? As Parrish drifted steadily on, the Test was carrying him inexorably towards the two rivers junction. From then on, he would be at the mercy of the tides, currents and the salty sea.

*

Chieftain Shimon had decided to bide his time before making his move on Dane-bre. He knew that going directly there and demanding to take charge being the only Chieftain would result in battle. With Parrish only one day gone and with no body to prove his demise, it would be seen as showing great disrespect and a huge insult to try and step immediately into his shoes.

But give them a few days, he reasoned.

Allow them to miss their leader, realize that after a few empty nights he would not be returning, then act whilst they were still undecided whether or not to embark on the selection of a new leader. That would be when the people there finally began to accept the truth and begin to mourn. And that also when their spirits would be at their lowest. Then would be the time to march boldly up, backed of course by all his warriors, demand entry as a Chieftain and take charge of this 'floundering' village with no one to guide it. Before the people of Dane-bre knew it, he would be in power, declare himself Chieftain of *two* villages, merge them into one great village and find himself in command of the biggest, most powerful village in all the south lands. With the combined strength of the warriors from two villages, he would be able to quash any other, and rise to be the greatest leader of all. Chieftain Shimon would have rubbed his hands together in glee, if that particular gesture had been known to him. His joy at Parrish's demise was undisguised, and quite repellent.

In Danebury there was indeed confusion and much distress over what had happened earlier that morning. People did not know what to think. They had never needed to think this way before. Before today, Chieftains simply lived and ruled, died and then were within a few days replaced by a newly selected Chieftain.

But now there was uncertainty. Even the holy man was unsure what to do, say or think. Only Klud, whose faith in his tall friend was unshakeable, believed his Chieftain to be still alive, somehow, somewhere. It would not be right though for him to be seen to disagree with or criticize the village shaman, so as confusion reigned in Dane-bre and plotting was afoot in Olann-bre, everyone in both camps was holding their breath, biding their time and waiting and watching to see how the next few days would unfold under Dannu's all seeing eyes.

5

Parrish drifted past the point where the rivers Test and Itchen converged and, unknown to him in his unconscious state, the water had turned salty. As luck, good fortune or the will of Dannu would have it, the second tide was on the wane and the buoyant little raft with its precious cargo moved steadily with the outflow, carried past the wooded shorelines that flanked him perhaps a kilometre away on either side. Calm waters and an onshore breeze were helping the raft along, all the time moving him further and further away from his beloved Danebury.

The calm was to be short lived. As he drew level with the spits of land at either side of the end of Southampton water, the shallows beyond, that were ideal for the site of a Short Sunderland flying boat squadron during the second World War, were interrupting the tidal flow. The water began to get choppy.

The raft began to bob erratically about and it was this jagged, uneven movement, rocking Parrish to and fro, that slowly brought him back to his senses. The rocking motion, causing his head to loll randomly from side to side, jarred his battered mind enough to finally jerk him into painful wakefulness. As his blurred vision fell into focus and his sense of balance told him he was on some sort of unstable platform, he tried to sit up. The uneven rocking increased alarmingly and he instantly splayed his arms out, palms down on the deck behind him to form a steadying triangular base. Then he saw the open water before him and the distant land mass on the near horizon.

"Wha ...?" was as far as he got before the pain pounded into his left temple. "Christ ..!"

He carefully and tenderly put his palm to the source of the pain and felt the break in the skin. There was a crust there and also clinging down the side of his face. Checking his palm he saw flecks of blood and through the pounding pain he began to recall what had happened there.

Taking a deep, calming breath he looked slowly about, careful not to move too much and risk dislodging himself from his perilous perch, and began to assess his situation.

Tree lined shores either side of him were receding over his shoulders, ahead was that open expanse of water and beyond it lay the rising green smudge of land.

Totally confused, he searched to no avail for a recognisable landmark. To try and clear his head he scooped up a palm full of water from beside the raft and splashed it onto his face. Salt!

Hold on, hold on, he thought. Let's work this out.

Sitting bolt upright made the raft suddenly rock rather precariously from side to side again and he froze, gave the unstable craft a few moments to settle down a bit, before slowly leaning back until he once again lay flat on his back, looking up into the cloud scudded sky. Now he was doing his best to ignore the pounding in the side of his head and, satisfied that at least for the moment he wasn't about to tip off into the briny, tried to apply reason to his situation.

He knew he had been on the east river and recalled the events leading up to the accident so, he reasoned, it seems he had not suffered any mental injury from that blow to the head. But there was a big blank gap in his memory between losing control of the river raft and waking up on the high seas. That's it! The sea! It would be his natural assumption that the loose raft would drift over to one or other of the river banks. Parrish allowed himself the smallest of grins then as he recalled one of his dad's favourite sayings. 'If you assume something, it could make an ass out of you and me'. He would waggle his finger at a young Shaun Parrish and say, 'be sure of your facts, son'.

So, *not* assuming that the raft would have floated to the river bank, logically it would have just continued on down the river Test. That meant the raft, with him aboard, had followed its route down through the last section of the Test valley to where his home town would one day be, past that point and out into ... Southampton water. Hellfire! As he joined up all the dots he started to jerk upright again but remembered just in time, as the raft gave him a warning bobble. Instead, propping himself carefully up onto one elbow he took time to survey about with more intent. Still nothing looked familiar but, reasoning that what he had deduced really had happened, the two points of land left and right of him, open water before him and a large land mass a couple of kilometres ahead could only mean one thing. His first thought was that it couldn't be, but it must! Parrish scanned the view for a third time, stunned, looked again at the land mass ahead of him and whispered to himself.

"Is ... is that the Isle of Wight?"

He knew then he was slowly but surely heading uncontrollably out into the Solent. And it was then also that he genuinely started to fear for his life. He was being carried by the tide out into open water. At the mercy of unpredictable currents on an unstable craft that might go anywhere, do anything and might even tip him off into the water. He knew swimming ashore from this far out was impossible. There was suddenly a distinct possibility that if he was not very careful, he might not live to see the morrow.

But his Army training was kicking in. Do what you can do and don't dwell on things beyond your control. Grasp the things that you *can* control and be as ready as possible for what might be ahead.

The one thing Parrish certainly could do was wait. It had once been said that he could out wait a stone. So he waited. Waited and watched, paying acute attention to the subtle and not so subtle changes. The slow shifting of the land masses from his perspective and the constantly moving waters beneath him, giving him information to help him gauge his speed and direction.

Dredging up from the bottom of his mind what basic knowledge he had of the geography of Southampton water, the Solent and the Isle of Wight, he formed a mental picture of the layout. The waters were as an inverted 'Y' shape with the island sitting in the bottom cleft while he was drifting down the stalk of the Y. He knew that the outgoing tide would carry him into the Solent then onward to either his left, east, or right to the west past the north shore of the island. If he went to the west the flow between the island and the mainland would speed up as it funnelled in between the narrow gap where a spit from the mainland reached out to within a single kilometre of the island. The tidal race was famously fierce and fast here, before it shot past the Needles and out into the English Channel. Parrish knew it didn't take a genius to figure out that if his little raft was unstable in slightly choppy waters, it had no chance in a fast tidal race.

However, if the little craft was carried the opposite way, east, the flow would be much more slow and stable, but the gap there between the two land masses was much wider. Possibly as much as seven or eight kilometres. As he continued to wait, he weighed up his options. West past the Needles meant that the shore, either one, would be close enough to swim to. Whichever way he went would be less than the total kilometre span of water. It was doable but his timing would have to be right. His raft would not survive the tidal race but neither would he if he got carried away in it too.

Going east out past the mouth of what would one day be the entrance to Portsmouth harbour, his actual speed across the ground, or seabed in this case, would be considerably slower but it then meant somehow paddling his dangerously unstable little craft to the shore. It would be a big ask to do this with just his bare hands, but trying to swim many kilometres in open water to safety was a non starter.

The day was beginning to draw on by now. It was still several more hours till dusk by his reckoning but Parrish knew he'd have to make a decision and take action before the light failed completely. To carry on aimlessly into the night was not an option.

The waiting began to grow in intensity. Subtle relocations of the main landmark he could make out on the Island, namely the mouth of the river Medina, proved that he and his little vessel were almost lethargically swirling about. Almost as if the tide, or Dannu, couldn't make up their minds which way to turn. But Parrish was patient and, sure enough, the ebb and flow gradually stabilised and he grew more aware, with growing disquiet, the he had begun edging towards the west.

"Well," he said sourly to himself. "Looks like I'll be going for a swim then."

One thing in his favour was that the dithering current and tide had pulled him a little closer to the Island before beginning to carry him off towards the setting sun. He could see the Island shoreline more clearly now. Small waves breaking in gently undulating white lines along the virgin shore and an unbroken tree line beyond.

About a click away, Parrish reckoned. Right, no time like the present. He gave a wry smile at his choice of phrase.

Carefully, so as not to disturb the little craft, he pulled his buckskin shirt off over his head and laid it out flat before him. Next he removed his moccasins, placed them toe to toe across the shoulders of the shirt and rolled them up in it. Then he looped the roll about his waist, the shoe filled bulk snug against his kidneys, and knotted the sleeves in front just under his navel.

Taking a deep breath he moved to the edge of the raft and, keeping a firm grip on some of the lashings, slid sideways and eased himself into the water. It wasn't as cold as he expected but he still gasped, and hung alongside the craft for several moments waiting for his breathing to settle.

It was at that moment he realised the troublesome little craft was in truth his life raft. As he bobbed in the water, clinging to it, he suddenly felt a real reluctance to let the thing go. Casting an eye towards the Island shore he couldn't tell if he was getting any closer to it or starting to move further away.

There was a real moment of affinity with the bobbing piece of timber construction and in a farewell gesture he gave it a last pat, took a deep breath and pushed away.

Not looking back he headed towards the shore, opting for a strength conserving breast stroke and skulled towards the landmass, which now looked alarmingly far away now that he was right down at sea level.

Parrish was certainly not one to panic. Steady, steady, he told himself and kept to his easy, regular pace, resisting the strong urge to try and reach dry land as fast as he could. Conserve your strength matey, marathon not sprint.

It did seem as if he was making very little progress and he could see that he was gradually moving along the line of the shore. He knew he was drifting to his right, while it appeared the shoreline before him was moving slowly away to his left, courtesy of him being carried along by the ever constant tide. It did nothing to ease his concern about not reaching his goal. But he concentrated on his rhythm and stroke. Do what you can do and try not to worry about things beyond your control.

Just as his steely reserve began to waver he suddenly noticed that the tree line did seem a little more distinct. He could now make out a few individual trees and then he thought he could vaguely hear the lapping of waves on the shore.

His morale picked up and he was again tempted to put in a sprint finish. Steady, he admonished himself for his weakness, steady.

Then something struck his foot.

"What ..?"

He skulled quickly around but saw nothing behind him and as he lost forward motion in the water and became more upright, his feet hit the bottom. He stood up, finding himself barely chest deep in water. Still thirty or so meters from the shore, he realised that the sea bed here must be gently shelving over some shallows.

"Hah!" he cried in satisfaction and with a huge sense of relief, waded gratefully ashore.

His elation was short lived. No sooner had he reached dry land and moved up past the high water mark to the start of the dense, undisturbed foliage, then all the events of the day caught up with him. The pounding in the side of his head returned with some vigour. He was swept by a great wave of fatigue and was suddenly aware that he had eaten nothing since breakfast time.

The pounding he knew would subside. It was no real hardship either to go twenty four hours without food. Soon though he would have to find water. But he could not deny the pressing weight of his tiredness.

Despite it still being a while till dusk, he pushed a short way into the undergrowth and found a space beneath the bracken big enough for him to lay down. Remembering at the last moment to hang his shirt out to dry over a low limb, he set his moccasins carefully to one side then lay back on the cool earth. Despite his sodden trousers, cold feet and his wet, bare chest, he was asleep in moments.

6

Parrish came too with the dawn. It wasn't the brightening light or the dawn chorus that brought him to wakefulness. It was the shivering.

He sat slowly up, clamping his arms about his torso and took a few moments to gather his thoughts. He recalled the events of the previous day and put his hand cautiously to the side of his head. The ache was much easier now, and he could feel the bloody crust beneath his palm, still adhering to his temple and cheek.

Doing his best to ignore the early morning chill he walked back out to the shore. The tide was half out, or in, he couldn't be sure but he walked barefoot out across the rock strewn gravelly mud to the water's edge and thoroughly washed his face. Despite the salt water sting, it was surprisingly refreshing and he immediately felt better. Still cold, but better.

Right. Going back to the high water mark he scanned the fore shore either side of him. Retrieving his still damp moccasins and shirt he dressed then did a short patrol up and down 'his' section of the beach. Passing by a number of long lengths of dried timber trunks and limbs much too big to be firewood, in a relatively short time he had collected a big armful of dried pieced of flotsam from above the high water mark, plus a couple of fist sized gnarly lumps of light brown flint. He knew he had zero skills as a shaper of stone and he also knew from his friend the village knapper that brown flint wasn't up to much. Dark, glossy black flint was the good stuff. Still, beggars can't be choosers and besides, he didn't need it to look pretty, just be sharp enough.

Displaying his complete lack of skill, he simply smashed the two hunks of flint together till one shattered. Combing through the splintered pieces he found one with a keen edge. First he whittled a point on a straight-ish two foot length stick and then cut a vee notch into the edge of a fairly flat piece of dry driftwood.

He was quite pleased with himself at successfully organising the pieces need to make a fire, that was until it took him a while to find something to use as tinder. Eventually he located a standing dead tree not too far away that he had earlier passed unnoticed while he was beachcombing. He pulled off some pieces of dry bark and with his ugly piece of flint, scraped at the insides until he had a ball of tightly gathered wood shavings. Readying the workings of the main fire into a small wigwam of sticks next to his main wood supply, it was now ready for his tinder.

Now came the effort. His Army survival training taught him that when going at anything to do with survival, 100% effort was required at all times.

Putting the sharpened end of his fire stick into the cleft of the vee he had already cut, he began to twirl the stick between his palms, working downwards each time to apply some pressure into the point where the two pieces of timber met. Friction would create heat, produce hot sawdust and hopefully, hopefully enough heat to make the sawdust ignite into a glowing ember.

This is so caveman, he thought, and allowed himself a grin, or was it a grimace, as he continued to work the stick. Watching for small wisps of friction smoke and its impending ember, he worked on. Beads of sweat began to appear on his forehead. Just as he was beginning to think it might be his hands that would burst into flames before his fire stick, smoke did indeed begin to wisp up from the cleft.

Parrish gently scooped the little glowing ember that suddenly appeared there and tipped it into his tinder ball, blowing softly in long bursts on it. Glow, glow, glow, smoulder, smoulder ... Yes! A flame.

The feeling of success cheered him immensely and offset the stinging of his sore palms as he turned and gently placed his little burning ball under his wigwam of sticks. A little more blowing and in moments he had a small but proper fire going. Parrish grinned and nodded to himself. If you have never experienced creating fire from scratch, you can't understand the fantastic morale boosting effect it has on a man.

He stoked his fire with more fuel from his wood pile until it was nicely ablaze. It was a clean burn too. The driftwood he had collected was so old and dry that it gave off virtually no smoke. His Army training was pleased about that. You can't be too careful in an unknown area. He chuckled again. Hark at yourself, as if anyone else would be marooned on the island. He took a few moments to warm himself before turning his attention back to the beach and sea shore.

Pulling his moccasins off again he wandered back out onto the wet ground between the high water mark and the lapping sea. Turning over rocks and looking into the small puddles of seawater he started finding what he was after.

Fortune was on his side, he felt, when he quickly found a couple of large whelks in one of the pools, but as he got his eye in he became aware that there was life all over the place. The immediate area around him was strewn with empty half shells from cockles. Wriggling his toes into the softer patches of gravelly mud he could feel hard nodules just beneath the surface. Digging down just an inch or so with his hands won him almost a dozen cockles in less than a minute. Then he spied clinging around the base of a suitcase sized rock a long string of mussels. He pulled them off till his hands were full of the shiny, purple-black molluscs, and carried his trophies back to the fire.

Raking the fire flat with his fire stick he set all the shellfish in it, hinge side down in the embers for the cockles and mussels, open side up for the two whelks. As they heated up he got a small green twig from the nearest tree and pointed the end. His winkle picker, which reminded him to put his shoes back on.

Once more he warmed himself by the fire while he waited for the shellfish to open, indicating that they were cooked. He had a sudden thought.

"Nah." He chuckled softly. "I don't think I need to worry about pollution here! And hey, is it five years or five and a half thousand years since I last ate sea food?" Eyeing the shells he added. "No garlic butter, but I s'pose beggars can't be choosers." And a full blown smile spread across his face as the first of the shells slowly began to gape.

Watching the steam rising with the heat as his shellfish breakfast became ready, he knew that water was his next priority. Strictly speaking, he knew that the search for drinkable water should have been his first and most crucial requirement, but he had not eaten for more than a day and now, because everything he'd needed was immediately available around him, he had readied himself a reviving meal for less than an hour's effort.

Hooking the hot mollusc morsels out of the embers he tucked in and found them quite acceptable. Tasty, fresh and energy giving. He did miss the tasty little condiments that would have enhanced them even more but it still pleased him just how good they did taste. Squaddies always bemoaned the fact that all foods consumed on survival exercises were universally disgusting and barely qualified as food at all! Still conscious of his immediate needs, he sucked every drop of moisture from each mouthful before chewing and swallowing.

Breakfast done, he scooped out a big hollow in the shingle beside the now dying fire and with a paddle of un burnt firewood pushed the whole lot, cooling embers, empty shells and any remnants of un burnt wood, into it. Scooping the dug out stones back over the top of it all, in mere moments any evidence of his being there was gone bar a slight mound of stones just above the high water mark.

For a moment he stood tall, surveyed his part of the beach again and patted his stomach. Not well fed, but definitely fed, and that's a good start.

Water next then.

He knew he could just go off into the woods and wander around for hours hoping he might find a small stream or some muddy puddle. Or he could have boiled up some sea water and let the steam condense into fresh water. After all, he'd already managed to get a fire going, but then it really helps things along if you have something to boil the sea water in!

His training and reasoning used the KISS method, taught by the military all over the world and easily understood in any language. 'Keep It Simple, Stupid.'

Parrish eyed the headland before him as he faced east and the rising sun. It was the western side of the mouth of the Medina River. He knew that one day a long time from now the famous yachting town of Cowes would be built there. But he also knew that, as its name implied, the Medina was a river. Obviously the river water flowed out from somewhere in the interior of the island till it reached the sea. Because the island was only about twenty four kilometres deep from north to south, if he followed the sea shore round the headland and continued along the river bank heading inland, it stood to reason that within a handful of kilometres travel the river would revert back from sea water to fresh. So, he surmised, abundant fresh drinking water, no matter how close to the source he had to go to find it, was no more than a maximum of fifteen kilometres away. And possibly a good deal less.

That'll do for me, he thought. Just a good stretch of the legs then.

And, once he had a ready supply of water and plentiful sea food to sustain him for a while, he could build a semi permanent shelter and apply himself fully to figuring a way to get back to Dane-bre while in reasonable comfort and safety. Get back to Juli, to his friends and to his people.

A firm determination settled on him. He nodded to himself, clapped his hands together and gauged the distance to the headland before him.

"Right then, Robinson Crusoe. Game on!"

Walking along the shoreline, he stayed close up to the trees just in case he needed to dive for cover, although why he would need to he couldn't say. It was just military thinking and training, so he found himself doing it without at first even realising it.

He applied himself to his task and started to take a closer interest in his surroundings. The shore was the shore and the tide was in fact coming in. A part of his mind noted the rising water while he concentrated more on the woodland close alongside to his right. A mixture of well established trees, which was good, and unblemished and dense ground covering scrub and bracken beneath the spreading branches.

He didn't want to put too much stay into his real first impression but along the kilometre or so to the point of the headland where he turned to head inland along the Medina estuary bank, it became noticeable that the ground level greenness *was* blemish free. Totally devoid of any animal tracks, runs through the low scrub, or burrows. It puzzled him. He wasn't expecting wildebeest sweeping across the plains or herds of buffalo, but no tracks of any kind? Signs of life were kind of glaring in their absence. Even around Danebury, where his people stomped all over the place, there was nearly always some sort of evidence of creatures that had passed by unseen. Parrish was no tracker but even he recalled seeing droppings and scrapes, or tracks and runs that had been used enough times to become permanent little pathways through the undergrowth. It began to remind him of his recent walk alongside the East river. Like there, the greenery here was virgin, at least for as far as he could see now.

Perhaps it's just this little bit of shoreline, he thought, shrugged and pushed on, pacing himself as he closed in on his first waypoint.

Cresting the curve of the coastline, the great sweep of the Solent suddenly opened up before him. Such was this vast open expanse of Mother Nature, the sweeping, open magnificent seascape, that it took his breath away. He always knew he had a great view from his cabin out across the valley beyond Danebury hillfort of the great forest under a big sky, but this! The glittering sea, the wooded shorelines to his left and right, the gaping mouth of Southampton water opposite him and the wide open sky unmarked by anything but clouds, stopped him in his tracks. For a second there he could have sworn he could almost see the curvature of the earth. Time stood still and for a moment, or many moments, he could not tell, he stood motionless, transfixed by the raw, untouched magnificence of it all.

"God bless, Dannu!" he whispered, then laughed at his mixed metaphor and, spell broken, returned to the task at hand. Trying hard to ignore the growing and persistent reminder from his body that he really could do with a drink, he turned south and set off along the western shore of the Medina.

After the wide vista of the Solent it was very quickly obvious that the river began to narrow quite soon after and within a kilometre the gap between the two shores was no more than a hundred and fifty metres. Looking further ahead to see just how quickly the river would narrow enough to become a stream, and hopefully drinkable, he was again stopped in his tracks.

In the mid distance, rising lazily into the air from somewhere further down along the opposite bank, was a thin column of smoke!

7

Parrish's first instinct was to dash up shouting 'Hello! Can you help me?' But he'd been there, done that and knew exactly how that would end. Instead, he sidled quietly into the woods to his right and, once he was sure he was completely concealed, began to push his way through the undergrowth making sure to keep an eye on the distant smoke plume through the gaps in the branches.

He'd not gone too far when he put one foot down on a particularly soft piece of grass covered earth. It was only when he lifted his foot to take the next step and it squished, that he stopped, turned back and inspected the bit of ground with the fresh, deep footprint. Deep and wet!

Closer inspection revealed a tiny trickle of water, coming from somewhere up on the higher ground, passing through his new indentation and then on down the slope through the dense greenery towards the shore.

Parrish pushed his finger into the moist soil and it did indeed come up wet. He tentatively licked it. Muddy and a bit gritty, but not salty!

Straightening, he turned his back to the river and looked up the slope. The gently rising greenery covered, wooded ground looked the same all around but after a moment to get his eye in he could see a slightly brighter green line of plants leading up from where he stood. Forgetting the mysterious smoke up river for a moment he started to follow the green line of this tiny trickle up, wading through the ferns and bracken. Perhaps two thirds the way up to the top of the rise he came to a bigger than usual bright green clump of ferns, clustered together and clearly growing more successfully than the plants around them. Carefully parting the fronds he checked down at their base and there, nestled in a small, gravel bottomed hollow no bigger than a large soup plate, was a small, gently bubbling and crystal clear spring. The natural bowl was no more than a couple of inches deep and less than two feet across but it was enough to put a huge grin on Parrish's face. Right now he couldn't recall seeing a more beautiful sight.

Parrish lay down flat amongst the greenery and, careful not to hit the bottom and so disturb any silt or sediment there leaned in and gently touched, almost it seemed kissed the surface with his lips, and took a tentative slurp.

Cool, fresh and delicious!

Taking his time and with lots of small drinks, Parrish slaked his thirst. Sitting back between slurps to let the tiny bowl of life giving water refill before drinking again he looked about him at the thick ground cover and wondered how many other tiny watering holes he might have passed before finding this little treasure.

No matter, he thought, this one is perfect, and chuckled.

Right then. He marked his precious watering point by making a tripod of long sticks tied together at the top with a handful of grasses. He set the tripod up over the tiny spring. The three pronged tip stood out above the surrounding ground cover but unless you were actually looking for it, it was fairly difficult to spot.

Now fed *and* watered, Parrish returned his attention towards the river below him, and the mysterious smoke column. He moved on through the greenery, just inside the tree line and drew closer to the source of the smoke plume across the river.

Just Like before, he recalled, as he closed the column split into several smaller columns as the view across the river slowly revealed itself to him.

It was an encampment.

Parrish called it that because it wasn't a village as he would recognise it. By the time he drew level opposite it, the flow between the two banks was less than about 60 metres wide.

There was no defensive ditch to speak of. The north and south edges, or up and down stream of the encampment, were about 300 metres apart and marked by a low palisade wall of posts. Like the ones surrounding Danebury, but these walls were no more than the height of a man and each stood just outside the path of a small stream, appearing from out of the woods behind to flow across the narrow beach and away into the river, again one at each end.

There then was the camp's very handy water supply.

Joining up the two walls behind the streams was a long stand of the same low posts no more than about 30 metres back from the shore line. Basically, the camp was a wide, oblong of enclosed land approximately 30 metres deep by roughly 300 metres in length with the long low wall at its back and the open shore at its front.

Different, thought Parrish as he viewed the odd layout, but his main interest was the contents of the camp.

There were perhaps two dozen dwellings, the huts no different to all the other huts on Dannu's land, but one thing quickly noticeable by its absence, was any sign of a shrine hut. Parrish watched the behaviour of the people milling around, going about their daily business, but as the time of day passed, he could see no sign of anyone giving any special deference to one particular Hut. Hmm.

The huts were set in a rough stagger along the length of the encampment well above the high water mark and the shingle shore, and the people were just doing what people do, with regular trips to the end streams for water.

What interested him most though during these first observations was the staggered line of long brown sausages that sat on the shoreline just above the high water mark. Canoes! Perhaps two dozen really basic looking dugout canoes.

This looked promising. As basic a water vessel as you could get but hey, they could be a way for him to get back to the mainland.

An agreeable grin settled on his features and he allowed himself to relax a little more, his morale boosted somewhat by this discovery. Settling down a little more comfortably in his spot amongst the ferns in a gap between two large oaks that gave him an uninterrupted view of the camp across the water, he started doing what he did best. He waited and watched.

As he had once done several years earlier, he watched the Neolithic people, looking for patterns of behaviour and trying to learn as much as he could. But unlike before, this time it was the differences between these people and his own that he noticed most.

The day wore on and he continued to gather information. Parrish had never considered himself much of a religious man and was surprised to find how much the lack of a shrine hut to Dannu concerned him. Watching the scene before him, he wondered, was he now really looking at a village of true heathens?

There was definitely no special deference paid to any one particular hut, but that deference was certainly being paid to one particular individual. The man wasn't dressed that much differently to any other person there, but he took the regular bows and nods of acknowledgment from others in his stride. Parrish knew he had found the camp Chieftain. He marked the man in his mind, committing the size, look and gait of the man to memory and the location of the Chieftains hut.

Now, once he had gained a rough understanding of the camps routines, he began to notice more about the people themselves.

And what he saw began to disturb him.

Watching intently, things started to become clearer and he began to understand they were in a somewhat difficult position, even if they themselves didn't realize it. At a casual glance the people seemed healthy enough. There were of course no fat people, but even from a short distance away he could plainly see that those opposite him were certainly very much on the slim side. It was not easy to spot at first. Their clothing was quite baggy and for the most part very loose fitting, which helped disguise their lithe, rather too slim figures. This then brought their clothing under his more analytical scrutiny.

Most of what the people wore was made of a coarse woven fibre of one sort or another. He recognised grass capes and other items, but nearly all their apparel was made of flax or some similar natural fibre. Most of the women wore grass skirts. There were a few leather items he could see, but not many. The Chieftain wore buckskins but even they were old looking and patched in places. And leather footwear was in short supply. Several people were barefoot. It didn't take Parrish too long then to string all his observations together. On suddenly realizing he could not see a single decorative animal skull or any bone work at all on display, did he finally reach his grim conclusion. Put all these little facts together with the other observations he had made during his time here on the island, and he could finally see what had happened.

With no signs of animal life at all in the forests he had travelled through, and now seeing the blatant lack of animal products among the people he now observed, he understood that they must have all but hunted the creatures on the island to extinction! So, unless they were growing some sort of crop somewhere beyond his vision, they must now be living just off the fish they caught and the food foraged along the seashore!

These people were obviously not about to die from starvation but he did wonder if they were getting all the minerals and vitamins needed for a varied and balanced diet. Looking back at his former life in the 20th century, he cocked his head to one side and said quietly.

"Well, I never did see a fat vegetarian!"

Bringing his mind back to the present, he thought about his beloved people at Danebury and how different life would be there without leatherwork in their lives. Or the bones they used for tools and other implements. It was an eye opener. He never realised just how much they were used in the day to day lives of his people. And even then, they all went to the solstice gathering at Avebury every year to barter for heavy leather and other goods because there were some things that even they could not produce for themselves. It must be a real and daily struggle for the poor sods here, he thought.

This realisation of the killing off of all or at least almost all of the usable animals on the island suggested to Parrish that the people of the encampment must have been isolated here on this island for a long time. Which meant something else must have happened too.

He now looked hard at the people themselves. He wished now he could be a bit closer but, even from across the river, he stared with brutal scrutiny at the populace. And it did look like he could see similarities. Stances, hair colour, and facial shapes he saw, especially whenever the people gathered to speak to one another. A lot of those opposite suddenly looked very closely related.

To Parrish's modern way of thinking he was shocked, and scowled as he found the thought of incest repellently distasteful, but had to accept the hard fact that the village he was watching had become trapped in its own shallow gene pool.

Not everything on Dannu's land was beer and skittles, he was sharply reminded.

"I don't like it." he said grimly to himself, realising what he had to do. He had nothing to barter with, even if he could get close enough to talk to those opposite without getting killed in the process. All he had he was standing up in! Being now fully in tune with the beliefs of Neolithic life, he found theft just as abhorrent as his people did, but... "I really don't like it, but it looks like I'm gonna have to nick one of those canoes and get well away from here."

8

The shadows grew long.

Parrish returned to his little watering hole and quenched his thirst again before settling back into his observation post and planning his boat theft to coincide with nightfall. With a smile he did wonder, in modern law, would this nautical criminal act actually make him a Neolithic pirate?

As the dusk began to darken, yet still providing enough light to see by, he slipped down onto the shore. Again his moccasins were wrapped in the shirt which itself was wrapped about his waist, and he quietly entered the water. After a chilling shudder he struck out with a strong, silent breaststroke for the opposite shore. He hoped the encampment would be running down for the coming night and that his crossing would go unnoticed.

The distance was no more than two lengths of an Olympic swimming pool and with just his dark, rhythmically bobbing head visible above the water, he remained unseen and his crossing was uneventful.

Reaching the far shore he snaked out on his belly, emerging slowly from the water like a crocodile, up the foreshore and towards the last canoe at the left end of the line. Still there was no shout of a raised alarm and he slid gratefully into the dark shadow behind the dugout canoe. Close up now, it was much bigger than he had previously thought. Easily twice as long as his body and, with a rap of his knuckle, proved to be a solid thing. Round bottomed, long and bull nosed at both ends, it was even more primitive than he had earlier thought. It really was no more than a hollowed out log perhaps three feet wide and maybe fifteen to twenty feet long. Oak too by the look of it. He realised that it must have taken quite a bit of work to hollow it out. He grinned. Someone was going to be cross in the morning when they found it missing. He peered over the gunwale and saw two paddles lying very handily in the belly of the canoe, along with a large coil of thin rope. Possibly some sort of long line fishing kit? He nodded. Nice. So far so good.

He lay in the canoes shadow for a few minutes, waiting for the visibility to reduce even further. He wanted to paddle away into the dark night, so no one would notice anything missing till the following day. By then he would be back at his original landing spot around the headland, and ready to paddle across back to the mainland at first light tomorrow.

The first flaw in his plan came when he jumped up with the intention to quickly drag the canoe across the foreshore and into the water.

It was really heavy!

Eventually, after some silent struggling, he had to go to the rear of the thing and push hard just to get it moving, and the noise it made as it scraped across the foreshore was horrendous to his ears, and yet still no one cried out.

From dripping wet and cold to sweating with exertion in less than 20 metres, he made it to the waterline just before the approach of his first heart attack! Saved by the more slippery wet ground at the river's edge. Pushing the canoe out into the flow till it became buoyant, he stepped into it, and almost immediately fell straight out of the other side! The thing was long, low, heavy, and rounded at the bottom and both ends. He found he had to squat really low into the boat just to prevent it being so top heavy as to immediately try and turn turtle!

Shit! He cursed, and I thought my little runaway raft was a poor excuse for a boat!

Sitting low at the rear of the canoe he grabbed a paddle and, with no further thought to the village people behind him, attempted to set off downriver towards the estuary mouth.

The damned thing was almost impossible to steer and wallowed most alarmingly with each paddle stroke.

It was a struggle just to make headway. Parrish had never canoed before but he didn't think that it would be *this* difficult.

He quickly came to two conclusions. Firstly, the little canoe clearly needed a two man crew. And secondly, if it struggled to make its way up the Medina River, there was no way it would ever cope with the Solent.

With great difficulty Parrish managed to make it to the turn of the headland without suffering any further dunkings, but there had been a couple of close calls along the way!

Once he was sure he was no longer in sight of the encampment, even though by now it was fully dark, Parrish could take the choppy, unstable ride no more. He headed to the shore, jumped out then, standing knee deep in the sea, steered his unruly canoe along the shoreline towards his original base camp. It was while doing this that he had a brainwave. With his arms outstretched and his hands gripping the gunwale, he noticed that as he waded alongside, the canoe wasn't quite so fidgety.

"That's it!" he shouted out at the dark. "Outriggers!"

Just like the Polynesian ocean going canoes. They had outriggers. A long parallel float fixed to one side that created a steadier platform.

He recalled seeing several long bits of flotsam along the shore when he had been foraging for food at the start of the day. And even more fortunate, if he was lucky the lengths of fishing rope in the canoe would do to secure the outrigger to it. Fantastic!

Fully around the headland, he ensured he was far enough back along the coast to at least not be seen by some opportunist canoeist who might paddle up as far as the mouth of the river. The headland curved back more than ninety degrees, so just a couple of kilometres around and Parrish felt safe enough to drag the canoe ashore, get a fire going and hunt up a couple of cross bars and a larger outrigger log for his stabilising float idea.

Fire lit, he next made some tall torches, set them ablaze and dug their ends into the beach so that they curved upwards like flickering lamp standards. Under their soft light he set too, making his dodgy canoe into a 'south seas' special.

The rope was a godsend, or maybe Dannu was smiling on him, especially considering the fact that at one point earlier he had considered slinging the big coil overboard. But that was more in frustration rather than to save weight, and common sense had prevailed.

It really didn't take him all that long and it was not even midnight when he finally sat back on his haunches to admire his handiwork.

"Not too bad." he had to admit. The whole thing just looked much more solid. With the cross spars tied on fore and aft, and an outrigger float almost as thick as his waist and as long as the canoe itself linking the two, it did at least *look* more seaworthy. If it goes half as good as it now looks, he thought, we might be in with a shout of getting back to the mainland.

"That'll do." he agreed with himself. "Now comes the really tough bit. I've gotta get myself a crewman." And that, he knew, meant going back to the Islanders camp again. "Hmm. Looks like I'm gonna get wet *again*!" he conceded with a wry smile.

Parrish trudged back along the shoreline in the dark, pacing himself for the five kilometre trek back to his previous starting point. At least undercover of the night he didn't have to sneak along in the tangled undergrowth beneath the trees.

He could see well enough to avoid any obstacles along the high watermark and other than feeling that he could do with more food, he was quite content to make easy progress back to the shore opposite the unsuspecting sleeping inhabitants of the island encampment.

Five kilometres was just a light stretch of the legs and it took little over an hour, even at his ambling pace, to bring the dulled glow of embers from the camp across the river back into sight. As long as Parrish made no noise he was happy to simply walk along the river's edge till he came parallel with it.

Standing facing the sleeping encampment across the way he put his hands on his hips and took a moment to contemplate, before a feeling of real determination settled upon him. He felt himself going into 'serious' mode, it did feel as if he was about to go into combat, and this time there was no jollity in him as he entered the water again.

Once again conserving his strength, he sculled with his efficient breaststroke across the river and emerged dripping and determined before the unsuspecting village. Paying no attention to the remaining canoes he padded silently on bare feet across the riverfront and in amongst the huts. Almost without a conscious decision he headed towards a hut with two free standing timber pillars before its entrance. It warmed him slightly to notice, even in the dim moonlight, that there were carvings on the front faces of the pillars. Small earth goddess symbols. Well, at least they were aware of Dannu to a certain extent.

Parrish's intended target was the head man. There were several reasons for this. By the gauging of the times, he would probably be regarded as the best man here. Secondly, once the rest of the village became aware of his abduction, it might take them some time before embarking on any course of action to find and retrieve him. This might gain Parrish some breathing space to get off the island. And finally, because the village Chieftain was the one individual he had really studied during his observations throughout the day.

The door blanket was tied in place but there were chinks of soft light showing around the edges. He realised that there were tallow lamps still alight inside which meant that there was still one or more active, or at least awake, persons in there. He took a moment to decide whether to try and sneak in, which would be difficult without having something to cut the ties that held the blanket in place with, or to barge in and tackle head on whatever he found inside. Fiddling with the ties of the door blanket would take time and also alert whoever was inside so, it looked like it was the bull in a china shop approach then.

Taking a couple of steps back and stooping low enough so as not to brain himself on the top of the door frame, he led with his right shoulder and barged through the hut entrance at the run.

It didn't go quite to plan. The blanket offered very little resistance, shredding as he went through it, and he stumbled on in, overbalancing and hitting the floor in a fall he managed to turn into a rather untidy forward roll.

Coming swiftly to his feet right next to the small central fire, he stood too in a fighting crouch, hands raised in readiness against attack.

He took in his surroundings in an instant. To his left lay the sleeping Chieftain. To his right on the other side of the hut were two sitting but still wide awake women. Behind them on a straw bed lay a sleeping babe.

The two women froze in shock and horror, one mid-stitch of some piece of cloth. Suddenly appearing as if out of nowhere before them crouched a wet, dripping, barefooted giant. Fierce looking, all the more so because of the fresh but healing wound to the side of his head and the bruising down the side of his face looking like wild war paint. They just gaped at him for several moments before their eyes flicked to something beyond him.

Parrish saw this and spun to find the sleeping man now scrambling to his feet. He had snatched up a flint dagger from beside the bed and bravely, but rather stupidly, lunged straight at the tall intruder.

Parrish didn't even flinch, he just let the smaller man come. Not quite awake but still very determined, the encampment Chieftain thrust out as he rose, his dagger aimed at Parrish's chest. Parrish simply grabbed the extended arm by the wrist, pulled his attacker to him and as he did so pivoted on the balls of his feet and drove his hip into the man's midriff. With a well-timed pull on the arm and an up thrust of his hip Parrish executed a perfect O-Goshi judo hip throw on the man, who was briefly aware of being completely upended before crashing painfully to the ground on his back.

Parrish knelt on the man's chest, twisted the dagger from his stunned opponents loosened grip and in a flash had it at the man's throat.

"Make a noise and you die." he hissed, then looked up at the two still agog women. "Make a noise and he dies. Understand?" the intensity in his voice was clear and they both nodded. "Good." he added. "Because I need to get off this bloody island, and you," he looked back down at the man pinned to the floor. "You are going to help me!"

9

The man with the knife at his throat saw the intent in the giant's eyes, and he genuinely feared for his life, but he was Chieftain, and with real gravel in his voice said quietly.

"I am Chieftain. I will not help you. Kill me now."

To his utter surprise, the giant actually smiled.

"Now *that* is the response I would expect from a true Chieftain. But know this. If you do not help me leave this island, I *will* kill you." He paused for effect. "But I do not kill without cause, so all I want is your help and I will allow you to live. So then, brave Chieftain, where is your will to continue to lead your people? Do they not look to you for guidance? Would you rather die than help me for one day? That does not seem to me to be the thinking of a man who leads. Your people would not thank you or think well of you if you died in your bed for no good reason or honour." He leaned in close and whispered into the man's face. "And I have watched you. I think you are a better man than that."

Just who is this man? thought the Chieftain. How can he read my mind? How has he watched me? How did he even get here? There are mysterious forces at work here. And to be beaten in combat even before I had stood up! He knew he had no defence against this giant and he had to admit he was also right. His words were wise words. Just offering help was indeed better than death, even if it was against his will. After a few moments he gave a pinched, restricted nod of agreement.

Satisfied, Parrish got up and hauled the man roughly to his feet. He kept hold of him with one hand, the dagger ready in the other. He may have agreed to help him, but Parrish didn't trust the man any further than he could throw him, which he knew was just to the ground at his feet.

Turning to the two women he opened his mouth to speak but paused, studying them for a few moments. They were of different ages but ...

"Are you two sisters?"

The women rose to their feet, being directly addressed by a man, and in unison shook their heads.

"No matter." His voice then took on a more commanding tone. "Give me some food. And a water bag."

They instantly jumped to his instructions and it took them no time at all to drop into a small woven fibre shoulder bag what looked like hardtack biscuits, pieces of dried fish and some early berries. No meat, he noted. And a hollowed out wooden cylinder plugged with a wide cork at one end with a string loop attached to the side. He heard water sloshing inside it.

The women stepped forward and each offered one out to him. Closer now the two looked so similar as to be a little disturbing to Parrish. They really could be sisters. Awkwardly while still holding the dagger and not letting go of his prisoner, he slung both containers over one shoulder.

"Thank you." he said kindly.

The two women seemed almost as shocked by his sudden appreciation as they were his explosive entrance a few moments earlier. They bowed to him and one of them said without thinking.

"We are glad to be of help."

Parrish knew it was an automatic response to a demand from a warrior but he smiled down at them.

"And I am glad of your help." he replied.

This brought the two women's faces up in surprise and they found him smiling at them. Their fear was suddenly gone as the huge man looked benevolently down. They were all at once charmed by this tall stranger. Then, in a gentle, quiet voice but laced with a hint of menace he said.

"And remember, no noise after we have gone. I am sure you want your Chieftain back in one piece. I have enough trophies so do not make me add one more. So, no noise until the morning, yes?"

The two women nodded, avoiding the angry stare their Chieftain was aiming at his tall captor. He was helpless in all this. He knew it and hated it. Yet he was all the time trying to understand his big captor. He had never heard of him or ever seen him before and he spoke with an odd accent to his words, but his words were strong, powerful and he sounded like a leader of men not a follower. His thinking got no further as the tall man shoved him towards the door.

"Thank you, ladies." Parrish gave a light bow to the two women, inadvertently charming them even more. And with that he dragged his prisoner out through the gaping door and into the dark night. "Come on matey," he said quietly in English. "You're gonna teach me how to drive a canoe."

Parrish frog marched the smaller man in silence down to the foreshore and shoved him towards the nearest canoe. Not letting the concern about his inexperience show on his face, even in the dark, he hissed at his prisoner.

"Help me get this in the water. You in the front, so I can keep an eye on you."

He let go of the man, half expecting him to try and run off into the night, but he did as he was told, through fear or respect, he dare not say. Side by side they gripped the gunwale of the dugout and with a great effort slid it across the beach and into the water.

The encampment Chieftain hopped into the prow of the canoe with an ease Parrish could only marvel at, squatted low in it and picked up a paddle there. Parrish in contrast stepped gingerly in with one foot, shoved off with the other and dropped with an untidy thud into the bottom of the boat. It rocked alarmingly and his opposite number automatically corrected the motion with deft use of his paddle. The man never said anything but Parrish's face burned as he could almost hear him mentally thinking 'you're not very good at this are you?' Or words to that effect!

They drifted out into the flow and sat motionless for several long moments before Parrish felt he had to assert himself again.

"Do not forget. I have my eye on you, so no jumping over the side and swimming ashore."

"Swimming?" replied the small Chieftain, trying the strange word on his tongue. "What is swimming?"

Parrish was slightly taken aback.

"You mean to say you spend your time on the water but do not know how to move through it?"

The man in the bow scoffed at his captor's ignorance.

“We travel on it, not in it. In it where it is deeper than a man is tall means death.”

Parrish felt the man wanted to add ‘you fool!’ to the end of his sentence but was biting his tongue. Mind you, during the great age of sail most of the sailors of Nelson's times couldn't swim either so maybe it shouldn't be quite such a surprise.

“Okay.” said Parrish. “Let us go. Downstream. Towards the sea. Nice and easy.” he added, hoping to disguise his ineptitude at the mysterious art of canoeing. But he was nothing if not a quick learner.

He followed his companion’s lead, squatting low in the boat, and slowly the pair paddled away into the night. He was sure the man grasped very quickly that Parrish was a novice, for even he was aware that the experienced man before him was making quite regular corrections to their course and their balance as they went along.

After a while of silently suffering their untidy, zigzagging course, down the river the already annoyed Islander could keep silent no longer.

“Where are we going, and is it far?”

Again Parrish could almost hear him mentally adding ‘because this is really painful’.

In fact, Parrish *was* beginning to master the paddling technique and with careful movements from the waist up could lessen the awful wallowing each time he stroked. He knew their path across the water was straightening.

Parrish nodded his head, forgetting that the man in front had his back to him, looking past the man and could see the headlands ahead of them, visible in the soft moonlight as a dark line before them over to their left.

“On to the headland and then left till I tell you to stop.”

“Left?”

“Sorry. West.” He apologised without thinking, hoping that his fellow paddler didn't take it as a sign of weakness.

They made the mouth of the river and the edge of the Solent without incident and turned to parallel the shore on their left.

Suddenly ahead, surprising Parrish, the small glow of his beach fire’s embers could be picked out in the virgin night.

Parrish told the man to stop paddling and they floated in silence for a moment.

"Before we go ashore, I will ask you something." he said. The man cocked his head but said nothing. "You are Chieftain. Are you also a man of your word? If you agree to something, is it the truth? Are you a man of honour?"

"Of course." the man in question scoffed. "Who would not be? It is you I do not trust. I think that you will kill me as soon as you no longer need me to paddle this canoe. It is clear you cannot do it by yourself."

That stung but it was the truth. Parrish bit back a sniping retort and continued.

"No matter, I will ask you now, will you give me your word of honour that you will not try to kill me or run away when we set foot on dry land? At least until you have heard what I have to say. I have no wish to kill you. In fact, I want to ask for your help. And if you agree, I might be able to help you in return. Will you give me your word?"

There was a long, tense silence as the pair bobbed gently just beyond the tiny white surf that marked the transition from sea to shore.

Finally the man in the bow grunted and nodding his head in an almost bow said in a begrudging tone.

"Yes."

10

It was a fidgety wait till the new day. Parrish, now in his slightly crispy but dry buckskin shirt and still damp moccasins, was desperate to see the state of the water in the dawn light. He really was desperate to get off the island and back to his life in Danebury. His wife and everyone else must surely be wondering where he was?

The island Chieftain seemed much more pragmatic about this whole strange event he was a part of. Parrish knew it was the much more stalwart way that the people of these times accepted their fate, whatever that might be. This included the matter-of-fact way they didn't contest the idea that if death was just around the corner, so be it. He really admired their straight forward attitudes, but disagreed completely with their acceptance of 'what will be will be', without doing anything to try and adjust, change or avoid the outcome. No need to die if you don't have to, he thought.

The false dawn duly arrived as it always did, and as the last vestiges of night receded and the men's vision began to clear, they were both stunned by what they saw. But both were looking at different things.

Parrish broke into a broad grin as the air cleared and the early light revealed a calmed, benign seascape before him. Just ripples of waves, the tide nearly up, no swell that he could see and the wind was light. It could not have been better. Luck, or with the help of Dannu? Either way he didn't question it, he was just grateful. Turning to his companion to point out their good fortune, he stopped to see the wondrous look on the smaller man's face as he was staring intently at the now revealed second canoe. The one with the never before seen outrigger attached.

Parrish swept his arm wide, indicating that the man was free to inspect last night's work. The little Chieftain walked down the beach to the modified boat, then slowly around it before closing in to examine it more closely.

"I ... I have never seen anything like this before." he gasped.

"I did it last night." Parrish grinned at the man's appreciation. "Before I nabbed you. Er, I am sorry about nicking another canoe."

The islander didn't understand the English words dropped into the sentence but he didn't care. He was just fascinated with the outrigger canoe.

"This will work?"

"I think so. I hope so. At least, I am ready to give it a try. It is my belief it will keep the canoe in balance on the water. As long as the water is not rough, I think it will work." Parrish eyed the watermark stain on the side of the canoe that indicated there was only perhaps six or eight inches between its waterline and the gunwale of the little craft.

There was a long moment before his little companion nodded. He clearly didn't fully trust Parrish's idea, but now he had seen it, it was obvious he wanted to try it out. Despite the fact that if it all went pear-shaped, he was very likely to perish in the waters of the Solent.

Although being keen to get on with it and sensing that his Islander crewman was also bursting with silent curiosity at how this new-fangled canoe might work, Parrish knew how to wait. He wanted a clear horizon, and to be sure that the weather didn't look like it might turn when they were in open water. He knew he had a while before the tide peaked and if they could cross when the tides were slack, then that would be one less thing to worry about. Zigzagging about on the briny trying to negotiate shifts in the tides was not his idea of a good time and definitely not something he wanted to add to his bothers. Straight across without getting blown around, dragged about by the tides or just plain drowning was his plan.

The sun appeared over the horizon. The sky remained clear and the wind remained light. The tide crept slowly in towards the modified canoe. Bonus there, he wouldn't get too knackered just getting the thing into the water. The little Islander kept looking at him and he finally nodded. It was time. He nodded again to the man and together they grunted with some effort and shoved the outrigger canoe into and across the tiny white line of surf.

The canoe became suddenly buoyant and both men jumped in and snatched up their paddles. It was instantly noticeable, at least to Parrish, how much more stable the little craft was. The pair stroked tentatively out onto the open water. Within a few moments of silent effort, from the front of the canoe Parrish heard a soft chuckle.

He's actually enjoying himself, he thought.

And away they went, the water also seemed to chuckle as it passed along the sides of the canoe. The men settled into it, a steady, deep stroking pace. Looking ahead Parrish tried to steer the craft towards a spot near the shoulder of coastline on the left or western edge of the mouth of Southampton water. The canoe immediately began to weave about from side to side under his clumsy attempts and also started to wallow.

"Stop!" shouted the man in the bow without turning round. "You are so clumsy, you will kill us both!"

Parrish's face burned at the truth and he drew his paddle into the boat and rested it across his knees. The outrigger helped everything stabilise and once they were again steady the islander said, again without turning around.

"I will steer. You are big and powerful. Just paddle as strong and as steady as you can."

It had been a long, long time since anyone had taken charge of Parrish, and at first, he was shocked and annoyed, but he could not deny the logic and after a long moment simply said.

"OK." There was a silent pause before he realised that the islander had not understood. "Yes." he had to add in the language of his people.

The man's head nodded and without another word, with him steering and Parrish acknowledging that he was now just the engine room of this boat, the two bent to their tasks and resumed their steady stroke off towards the mainland shore, more than two kilometres away in the distance.

In fact the straight line distance from their departure point between what would eventually be known on the Isle of Wight as Gurnard point, and its opposite point on the mainland that would one day be Calshot, was in excess of five kilometres. Ironically, because of their most basic navigation in aiming direct line of sight for the point of land that was the corner of the mainland at Calshot spit, they were not crossing the Solent at its narrowest point. Heading for a low promontory six kilometres west along the mainland at a place eventually known as Lepe would have reduced their canoeing distance to under four.

But this was lost to the pair as they canoed out across the open expanse between the two land masses. Travelling while the tide was on the turn and at its highest was a blessing to the men, otherwise they would have truly been at the mercy of the sea. But that was the last thing on their minds as they drew further out into the Solent. The further they went the more exposed they felt. The sea was bigger, they felt smaller and their little craft seemed more and more flimsy.

Parrish fought against his own growing anxiety by concentrating on his strokes and looking straight ahead, which of course included the back of the man sat in front of him. He suddenly noticed the islander's stroke falter. Once, then a second time. Then the man stopped paddling altogether. Parrish stopped too and their forward motion slowed, ceased and suddenly they were just bobbing gently up and down on the water.

"What?" questioned Parrish. "What...?"

The Island Chieftain swivelled slowly at the waist and looked back over his shoulder at him. He said nothing but the fear was there in his eyes.

"It's OK." Parrish said quietly, forgetting that the man would not understand. But he knew that it was not so much the words, more the gentle, calming tone and confidence he was trying to convey that was more important.

"There is no problem. *No problem*. Yes? We are good. Do not think of the water as water. It is just a flat plain we must cross. Do not stop paddling and just look to the higher ground in the distance." He pointed with his paddle beyond the man. There was a tense moment before the Islander took a deep breath, nodded and turned back to face their destination. Parrish saw the man's back and shoulders expand as he took in a long breath then dug his paddle almost aggressively into the water beside the canoe.

Parrish exhaled forcibly, releasing his own fear and tension, and took a moment to view the scene around him. Everything was far away. The land masses in the distance fore and aft, the vast expanse of the Solent, its surface glittering in the early morning sunlight and, he knew, not a single living soul for miles in any direction. No wonder the little man freaked, he thought, shook his head and digging his own paddle in quickly matched his partner's strokes.

The rest of the crossing went without incident. As the shoreline of Calshot drew nearer both men felt a growing sense of relief and Parrish could see his lead man's shoulders visibly relaxing as they got closer.

The first sign that their crossing was over was both men unexpectedly and simultaneously striking the bottom with their paddles while still some 50 metres from the shore.

"Ha!" shouted the Islander and without a second thought leapt out of the canoe and found himself standing only knee deep in water. Hiding his own relief, Parrish joined him and splashing through the shallows together they ran the canoe up onto the stony beach.

The men walked up the shingle and to the tree line. To Parrish it looked no different to the tree line on the island. The pair turned, sunk to the ground and looked out across the water. Back the way they had come. The tension flowed out of them and they were suddenly aware of the sound of the lapping waves, the gentle rustle of the foliage behind them and the birdsong in the air around them. Parrish looked at his companion, who looked back in satisfaction.

Parrish chuckled. "Do not look so pleased with yourself. You still have to go back. But at least you know it can be done." he added as the smile fell from the Islanders face.

"Yes." He didn't seem overly convinced.

"When you are rested, not before, eh?" The man nodded. "But before then we need one last talk. That is if you are ready to listen?"

The little Chieftain looked at the beached outrigger canoe, away to the island in the mid distance then back to the giant seated beside him. As he had been told earlier, he had nothing to lose. He nodded.

Parrish took a deep breath.

"OK. I will leave you now, but I want you to think on what we spoke of last night. You need new blood, you need good tools and you need to renew yourselves with Dannu. All these things can be yours, to be bartered for at the great gathering near her temple at the high of the summer sun. This is now within your reach, because you and your people can now cross the sea with canoes like that." He pointed. "As long as you take care to watch the weather and water, yes? So, the choice is yours. Watch for the sign. When the time is right, and I believe that time is not too far from now, I will send someone to lead you. From here." He pointed at the ground at his feet. "Right here. There will be a smoke signal. It will burn for three days and no more. After three days it will be too late. Watch for the sign. And then you come or you do not come, but I give you the choice."

The two men eyed each other in silence. The small man's mind was clearly working and Parrish let him think on it for several moments before trying to tempt him a little more.

"You can now at least cross the water when it is calm, which means you can hunt every now and again. I am sure you can build more canoes as good as this." Again he pointed at the little boat.

"Better than that." said the islander almost without pause.

"Yes. So your lives are already better. They can be even more so if you come. So the choice is yours. Watch for the sign." Parrish didn't get an immediate 'yay or nay' so just shrugged. "I will leave you then. Safe journey back." He rose to his feet.

The island Chieftain stood up with him, faced his tall companion and offered a small, acknowledging nod.

Finally, thought Parrish and nodded formerly back.

"I will not say what me or my people will do, but I can say that we will watch for the smoke." the smaller man growled.

"Good enough." Parrish turned to leave.

"Just who are you, tall man?" It was more an instruction than question.

"I am Parrish."

"And I am Chieftain Garth." Again the pair nodded to each other.

"Be well, Chieftain Garth."

"Parrish." came the blunt reply with a dismissive nod.

The Chieftain of Dane-bre just snorted through his nose, turned away, pushed into the dense foliage and in moments was gone from sight.

11

Men were on the march.

Ten warriors in all, with a Chieftain at their head. Shimon had decided now was the time to make his move. The spirits of the people of Dane-bre must surely by now be at a low ebb. They would be sad, confused and without a leader. All he had to do was exert his rightful power as a Chieftain and before they knew it, he would be head of Dane-bre and all it contained.

In fact ten men were he thought enough warriors to be imposing, and to back him in case of an isolated spot of trouble, but there was no need to tell anyone else that they constituted more than a quarter of his total fighting force. He was not a vindictive man. Yes it would be good to sit at the head of a powerful, successful and flourishing village like Dane-bre, but he was also trying to ease the burden and stresses on the under-manned and under-provisioned people of his own village. Times were hard at Olann-bre and he was having to make hard decisions to try and ease their lives. And if that meant treading all over the lives of an adjacent village to do that, so be it.

But first he had to get there. So, as Parrish had done several days before, he and his men were making their way upriver towards the shallow, or rather shallower, crossing point where a man had a better chance of surviving the dangerous waters of the dividing waterway.

It had not escaped his notice that a link rope across the span gave those who had to cross the river more confidence, and something reassuring to hold on to!

The bravery of the first warrior to cross was not in question, and once he'd safely forded to the opposite side, posts were quickly sunk and a rope secured. The others, Shimon included, crossed wet but safe, and set off back along the other bank towards Dane-bre.

The first the people of Danebury had any inkling that something was afoot was a report from the parapet that a band of men were on their way up from the east river.

They were spotted early enough and so by the time they had reached the approaches to the hillfort a type of welcome committee had already gathered at the approach to the snaking pathway that led to the hillfort gates.

Klud, as de-facto leader was at its head, Tomps one pace behind him, followed by a mixed gathering of warriors and women, all wanting to see and hear what was about to unfold. Those of Danebury soon outnumbered the approaching group but there was confusion.

Clearly they had not come for battle, being small in number and also plain and bold in their approach to a potentially hostile hillfort. And everyone there recognised Chieftain Shimon at the head of the group. There were mumblings in the Danebury crowd and they were not sounds of confidence. This greatly pleased Shimon as he drew nearer to them.

He stopped a safe ten or so paces short of the lead man and held up his hand to halt the men behind him. A brief staring match ensued. Klud dearly wanted to know what the Chieftain had to say, despite his natural instinct to simply attack and take some trophies. He had never before been in a face to face confrontation that hadn't immediately resulted in mortal combat. But the man before him was a Chieftain. His word was right and even though he was not Chieftain of Danebury, the warrior still deferred to the leader before him, as protocol demanded.

This indecision made Shimon smile all the more. And he let the crowd before him sweat just a little before he spoke. In a clear, commanding tone he said loudly.

"You all know who I am. I am Chieftain, and I have come here to save you from yourselves. Without a leader you will all soon be in trouble. No decisions can be made. Who will know what is best? Who will settle disputes? Who will lead you through the winter storms? We all saw Parrish carried off by the great river, back into Dannu's arms. He is gone now and you are all without order or direction.

So, it is my task to bring order back to this part of Dannu's land. Step aside. I will enter your fort and become the Chieftain of Danebre. Who else has the right? Am I not already Chieftain? Step aside and I will lead you back onto the true path. The village of Dane-bre can still flourish, with me as your rightful Chieftain!"

It was quite a speech and there was at first a sea of gaping mouths opposite him, then serious mumbling and discussion.

These were simple people who just carried on with their lives and once they had chosen their own leader were happy to, and in truth had no choice but to, follow his directions and orders for the well-being, continued existence and hopefully flourishing of their village.

Shimon crossed his arms over his chest with easy authority and braced up before these now indecisive people.

Like everyone else there Klud let all this unfold, listening in silence. Then in its aftermath, he stood wide footed, rested his fists on his hips and braced up himself. He looked the Chieftain in the eye, in itself almost an insult.

"Parrish is Chieftain of Dane-bre. I do not believe he is dead and until he returns, I will look after the village. It is a great honour that he has trusted me with and I will not fail in my duty to that honour. Go back to your own village and leave us to await the return of our Chieftain."

It too was a great speech, this time the crowd gaping at the power of Klud's words. Even Klud himself was slightly amazed, wondering where his bold, Chieftain-like words had sprung from.

Chieftain Shimon began to see that the confusion in the crowd behind the insulting warrior at their head was waning, as was the power of his attempt to wrest control of Dane-bre from these people.

His natural instinct as a victorious warrior who had risen to be a leader of its village rose to the surface. He was a Chieftain and he was used to his word being obeyed. Any of his remaining diplomacy vanished. His jaw set and his voice, still loud, had real edge to it. He eyed Klud and the young warrior beside him, who looked like he was about to spring into action at any moment.

"Step aside!" He barked. "Your Chieftain is dead. Your village is mine. Step aside or I will kill you, and the boy there, and take my rightful position as Chieftain of Dane-bre!"

Unexpectedly, a voice from beyond the rear of the crowd called out.

"Is that so?"

Every head turned, recognising the voice. For every instant scowl on the faces of Shimon's men, there were all at once twice as many grins on the faces of the people of Danebury. Brightest one of all was Juli's as she saw her beloved husband approaching.

He looked dishevelled, tired and his face was a mass of bruising down one side and an ugly scabbed over wound was clearly visible along the hairline above his left temple. No matter. It was Parrish!

He had been quietly walking around the southern lip of the defence ditch on his way to the entrance when he had come across the growing gathering and heard the exchange of words. As he reached the back of the crowd they parted for him and allowed him easy passage to the front. Even before he had reached the confrontation at the heart of everything he spoke in a soft but commanding voice.

"If you kill Klud and Tomps, which by the way I think you might find difficult, you must then try to kill me!" He stopped alongside Klud and patted him warmly on the shoulder. "My friend here has been taking care of Dane-bre for me, and it seems doing a fine job of it. But now I am back to take charge again."

Klud's chest swelled at the compliment. Tomps broke into an even wider grin but Parrish remained straight faced as he watched the impotent rage boiling up behind Shimon's eyes.

For the man knew his chance had gone. Parrish was not frightened nor confused. He was certainly not a man to take on in combat. And he was certainly not afraid to use deadly force if it was required. Almost as if Dannu's man was reading his mind, the tall man stepped forward and spoke quietly, so that only he and the warriors Klud and Tomps could hear.

"So you are no longer needed here. I think you should leave now. Return to your own village, my friend." There wasn't an ounce of friendliness in his tone. "Or I think it might get a bit messy for you and your men." He added levelly.

Shimon looked into his eyes, then at an eager looking Klud and Tomps, and noted the massing warriors of Dane-bre who were keenly gathering behind the trio, now growing confident of what might follow next now that their venerable Chieftain was back. The thwarted Chieftain of Olann-bre held out for several tense seconds to save some semblance of pride, then gave Parrish a brief, tight nod, turned and without a word marched off back down the slope that led away from Dane-bre and back to the east river. His men duly followed and Parrish watched in steely silence until he was sure they would not turn back at the last moment and do something stupid.

Finally satisfied, he turned to face his people and offered them all a cheery grin.

"Welcome back, my Chieftain." Klud acknowledged formally, bowed then as he straightened broke into a huge smile.

"It is good to be back." He laughed, and as if that were a cue everyone else there laughed and there was happy chatter. Juli made her way to the front, her eyes glowing. She wanted to rush to her husband's arms but was halted, inadvertently saved from a public indiscretion by Tomps, who blurted out loudly.

"But my Chieftain! What has happened? Where have you been? How ..."

Parrish silenced him with a raised hand.

"All in good time, my young friend." He smiled. "First, I need to clean myself up, get something to eat and speak with my wife." He winked at Juli and she tried, for the most part unsuccessfully, to hide her joy. "Then I really need some sleep. And after that I will call a small gathering and then I will tell all."

The Chieftain, *their* Chieftain had spoken. Everyone nodded. They would of course obey his wishes. A final mass bow then everyone turned to face Dane-bre. The people once more parted to allow Parrish through and he led off towards the great gates.

Klud was at his right, Tomps on his left. Juli was but a pace behind, as it should be. Everything was once again right with the world.

12

In actual fact, Parrish was in his bed before the sun had set, and slept right through almost till noon the next day. Indeed, the sun was very nearly at its height and Julie was beginning to wonder if her husband would ever wake. She had made sure everything was in order in case there was anything he might need. Food was ready to be heated, fuel for the fire if needed, a good supply of water, and clean clothing. And so she sat patiently, silently watching her husband as he slept. Recharging his batteries he had said, whatever that meant?

Finally he opened his eyes. The first thing he saw was his wife. Then his eyes flicked to the cot where Chris slept. It was of course empty. The little lad was out and about somewhere, but the scene put a huge smile on Parrish's face. He yawned, sat up then opened his arms as Juli went to him, and enjoyed a good hug with her.

"Breakfast?" she asked as if nothing untoward had happened in the last few days bar his sleeping late.

Parrish nodded, detecting the slight chiding in her voice. He looked to the open window port.

"Is the day far gone?"

"You have missed almost half of it, my love." Julie laughed, kissed him then made to prepare some food.

Parrish stretched, scratched and reached for the water bowl to splash his face. Better. Getting dressed he said.

"I am going to need a runner. To tell Klud, Tomps, Gant and the Holy one to meet me in the Chieftains hut. They need to know what is going on and what happens next. And to tell them to bring their wives, so that means you are coming too." Juli froze in her tracks and looked at him with a mixture of curiosity and apprehension. "There is no need to look so worried. You and the other women are only there to listen. I just want everyone to know what is going on." He winked at her.

Juli half smiled. It had not occurred to her that he might know about the female grape vine in Dane-bre. But yes. Dannu's man knows all, she realised.

Parrish noticed none of this. Only moments after he stepped out from the threshold of his cabin he had hailed a small boy he could see near one of the huts.

Leaping to his Chieftains command the lad raced eagerly off into the village to pass on his message to the chosen men.

"A quick bite to eat," he smiled at Juli, "then we will go down to the Chieftains hut and await the others."

She nodded back and set too, knowing full well that it was his way of ensuring that everyone else would be there in good time before he arrived. It did not do to keep a Chieftain waiting and Parrish was making sure there would be no chance for one of his friends to insult him, and themselves look bad, by being late. It was another reason she loved him so.

A short while later, everyone who needed to be was gathered in the roundhouse that was the empty but official residence of the Chieftain.

Klud, Tomps, Gant and the Holy man were sitting cross legged in a semi-circle facing Parrish. He too sat and looked back at his men. His friends. Klud was his right hand man. And as solidly dependable as the great grey stones at Dannu's temple. Tomps was the keenest follower of his friend and mentor. Gant was the great organiser, quiet yet efficient. And the Holy man was, well, the holy man! Behind each of them, a short space back, silent and respectful sat the wives, all wide eyed and ears open. Juli sat alongside Klud's wife and Parrish gave her another wink. This time she remained flat faced, while Parrish had to smother a smile of his own.

Then he eyed the men before him, took a breath and steadily relayed all that had happened after he'd been knocked out during the failed ferry crossing. There were wide eyes, gasps and the shaking of heads as he told each part. Finally he explained how he thought the Islanders had hunted their land till it was empty and the lack of people to continue their existence on Dannu's land. And also their lack of respect, forgotten not deliberate he added, for the Goddess herself. The Holy one in particular was greatly shocked by this. Secretly, Parrish was glad of the little man's reaction because he thought he might have had trouble explaining what he wanted to happen next, if those before him had shown a complete disinterest in the whole affair.

"So now you know." he concluded. There were silent nods from his men and wide eyed stares from the women behind. "Now, what I want to do is help these people to come back to Dannu." That got everyone's attention. "I have given them the means to travel across open water to reach back to the mainland." They all understood he meant the thing he had referred to as an outrigger canoe. "They need meat for food. They need goods and good tools to ease their daily lives. They need new blood to be added to their village and they need to return to Dannu's arms."

"And how is all this to be done?" It was the Holy man who got there first with the all-important question.

"I am glad you asked, my friend, because part of doing this calls upon you and your special holy knowledge."

"Huh?" was all the Holy man could manage.

"I will explain." Parrish said rather casually, and he could almost see everyone, and he meant *everyone's*, ears flapping then. Chieftain's never explained. "Once the Islanders have crossed the salty water, they can hunt as they travel and get that badly needed meat. And it is my plan that they should travel to here." Eyebrows went up at that. "And then we at Dane-bre can lead them on to Dannu's great temple for the gathering at the highest high of the sun. There they can be rejoined with Dannu. Then after, they can trade for goods and even for women. It is my hope that we can add their number to Dannu's great flock and help them with their daily lives."

There was a long silence.

As the seconds drew out Parrish thought that he might have asked, or expected too much from his people. But then Klud came to his aid asking the simple but difficult question.

"How do we do that?"

Parrish gave him a grateful smile.

"I am glad you asked that too." he smiled. "I need someone to go and meet the island clan and lead them back here. They have not left their lonely place for many, many seasons and their knowledge of this place has been lost. But more importantly, is just *when* they are to be led here." He turned his full attention to the Holy man. "I do not know how you do it, but I know that you can work out how many days before the day of the highest sun. You somehow know the right day when we have to leave Dane-bre to get to Dannu's temple to be there on the right morning. I am hoping that you can work backwards from there and tell me the right day to send my messenger to meet the Islanders."

"Go on." said the Holy one slowly, suddenly cagey that he may have to give up a secret of his religion.

"I want seven days warning. Er ... what I mean is I need two days to reach the edge of the salty water. Then three days to await the arrival of the Islanders. And two more days to get back to Dane-bre before we all set off to Dannu's temple. Can it be done? Can you do it?" Parrish found himself holding his breath while the little man paused. As Parrish watched he tried to imagine the little man doing some sort of mathematics in his head, but knowing these people, he found it difficult. Once more he realised that even after all the time he'd spent here, he was still underestimating these resourceful people.

"I will not tell you how it is done," he said eventually, "but yes, it can be done."

Parrish sighed in relief and nodded his satisfaction.

"Good. Very good. I do not need to know how you do it, but I trust I can rely on you to tell me *when* I must send my messenger on his way?"

"Yes." the Holy mans reply was curt but definite.

"Outstanding." whispered Parrish in English under his breath. "Very good." he said again in the language of his people and nodded a bow at the little man. This got a nod back.

"But who goes, and where?" asked Gant.

"I will give directions to the man who will go," he answered. "And, I will be sending Tomps."

The youngster's eyes lit up. In contrast Klud looked crestfallen. He eyed Parrish.

"Why Tomps?" he growled, feeling an insult at not being chosen.

"Why, it is obvious." Parrish quickly tried to pacify his friend. As he spoke he pointed to each man in turn. "The holy one is needed here to guide us all to Dannu. Gant is needed here to organise extra camp materials, fuel and possibly even food for so many people.

Tomps is young, fast, and a good fighter, but also ready to obey my orders *not* to kill anyone unless he really has to. And I bow to his decisions if and when that is needed. You are too good a warrior to hold back in battle, my friend. Besides, I need you here by my side. You are my right hand. I will need your help to arrange extra men, women for chores and to keep control. If even for a short time we are twice as many, I could not be everywhere at once. I will need your wise words and actions to guide me, my friend."

Every man there smiled then, each accepting their tasks and seeing the bigger picture now that the Chieftain had explained it all. And all the while the silent women to the rear were goggling at being present to see such a never before heard of meeting, and at the scale of Parrish's plan.

The Chieftain scanned the faces before him, smiled and asked, "Any questions?" It was a normal action at the end of any briefing but those before him just stared back. Of course not, he realised after a moment. "Well then," he hurried on. "I think that is about it." He turned one last time to the Holy man. "Just let me know when I should send Tomps on his way, and we are done."

The Holy man nodded but Parrish was already rising to his feet. Juli jumped up and fell in behind him as he left the hut. All the other men filed out after him, followed by the other two women, who quickly dispersed back towards their huts, eager to get away from the disturbingly unusual event. Gant and Tomps walked away together, keenly discussing what had just transpired, leaving Klud and the Holy man alone under the hut porch, watching Parrish's receding back as he strode away through the village.

There was a stony silence before Klud spoke quietly.

"I cannot say that I fully agree with this. Parrish is a good man, but sometimes his goodness is his undoing. And it is not always he that suffers for it."

The Holy man was about to snap at the warrior beside him for daring to criticize the Chieftain, but he too had witnessed events in the past which Parrish had set in motion that had unfolded in unexpected and sometimes deadly ways. Instead, he chewed his lip in thought before slowly nodding in agreement. After all, did Dannu's man not say only moments ago, Klud speaks wise words. With a nod of acknowledgement, the pair went their separate ways.

13

And that's how it was for some time after. Word of his great scheme spread like wildfire through Dane-bre. Parrish knew he could rely on the women to spread the news. Everyone was by turn curious, excited or confused, and there was a heightened sense of anticipation for several days. But village life continued on as it normally did, and when nothing out of the ordinary happened after many days, the increased excitement waned and the whole thing seemed then to be no more than a storm in a teacup. If there had been teacups, or even tea for that matter, thought Parrish.

The Holy man no longer felt any pressure to act. The warriors were simply waiting on Parrish and he was keeping anything extra that he might know close to his chest. In actual fact Parrish himself was trying to count the days and to work out just when Tomps' 'go date' was approaching, but apart from knowing that the moon was already halfway through its cycle, he was as clueless as everyone else!

Which is why it almost seemed like a bolt from the blue the morning Parrish stepped out of his cabin door to find the Holy man waiting for him.

"Yes?"

The little man had never been known to mince his words and simply said.

"It is time."

"Time?"

"Yes. From tomorrow Tomps will have this many days to leave and return before we must all set off for the great temple of Dannu." He held up his hands with splayed fingers and thumb on one and two fingers extended on the other. Parrish's first thought was, you sly bugger, you can count after all, but all he said was.

"Thank you. I am grateful for your efforts. There are just a few things to be done now but we can finally get going on this."

He bowed to the Holy one, who bowed back but remained flat face. The little man was pleased to be of help to his Chieftain but as he looked into his Chieftains eager face Klud's words came ringing back to him. Without another word he turned away and left the tall man to his tasks, whatever they might be.

Tomps was duly sent for and arrived in a combination of excitement and trepidation. Parrish smiled at the expression on his face and ushered him inside with a chuckle.

Juli bowed to them both then kept discretely back but within easy earshot in case they needed anything, and also to try and understand what was going on.

Parrish led Tomps over to his table and allowed the lad a few moments to gaze upon what lay there.

It was a map. In fact, as far as Parrish was concerned it was barely worthy of the name, but in essence that's what it was.

An irregular, roughly two foot by two foot square of scraped smooth sheepskin. Clean, supple and with black charcoal squiggles on it. At least, that was how it looked to Tomps.

Parrish thought it the worst attempt at a map he had ever seen and was almost ashamed to admit it was his own work.

A gently wavy line starting near the top of the map next to a large black dot, which Parrish had placed to mark the position of Danebury, made its way part way down the skin. Then it joined to the tip of the left fork of a tongue that angled on down, leading slightly towards the right bottom corner of the skin. This was a rough representation of Southampton water. Before it reached the bottom of the skin the two sides of the tongue lines shot off left and right to disappear off the sides of the skin. Right on the bend of the left line was a big cross. Even Parrish found it hard to believe that he deemed it necessary to resort to 'X marks the spot'! At the bottom of the map, sticking up like the split tip of an arrowhead were two triangular peaks. This represented the northern tip of the Isle of Wight and the open mouth of the Medina river. Down the right hand edge of the map was a big arrow pointing at the bottom of the skin. And he had even drawn little wavy lines to represent the water area.

There were no words on the map. Tomps could not read. There were no contours on the map. Tomps would not understand altitude. There were no distances marked on the map. Tomps would not understand scale. The more Parrish looked at the map the more he felt it was a shoddy piece of work and he so hated that. He just hoped it would be enough for Tomps not to get lost.

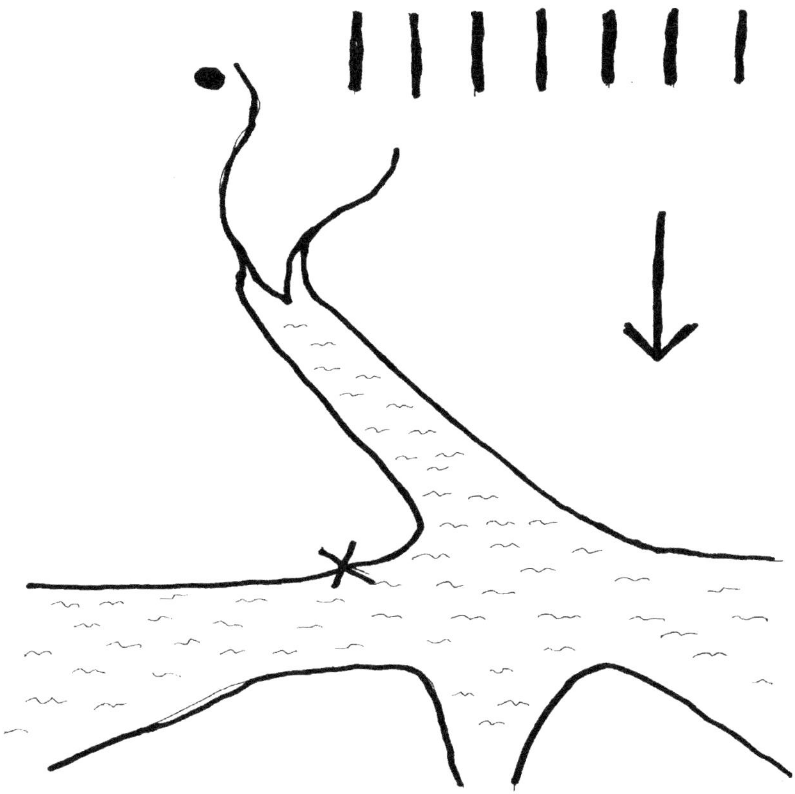

Along the very top of the map were seven heavy vertical lines, each as long as a man's thumb and well spaced across the top of the skin. Tomps made to run a finger over them but Parrish stopped him.

"Not yet." He said mysteriously and looked sideways at his friend. "I will tell of those at the end, and talk you through all of this," He waved his hands above the skin map. "And I hope it will help you do what I ask."

"I will not fail you, my Chieftain." Came the firm reply.

"Good man." Parrish clapped him on the shoulder. "Right then! This, my friend, is your map."

"Map?" The young warrior tried the English word on his tongue.

"A picture that can show you the way." Tomps just looked at him, puzzled. "It will become more clear as I show you." He pushed on. "This mark," he pointed at the black dot. "is here. Our village. And this wiggly line is the East River. It leads southwards and where it meets a great, wide river." His finger followed the line till it met his wavy line covered rough drawing of Southampton water. "The wavy lines just mean that all this is water, but you will see it for yourself when you reach this point. At the bottom here." he indicated the cross. "This is where you will wait for the Islanders. Yes?"

Tomps still looked confused.

Okay, thought Parrish, different tack. As he continued speaking his finger traced the route from dot to cross.

"This is Dane-bre. Go to the east river and then head south. Keep the river close on your left and follow it. You will eventually come to a very wide river with salty water that you cannot drink. Carry on, still keeping the water close on your left. Where the land meets this water it is called 'the coast'. Stay on the coast. You will find your travel easy along the edge of the water. With the water still on your left and the forest on your right, travel on until your path turns to the right. There, across the water from where you stand, you will see a distant land. That is where the Islanders live." It was already a lot of information for Tomps to take in and the youngster looked unsure. Parrish patted him on the shoulder.

"Do not be so worried. This map is just a rough guide. I thought it would help to guide you. Look, to know which way to go, do you see the arrow I have marked here?" He pointed to the arrow drawn on the right hand edge of the skin.

"Yes."

"That arrow must be pointed at the horizon beneath the sun when the sun is at its height. That way will be south. Wherever you are on your route, at midday if you hold the map out flat and turn it till the arrow points at the horizon beneath the sun, that is south. Then the map will tell you which is the direction back to Dane-bre."

Parrish knew his young friend could tell north from south and east from west, but he was trying to link the points of the compass and the map together in the lads mind.

"I ... see." Tomps still wasn't too sure.

"Trust me." Parrish smiled and Tomps just nodded. "Okay. I will make it as easy as I can. Keep the river and then the salt water on your left as you travel south. Once you have turned for home, keep the water then the river on your right. This map is to help you find your way, plus other things."

"Other things?"

"Yes. Two things you need to know. The cross." He pointed again. "It shows where you must wait for the Islanders, and to signal them. When you get there get a good smoky fire going and keep it going. I hope they will be watching for it."

"How long must I wait?" It was finally the right question. Parrish grinned.

"That is where the marks at the top of the map come in. As you travel, at the end of each day when you settled for the night, rub out one of the marks with your fingers." He hovered a finger over the first mark. "I have walked this route already. It should take you no longer than two days to reach this cross area." He covered two marks with his fingers. "By the end of the second day you should be roughly where the cross is on the map. Next morning start your smoking fire. At the end of each day, rub out another mark. If no one appears by the time you have rubbed out three more marks, return home alone. Do not wait any longer." He covered three more of the dark slashes and Tomps nodded. Rubbing out a mark each evening he could do. "You should then be back here at Dane-bre two days later." With that he covered the last of the two marks with his hands.

"I think I have it, my Chieftain." Tomps didn't sound too sure though. Parrish laughed.

"It is not as hard as it seems, my friend. Stay close to the river and keep it on your left shoulder. It is where you set up the signal fire that counts. If the Islanders do not see it or choose not to come, no matter. Just you come back safe after three days waiting."

Tomps nodded. It was a lot to take in.

"I have faith in you, my friend." Parrish clapped him on the shoulder. He got a weak smile in return. "Go and think it over. You leave at first light tomorrow. I will be there to see you off."

Tomps nodded and turned to leave.

"Do not forget your map." Parrish smiled again

"*My* map?"

"Of course. If it can be of any help as you travel, you will need to have it to hand." Parrish rolled it up and offered it to him. "If nothing else, you will need it with you so that you can rub off a mark every evening." If this was going to work at all, he thought, timing was everything. At the very least he wanted Tomps back in time to go with the rest of the village to the solstice gathering. If the Islanders missed it then that was their look out. He had done what he could.

Tomps took the skin roll, bowed to his Chieftain and without another word left the room in thoughtful silence and exited the cabin.

Parrish looked at his wife, who just stared back in astonishment. She had never seen anything like it. He shrugged. It was the best he could do.

"I think he grasped the idea." he said to Juli, then shrugged and slumped onto a stool. Had he asked too much of his friend, he wondered?

Juli sat down beside him and leant against his shoulder to try and offer some kind of support. But she had nothing to say.

The false dawn was lighting up the sky. The rim of the sun was almost at the horizon and Tomps stood outside the door of his roundhouse. Karin handed him a water bag and another, well provisioned carry bag. Her husband slung the bags, one over each shoulder so that the straps crossed his chest like bandoliers, and their contents hung on each hip. Into the food bag he slipped his map roll. He next closed the toggle of his cape at his throat, the woollen garment draping over his shoulders and down his back and for the most part covering his food and water bags. Karin handed him his battle club.

It was a modified one of his own design. In truth it was just a normal club but the handle had been extended to double the length. If Tomps had set the end of the shaft on the ground, the big flint mace head would have been at his navel. He grasped it at the neck and its balance was such that it automatically swung and settled at a 45 degree angle.

"Be safe." Karin said softly, so softly that she wasn't sure Tomps had heard, but he turned, smiled at her and gave her an almost imperceptible nod. Karin did not smile in return but a warm glow filled her. She bowed deeply to her husband. When she looked back up he had already turned away and was striding off towards the great gate. A glum look settled on her face and she went back inside.

Tomps had expected to meet Parrish when he stepped out of his house but there was no sign of the man. No matter. He had his new goal and he was determined not to let his Chieftain down. At the gate he slid back the bar, remembering how he and Parrish had fought and won against a superior number of warriors at this very spot the previous autumn. But now he was alone.

With some effort he pulled the big gate closed behind him and turned to set off down the approach path. There at the bottom stood a tall silhouette against the early light. Tomps grinned in recognition and nodded a greeting.

"My Chieftain."

"My friend." replied Parrish unknowingly giving the young warrior what he considered the greatest compliment. "I will walk with you to the East River." Tomps fell in beside him and they set off in the brightening dawn. Light flecks of cloud high up in the sky grew golden red edges as the sun started to appear over the horizon. It promised to be another fine day.

Parrish spoke quietly, voicing his thoughts on what might happen. Finally, he looked his young companion in the eye.

"You are happy you know where you are going? Would you like me to explain it again?"

"No, my Chieftain. I have looked at the map a lot and I believe I know what it is you ask of me."

"Good man." said Parrish and again lapsed into silence until they drew close to the river. Then he stopped the warrior with a hand on his shoulder and they turned to face each other.

"Tomps. Now listen, this is important. Do what you can, but not too much. If the Islanders come to your signal, I do not know what they will do when they see you. I know I said that you can fight without killing, but do not hold back from defending yourself if it gets too dangerous." he paused and took a deep breath. "I do not want you to die for me just because I wish to help the Islanders. If they are too proud or too stupid to accept help when they need it and it is offered, that is their problem. Protect yourself Tomps. If you can help them do so. If not, well, protect yourself. Kill if you must and get away by any means. I would rather have you alive than any number of Islanders."

"I am ready." Tomps waved his club out before him. Parrish noted it fully for the first time

"Ah. I have seen one of these before." he said, not adding 'in the Imperial War Museum' to his sentence. Tomps face fell. He thought his new club was unique. "It is called a war hammer. I am told they are very, very good during a battle. Well done." Tomps' grin returned.

Parrish paused to think of something that Tomps would easily understand. He rested both his hands on his young friend's shoulders and looked him in the eye.

"Understand this. I would be *very* angry with you if your skull ended up as someone else's trophy. Do not die because I may have sent you on a foolish errand."

Tomps stepped clear of his Chieftains grasp, bowed very deeply and said solemnly.

"I understand, my Chieftain."

Parrish looked so deadly serious that Tomps repeated himself.

"I understand. I will not dishonour you."

"Good enough." Parrish said rather magnanimously and returned the warriors bow.

Tomps smiled then. "I will be back." he said confidently. "With or without the Islanders, but I will be back on the last rub of the map."

"Then, safe travel my friend." Parrish held out his right hand. Tomps grasped his Chieftains forearm, his own was gripped and they were locked there for one deep moment before they released. Without further ado Tomps turned and set off towards the south, alongside the river.

Parrish stood and watched him go, keeping any other thoughts he had then to himself.

14

As the day progressed Tomps found himself making good, steady progress. He knew he was heading southwards into unknown territory, but was quietly confident knowing that Parrish had already passed this way and arrived home safely. So the Neolithic warrior did not expect anything immediately deadly to cross his path.

The woods were open in places, very dense in others. As long as he could see the glittering water of the river to his left, or at least hear it if he had to occasionally divert slightly away to go around obstacles that temporarily blocked his way, he was quite content to move along at the steady pace that all the people used whenever they travelled cross country. Stopping for food and drink when he needed it, drink mostly, he marched on, reminding himself to ensure that his water bag was full before he reached the mysterious 'undrinkable' water of salt that Parrish had spoken about.

Unknowingly, he had covered some fifteen kilometres, or eight to ten miles, before the end of the first day. He set up his little camp in the wilderness just short of where the river Test began to pour out into the wider, tidal waters. He topped up his still more than half full water bag and settled back into a cleft between two big buttress roots of a magnificently huge old oak tree. He had no real need of a fire but lit one just to cheer himself and, in the unlikely event that some aggressive animal might come close, it would ward the intruder off. Before the light finally went, Tomps rubbed off his first map mark then leaned back against the sturdy oak and listened to the sounds of the great forest. Insects still flitted and hummed. Bats would soon be on the wing and Tomps, rather than being frightened to be in this unknown part of Dannu's land, snuggled down into her arms and in moments was fast asleep.

He was up and away again bright and early next morning, not long after sunrise. There was a lightness in his step. He always accepted that the comfort and ready to hand things that eased his life in his own house were a source of confidence and some small pleasure but there was no denying his joy at waking up in the greenwood. What could be better than the warm sun on your face and the smell of the wild world in your nostrils. Insects were abounding and he could hear some kind of wildlife moving about somewhere in the distant undergrowth. Dannu in all her majesty. This was what it meant to be alive.

He went to the water's edge and strip washed with no feeling at all of any self consciousness, drank, ate some jerky and set off once more. He knew where he was going and really didn't need to reference the map. It was in his mind and he could call up the image at will.

Unknowingly, he had already mastered a skill that all good outdoorsmen have. Once a map had been fully studied and the objectives realised, the map itself was only referenced occasionally, to check progress or to mark off a landmark to update it. The old saying was 'As you travel, you should have the map in your head, not your head in the map'.

Setting off, he'd not been travelling long when, after moving slightly inland to negotiate a small creek, he returned through the trees to the water's edge just where it opened up into Southampton water. The far bank had suddenly moved away from him and he was confronted by a great open swathe of gently moving water. It stopped him in his tracks and he stared for several long moments. It expanded out and away to his right quarter and the distant tree lined shore opposite was further away even than the distance between the gate of his village to the bank of the great river.

He smelled the difference in the air too and walked slowly down till the water was lapping at his feet. He could not know, but it was almost high tide. Even so the unknown smell of seaweed and salty air filled his senses.

Parrish had said that the water here was undrinkable, so obviously he had to taste it. Scooping up a palmful he slurped it into his mouth. And spat it straight back out. Ugh! Of course, his Chieftain was right.

After a few more moments taking in the sight of the vastness of the water, he remembered that Parrish had called this place where the land met the salty water 'the coast'. So, he was now on the coast, his passage tallying with the map, and the image before him of the moving water somehow corresponded to the little wavy lines drawn on it by his tall friend. It was all new, vast and unknown to him but he was not afraid. He couldn't help it, he just grinned broadly at the beauty and spectacle of it all.

"As my Chieftain would say," he whispered almost under his breath, "Nice!"

With a fresh wonder at this new part of Dannu's land before him, he nodded to the scene then turned and again set off southwards along the shoreline.

He kept going along the shoreline for most of the day. After a while he noticed with amazement that the edge of the water was receding and wondered where it went and if it would all go away completely. But that was beyond him and anyway, the water would just do what it did.

The day passed pleasantly enough for Tomps. He kept a wary eye out for trouble in these unknown parts but everything seemed quiet. He did notice that, as the hunters of Dane-bre had always said, game of any sort seemed much thinner on the ground here.

The sun was drawing lower to the horizon by the time Tomps reached the corner of the coast and the full vista of the Solent and the Isle of Wight opened up to him. It again stopped him in his tracks, but not now for so long. He had watched the view gradually opening up as he travelled and as he stood gazing out across at the islands low horizon, Tomps was more amazed that an entire tribe of people had somehow long ago crossed the water and since become trapped there.

Giving only a cursory glance to the bare shingle spit that swept away to his left, following his Chieftain's instructions and the map he now held, he turned right and travelled a short way along the shore.

As Parrish had found out when he and the island Chieftain had beached here not too many days before, the ground sloped slowly to create the shallows. Correspondingly the shingle beach above the high water mark angled up gently to provide a wide swathe of foreshore before it met the edge of the greenwoods.

Tomps picked a spot that he thought roughly corresponded to the cross on his map and moved up off the shingle and to the edge of the woods.

In fairly short order he had cleared a patch of undergrowth and cut into the greenery, making himself a crescent shaped alcove with the protection of the trees at his back and on both sides, but giving him a clear view out across the Solent.

The green shrubbery he had cleared was stacked to one side. No need to waste 'smoke making' fuel for his signal fire tomorrow.

By the fading of the remaining light he had set up his camp and built a basic wikkiup for shelter in case the weather turned. Pulling up a dried length of tree trunk from among the flotsam that gathered along the high watermark, he leaned back on it, made himself comfortable and looked out. Where all the water had gone baffled him. He also saw the odd, strange looking creature moving about across the exposed wetland. They were only crabs but Tomps had never seen their like before and kept well away.

The sun finally set on this second strangely different day for the young warrior. He settled down, took great satisfaction in rubbing the next mark off his map and fell asleep thinking of how much wood he would need to gather to keep a fire going every daylight hour for the next three days.

He never needed three days' worth of fuel. The next day he burned his 'smudge pot' fire from dawn till dusk, the column of white smoke from burning greenery hanging in the air before wafting away on the light breeze. Tomps just waited. Another mark was rubbed from the map.

It was towards the end of the second day when the Danebury warrior, who had now become quite adept at scanning the view before him, noticed small dots suddenly appear at the distant edge of his vision.

The water of the Solent was fairly calm and so he watched as the late afternoon sun threw its light side on to the dots, which began to reveal themselves as distant people in what Parrish had described to him as canoes.

His mouth dropped open as the flotilla of little craft drew ever nearer. He had never seen anything like it before.

There were in fact over twenty long canoes with their new-fangled out riggers fitted. The island tribe had utilised everything they had that would float to get the entire village across the water. Fore and aft of each canoe a warrior paddled. In the middle of some of the craft sat two or sometimes three people, more warriors and women and children. A few of the canoes carried mysterious mounds of kit, covered against water ingress. The boats were well spread to avoid any contact but still close enough to gather together to offer help if anyone got into difficulty. Only their Chieftain had made this crossing before and so there were many concerned and nervous faces among the canoes occupants, unsure of crossing the open water.

Tomps stood at the top of the shingle slope, leaning on his war hammer like a walking stick, watching their approach.

The flotilla drew near and as the first canoe grounded noisily on the shingle the two paddling warriors dropped their paddles, snatched up stone axes that had lain hidden in the bottom of the canoe, leapt out and charged up the shingle towards Tomps, yelling a battle cry. Their Chieftain, still in one of the canoes out on the water, could do nothing but watch, tight lipped.

Tomps went from idle spectator to battle ready fighting man in an instant. But he recalled his Chieftains words and gripped his war hammer just beneath the stone head, lifting the foot of its shaft clear of the ground.

The two island warriors rushed him, the first man three or four clear paces ahead of the other. Partly so they didn't get in each other's way, partly because they had set off at the run already that far apart.

Tomps let them come. As the first man drew close the Danebury warrior flicked up the long handled weapon and leaning forward jabbed the handle base out like the point of a sword. Out and into the oncoming man's midriff. Compounded by his own momentum, the blow was fierce and the island warrior's breath whooshed out of his body and he doubled up. His continuing momentum carried him on towards Tomps, who stepped deftly aside, reversed his grip on his club and struck again with the handle end, bringing it down sharply with a loud whack on the back of his would be assailants head. The man sprawled face down onto the shingle, unconscious.

The second man suddenly found himself running hard towards the strange warrior, but with his fallen friend now spread eagled on the ground between them. He angled in towards Tomps intending to engage him but had to glance down to be sure he didn't trip over his friend on the ground.

And Tomps struck again.

He let the shaft of the long club slip through his hands until he re-gripped it near the end. With the added reach the war hammer offered he thrust outwards and up, the blunt top of the stone mace head thudding into the second warrior's face. The man's nose burst like a soft fruit. With blood streaming from his face and his eyes watering so badly he could not see, he completely missed Tomps swinging his club round in a wide arc, to come in low behind his legs and sweep them out from under him. This second warrior fell onto his back, losing his grip on his own club in the process. Through blurry, pain filled vision, he squinted up to see the man who had just bested him put one foot on his chest, jam the head of his long handled club into his throat, and say softly but full of menace.

"Now you just stay right there."

The sound of another canoe beaching made Tomps look up. The man who stepped out was in no rush and had an air of authority. He strode towards the Danebury warrior but before he could say a word Tomps called out loudly.

"I was told not to kill if I did not have to, but the next man who comes at me dies here!"

15

The island Chieftain stopped well short, safely out of Tomps clearly deadly and efficient reach, and pondered briefly on whether to bark out a command for the respect due a Chieftain. But instead he just stood his ground.

"We have not come to fight with you. I am the leader of this clan. I am Chieftain Garth" He waved an arm loosely to indicate the others behind him now beginning to come ashore in ones and twos.

Tomps gave a light bow of respect but did not lower his guard.

"And these two did not come to fight?" He pushed his foot down on the chest of the man beneath his moccasin. A small 'oof' came up in response.

Chieftain Garth gave the prostrate figures a considered look and simply said.

"They were ahead of me and, warriors are warriors."

It was as close as Tomps was going to get to an apology from a Chieftain and he nodded again, removed his foot from the chest of the man beneath him, stepped aside then bowed formally to the leader before him.

"I am Tomps of Dane-bre ..."

".. and Parrish sent you." The Chieftain finished the sentence for him and offered a disarming smile. He swept his hand forward and some of his people went to assist the two injured men. Tomps gave them more room and a few of the helpers, warriors, gave the young man a respectful sideways glance. The Chieftain closed with Tomps and together they turned away to confer.

"A fine display of your fighting skills." Garth said as they walked away. "I would like to see more of it sometime. But now, let us talk and decide on what we do next, yes?"

It was a great compliment to be asked by a Chieftain to assist in a decision by him. Tomps understood that he was as much in control as the Chieftain but still accepted it for what it was and bowed again.

"You are as wise as Parrish said you were when he described you to me. It would be my great honour to assist you if I can. I will explain Parrish's reasoning's for our travels and you can make your thoughts plain to me. I will not disagree with you. You are Chieftain after all."

Chain of command established, Chieftain Garth smiled and then patted Tomps on the shoulder.

"Wise words, my friend." He said. Tomps wasn't too convinced about the 'friend' part. "Let us draw up a plan for the morrow." Garth added with a grin that didn't reach his eyes.

The pair moved away to Tomps little campsite while the island villagers decamped en mass onto the shingle beach. Pulling their canoes well up past the high watermark they set about making fires for cooking and warmth.

After a fairly brief discussion with Tomps where the Danebury man informed the Chieftain about the lay of the land on the route ahead, and how long he thought it should take, it was officially the Chieftains decision that they would camp on the beach for the night and set off fresh in the morning. There wasn't really any other option this late in the day, but proper protocol must be observed and once it was agreed, he returned to his people and made the announcement.

From his little alcove in the greenery Tomps looked on in silent amazement as the Islanders flipped their canoes on their sides, out riggers sticking skywards, linked them together in pairs to make the strangest looking of tepee's, and in a matter of moments an ad hoc village had sprung up on the shore before him.

Fires were going, bedding was being laid out under the protection of the canoes and women were bustling about at their business. By the time the bottom edge of the sun was kissing the horizon everything was set. The islander's had quickly settled into their temporary village on the shingle beach, with Tomps still manning his solo camp some twenty paces back from them at the edge of the forest. The light thrown from his small campfire was completely swallowed up by the many fires of the village at the water's edge.

Everyone had settled down around their campfires.

The food was ready and being distributed around. Chieftain Garth looked away from the people before him, over his shoulder and off towards the lone figure from Dane-bre. Illuminated by his own small fire, he saw the young warrior bite a chunk off a strip of cold jerky. Another sly smile flowed onto the Chieftains face.

A young woman from his village passed by that moment, carrying a large clay bowl of hot fish stew, on her way to her family.

"You!" Garth barked, stopping the girl in her tracks. He did not know her name but knew she was unmarried and, from his point of view and for his purpose, not too unappealing. She would do.

The girl looked immediately frightened, coming under the direct eye of her Chieftain. She bowed deeply.

"Take some hot food to our friend over there." Garth pointed with his wooden spoon.

"Me?" She gasped. "Now? I ... I mean yes, my Chieftain. Of course."

Garth bit down on his anger at being questioned, especially by a woman. But he had a bigger and better idea now to play with.

"Yes!" He snapped, then his voice softened. "Go to him." He waved his spoon again. "Tend to his needs. Stay with him. I want you to find out what you can about him. About his village and anything else he might talk about." His eyes glittered at the cunning of his plan. "Then come and tell me everything."

"But what if he sends me away? I..."

"Just go!" Garth barked again then abruptly turned his back on the girl, dismissing her. He cared not if he had put her in a difficult if not impossible position. She was duty bound to bow to his wishes.

Dismayed, the girl looked down at the stew her family was now not going to eat. Then up at the stranger in the distant camp. With a gulp she plucked up her courage, turned her back on her village encampment and set off towards the stranger in the woods.

Tomps looked up as the girl approached. She knelt before him and offered out the huge bowl of stew.

"Eat?" she asked. Tomps eyed the contents then looked up with a quizzical eye.

"All of it?"

"It ... It was for my family but..."

"Then take it to them." he interrupted. "And come back with a proper portion."

She nodded but he had already returned his gaze to the fire. Jumping up she returned to the encampment, giving her Chieftains own little gathering a wide berth. He noticed her passing but did nothing, already curious.

A short while later she returned to Tomps camp, this time clutching two much smaller bowls of stew. This time each one was accompanied by a crust of bread. Again she sat and offered them out.

"That is better." Tomps approved. The girl nodded. Tomps looked over her shoulder and caught Chieftain Garth glancing in their direction. He quickly looked away.

"Sit with me here." Tomps invited her to his side to share his fire. She duly sat, fear and confusion on her face. He smiled at her then, surprising her, and spoke more softly, so that only they could hear each other.

"My name is Tomps. I come from the village of Dane-bre." He said proudly. "And you are?"

"I am just a girl." She bowed her head as if in apology.

"Greetings." There was a pause. "Thank you for bringing me the hot food. Does it surprise you that I say this to a woman?" The girl just nodded. "Well, the hot food is clearly welcome, and I give you the words for the benefit of your Chieftain. He sent you to speak with me, did he not?"

"Yes..." she hung on her next unspoken words, neither willing nor sure whether to speak further. Tomps helped her out.

"To find out what you can about me, where I come from and what happens next."

She goggled. "How could you... you are a very wise man." She changed her question to a compliment to save any insult and possible punishment.

Tomps laughed, again surprising her.

"Not I. My Chieftain said this might happen. He is the wisest of men and knows many things. So I am not offended at being asked, even by a woman. But let me tell you what we shall do together. I will tell you only what I think Garth needs to know. Then, you can tell him all you have heard without keeping anything from him or even having to lie to him. How is that?"

She could do nothing but nod in agreement.

"Good." Tomps nodded also. "Okay." She didn't understand the strange word but never said. Tomps continued uninterrupted. "I give you permission to speak freely to me. Ask your questions. But first, tell me your name and then we shall eat this fine looking stew."

"Greta." She smiled shyly. "My name is Greta."

"Okay Greta." He almost smiled back. "Eat."

Unsurprisingly, the conversation wasn't exactly gripping. Greta, like all females in these Neolithic times, had more or less been trained since birth to NOT ask questions of a warrior.

Moreover, she did not know exactly what her Chieftain expected of her, and each question she did ask came out really tentatively and was very, very basic. Tomps, on the other side of the conversation, was mindful of *his* Chieftains words and had to think carefully before he replied, lest he reveal some piece of information that he thought Parrish might not be happy about becoming common knowledge.

After a while of awkward stumbling and stuttering verbal sparring, the pair finally settled on talking about their families and day to day common events that went on within a Neolithic encampment. Such as how did island life compare and contrast with that on the mainland.

This more common ground was the real ice breaker and the pair began relaxing and surprisingly, they spent a pleasant while in small talk.

A while later and the fires began to burn low and the hubbub of noise quietened. People were settling down to sleep. Tomps half expected Greta to make her apology and return to her family but she laid back near him and closed her eyes. In a short while her breathing regulated and Tomps knew she had fallen asleep. Only then did he slip his map out of his food pouch and quietly rub off another mark. Tucking it back safely away in the leather bag and using the pouch as a pillow he lay back himself. He was about to pull his woollen cape over himself when, still asleep, Greta rolled onto her side and innocently snuggled up against him. Tomps made to push her away but then, well she was friendly enough, and had brought him food. With a sweep of his arm he flipped his cape across them both and settled back again, enjoying the girl's closeness, the smell of her, and the warmth of her body.

16

Tomps awoke bright and early to find Greta waiting for him, another clay bowl in her hands. He rubbed the sleep from his eyes and as he sat up, she knelt down before him.

"Here." she said, smiling inside that her timing was perfect.

Tomps took a moment to orientate himself in his surroundings then peered over the rim of the bowl. There was some kind of wheat or grain porridge, piping hot. It also had some strands of an unidentified green plant in it.

"I hope you like our porridge." she said, flat faced and with their merest nod he took it from her. It smelled good and felt nice and warming through the sides of the bowl. He readily accepted the offered spoon too and, sitting up straight, dived in. It *was* tasty. There was some kind of sweetener in it, honey he suspected, and those occasional pieces of greenery he ate had a hard bitterness but was not unpleasant. He ate heartily and when he was finished, he asked.

"Very nice. Tell me, what were the green bits? I have not tasted anything like that before."

"Seaweed." she said very matter-of-factly.

"Weed from the sea?" he said, slightly concerned. "Weed from the undrinkable water?"

"Yes. We have found it to be a very good food."

"Well, okay then." He could do nothing else but agree.

Tomps retrieved his water bag, rinsed out the porridge bowl then poured some clean water into it. Pulling off his shirt he splashed water on his face, then dried it with his woollen cape and rubbed his chest, armpits and arms with the now damp cloth.

"Er.., why did you do that?" Greta was still careful about asking straight forward questions but her curiosity was piqued.

"I clean myself." Tomps stated. "It is something I learned from my Chieftain. When he first came to our village we thought him strange to do such a thing. Now most of my village does the same. He says if you keep yourself clean it will help keep you from being sick." Greta looked dubious. "In the many seasons since my Chieftain has led us, it has been true. The sickness in our village is now much less."

Greta bowed to his superior knowledge but didn't feel inclined to strip off herself at that moment.

"You have already eaten?" Tomps abruptly changed the subject. She nodded. "Does this mean you will be with me all day?" She nodded again. "Good." That pleased her more than she expected. "Then I shall pack away my things. You can clear the rest of the camp. And after we shall wait till everyone else is ready and then we shall set off." Even Tomps was surprised just how much authority his voice carried.

Without a word Greta bowed to him and together they prepared to leave the edge of the Solent.

It took a little while for the islanders to make ready. Fires were extinguished. Packs were loaded and secured. Many women were burdened with backpacks or bags. The men carried what they had to along with their personal weapons. All the canoes were pulled well up above the high water mark, almost to the edge of the greenwood, and inverted so they laid hull up so as not to catch any rainwater. They were quite a sight, like a regimental line of beached whales, a long row of well spaced hulks awaiting their owners return at some later date.

Garth finally approached Tomps. Greta stepped back and bowed deeply. Tomps bowed too. The Chieftain feigned indifference and simply said.

"We are ready. Lead on, we will follow."

Tomps got the distinct impression the man didn't like deferring his leadership one bit to some young unknown upstart so he simply bowed lightly, spun on his heel and led off along the shoreline.

With his war hammer gripped in one fist, cape flowing down behind him and his unstrung bow and arrows in a quiver slung diagonally across his shoulders, as he strode away he was quite a picture. As soon as Garth had turned back towards his people Greta smiled at her new companions back then skipped up beside him. Her pack was quite small, not unduly heavy and he had given her permission to walk beside him so they might talk further. The next few days looked to be exciting and unpredictable and, truth be told, she was quite excited at the prospect.

Contrary to her expectations, the day progressed slowly.

Tomps led the way and at first was quietly thrilled at the feeling he was emulating his hero. So this is what it is like to be Chieftain Parrish when he leads the whole village out from Dane-bre. It was a powerful, heady feeling, but as the day progressed he found it becoming a strain as he came to realise that it wasn't just a case of striding manfully out towards the horizon and expecting the people to simply follow on behind. He had to be constantly alert. To always be aware of the route. To keep a constant eye on the people behind him, from the keenest warrior to the most wayward self-absorbed child. Seeing how some struggled under their burdens. To go as fast as the slowest person and to watch for stragglers. To try and keep everyone together. How some struggled over obstacles that others didn't even consider obstacles. Tomps began to see that being a Chieftain wasn't as easy as Parrish made it look.

So the whole troop made slow but steady progress. There was little talking. Chieftain Garth had to be seen to be at the head of his village yet had to defer to Tomps because he did not know where they were going. Tomps could feel the man's angry eyes boring into his back the whole time.

Greta sensed his discomfort but was not familiar enough with her new charge to offer much verbal comfort. She was still uncomfortable and unsure of the new freedom he had given to her. Happy to walk alongside but reluctant to talk and also aware that the warriors of her own village thought she was showing disrespect and insult to be so boldly parading alongside a warrior. Even if that warrior was from another village!

The slow pace meant that eventually, by the time the sun was low and preparations were being made to set up camp for the night, the people had covered perhaps fourteen kilometres or around eight miles.

Tomps realised that they had stopped quite near to where he had camped at the end of his first day on the outward bound leg of his trip. He saw then that with perhaps a little helping of Dannu's good wishes, they might make it all the way back to Dane-bre by the next night. Yes, with luck they could complete the journey with a mark to spare on his map.

He still bedded down away from the Islanders, keeping both to himself and a wary eye open. It wasn't that he did not trust Chieftain Garth's word, but that first clash with the two men on the shore of the Solent made him realise that the Chieftain did not keep a very tight control over his men.

Greta supplied more hot food, which was very welcome, and she also tried some small talk by asking about his family, noticing by the end of the day how tired he looked. She smiled at him a lot now. Tomps found it rather disconcerting, even though he had given her permission. Disconcerting too because he liked it a lot more than he thought he should. He was beginning to see that she was looking very comely to him.

When night had fallen and the people quietened down, Greta snuggled uninvited up beside him and, almost of its own accord, his arm snaked around her shoulders and drew her close. Tomps quietly rubbed the fifth mark off his map and settled down for a comfortable night's sleep with the new lady in his life.

It was the next day when the Islanders started to show their true colours.

Tomps had tried his best to cajole the people to set off as soon as was possible and, rather begrudgingly, they were all again moving across the Neolithic landscape not too long after sunrise.

It was early in the afternoon, or at least some while after the high of the sun, and Tomps knew they were getting nearer to Dane-bre. This estimation was of course crude but he was within 5 miles or roughly 8 kilometres of his destination.

Suddenly a cry went up and as he looked back from his position in the lead, he could see several people pointing. Squinting through the trunks of the forest that grew ever denser as it expanded away into the distance, he could just see movement in the dappled shade there at the base of some of the trees.

A herd of pigs had been spotted. A large boar, two or three big sows and over a dozen piglets, snuffling about in the undergrowth.

With an uncontrolled cry, many of the warriors instantly dashed off into the woods and in moments all the men in the village rushed away between the great trunks.

"Well," said Tomps disappointedly. "It looks like we will be here for a little while." He turned to Greta, who was quite happy to shrug off her pack, but could not understand his obvious annoyance.

Although he had no concept of measured time, simply squatting down to wait, it was a good hour or so later when the men of the village returned. They were all jolly and cheerfully congratulating each other. The larger animals were swinging lifeless under wooden poles between two men, while all the dead piglets were slung across the shoulders of other warriors. Garth didn't need to instruct anyone. Fires were soon going and a lot of people set to, gutting, skinning and then processing the carcasses for bones for tools, sinew and gut while the meat began to cook.

Tomps just looked on as everyone got busy, and Chieftain Garth approached, a very satisfied grin on his face.

"A good hunt!" he boasted to Tomps. He looked into the young warriors expressionless face. For some reason the Dane-bre man did not share his enthusiasm.

"You killed them." He replied flatly.

"They were meat." replied Garth, speaking to Tomps as if he were explaining something very obvious to an innocent child.

"But you killed them all." He said again.

"They were meat!" repeated Garth more forcibly this time and, not getting the joyous reaction he was expecting, scoffed and turned away, back towards his happy people.

As the man strode off, Tomps shook his head, sat down and stared into the flames of his fire. Confused, Greta just sat down beside him and heard him mumbling quietly under his breath. She wasn't quite sure what he said, but it sounded very much like ...

"No respect."

So the remainder of the afternoon was spent working on the remains of the slain animals while the meat slow roasted over the fire. There was clearly more meat than could be eaten so when it was ready, the best cuts were consumed first.

Everyone feasted and Tomps watched as the islanders gorged themselves and relished every mouthful of this, for them, rare chance to gross out on meat. He of course accepted the huge portion of pork thrust into his hands. Who would not accept the offer of free food, and it was very good, but he did not take much enjoyment from it.

Finally, stuffed and satisfied, the villagers settled down amongst the scattered debris that remained of their feasting, and relaxed into the evening glow to talk, laugh and look forward to a good night's sleep with a full belly.

Greta ate alongside Tomps and tried to be cheerful company, but the warrior's face seemed reluctant to break into a smile at her villages good fortune. She did not understand.

At last night fell and the campfires began to burn lower. Greta snuggled up against Tomps and said quietly.

"You are not happy. Is there nothing I can do to cheer you?"

"It is not you." Tomps didn't feel like explaining. "If your leader and betters cannot see what has happened here, then it will take a greater man than me to tell them." I know Parrish would tell them exactly what they had done, he thought but never said.

"Warrior Tomps." said Greta softly, catching his attention. "Can I do nothing for you?"

"No." He smiled then, pleased at her attempts to please him. "It is a well meant offer and I truly thank you for it. But now let us not think on it any more. I would have us all start again early in the morning." He now just wanted this whole trip to be over. Plus, he had lost the day in hand and wanted to get back to his own village at least in time to join them when they all set off to go to the great temple of Dannu.

He could see that a late start on the morrow would mean perhaps missing the mass departure from Dane-bre and then either having to leave these barbarians to catch up with his friends and village, or worse, have to lead these ignorant people all the way to the Great Temple. And he didn't fancy either much.

"There is something that I can do." Greta interrupted his train of thought.

"Huh?"

"Tomps, I ... I have my right of seed." she said in all seriousness. Was there also a hint of hope in her eyes?

"Oh. Well ..."

Without another word she rose to her feet and rapidly stripped out of her clothing.

Tomps watched in silence and was only half surprised to find himself aroused by the sight. He had after all found her more and more appealing these last few days.

She lay down beside him and waited on her back while he undressed. This was not her first time and she waited for his penetration, knowing what came next.

Tomps lay down beside her and for a moment everything was still. Greta briefly thought that he might refuse her but he was just settling his mind. Where the couple touched he could feel her glow and he couldn't help it, a smile washed onto his face. Propping himself up on one elbow he eyed the contours of Greta's body and suddenly felt a burning need.

Manoeuvring himself on top of her he looked into her eyes. The glow was there also and at that moment he knew that this was not just duty. Slowly, gently he eased himself into her. She just lay passive beneath him but he expected no different.

Greta in contrast immediately expected the rough pounding and thrusting to start but to her utter surprise he just continued with slow, steady thrusts as he let his full weight settle on her and took her into his arms. His breath was on the side of her neck, which she found to be surprisingly pleasant and as his measured thrusting continued the first waves of unexpected pleasure washed through her.

Her loud gasp of surprise was very gratifying to Tomps and he smiled all the more and slightly increased his pace. Greta began gasping, the gasps in tandem with each thrust. Unsure what was happening but realising that it was in no way painful or uncomfortable, she wanted more. To Tomps utter joy she began to push back against him with her hips and as if it were a sign, he pulled her to him with his arms. She responded in kind and reached around him. Her palms pressed on his back and urged him on.

They were together in this now and Tomps was taking real pleasure in carrying Greta to somewhere she had never been before. She now began gasping loudly and releasing moans of pleasure out into the night air. She had never felt it's like before, and it was wonderful. Then her first orgasm came. The waves of feeling rushed out from where their bodies were joined. Rushed out to the very ends of her being. She cried out and clenched all her muscles around the wonderful man who was doing this to her. Her speech was lost and it was all she could do to pant loudly for breath.

This pleased Tomps immensely and to try and hold onto that moment he increased the speed of his thrusts even more. But he was drawn along with her and as he managed to raise her to a second orgasm, he peaked at the same moment. She cried out again as Tomps pulled her so tightly to him and with a final thrust of his hips, his seed thundered into her.

They clung to each other, both panting and gasping in satisfaction and holding onto the moment for as long as they could. After the timeless feeling of togetherness they released their breath, the glorious tension of their muscles eased and with a great whooshing out of sighs the couple slumped together.

Tomps raised his head and looked into Greta's eyes. How they shone. In a totally un-warrior like moment he smiled broadly at her, hugged her tightly again then in an almost instinctual act, kissed her on the mouth, as he had seen his Chieftain do to his own wife several times. Greta didn't know why he did this, but she pressed her lips back onto his, another never before experienced but surprisingly pleasurable feeling.

"Oh ... oh." Was all she could say after they parted.

He put a gentle finger to her lips.

"No talk. It is as my Chieftain says, Just feel. I am happy that you are happy."

"I am more than happy." She said, blatantly ignoring a warrior's instruction as she wanted somehow to express how she felt towards him. "I have never known anything like that before. I ... it ..."

Tomps smiled at the compliment.

"I know. I must say that it was a great thing for me also." He looked into her bright eyes, considering for a moment. "When the time comes for us to part, I think that I will go to your father and speak with him."

Greta grinned afresh as she realised what that meant.

"I would gladly be a wife of yours." She breathed and her eyes glowed even more.

Tomps grinned too and then lay back beside her.

"No talk." He repeated. "Sleep now." He pulled his cape over their bare bodies. She came to his side and snuggled up. Tomps pulled her close and gazed up at the clear night sky. His silent grin was almost as bright as the stars above him and he only just remembered to rub the last but one mark off his map before falling asleep.

17

Cajoling the people with promises that they were very near to Dane-bre and the moving on point towards the great gathering at the temple of Dannu, Tomps got the Islanders packed up and moving not too long after sunrise. Looking back as they moved away he sourly viewed the debris and scatter they left behind after their 'glorious' feast. He felt a pang of disgust and guilt and mentally apologised to the Goddess for the disrespect to her land and the animals.

He knew they were a fairly short travelling distance from his home and was looking forward to getting back to familiar surroundings. Even if he might barely have time to catch his breath before moving on again with his own people, it still made him smile.

Greta was at his side and his good humour spilled over onto her. He was glad to speak of his family, his wife and the village itself. It had not occurred to him until he had left on this trip, his mission as Parrish called it, just how much he suddenly missed and therefore loved Dane-bre. Greta was also overtaken by his jolly demeanour and they fell into a comfortable companionship as they walked northward.

Chieftain Garth and his people followed on a short way behind. The Chieftain was not feeling the joy of the two youngsters ahead of him at all. In fact every step that he had to follow behind the young upstart displeased him. He was critically aware of how it was making him look second best to his own warriors. Their mood matched his, not so much at the undermining of their Chieftain's leadership, as to the blatant display that a mere female of no standing in their society was so freely conveying and openly consorting with a warrior. Such a display of disrespect needed to be severely punished in their eyes.

Other than a disconcerting prickle on the back of Tomps neck, he chose to ignore the angry shadow at his back. He knew that only a short while more and then he could turn the whole bunch of them over into Parrish's keeping. Hah! The great man would no doubt put them in their proper place. This thought made Tomps smile all the more.

Indeed, Parrish was making sure things were in their proper place. He was making final checks of his house, it stores, the damped down fire and anything else he could think of. From ensuring there was ample firewood ready when they returned to checking the dry stores to ensure there was nothing that might rot or putrefy in their absence and attract pests, cause a stink or even become a health risk. Similar checks were going on throughout Danebury as a final act before the village set off on its own pilgrimage to the great temple of Dannu.

The people there had also risen early but they were in no great rush. Once the Chieftain was sure that everyone else was happy the village was set fair, then they would swing the great gate shut behind them and set off towards the northwest.

The holy man was first at the gate and waited patiently for the people to come to him in their family units until everyone was there. The Chieftain was always last in this respect. He would come down from his high house on the hill, checking as he went that no one was left behind, then give the nod for the exodus to begin.

Parrish gave a final glance around and nodded to Juli. Her pack was fairly small and light. He did not know what was in it but knew she did not need to barter for much at the gathering. If she really needed an item all he had to do as Chieftain was ask and it would be produced. He very rarely used this product of his position but it was a nice thing to know and to be able to fall back on if necessary.

Juli scooped up little Chris, who clearly thought he could run anywhere he wanted to go but was just as happy to be safe in his mother's arms, and the three of them went out into the clear air of the day. Parrish tied the door blanket shut, straightened up and turned to scan the land out beyond the confines of the hillfort as he always did from his threshold, looking finally down and away towards the East River.

Almost at the same moment as he saw the group of people walking down alongside the river coming from the north, he recognised them. In an instant he understood. They had obviously crossed at the crossing place further upriver. Smaller in number than the people of Danebury, these were the people of Woolbury. Parrish guessed not more than seventy souls, all led by Chieftain Shimon. A small smile spread across Parrish's his face. It was unexpected but he quickly realised that it made good sense. They were a smaller group, thus more vulnerable to attack from a full size village. So, although not overly friendly, they were not openly hostile to the people at Danebury. It looked like Shimon had done the sensible, very Chieftain like thing, and come to throw in his lot with Parrish and his people, at least for the duration of the solstice armistice. Strength in numbers for the journey across open country to and from Avebury. Yes, there was sound logic in Shimon's reasoning.

He was just about to set off down to meet Shimon and ensure the smooth transition to the joining of both villages for the journey when a cry went up from someone near the gate. More of Parrish's villagers joined in and suddenly everyone was looking to the south, downstream.

Parrish followed their gazes and saw a second large group emerging from the trees. At their head, separated by a fair gap, was a lone pair and even at this distance he felt sure that one of them was Tomps. Open mouthed he watched on as with terrible timing, both villages along the edge of the east river spotted each other. From his high point at the top of Dane-bre Parrish's skin prickled as he saw the change in demeanour of them all and almost at the same moment each village went into defence mode. He knew next they would go on the attack. Horrific realisation crossed his face as he could see then the imminent clashing of two unknown villages. In moments there would be carnage, men killing for trophies and mass death.

"Shit. Shit. Shit!" Parrish shouted in English to no one in particular. Juli spun at the dread in his voice and saw the look on her husband's face. "How the fuck do I stop this?" he gasped.

Juli felt a great fear then, knowing her husband would throw himself between the villages and die if he had to, to try and stop the battle if he could.

"I have only seen you stop a whole village once before." She said, the words spilling from her mouth before she could stop them, dread in her own voice.

"That's it!" he blurted again in English as realisation dawned.

Spinning on his heel he charged back into his cabin, bursting the door blanket asunder as he charged straight through it. Mere moments later he re-emerged and Juli looked on in horror at the object clutched in his fist. It was Dannu's Man's black death giver.

Checking the safety on the handgun he had brought back with him from the 20th century, Parrish tucked the weapon into his waistband and sprinted off down towards the main gate.

All this time the two disparate villages drew slowly closer. Tomps suddenly found himself in a no man's land between the two groups, standing approximately forty paces from each one. To her credit Greta had remained by his side. She looked terrified as she scanned back and forth between the people of her own village on one side and the unknown people on the other.

Tomps dropped his war hammer in the attempt not to look threatening and raised his hands, shouting loudly.

"Do not attack! There is no threat if you do not attack. We are all here to go to the temple of Dannu!"

His basic diplomacy fell on deaf ears. Fear of attack from any other village, and the natural aggressiveness of the Neolithic warrior, was too powerful to resist. Tomps had had no dealings at all with Shimon's village but he had led Garth's people for several days. Perhaps they would listen to reason. Turning his back on the people of Woolbury he faced Garth and his men and shouted again.

"Do not attack. Do not..."

The man immediately to Chieftain Garth's right already held a half drawn bow in his hands. Tomps recognised him instantly as one of the men he had bested that day on the beach, the disfigured nose a giveaway. Even as Tomps was trying to finish his sentence the warrior with the broken nose drew his bow and brought it up to aim. At that instant Tomps saw that the man was aiming at him! This was not self-defence he realised; this was revenge.

The Danebury warrior burst into a sprint towards the archer who, at that moment also realizing he was now coming under direct attack himself from his intended victim, rushed his shot. The arrow whooshed across the short distance and missed Tomps, close enough though to pluck at the shoulder of his buckskin shirt as it passed by. A moment later Tomps was on him, bare handed but filled with deadly determination to kill the man who had just tried to kill him. At that instant, with the release of the arrow and when he had burst into his run, it was as if it were the signal for everyone else to jump to the attack. The warriors of both villages were galvanised into action and charged across the gap between them, axes and clubs raised, great yells coming from their throats.

But the delay caused by Tomps failed attempts to stop the clash of the villages was not all in vain. It had given Parrish enough time to clear the village gate and charge down the slope towards the two groups. But he knew he could not get between the two groups in time as he witnessed Tomps gesticulating, then that initial shot that seemed was the silent signal for the ensuing battle to start.

The two villages clashed together, even as Parrish ran up to the battling crowd.

"STOP!" he yelled at the top of his voice, but he could not make himself heard. Men were already being struck down.

He raised the pistol into the air and squeezed the trigger. The deafening crash of the weapons discharge stopped almost everyone then in their tracks. People from all across the conflict froze at the sudden assault on their eardrums and heads turned to see where the sudden, arresting, unexpected and painfully loud sound had come from. They all saw the tall man, many of his own warriors pulling up behind him now, standing alone with a mysterious black object in his raised fist.

By now Tomps had knocked his own opponent brutally to the ground and was about to smash his fist into the man's throat when the crash of the gun rolled out across the countryside. He too froze and looked up to see his great friend and Chieftain in full command, his feet planted wide apart, chest heaving and his face like thunder. But Parrish never saw Tomps. Never even glanced in his friend's direction. His full focus was fixed on another man he already knew. Chieftain Garth.

The island Chieftain was sat astride a fallen warrior from Woolbury who he had beaten to the ground with his war club. Garth looked too at Parrish but chose to ignore his order. Perhaps it was because he did not understand what the object in Parrish's hand did. Perhaps it was because he had at no time being told or realised that Parrish too was a Chieftain, or perhaps it was simply because Garth was a Chieftain and no one told him what to do, and certainly no one was about to stop him from claiming a new trophy. After giving Parrish the briefest look of complete contempt, he turned to look back down at the man beneath him and drew his war club back to strike the killing blow.

The Chieftain of Dane-bre did not give second chances.

Before the blow could fall Parrish brought his handgun to bear and shot Chieftain Garth through the chest. The second loud report made everyone flinch. Those of Danebury and Woolbury had seen the black death giver and its lethal work once before.

Chieftain Garth jerked in surprise, shocked disbelief on his face as he looked sideways and up at Parrish who was still standing some ten paces away. Then his eyes glazed over, the club fell from his numbed hand and he slowly tilted away to one side and flopped limply to the ground, dead.

Everyone stood, shocked at the sudden end of the man, struck down when he was not within the tall man's reach.

The quiet was broken by the moans of men, injured on the ground. Parrish breathed deeply, looked quickly about then barked out.

"Each village is to help their wounded and attend to their dead. Both villages will part without more fighting. You island people go back into the trees and wait till I come to you. Shimon, gather your people and wait by the river. I will be with you shortly."

There were no arguments, just nods of compliance. No one was about to argue with Dannu's Man. People quickly turned away and went to the aid of the fallen.

Tomps strode purposely over to his Chieftain and stood before him grinning.

"I am very glad to be back, my Chieftain." he said.

"It is good to see you too, my young friend." Parrish replied without humour. He was still trying to shake off the after-effects of coldly gunning down a human being. He tucked the pistol back into his waistband and nodded to his friend.

"It looks like you have had a very interesting time."

"Yes, I did." agreed Tomps. "And I met someone I would like to show you. This is..." he turned but found himself alone. "Huh?"

A short distance back some of the women, including Karin, Klud's first wife and some women from the island, we're crouching around a body on the ground. Tomps rushed over and looked down in horror. The kneeling women were tending to Greta's body. A single arrow stuck starkly up from her chest, deeply embedded just below the neckline of her bodice.

Tomps just stared down. One of the Islander women looked sadly up into the warrior's distraught face.

"She only said four words." The woman whispered.

"What?" Tomps blurted out. "What words? What words did she say?"

"All she said was, 'Tell Tomps, thank you'."

The Dane-bre warrior stood in silence. He trembled slightly and clenched and unclenched his fists several times. Then without another word he spun on his heel and set off back towards the island people. At the front of the group stood, among others, the man with the disfigured face who had fired the fatal arrow. As Tomps closed fear swept across the man's face, for despite fumbling with the dagger at his belt, he knew he had no defence against the Danebury man.

But Tomps was stopped short by a restraining hand on his shoulder. He spun again and found Parrish there, towering over him. With a firm voice the tall man said.

"No more killing today, Tomps."

The Neolithic warrior squared up to his Chieftain. Properly squared up to him and Parrish saw the fire and anguish burning in the youngster's eyes. He realised that someone this boy loved had just been killed. He could also see a wild rage in him and he seemed barely in control. Looking deep into the young man's eyes, Parrish repeated more softly this time.

"No more killing today."

Tomps glared for a moment more, then the fire seemed to go out of him and his eyes dimmed. He now saw who faced him as his sanity returned. Parrish noted the change and also saw something in the boy die. His youthful enthusiasm, boyish upbeat demeanour and readiness for some fun suddenly vanished. It was replaced with a harder glint and Parrish knew in that moment the youngster was a boy no more. A sadness swept over him and he just looked at the angry man before him.

Tomps gave his Chieftain and acknowledging nod, but no more, then turned back to the island warrior with the broken nose, who seemed rooted to the spot.

“Two times now we have met and you still live.” He hissed. “After today, if you ever come within my sight again, I will kill you where you stand. No matter who tells me not to!”

And with that he blatantly exposed his back to the stunned warrior and walked away past Parrish, not even acknowledging the tall man. Away back towards Dane-bre, not trusting himself to look back at his lost love, and leaving the women to take care of the body.

18

It took the remainder of the morning to sort out the bloody mess that was the aftermath of the 'battle of Dane-bre'.

At Parrish's count there were four dead from the Woolbury camp and five from the Islanders. It took a bit of persuading to allow the dead to keep hold of their heads but when Parrish refused to allow their bodies to be held up for the sky spirits unless they were whole, the different factors finally relented. The two holy men prepared the souls of the dead for departure in a rather hurried ceremony in the shrine hut, before all nine bodies were carried over to the trestles standing on the knoll in the east. Feast time for the crows, thought Parrish, but wisely kept the thought to himself.

It also became suddenly clear to him that all the victims in a Neolithic fight were either dead or walking wounded. It was a further surprise to find that none of the injured was so badly hurt that they had to have intensive care. Combat was definitely an all or nothing conflict with these people! Parrish was quietly grateful because it made his hastily re-jigged preparations for the long walk easier.

He was happy enough for the people of Woolbury to join his own people on the walk to Avebury but he did impress upon Shimon their agreement of no fighting unless on their specific say so. Shimon just nodded and offered that his people would walk close by, but not mingle. Parrish readily agreed. He knew the women would no doubt greet, mix and talk, but it was a wise move to keep the warriors at least a little distance apart.

When Parrish went to the Islanders, all squatting in a big, confused bunch in the tree line by the river, he did not hide his displeasure at their actions. Part of his displeasure at them was for the grief they had inflicted on Tomps. But he knew the people of the times seemed somehow to shrug off death and he was confident his friend would quickly bounce back. He had spoken with Tomps and although the young man was still sullen at his loss, he relayed to his Chieftain everything that had happened. Parrish had to agree with his young friend's opinion. Barbarians with no respect for Dannu.

He instructed the island clan to follow on behind the two village group that would be travelling ahead of them. They had no concept of measured time in hours so Parrish just told them that they could find their way to the great temple by following their tracks. But he was in no mood to be benevolent. He told them flatly that they must stay well back until they all reached their destination.

"If I so much as see you behind me." he growled. "I will turn both village's warriors on you and wipe you from the face of the land." Fear showed on all their faces at that. Then he softened his tone. "You must understand that you need this more than we need you. Do not be stupid and throw it all away for want of a few trophies. There will be peace at the gathering and past errors will be forgotten. Just follow our footsteps to the temple and once there trading, tools, new blood and Dannu are all yours for the asking." If you can curb your bloodthirsty aggressions, he thought but did not say out loud.

There was a small sea of uncertain nods in answer and he just gave a short nod in return and left them to stew on his words.

Finally, with the early summer sun cresting the sky at midday, the people of all the villages gathered up their equipment, children and weapons, and at Parrish's signal set off towards the north-west. Looking back at the never before seen biggest ever crowd of Neolithic bodies as they moved away from the hillfort, he turned to Klud and said.

"If the Islanders can keep their peace long enough to get to Dannu's temple, we should not have any trouble. But let us keep a good eye on them, yes?"

"You are right of course." Klud nodded in agreement. "But they will have their minds on other things for the moment. That will keep them busy for a while."

"Oh? What is that?"

"They are now without a Chieftain. A new leader must be chosen, and that before they arrive at the temple. As you know, a Chieftain must present his people to the Goddess."

"Of course." Parrish mentally admonished himself. How could that have got past him? Mind you. A lot had gone on this very morning.

"And..." added Klud with a knowing smile. "As the killer of their last Chieftain, you will need to have the mark put upon your neck."

"Oh..." Parrish's face fell.

Klud stifled a laugh, clapped his tall friend on the shoulder and walked off to join his family, a broad grin on his face.

The massed people walked on across the Neolithic landscape, together but in their respective groups. Initially, as everyone settled into their pace, there were numerous surreptitious glances back and forth across the gap between those of Dane-bre and Olann-bre. The wary eyes soon became less alert as the drudge of the trek took hold. Even looking behind for the not seen but keenly felt presence of the Islanders behind them became less frequent as everyone settled.

Then one or two women sidled out to meet one or two women from the opposite group. Items began to be exchanged. Perhaps a small piece of equipment, maybe a few bone needles or strip of cloth. A handful of early fruits were offered for some dried meats. Parrish noticed and he smiled at the tentative starting of trade. It really helped to ease some of the tension. He nodded his approval across to Shimon, who reluctantly nodded back. Parrish smothered a smile, Dannu bless the girls, he thought.

By the end of the first day, when everyone pitched up for the night, smokeless fires were allowed considering there were so many warriors present, and the women almost, as if it were expected, grouped together and had a mass cook up, preparing a meal for everyone. The holy men from both villages worked as one, passing among the people and eating together as a sign of the solidarity of their belief. It warmed Parrish's heart to see what he hoped were the embryonic stages of perhaps a basic coalition between the villages. Shimon nodded in approval too although for him it was more that his village was reaping the benefit from the extra food and protection in this great group.

As the light faded Parrish walked out beyond the circle of light and people of the double camp and gazed back the way they had come across the dark landscape.

Away in the distance the faint glow of fires from the Islander encampment could be seen. Klud stepped up beside him and they stared off at the soft glow on the horizon.

Shimon suddenly appeared, coughing to announce his approach then joined them staring out into the night.

"If it was just my people alone out there in Dannu's land." he said. "I would not signal to anyone who might be looking, just where I was."

"Nor I." said Parrish without looking at the Chieftain. "They have been alone for so long and they have forgotten so much."

Despite being flanked by two Chieftains, Klud felt compelled to add his own thoughts.

"As long as they stay back there till we reach the temple." He said to no one in particular. "There they can be taken into Dannu's care. I am getting an ache in my neck looking back over my shoulder all the time." To his surprise and pleasure both the Chieftains chuckled.

"You speak wise words, my friend." agreed Parrish. "With the good wishes of the Goddess, they will keep their distance tomorrow and then we will be at the temple. I will be quite happy to be rid of them too."

"You also speak wise words." said Shimon flatly and, as if for him that was the end of the conversation, he just spun on his heel and headed off back towards his people.

"He is in agreement with us." said Klud when Shimon had gone. "But I still do not think I will turn my back on him or his people."

Parrish chuckled again and patted his friend on the shoulder.

"As I say, you speak wise words, my friend."

They smiled together in the dark, shared one last glance at the glow on the horizon then also spun on their heels and returned to the warmth of the fires and their people.

Everyone was up with the dawn. Food was readied and consumed, camps were broken, packed away and once more the people from the Danebury area set off towards the northern edge of Salisbury Plain.

Parrish waited till his people were up and moving, letting them move away before he did his final check to ensure nothing and no one had been inadvertently left behind.

Seeing it all clear, he let a small smile spread across his face as a final glance back at the way they had come gave him a brief glimpse of a lone scout off in the mid distance. The man hastily dived out of sight but the nearness of a warrior clearly from the Island clan did not unsettle Parrish. He knew the islander was just confirming that his people would not stumble into the lead group by setting off too early themselves. Acting as if he had seen nothing, Parrish casually sauntered away to rejoin the rear of the moving mass out ahead of him.

The two village group made slow but steady progress across the remainder of the Plain. All things being equal, Parrish knew that the pace was standard and they would easily be descending into the Vale of Pewsey before nightfall and there have one more camp before the final push to the Gathering Point the following morning. He glanced across to his holy man, nearby. The little man felt his Chieftains stare and, returning it, nodded as if he could read the tall man's mind. Parrish nodded back and they both turned to look towards the future.

The massed people were now almost that, a single mass of people, by the time they had all settled down in the dense woodland of the Vale of Pewsey for the second night's camp. The two villages remained in their individual clans as they created their fires and made ready for sleep, but the division between them was now not so clear cut. Now they were but a short morning walk away from the Gathering Point the next day and the two village holy men were already passing among the people. Calming them, reminding them of their reverence and in many other subtle ways making sure the people were in the right frame of mind to worship the Goddess.

Less belligerent and more benevolent was the silent thought that came to Parrish's mind and brought a grin to his face as he watched the shamen at their work. A sight admired all the more when he realised the two men were overlapping to the warriors and women of both camps. For the rest of the year Parrish knew that *his* holy man was fiercely proud and protective of Dane-bre, just as he had no doubt the Olann-bre holy man was of his own village. But now they were of one mind. Their loyalty now was first and foremost to Dannu. All were equal in their given status under the eyes of the

Goddess and her servants and it was becoming plain to him now that as the holy men moved amongst the peoples, they were all now coming to realise it during this short, special time of the year.

It warmed Parrish's heart and he once again felt the love for the people of these times, and especially for those who were *his* people, create a warm glow within him. Several individuals he passed gave him subtle but still noticeably curious glances, until he realised he was swanning about with a silly grin on his face. He mentally ticked himself off and quickly re-established a more stern and Chieftain-like countenance.

But it didn't diminish the glow.

19

The following day, around mid-morning, the massed group of Dane-bre and Olann-bre ambled into the gathering point from the well-used track that approached from the East. There were already several different village groups there, well spread around the huge area of open ground.

The size of the crowd led in by Parrish grew lots of confused and curious glances. The initial surprise dimmed quickly when, as soon as they passed into the open, the band split into two groups and found themselves separate spots to settle in. Parrish didn't get so much as a thank you nod from Shimon. He and his villagers just walked away. Parrish did not care. He was happy enough to have been of help. After all, it was his original idea to site the once lost village of Shimon's on the hill on the far side of the east river. But now these people were safely under the protection of Dannu and her servants, he understood that they would want to appear to be masters of their own fate.

Klud looked to his tall friend, who just shrugged back, dismissing the moment with a casual wave of his hand and set off to the officially greeted by the holy men waiting inside the central shrine hut that straddled the boundary palisade wall enclosing the northern aspect of the wide, horseshoe shaped gathering point. The Neolithic warrior tipped his head in return, more in acknowledgement that his Chieftain was the better man rather than thinking that just walking away after being escorted safely to the temple of Dannu was something a lesser Chieftain might have taken as a great insult. More to the point, Klud was keenly interested in what would or would not happen when the uneducated island people behind them eventually arrived. That he thought would be quite interesting to witness.

In fact two more different village groups had arrived and settled themselves before the Islanders eventually walked uncertainly in. They were astounded by the massed villagers before them and stood in utter confusion at the mouth of the pathway for a long time, unsure of what to do. Only after a quiet word from Chieftain Parrish, standing in silent observation in the doorway of the shrine hut, did a small committee of three holy men step out and go to greet the people where they still stood. They had not realised that not only had the Islanders never been here before, but they did not have a holy guide of their own to help them out with advice to their new leader.

Parrish looked on, not just to see the struggle, but to try and identify the newly elected leader. But no one stood out from the strange crowd. Warriors naturally bristled to project confidence and aggression. The women clustered together like herd animals for protection. Once again Parrish noticed that many of the women were extremely similar in look, build and colouring. He doubted he was the only one who realised that this was a blatant display of the result of inbreeding. But mostly he was surprised that no man stood out from the crowd as a leader of men. There were no orders or directions. No deference that he could see to one particular individual from all the others. It bothered him more than he cared to admit that he could see no real leader and no definite hierarchy or structure to the village before him. He recalled Tomps telling him that Chieftain Garth had appeared to have a rather loose grip on the control of his men. This new leader, whoever he was, seemed to have even less!

Groups continued to turn up intermittently through the day.

Before the daylight began to fade it was evident that just about all the known villages of the south land's had arrived in good time. Well over a dozen great clusters of people, most more than a hundred strong, had found themselves a place in the wide expanse and were settling in nicely. Cooking fires burned small and hot, some warriors were already renewing contact with friends and acquaintances from the last gathering and the general hub-bub was of a good humour. All that was apart from the obvious wariness that radiated out from the unknown group at one end of the gathering point and was reflected back towards them from everyone else. They kept to themselves and no one apart from the women of Dane-bre and a few of the women from Olann-bre seemed willing to get involved with them. Juli, Karin and the others of Danebury did not fear the islander group. They felt safe under the protection of Dannu's Man and, although respectfully avoiding the island warriors, as was right and proper, the ladies were already engaging in some barter and trade with their female opposite numbers. A few women from Woolbury were bravely but tentatively joining in too but men from their village had recently been slain at the hands of the islander warriors and goodwill towards them was in short supply.

Parrish and Klud watched judiciously from the sidelines. Both were thinking the same thing.

"The island people look on edge." Parrish commented to Klud, a casual remark if one did not know the Chieftain of Dane-bre very well.

"Yes." Klud nodded. "They have not settled. Their new leader has no fine or powerful words for them, I think. They need to be calmed. Do they not know that there is no threat to them here?"

"The holy ones are doing their best to keep the peace here but the big problem as I see it is that the people from the island have no real respect for Dannu. And here, that is what really keeps the peace."

"You are wise as ever, my friend." Klud nodded again without looking at his tall companion. "They should be very careful not to offend the Goddess. Her punishment can be swift and terrible. Also, I have spoken before about keeping a watch on Shimon and his warriors, but even more so I feel it would not be at all wise to turn your back on these island people."

Parrish turned to his friend and Klud looked up at him.

"If we keep this up, word will soon be spread that we are the wisest two people we know!" He laughed out loud before his face turned deadly serious. "But you are right. We need to keep an eye out."

As one the pair gave a last look at the group that still managed to remain alone amongst all the other groups, then turned and went about their business before the light faded completely. Expectation was building. Tomorrow was Dannu's day.

Parrish was nudged gently awake by his wife. She sat back and watched as he sat up, rubbed asleep from his eyes then stretched his arms wide. All this followed by a great yawn then he turned to her and smiled. She smiled back at him as he completed his morning 'wake up' ritual, A smile permitted because it would be unseen in the dark. The clear sky was full of stars and Parrish stood and looked about him. Despite the lack of a moon he could still just about make out shadowy movement around him nearby. Juli rose, stood beside him and he slipped his arm about her. The growing excitement around them was almost palpable. And why not? thought Parrish, hell, even I'm excited. It's the solstice!

He was seriously looking forward to the happy ambience of the massed people moving with their holy guides along the stone lined avenue that led all the way to the greatest henge and stone circles in the land. Avebury. Today everyone got to worship at the great shrine and every individual would get their chance to briefly touch the symbol of the Earth Goddess. What was there not to be excited about?

He took the drink he was offered and looked to his wife.

"Are you OK?" he asked. "Everything ready to kick off for the big event?"

She smiled at his odd turn of words but like Klud, always seemed to know what he meant.

"All is well, my husband. People are waking and looking forward to the start of the walk in. We are now waiting for the sign from the holy ones."

"Good point." he replied. "Come to think of it, just where is our man?"

"He has just gone to gather with the others. They are waiting at the entrance to the shine hut. As soon as he saw you awake, he set off. Everyone else in Dane-bre is ready."

Parrish momentarily felt embarrassed that he was the last of his people to rise but then grasped that no one would move until he was ready. The holy man of the village would check on everyone else and when the last man, namely he, was awake then and only then would he say his village was ready. It all made sense now and Parrish tucked the snippet of information away in the back of his mind. Dannu's servants were indeed very well organised. He could see it now. Each holy man would make their own way to the shrine hut on the fence line to declare their village ready. As soon as every representative from each village had arrived, only then would they all be ready to go. And all done in the dark too, he thought. Nice work!

Parrish watched his people near enough to him to be seen at least in silhouette. Some nodded back to him and they all waited eagerly but patiently for the word to go.

Almost imperceptibly at first, people began to move. He registered it first by sound rather than seeing anyone but gradually a very slow momentum began to carry the people towards the central shrine hut. At that point, right across the crowd, warriors began to lift lighted torches into the air above themselves. Lit by the nearest cooking fire embers, they sprung to bright life in their tens, then hundreds. The people were soon shoulder to shoulder and gradually this long funnelling of humanity squeezed down to a two person wide stream that flowed into the hut, past the statue of Dannu there and out the other side, where they congregated at the start of the stone lined avenue. It was for Parrish that first symbolic moment of unity as they were forced together through the narrow tract of the hut. Cheek by jowl, his father used to say. Shoulder to shoulder. Man beside woman, warrior by child, woman alongside leader. It somehow, at least for a short while, squeezed the rigid hierarchy out of the people and they were emerging on the other side with one aim and appreciation. Now there would be good will, friendly talk, unhindered mingling, the prospect of trading to come, and honouring Dannu the Great Goddess.

Parrish was suddenly struck by the realisation that it was more than likely the whole layout of the gathering point, the high palisade containing wall and the necessary funnelling of the people through the narrow gap to begin their approach to Avebury was carefully designed and managed. It was very clever, he saw, and a fresh new appreciation rose within him of the whole cult of the Earth Goddess. This was not his first time here but still he was learning new, unexpected and enlightening things. He couldn't help it. Like everyone else that he could see around him under the flickering torch light, a happy grin settled on his face and he was genuinely looking forward to this morning's remarkable event.

20

From the rear, a runner passed the massed people and reached the leading group of holy men, informing them that everyone had now cleared the shrine hut at the gathering point. He did feel that he had to add that the last people through were the islanders, but everyone was now ready to be led off. With a respectful bow the young apprentice stepped aside and took up a position alongside the nearest standing stone. It was a purely personal thing but as his task was to follow on behind the last of the people, he got to enjoy the sight of the massed men and women of the southland's flowing past him in their hundreds. It was a sight he never tired of and the opportunity to people watch hundreds of individuals was a rare and wonderful thing. The smile on his face was a genuine thing and as the throng passed him by, he silently wished them all well. Bless the Goddess.

The holy men led the people in respectful pomp along the stone lined avenue. The great monoliths were more or less evenly spaced apart on either side, alternately pillar then lozenge shaped, creating an 'open' corridor about thirty meters wide. Parrish noted to himself that each one must easily go at least five or six tons in weight and the pillar stones were a good ten to twelve feet tall. Lit up as they were by the unevenly flickering torches as they were passed, the uneven light seemed to make their still, rough hewn surfaced grey bodies flicker and undulate. And with the blackness of the night pressing in behind them, to the steadily moving crowd it almost appeared as if the people were motionless and the stones themselves were mysteriously marching away backwards past them. It was at once both mesmerising and somehow soothing. As if the land of the Earth Goddess, on this special morning, was magically coming to life to welcome the people into Dannu's world.

There were some quiet mutterings of appreciation and the occasional mother's voice softly calming or reassuring a babe. Yet even these sounds were somehow elemental and in keeping with the feeling of the event as everyone held a hush of wonder and worship. Parrish had to think for a long moment before he could put his finger on just where he had experienced this feeling before. Then it came to him. That quiet warmth from the watching people in the pews as they witness the bride to be being walked with radiant pride up the isle on her father's arm. Only here the feeling was tenfold. Of calm, pleasure, full of warmth, rising expectation and good wishes for the imminent event to come.

There was no hurry and the avenue was two and a half kilometres long, but in what seemed to be almost no time at all, the end of it came dimly into view, initially just for the holy men and those people at the vanguard of the great throng.

Parrish knew the layout here well enough and even though he couldn't see, he still steered his gaze left and right, trying to see through the impenetrable dark the entrance to the great stone circle of Avebury. He was well aware of the two enormous lozenge shaped sentinel stones that guarded the south eastern entrance to the great temple. They loomed up in the torches half light, towering over the humbled people as they passed by. But Parrish really would have liked to catch an early glimpse of the truly massive ditch and embankment that encircled the whole complex. Sure, it would be visible to all when the massed people eventually left the henge but to Parrish, the sheer effort of work that must have gone into its construction never failed to stagger and impress and he could have happily stared at its majesty for hours. He realised that he loved this place too and now, as everyone passed through the portal and began to gather under their torch lights, moving slowly around to fully encircle the separate, smaller stone circle in this south eastern quadrant of the great henge, he truly felt one of the Neolithic throng. And, he didn't care a jot if the silly grin on his face was as silly as everyone else's silly grin. For this one glorious moment, everyone was happy.

The people were silent, plainly waiting for something to happen and everyone felt reluctant now to speak at all and risk breaking the reverent, church like atmosphere.

They stood that way for a while, no sound bar the soft fluttering of the flames. Waiting. Then, almost imperceptibly at first, the false dawn started to lighten the sky away to the east. It changed the colour of the sky from black to midnight blue, through the many shades of an ever lightening mauve to a glowing, ember red. It promised to be another fine and sunny day. As the sky lightened people began to extinguish their torches, dropping them to the ground and rolling them with a foot in the wet, dew covered grass. They reluctantly died in their hundreds with protesting hisses.

Parrish used his extra height to its full advantage, scanning the area around him as the stones he knew were there began to reveal themselves in the strengthening half light. The great slabs of rough hewn stone seemed almost to creep stealthily up out of the receding night until they had surrounded the gathered multitude. Further back, behind the hulking megaliths, was that shadowy, high wall of clean chalk, sweeping right round to fully encompass everything and everyone, the portal to the south east where they had entered the only break in the barrier.

As the last vestiges of night slid away beyond the horizon and the early glow of daybreak fell upon the white chalk face, the light was instantly reflected back into the man made arena and everything became clearly visible, as if some mysterious, unseen hand had switched on invisible flood lights. The effect made many people gasp. Parrish, who benefited from his totally unrestricted view of the whole event, nodded in satisfaction, for it was enough to take anyone's breath away.

Surrounding the hushed ring of well over a thousand Neolithic people, where warriors unabashedly rubbed shoulders with women and children, was suddenly revealed the circle of Avebury. Massive stones, most at least four meters high and some half as much again. Beyond the dark, perpendicular slabs was a wide ditch that was deep enough to render its bottom invisible from where the people stood. Banked up behind the ditch was a steep wall of pure white, immaculately clean chalk, at least seven meters high, towering over even the tallest of the great stones.

Parrish looked slowly about. He still recalled the photo's his platoon had been shown of this place when the light infantry were briefed on the importance of not damaging or destroying ancient earthworks or other archaeological sites during their exercises in the Salisbury Plain area. Those images paled into insignificance compared to the sight before him. Just drab, faded and feeble images that completely failed to capture the majesty and grandeur of how it had once been.

As it was now. A mind staggering, gargantuan and unequalled Neolithic monument to human endeavour, commitment and religious belief. Greater even than the more famous Stonehenge circle. Yes, this was Avebury!

The magnificent stone circles of Avebury were first 'discovered' by the man many consider to be the founding father of archaeology, John Aubrey, when he was out fox hunting. It was January in the year sixteen hundred and forty nine. He wrote of it in his journal that Avebury:

'does much exceed in greatness the so renowned Stonehenge as a cathedral doeth a parish church.'

The sheer volume of manpower and effort required to build such a monument in those ancient times supports his sentiment.

The chalk bottomed ditch measured three hundred and forty seven meters across its inner diameter and was between seven and ten meters deep, enclosing a level area of twenty eight and a half acres. The seven meter high outer bank has a median circumference of one thousand three hundred and fifty three meters, in itself an incredible feat of Neolithic engineering. The volume of the ditch equates to an unbelievable three million nine hundred thousand cubic feet. The material from it had undoubtedly been used in the construction of the bank beyond it and so, using just antler picks and shoulder blade shovels, the people who laboured in its construction had removed from the earth two hundred thousand *tons* of chalk!

Independent of the many smaller stones lining the avenue that linked the ring to the Sanctuary beside the river Kennet, the twentieth century man remembered the stats banged out to the soldiers there at that distant, long ago MOD briefing. They were trying to impress upon the ignorant squaddies the scale and magnificence of it. The megalithic outer ring of Avebury has a circumference of three hundred and thirty one meters and contains one hundred and thirty roughly shaped sarsen slabs. These huge stones, weighing as much as sixty tons each, fall into two basic types, tall and straight sided or diamond shaped. Amazingly, he could even now recall it almost word for word. The largest pair flanked the entrance to the temple, which everyone here had passed between as they completed their long walk. The skill, care and expertise of positioning and erecting these stones paralleled the remarkable feat of the construction of the ditch.

In the centre of the great ring are two smaller stone circles. Both lying on a north-north west to south-south east alignment and one hundred and three meters across, they each consist of thirty high, broad slabs of sarsen stone. One lay in the north-north east quadrant and the other in the south-south east. Inside each circle lay a single large, sculpted oblong stone resembling a sacrificial altar.

It was the south-south east circle of stones that was at the hub of the ring of people, and he returned his attention to its centre as the brightening of the sky signalled the imminent arrival of the sun. The altar stone at its centre was perfectly aligned with the impending midsummer sun rise. Around this stone stood a ring of flower and feather men that Parrish did not recognise, even among the holy men he had seen since his arrival at the Sanctuary gathering point and his previous visits to the temple and its village beyond the stones.

These men were older than most of the people who now watched them with baited breath. Their clothes were impressive if not too functional, plainly made for ceremonial use. They wore hats of fur that were crowned with fans of display feathers from the tails of some unidentifiable but colourful wild fowl. Their tunics were similarly adorned and the men wore the tasselled leg straps that Parrish had seen for the first time on his own village's holy man. Around the men's necks hung strings of drilled stones of varying shapes, tiny miniatures of the great stones that now encircled everyone. Across their shoulders like mini capes were tied wraps of woven grasses, decorated around the edges with bright spring and early summer flowers. Their entire outfits were unmistakably symbolic to every aspect of the Earth and its life giving properties.

As one, this ring of undoubtedly highly revered men raised their arms into the air above the altar stone. As the very top of the suns orb became visible above the rim of the eastern edge of the earthen bank they started to chant. The chant was at first softly melodic and low in tone. As the men began to increase their volume it turned in to a song. The words were lost on Parrish, the language unrecognizable, but it was undeniably a good song. After only a short time he had to make a conscious effort to prevent himself from swaying to the steady rhythm. The holy men from the visiting villages, positioned at roughly equal spaces around the inner edge of the ring of villagers, started to join in.

The swooping and rising pulse of the song filled the bowl, it giving the sound of a throbbing resonance as the musical strains rebounded from the walls of the earthen amphitheatre. The glorious chant had a spell binding, mesmeric effect on the hushed crowd and Parrish could see many people near him starting to sway ever so slightly, like corn ears in a gentle breeze.

During all this time the sun was rising steadily over the rim of the circular temple. Its bright rays illuminated the western side of the bowl. The line of shadow that marked the leading edge of unobstructed sunlight crept slowly back across the upturned faces of the crowd, towards the inner ring of stones and the central altar stone. Parrish watched, eyes aglow with anticipation. The people's faces seemed to light up with joy as the warm rays illuminated them, many apparently unable to stop themselves from smiling, no matter what their sex, age or standing in their own community. No one objected. Even the giant stones beyond the crowd seemed to drink in the light. They seemed to swell in it, their surfaces changing dramatically from a dull charcoal black to a lighter, warmer, greyish white.

The sun's rays crept closer and ever closer to the inner circle of stones with the singing, chanting holy men and the almost magnetic altar stone at their centre. As the golden light at last reached the old men they brought their joyous song to a rousing crescendo and then, with perfect timing, every single chanting holy man inside the giant ringed temple of the Earth Goddess stopped. There was total silence. All eyes were focused on the altar stone. The sun's rays finally fell upon it.

The light caused an astounding transformation. It changed the stone from being a flat, black hulking table top of rock into a bright, almost living beacon! It took on a sudden, golden hue and gave the appearance of reflecting back the rays of the sun. Parrish had of course witnessed it before but it still astounded him. The stone just seemed to glow with a soft, warm light, as if the whole solid block of rock had become a hollow model of frosted glass, lit from within by bright candles. From all around the crowd came gasps of wonder, amazement and blissful satisfaction. Parrish had to resist the urge to punch the air in joy.

The two holy men who stood at each end of the long stone, seeming almost supremely indifferent to the spectacle before them, lowered their hands onto the bright rock. The rest took a few measured paces back, keeping their own hands raised high in the air. Without a single word of command from anyone, the massed people of Neolithic southern England began to walk in single file into the inner stone ring from each end, past the retreated holy men.

As they came alongside the softly glowing stone each person reached out and trailed or rubbed one hand along its top surface, glad and grateful for this once a year opportunity to touch the life giving warmth of the all powerful Earth Goddess.

There was no pushing or shoving at all from the crowd. They were all eager but no one was in a rush, everyone certain that they would be able to feel the warmth of Dannu long before the rock faded back to its former state of lifelessness.

The old holy men watched solemnly as the multitude passed slowly and simultaneously along each side of the stone.

Parrish remembered that the stone felt hot enough to burn the skin, at least to those of the religion who were 'in tune' with Dannu. He let the palm of his outstretched hand float just above the surface of the altar as he walked slowly by.

Trying hard to act as if nothing had happened, he followed Juli and flowed with the procession out of the other side of the inner stone circle and rejoined the rest of his village. Like all the others that had already passed the stone, they were watching the rest enjoy their brief moment of closeness with the Earth Goddess.

As the number of people still waiting to touch the Goddess dwindled, it became clear that the island villagers, unsure of themselves, were deliberately hanging back and eventually they were the last group to approach the glowing, unearthly looking altar stone.

A rather inconspicuous looking individual, at least he looked just that to Parrish, led the group to the edge of the stone. If he is their new Chieftain, he thought, he doesn't seem very commanding.

The islanders extended their hands and began to file past the altar between it and the lines of holy men. Almost immediately the great slab of rock dimmed. It didn't switch off or go out, but the bright glow emanating from it lessened significantly. There was a universal gasp from the watching throng, and the whole island group under their gaze stiffened visibly in defence, but continued to file past the stone.

The holy men beside them appeared totally unmoved by this

unusual occurrence but Parrish was quick enough to notice a few darting glances on the faces beneath the rims of the fabulous head dresses.

Finally the long procession past the altar stone was done. Once all the people had gathered again beyond the smaller ring of stones and after a respectful silence, the old holy men once more burst into song. It was a different chant but still one of rejoicing. Just about everyone, bar the still rather bewildered islanders, was cheerful and smiling, for that brief moment all taboo's, restrictions and restraints forgotten. Once the second song had been sung and the last words died away, the holy men clapped their hands loudly and bowed deeply to the altar stone. Every single person in the great stone and earth circle of Avebury did the same. There was another long moment of silence, and then the people nearest the entrance to the temple turned and quietly made their way out of the earthen ring. Gradually everyone else followed suit, reluctantly leaving the still glowing altar stone to the private delectation of the old holy men of the temple.

The great Neolithic throng ambled in a now much more disorganized manner back down the stone lined avenue towards the Sanctuary. The quiet hub-bub of different voices had a hallowed edge to it as the people talked in low tones of their brush with Dannu. No matter how many times it was experienced, touching the Earth Goddess was always a moment to savour, not to mention being a great honour.

Parrish turned as the village holy man appeared by his side. The little man never said a word as they walked along together, apparently waiting. Finally, the tall man smiled and obliged him.

"I noticed the reaction of the stone towards the island people, as I am sure did everyone else. Does it mean what I think it means?"

"And what do you think it means?" asked the shaman.

"That the Goddess sees the lack of respect for her in the hearts of the islanders." After a moment he felt compelled to add. "Just as I do."

There was a long silence before the holy man said quietly.

"I hope for their sake they do not offend her anymore." He paused then added. "Because her wrath is swift and terrible."

"You speak true words, my friend." Parrish could not deny it. "But at this moment I am more worried about what her people here might do if *they* see such a lack of respect."

‘Cos no one likes to see their gods rubbished, he thought, but kept those words to himself.

21

Now returned to the gathering point, there was jollity and camaraderie. Breakfasts were heartily consumed and old friends were reunited, acquaintances made and new friendships forged.

Trading began in earnest, these early beginnings of commerce helped along with food and drink. Parrish watched with great fondness and some amusement. Sometimes it seemed that deep conversation and stiff bargaining went on over what seemed to him to be quite trivial items. Yet he knew those pieces of thick and stiff leather for the soles of shoes, or well spun wool yarn, tight and thin for good stitching, was as precious as gold used to be in his old life.

In fact, despite the fact that the Islander warriors he had coaxed into coming to Avebury were still reluctant to mingle and were constantly wary, the women of that clan were doing what Parrish could only be described as brisk business.

Their similarity in look and build that spoke to the rest of the gathered masses of in breeding, did not deterred them from serious bartering. The women of the island were still considered handsome by some of the men from other villages and Parrish saw at least a couple of the ladies bought as wives to different tribes. More important to him though was that he saw some women from the other tribes moving to the island clan. Not all of them looked that happy about it but had no choice. Parrish hated to see what amounted to a slave trade going on before him but this was now and it was the way of things, and he knew that this new blood was vital to the future well being of the Islanders.

Trying to concentrate on the finer aspects of the trading sessions instead, he quizzed Juli, who he had already seen doing deals with some of the island ladies, just why their goods seemed to be so desirable.

She nodded at him knowingly.

"It is a good year to be here for goods." she smiled. "The island people want our wool and our leather." Parrish nodded at that. More proof, if proof were needed, that the more 'useful' wildlife on the Isle of Wight had been hunted to near extinction. Unknowing of his thoughts, Juli continued. "But they have their own goods. Their fishbone needles, carved brooches and clothing pins are of the greatest quality. They are skilled in weaving and knotting the finest netting too. Also, it appears that they grow something called flax and it is a very different material for clothing.

"Ah." Parrish had not given any thought to clothing. As far as he was concerned leather was good for buckskins and wool was, well, wool! But he only had a vague recollection of flax and that was from his history lessons at school. "Well," he said. "I am sure you ladies know what you are doing."

Juli smiled again and nodded. She knew he understood the female subculture of support and exchange that the women of the villages ran to assist each other. But he also chose not to delve too deeply into it. He understood the ladies knew he knew, and that he kept this knowledge to himself. They were grateful for that and loved him for it.

So the first day of barter, exchange and mingling seemed to go well and Parrish heaved a sigh of relief. Everything appeared normal and the prospect for bother or any sort of trouble looked to be unfounded. But his relief was premature.

Not able to be everywhere at once he could not see the little niggles and growing animosities coming from the outsiders. They were unsure. Had certainly noticed the reaction at the stone circle when the altar tone 'treated' them differently, and the way it made, if not the gathering women, then certainly all the other warriors there be standoffish unless they were trading directly with them.

If Parrish had but known he could have spoken with the Islanders new, somewhat ineffective Chieftain and helped if it had been called or asked for. The island warriors began to get what Parrish would have called 'skittish'. Before he was even aware or had a chance to diffuse the situation, the inevitable happened.

The second morning arrived to an overcast sky and Tomps was making his way back towards the people of Dane-bre. He had been to the river, just to sit at its edge, gaze into the never ceasing flow and contemplate the loss of Greta. In his melancholy state he did not notice his passing so close by the clustered Islanders.

The first he knew was the angry murmurs that came from the seated warriors nearest him and as one they rose to their feet. This was the man who had led them far away from their home and had led them into a conflict where several fellow warriors *and* their Chieftain had been killed. Tomps turned toward them in surprised realisation, suddenly finding himself so much closer than he had intended. But even more surprised was the island man with the broken nose who had been sitting with his back turned. As he lifted to his feet and turned to see what all the fuss was about, he suddenly found himself face to face with his nemesis. The last words Tomps had spoken to him still rang in his ears and he panicked, yelled out a cry and, snatching his flint dagger from his belt lashed out in a mad defensive gesture.

Tomps had quick reflexes but barely had time to raise an arm in protection. It was enough to save his life. The target of the strike was his throat, but the up sweeping strike went across the outside of his right forearm, over the crook of his elbow and on up as far as his shoulder. The muscles there opened wide and blood spurted as the razor sharp stone edge opened a four inch gash across his forearm and a long twelve inch slash up his bicep all the way to the point of his shoulder. He cried out in pain and staggered back. The Islander, seeing his greatest fear still not dead, and knowing how deadly his assaults were, had no option but to press home his attack if he himself was to continue in the land of the living.

But other warriors had been alerted. Fortunately for Tomps several were very nearby and they saw the incident with horror. They were not shocked by the deed. Warriors were not offended by violence. Such things happened. It was where the deed was done. No one fought at the temple of Dannu. No one showed such disrespect. No one wanted to risk the anger of the holy men or worst of all, feel the wrath of the Goddess.

Just as the broken nosed warrior leapt onto Tomps, he was pulled off and restrained by two close by warriors from another clan. Danebury men also came rushing to Tomps assistance while the island warriors crowded quickly in to back up their own man. Within moments several dozen warriors from several different clans were facing off against a bank of warriors from the Isle of Wight. The Islanders were reluctant to make the first move. They at least had the sense to know that they were greatly outnumbered. Fortunately for them, the steadily massing warriors from several villages facing them had reined in their own instinct to attack out of their strong respect for Dannu in this most holy of places.

Parrish was suddenly there, rushing into the middle of the potential disaster, arms outstretched and shouting at the top of his voice in English.

"What the fuck is going on here?!!"

The loud unintelligible words froze everyone as Parrish assessed the situation. He saw the Islanders ready to fight. He saw Tomps bleeding on the ground and he saw the broken nosed man still being held in the grip of several warriors he did not recognise. At once it all became clear. And he finally saw that it was all his doing. His patience snapped but he too controlled his anger out of respect to Dannu.

"You have had every chance to make the most of this time. And this is how you act!" He barked, the words were chipped flint in the air. "You showed no respect to the people here, to me, to my men or to Dannu. You can thank the Goddess that you are still alive, and only because everyone else here has respect for her. So now I say enough is enough. We do not need or want you here anymore. Gather your things. You leave now!" he pointed beyond the now huge, gathered crowd, over their heads and away to the exit of the gathering point. The Islanders just stared at him.

"NOW!" he shouted and glared at them. The watching warriors and women, even from the other clans that he had never met before, were open mouthed at the power of his anger and command.

Without another word the Islanders just bent and started to collect up their goods. Parrish stood motionless, arms crossed aggressively over his chest. Klud was by now at his side and holy men had also appeared. His own holy man stepped up close on his left. Parrish wanted to go with Tomps, who was now being helped away by some of his men, blood streaming down his arm. Hopefully, he was not too badly hurt. Instead, he turned to his holy man and said quietly.

"It will take a short while for these people to make ready. They are going back where they came from. Perhaps a holy man might go with them and try to teach them some respect?"

Without a word the little man dashed off, while Parrish resumed his steely eyed watch. Even he could not believe that after this latest outrage, he was still concerned with the welfare of these idiots. But this was it. He would help them no more.

Fuck 'em, he thought finally, and mentally gritted his teeth in frustration.

There was no way to measure it but definitely not more than a quarter of an hour later and the Islanders were stood in a tight cluster. All armed, most with goods in their arms and more of the same in the women's packs. The newly bargained women amongst the group were wide eyed. What had they been sold into? Parrish noticed two holy men slide silently in amongst the group. No doubt on orders from Dannu's high priest.

The puny Chieftain finally stepped hesitantly forward. He plainly looked terrified. Parrish never wasted any words on him. He just pointed to the exit again.

The massed crowd between it and the Islanders parted like the Red Sea to create a passageway. Without a word the timid Chieftain led off and his followers tramped silently through the crowd, a hushed walk of shame. They were across the gathering point, into the woods along the worn pathway and gone from sight in a short time.

When the last of them had disappeared, the sea of faces turned back to Parrish. He finally let his arms drop to his sides and forcibly exhaled.

It was difficult to hide his frustration, anger and personal sense of defeat that his hopes and plans to integrate a new clan into the cult of Dannu and the social system here in the southlands had come to nothing. His efforts resulting in only physical and mental injury to his friend Tomps, a lot of unnecessary deaths beyond the walls of Danebury, and now here, a blatant display of disrespect to everyone and everything Dannu and the belief of the people before him stood for. And there had almost been a mass battle at their most revered time of the year. He scanned the sea of faces.

“I am sorry that it has come to this.” He opened his arms to the people before him. “Please, forgive me. I had hoped they would learn to love Dannu as we all do.”

He bowed deeply to the crowd then turned away, heading quickly off to see how Tomps was.

There were open mouths in the crowd, amazed at the display of both power and piety from Dannu's man. No sooner had the tall man left when there was a great hub-bub of discussion as the crowd broke up.

22

There was a slight hiatus after the confrontation, while the gathered clans talked amongst themselves, having ideas about what caused it and forming their own opinions on the whole extraordinary event. No one was in any doubt that tongues would be wagging for a long time after the solstice gathering was over.

Parrish cared not. He went to his young friend's side to see what was happening, how Tomps was and if he could help in any way.

The blood flow from the young man’s slash injuries had been staunched by tightly bound bandages which held the edges of the wounds together. Parrish could detect a faint smell of the healing poultice. Smears of it had clearly been applied and he was greatly impressed that they could get their hands on some of it. Here of all places, and so quickly too! He never asked though.

Karen was just finishing the bindings on Tomps’ arm when he arrived. He caught the brief, warm yet pain twisted smile his young friend gave his wife. At least Parrish was happy in the knowledge that even through the pain of the loss of Greta, Tomps was not feeling any less towards his wife. Karin gave her Chieftain a brief smile when he offered to help, the gesture quickly dropping from her face as she returned to attending her husband.

“I honour you for your offer.” Tomps said from his sitting position by the fire. His face was pale from shock but he was determined to do the correct thing. “But do not concern yourself, my Chieftain. The wound is being tended to and I think I will not die.”

Surprising himself, Parrish laughed. That was more like it. That was the Tomps that he knew.

“Good man. Well, it seems the other man's knife was sharp, so if the wounds are kept clean and heal well, you should not have scars that are too ugly.”

Tomps nodded. His abiding thought though, was that as he now seemed to be going to live, he would also carry scars on his body just like his Chieftain did. And there was still the unresolved issue of his feud with the broken nosed islander who had once again attacked him.

"I am still alive. Thanks to you." He managed a seated bow. "I am in your debt."

"Not me." said Parrish. "I rocked up after it had all happened. But happy enough to have stepped in to stop any further bloodshed. You just pay attention to getting well, my friend. Tomorrow we will set off back to Dane-Bre. I will be glad when we get back home. This has not been the best of days at the gathering point. And I know I am responsible for that." Both Tomps and Klud were about to protest that claim, but Parrish waved them silent. "No matter. It is done." He turned to Klud. "Just let the people know, if there is any bartering they still wish to do, it must be done by the end of the day. I think it would be a good thing if we leave here fairly early tomorrow morning."

Anyone in the gathering point who was paying attention would notice the subtle change in the atmosphere once the word got about. The knowledge that Dannu's man would be cutting the people of Dane-bre's stay short somehow quietly galvanised everyone. There was no rush or panic, but the bartering, chatting and exchanging going on across the great space just seemed to go up a gear. No one wanted to be left alone at the end of play tomorrow. Deals were being quickly concluded and the first instances of pre-packing before next day's exodus could be seen.

Parrish did not notice, or at least he did not appear to notice. How the different villages conducted their affairs was not his concern. On the other hand, Klud, Juli and many others of Dane-bre saw the increase in activity and they were proud of their Chieftain.

The power of his words was indeed mighty.

The following morning was bright and clear. There was once again a sense of calm and a pervading mood of camaraderie among the clans in the gathering point. The occasional holy man could be seen speaking with Chieftains and the people were damping down their campfires, having eaten well in preparation for the long walks to wherever their villages were and however long it took for them to get there. Being well fortified before the off was a necessity.

Parrish was walking slowly around his own enclave of people, checking that everything was ready and no tasks were undone or not completed before he gave the signal to leave. He could think of nothing worse than doing half a deal, barter or arrangement and having to wait a whole year to complete it just because The Chieftain shouted 'let's go!' before everyone was ready.

He took his time, speaking to several of his people as he walked among them, getting smiles and bows in returns. Klud was always ready, of that he had no doubt. Karen was packed and now gently fussing around Tomps. His strapped and bandaged arm was being favoured and treated very carefully. Parrish didn't doubt it was very painful and the young man was working hard to ensure it was not accidentally jarred or knocked. His right hand was tucked into his tunic belt to keep the limb still but Parrish heard a sharp intake of breath if he moved too quickly.

"I think some sort of sling would be better." Parrish piped up as he met the youngster. "You can make a comfortable one out of cloth, but for now ..." He asked Karen for a long leather thong. She obliged by pulling a belt out of her pack. Parrish quickly felt its thickness and knew she must have bartered it for this item. The leather was definitely too thick to be sheep hide.

Connecting the two ends together with its loop, hole and awl buckle, he placed it over Tomps head so that the loop of strapping hung down over his chest. Gently he helped Tomps pull his hand out of his waistband, crooked the elbow then pulled the leather loop over the hand till it sat at Tomps wrist. The youngster gradually let the strap take the weight of his arm. He smiled at his Chieftain at the more comfortable position.

Parrish smiled back. "I cannot stop it hurting, but I hope that will help a little." Tomps made to bow but Parrish stopped him with a gentle hand on his good shoulder "No more movement than is needed." he ordered and Tomps just smiled. He turned to Karen. "Look after him. If he is doing too much or hurting himself by being brave or stubborn against his pain, you come and tell me, OK?" Karin bowed, and Parrish moved on.

He nodded to Gant, who nodded back, and moved on again before passing Anna. She had her eyes down, trying her best to be just one of the Dane-bre women and not to stand out. He knew it must still all be so new to her, still finding her feet, yet to make friends or find her place among the Dane-bre throng. He stopped alongside her and, without looking directly at her, simply said.

"Okay?"

"Yes, Chieftain." was the mumbled reply.

Parrish just nodded and moved away, but he felt for the girl.

Finally he returned to Juli and everyone looked to him expectantly. It was only then that Parrish looked out beyond his people to the other clans all standing around in silence. They were all looking at him too.

"What ...?" He frowned. "What is going on?" he whispered to Juli, who smiled that knowing smile when everyone but he could see what was going on as plainly as the nose on their faces.

"My husband." she whispered back. "Everyone knows you are leaving early. They all want to follow in your footsteps. No one will depart until you do."

"Oh ..." he looked up sideways at them then whispered again to her. "Really?"

It was all she could do not to laugh out loud.

"Yes, my love."

"Well ... in that case, I think we should be off then."

He braced up and rose to the occasion by giving a great, majestic scan of the vast sea of faces that were all turned his way, then pointed to Klud.

"OK, my friend." He barked loudly. "Away we go then!" And the whole of Dane-bre nodded, picked up their packs, goods or weapons and were ready to go. Parrish stepped up to the head of the people and turned to face across the great clearing towards the exit path.

Just like the day before, but this time with honour rather than disgust, the crowd before him parted to create a wide path to the exit.

Parrish thought it was all a bit much but he led proudly off and everyone else in the village of Dane-bre followed. Their chests burned warmly with the great pride they had in their tall Chieftain.

Parrish unexplainably felt he could breathe more easily once he was out from under the watch full eyes of everyone. Now he and his people were well out into the landscape, a good way across the Vale of Pewsey and heading inexorably back towards home. This he enjoyed. More like being on a patrol, he felt, only with a lot more bodies under his command. The sun was not yet at its height but already Parrish had posted outliers either side of the main group and a couple of scouts on point, a kilometre or so ahead. The chances of an incident of some kind were slight, but Parrish simply rested easier knowing his men were out there. He allowed himself to relax a bit more.

No one stopped for a midday meal or rest. The pace was slow enough and steady enough not to tire anyone and the people settled into the slow rhythm of cross country travel.

Parrish had eaten what Juli had passed to him and was just about to turn his attention to the campsite for the coming evening, when Tomps fell in beside him. His injured arm was in a cloth sling now, knotted at his neck and adjusted in length to allow his arm to rest across his lower chest at a comfortable height.

"How are you doing?" Parrish grinned at his young friend before the lad could speak.

"Oh...... I am good." He glanced at his bandages. "It pains me but that is of no importance. But I would speak with you?"

Parrish smiled at the youngster's bravado. He knew it must be hurting like hell.

"Go!" was all the Chieftain said.

"I have been thinking." Tomps started again.

Good man, thought Parrish to himself. And I think there's the makings of a section commander in you somewhere. "Go on."

"After you sent the Islanders away. A day ago ..."

"Yes?"

"Well... I am right when I say that their knowledge of Dannu's land beyond their island is long forgotten?"

"Yes."

"Then I think that they will return to their home by the only route they know."

"That makes sense."

"Right past a completely empty Dane-bre!"

"Shit!" blurted Parrish in surprise and sudden realisation.

"... And they have no respect." Tomps continued, taking a modicum of pleasure at being able to startle the Chieftain so. "So I am wondering if they will perhaps go inside Dane-bre."

"Tomps, that is the wisest thing you have ever said to me. And I think you may be right. Shit! I hope they do not burn the place to the ground."

Tomps private glee suddenly turned to horror. "You do not think that ...?"

"I cannot say. And we will not know till we get back home. But it is a good point well made my friend." He looked about him at all the clear, innocent faces on the march. "I cannot make the people speed up. And whatever we do the Islanders will be long gone from Dane-bre by the time we get there. Can I trust you to explain this to Klud and Gant but to no one else. Keep it to yourself and be ready when we get home in case people need help depending on what we find there."

"Yes, my Chieftain."

"Good man." This time he said it out loud, went to pat his friend on the shoulder but stopped just in time. He pulled his hand back and raised it to his chin, then stared off towards the far horizon, suddenly lost in deep thought.

Tomps understood the conversation to be at an end, nodded and moved away, just in time to hear the Chieftain curse under his breath one more time.

"Shit!"

23

The return march to Danebury was a fraught one for Parrish. He tried to push the concern for his home and the home of his people to the back of his mind but it was always there. The innocent, unknowing crowd he led moved steadily along, yet whenever Parrish caught one of his friend's eyes, there was a knowing glance or nod and it gave him no comfort to know they were as concerned as he was.

Juli picked up the disconcerted mood of her husband. But she would not ask him why he was so. He was her husband but no one asked a Chieftain to explain. And Parrish didn't want to burden his wife with his worries. Telling her would achieve nothing, for it was a worry that nothing could be done about until the whole village had completed their return trip.

The overnight camp went as well as ever although there was some surprise that not just the Chieftain, but his friends Klud, Tomps and Gant were all very keen to ensure that everyone was up, ready and once again moving on as quickly and as early as possible.

Shortly before the high of the sun, when by Parrish's estimation they were still a few kilometres short of Danebury, Shimon signalled to his people. They all followed his lead and en-mass the whole population of Olann-bre peeled away from the Dane-bre clan and slowly headed off in a more northerly direction.

Parrish understood what was happening. They were in effect cutting off the corner and heading directly for the east river crossing point some six kilometres upstream from the villages locations. It made sense. The people of Olann-bre were happy enough to accept the added protection of travelling with his people as their own under strength village crossed Dannu's land. But now they were almost in sight of home they were happy to make their own way.

There were clearly audible scoffs from some of Parrish's men as they realised what was happening. Not knowing, or caring about any concerns Chieftain Parrish and his friends might have about Dane-bre, without so much as a by-your-leave Shimon led his people off towards the north through the trees.

Some of the Olann-bre women waved a farewell to their new friends of Dane-bre, but neither Shimon nor his warriors gave a backward glance. The tight group of people just ghosted quietly away amongst the trees and were soon gone from sight.

Finally, around mid-afternoon on the second day, the people made their final approach to Danebury. Those three who were in the know gathered alongside their Chieftain as the hillfort came into view, still a kilometre or so away.

The men studied it intensely for several long moments in silence as they drew ever nearer. At this distance nothing seemed untoward.

"Well," said Parrish eventually. "At least it hasn't been burnt to the ground."

"Yes." agreed Tomps, Klud and Gant nodding too. "Perhaps they simply went straight on by?" He added hopefully.

There were more nods but it was a forlorn hope. As they drew closer there were a few cries and pointing of fingers. Several dead sheep carcasses could be seen strewn about near the start of the approach path. Concerned eyes cast their gaze to the flock that still grazed innocently away, near the forest edge. Parrish had no way of telling but to him at least it didn't look that much smaller a flock than he remembered. Thank Dannu for that!

Parrish called a halt before the crowd reached the village entrance as more and more people began to make the connection between Parrish banishing the Islanders and what was being discovered here and now.

"People." he said loudly, catching everyone's attention. "I had hoped that this would not have happened, but I think that the people from the island may have visited our village on their way back to where they came from. Prepare yourselves." His explanation confirmed their fear and there were murmurs of concern from some of the crowd. "I think it is likely that they would only take what they could carry but we can overcome any difficulties that may cause." He could say no more as he gazed back at the dismayed looks on the people's faces. The thought that their homes had been invaded, their private quarters defiled and the mortification of how a great act of theft, the one act abhorred more than any other, had been inflicted upon them. "Now, let us see." He said quietly and slowly led the way up the approach path.

The first sight to greet them was the great gate, swung wide, the way into their homes open and unguarded. That in itself was a heart breaking sight.

The crowd entered the hillfort, slowly fanned out and headed towards their individual huts. Even at that point it was clear that Dane-bre had been violated. The village had been ransacked. Sundry items from inside the huts had been thrown out onto the ground. Broken pottery, odd discarded items of clothing, tools and utensils were scattered about. Families dashed into their roundhouses and there was an awful, hushed silence as each warrior and his family found their homes trashed. Parrish's cabin had not escaped the carnage either, with broken bits of furniture strewn about and everything upturned. It was burglary and vandalism on a village wide scale. Every house had been violently searched for any useful items that could be carried away. After a long silent survey of their houses, the people re-emerged into the sunshine and looked to their Chieftain for guidance. Parrish could be found outside the entrance to the great shrine hut. The holy man emerged from it, white faced. Parrish realised it was the very first time he had ever seen the shaman genuinely furious.

"In there as well?" he asked, not needing to know the answer. He just got a tight, angry nod in return.

Gradually the whole village gathered before him outside the great hut, ashen faced wives and grim faced warriors. Some of the younger children, not understanding but feeling the mood were crying. You could almost feel the anger radiating from the men. They all looked to their Chieftain.

Parrish was about to speak to them, struggling to think of some wise or comforting words, when Klud and Tomps suddenly pushed through to the front of the crowd. They had murderous looks in their eyes and Tomps was gently fingering his bandaged forearm. Another of the unwanted gifts from the Islanders.

"My Chieftain." Klud spoke up. "Tomps I have looked about and we have found something."

"Oh?" Parrish looked searchingly down at his friend and everyone else there pricked up their ears.

"Yes. Several of the outside hearths are still warm and there are sheep remains. Bones, bits of burnt flesh and some entrails scattered around them."

"My Chieftain." Tomps stepped in. "It is like before when I was leading the islanders here. When they find a meat source, they kill more than they need, then they feast."

Parrish saw what they were getting at. His mind did some quick rough and ready calculations.

"So ..." He spoke slowly as the implications all came together in his head. "What you are saying is that, if they travelled across country at the same pace as us, which is likely, the Islanders would have arrived here late in the day yesterday."

"Yes." Tomps nodded. Gant began to nod too, although Klud was initially not quite as quick on the uptake. He continued to stare at Parrish. He had learned long ago not to speak until the Chieftain had finished speaking himself.

Parrish continued. "And as they have found an ample meat source of our sheep, they would have feasted." Which explained the carcasses.

"And then it seems they rested for the night and slept it off." Tomps finished his conclusion.

Klud began to understand now.

"The cooking fires embers are still warm." he said. "So I think, as do my good friends," He nodded to the warriors beside him. "that the Islanders could only have left here a short while ago!"

There were some gasps from the crowd and then growls from some of the warriors. Parrish knew what was going through their minds. He could not fault his men's reasoning. The Islanders were most likely only a few hours, or half a day at most, away from Danebre, heading south back towards the beach where their canoes waited.

The warriors before him now knew that the people who had defiled their village, ransacked their homes, invaded their privacy, committed mass theft against not just the individuals who lived here but the whole village and damaged its livelihood of the sheep flock, were perhaps less than half a day gone.

Parrish looked at all the people before him. His people. His friends and their families. He knew what they all wanted to do now, but all *he* wanted now was to keep them safe. Homes could be repaired, missing items could be replaced. He didn't give a shit now about the thieving bastards from the Isle of Wight, but cared *so* much about the people in his charge.

Klud stepped up close to his tall friend. He could see the conflict in the Chieftains eyes. He understood how Dannu's man thought. Not like other men. Yet it was Klud's task in life to explain to his friend how things were. He looked Parrish in the eye and spoke in a firm voice.

"Parrish. You cannot just leave this. It must be acted on. Can you not see? It is not just an insult to each warrior whose home has been robbed and broken. These people with no respect even for Dannu." He pointed past the holy man to the shrine hut behind him. "Have attacked our homes, our flock and stolen from us. This is more than just an insult. It is the greatest insult to the Great Goddess, to all the people here, to you the Chieftain and to the village of Dane-bre itself. It cannot be left un answered!"

There was total silence when Klud had finished. Even Parrish was astounded by the sheer eloquence and power of Klud's words. Great words that would ring in the ears of the people for a long time to come. There was a great murmur of admiration for Klud, then every eye in the village turned and looked expectantly to their Chieftain.

Parrish just wanted to keep his people safe. To keep them from harm. But it was an impossible wish. He knew it and knew what must be done. It broke his heart to say the words but he stared for a long moment at Klud before a look of grim resignation settled on his features.

"You are in the right of it, my friend." He looked out at the crowd. "My warriors, gather your weapons and enough supplies for a few days. Meet me at the gate shortly." There was another great murmur of ready agreement and satisfaction from the people which he pointedly ignored. "Women of Dane-bre. While we are gone, do what you can to sort out some of this mess," He swept the site before him with an arm. "We will be back as soon as we can." He returned his gaze to Klud, Tomps and Gant at the front of the crowd. “Know now, if we do this thing, then we do it my way. OK?”

“Yes, my Chieftain.” the three chorused.

He was about to suggest that the injured Tomps stay behind in his present state but the look in the young man’s eyes killed the words before they had lived.

“Grab your kit and meet me at the gate.” Was all he growled, and turned away as the crowd dispersed with a sudden and brutal urgency.

24

It didn't take too long. Angry men are motivated men.

Parrish waited by the great gate. Over one shoulder he had a small satchel containing jerky, fruit and a flat bread, plus a water bag. He carried his longbow and a quiver of arrows across his back. As his men began to gather before him, they were all similarly kitted out. Hidden in Parrish's inside pocket was the pistol he had brought back from the 20th century, but he sincerely hoped that he wouldn't have to use it.

Waiting patiently till every warrior was before him, he scanned the crowd. In the past he had seen looks of undisguised glee on their faces when readying for battle. They were happy at the prospect of gathering trophies and gaining honour. If they survived. But this time the mood was dark. A great wrong had been perpetuated against not just themselves and their homes but also against their religion and their Goddess. A brutal slight on the very things they believed in. Their quest now was not for glory, but retribution. He saw that the intent of every man before him was to right this wrong with violence and mass murder.

After a final check on the men, Klud stepped up. Tomps was at his shoulder.

"We are ready, my Chieftain." His great friend said calmly.

Parrish nodded. He looked at Tomps. The boy's right arm was still in the sling. A war club was tucked into the left side of his belt. All Parrish did was raise his eyebrows in concern. Before the youngster could speak Klud stepped up to defend him, slightly misjudging the gesture.

“His wound would make it difficult for him to carry so we have shared his load amongst us.”

Parrish knew his ‘load’ would be no more than what everyone else had, but the gesture summed up the camaraderie and solidarity that bound the people of Dane-bre together.

“Good.” He looked again to Tomps. “And you are happy to make this journey again?”

The young man bowed to his Chieftain. “I am.” There was a pause before he added. “And only if you order me not to go, would I stay behind.”

There were a few murmurs from the men. In admiration or concern over almost inviting a challenge to the Chieftain, Parrish wasn't sure. He just grinned at his young friend.

“As if.” He said and the lad smiled back at him. “Just take care of that arm.” Parrish couldn't help but voice his concern though. “And remember, when we meet with the Islanders, I suggest you keep back during the first moments when battle is joined. I do not question your bravery for a single moment, but a man who fights with one arm must choose his enemy if he can. Do I make myself understood to you?”

“Yes, my Chieftain.” The lad looked a little crestfallen.

Parrish rested a hand on his friend’s good shoulder. “You already have huge honour. Coming with us is a great thing in itself. If anyone can win a skull with one hand, it is you. But taking on several men at once is too much for any man. I would have you return safe to Dane-bre. It would not please me at all to have one of my best warriors throw his life away just to prove he is the equal of everyone, even when injured.”

Tomps chest swelled at the accolade and his smile returned.

“Yes, my Chieftain” he said, now in a happier tone.

Parrish looked to his smiling men, then over their heads to the gathered women listening quietly behind the warriors. He saw the concern on the women's faces. His focus centred on ‘his girls’, who were in a small cluster at the head of the group.

Juli looked directly at him and he winked back. She could not bring herself to smile in return. Beside her was Klud’s first wife, her face deadpan. Karin was there too, not hiding the concern on her face about the prospect of her husband fighting battle hardened Islanders with only one good arm. To his private pleasure Parrish also spied Anna, close in behind 'the girls'. Maybe she was now trying, or perhaps being helped, to integrate with the rest of his village. One good sign at least, he thought.

There was no need to tell anyone what their tasks were, so he just gave a general nod, turned and led his warriors out through the main gate.

And so began the strangest pursuit ever heard of across Dannu's land. Parrish and his men set off after the Islanders. His men were intent on catching their prey before they could escape across the sea, while the islanders were completely unaware that there were warriors determined to run them to ground and destroy them before they could reach the water.

Tomps was right in his original assessment that the Islanders had almost half a day's start. Parrish and his men were away from Danebury in the late afternoon and, though they all set a good pace, the coming of night meant that they had only gained a short space of time to their intended target.

Tomps approached Parrish, a serious look on his face. He bowed.

"Yes?"

"My Chieftain. If we carry on through the night, even if the pace is slow, would we not catch the islanders earlier tomorrow?"

Parrish knew his friend was keen, despite his slashed arm and he knew that the point had been put in an observational, suggestive way rather than as a direct question. The youngster's warrior skills were constantly improving. He smiled.

"If we did that, everyone here would have walked for a day, a night and at least part of the day tomorrow, before being expected to do deadly combat with a freshly rested enemy. Tell me, how well do you think they would fare? I know you have a personal score to settle with one man in particular, but resting tonight is the wise thing to do. Do not worry, my young friend. Your own enemy will get what is coming to him, but you must be patient. At least for a little while longer."

Tomps nodded in deference to his leader's wise words.

"You are right, as always. Forgive me. I was foolish to try and think your thoughts."

"You keep thinking my young friend. It is a good skill. And just between you and me," He leaned in close and lowered his voice. "I do not claim to know all and sometimes a second set of eyes on a problem can be very helpful." He winked.

"It is my honour." Tomps smiled back, bowed and returned to his campfire. Parrish smiled at the young man's back.

Almost at the same time, but several miles apart, both groups settled in for the night amongst the tall trees.

The Islanders were oblivious to both their pursuers and any stories, folklore or hunting knowledge of the land they were crossing. Their bedding down in blissful ignorance was in complete contrast to the men of Dane-bre. Those men did not hunt to the South. The animal life there was known to be much less, it was an unknown area and only recently from Parrish and Tomps had they heard confirmation of a giant tract of undrinkable water and a mysterious island beyond it. And regarding that island, all they knew about this place was what they had gleaned from the contact with the Islanders themselves. And everything they had learned was bad, disrespectful or was just unconfirmed stories.

Parrish never said but he certainly noticed the men with him had set bigger than necessary fires and all camped as close together as they could. After all the bravado at the gate of Danebury, they were now being cagey and not taking any chances in this unknown part of Dannu's land. It was safe to say one set of people slept better than the other.

Parrish's men were up at first light. There was no sun this day. The sky was dull, grey and overcast. A light breeze rippled the leaves in the high branches. He stood and considered the conditions for a few moments. It might be a little more brisk over open water but in no way would it deter the people from the island setting off back to their home turf.

With it being only four days after the solstice, dawn meant around 05:00 hours by Parrish's twentieth century clock. It did mean also that they had broken camp and were once more on the move much earlier than the less hurried or stressed island villagers. More time had been gained and Parrish knew that if they pushed on once they reached the shore of Southampton water he and his men could reach the departure point on the Solent where the outrigger canoes waited, well before dusk. Whether or not the canoes, and thus the Islanders, would still be there that late in the day was another matter. Parrish knew that whatever would unfold this day was in the lap of the gods. His people were hoping for a chance to right wrongs and for glory. However, if the Islanders got clean away, the warriors of Dane-bre would be bitterly disappointed but at least they would all return home alive. Personally, the Chieftain of Dane-bre didn't have an issue with that!

Not much more than an hour after the Danebury men had set off from their campsite they came to the woodlands edge and the broad, shimmering expanse of Southampton water opened up before them. He had no idea of the timing, but the tide was almost fully up and it took a moment before Parrish realised that as one the men behind him stopped and goggled at the sight. Once again he swept the view with a practiced eye. It was completely unsullied by the buildings, bridges or ships he remembered but even so it brought a warmth of familiarity to him. He smiled as he saw the looks of wonder on his men's faces and allowed them the time to take it all in. Many walked down to the water's edge and just stood in silence. Several scooped up a handful of the water, slurped it in then spat it back out. Parrish smiled, caught Tomp's eye and the young man smiled knowingly back.

After a few moments or so he called his band to order. They turned to him with yet another sense of wonder at their great Chieftain, who knew and took all these previously unknown wonders in his stride. They gladly rallied to his call for there was no fear in them now. They were being led by Dannu's man and that meant that the Goddess was with them.

The contingent all headed off along the shoreline and Parrish set a brisk pace. He did briefly consider dragging his feet in the hope that when they arrived at the islander's departure point, all the people would have already gathered up their canoes and be long gone. It would save the lives of his men but he knew it was imperative that a solid conclusion was reached and a line drawn underneath this whole sorry episode. Otherwise there would be dissent in Danebury for a long time to come. If wrongs were not righted, and seen to be righted, unhappy and unsatisfied thoughts would linger and fester. It was quite something, he realised, to make a decision that accepted the fact that some of his men's lives were to be given for the well-being of the whole village. He didn't like it but it was necessary. There was a sudden understanding smile on his face as he recalled all the times when as a humble foot soldier, he'd questioned and criticized the decisions and orders of his superiors. He thought they were idiots and had no concern for the lowly privates, corporals and sergeants under their command.

Now he understood and after saying once that even he could have done a better job than the top brass, he wished he could take it all back. Being in charge was no picnic. Sometimes what looked stupid was in fact a difficult decision which could result in ending men's lives. The smile dropped lead like from his face as he looked at his men, some he realised would not be alive at the end of the day if they managed to catch the Islanders at the shoreline. He exhaled forcibly.

Sometimes, being in charge sucks!

The dull sky did nothing to brighten the mood of the men and they pushed along the edge of the tree line between the forest and the high water mark. Ominous looking darker clouds were slowly gathering away to the east, the tops of them visible above the mighty oaks on their left. The easterly breeze coming over the trees was still light, so no one was concerned.

If Parrish had known, it was fourteen kilometres or about nine miles to the edge of the Solent. The steady pace enabled his war party to complete the distance in a little over five hours. This time scale of the modern era meant nothing in itself, but the men made the turn of the coast before midday. No sooner had they veered eastward along the Solent shore when the site where all the canoes had been beached only a few short days earlier came into view. And what a sight it was, framed by the water on the left, the greenwood to the right and with a towering backdrop of darker clouds beyond.

But no one was looking at the view.

25

As far as Parrish was concerned, their timing could not have been worse.

If they had been earlier, the islanders would have been caught off guard on the beach. Even better, if he and his men had arrived later, the islanders would have been gone, well away across the sea and beyond their reach.

If the Islanders had long gone Parrish's men would have been bitterly disappointed. If they were still on shore, they would have gone into battle but as everyone took in the sight before them, it was clear that they had caught the transgressors right at the point of departure. The people of the Isle of Wight had already loaded their crafts, most were already on the water and the last few canoes were being launched as they watched.

As the last island warrior pushed off and jumped into the stern of his canoe, the men of Dane-bre bellowed in rage and charged along the foreshore, even as their enemy was escaping to sea. Parrish kept pace and they all covered the few hundred metres along the beach as fast as they could, but by the time he and his men reached the departure point all the canoes were safely out of range. Hot, impotent rage burned in their eyes as they stared in fury at the little bobbing boats, just out of reach.

Most of the outrigger canoes were fifty metres or so from the shore already, beyond arrow range and heading out. On hearing the shouts from the men of Dane-bre the paddling stopped and the occupants turned to stare back. Some of the canoes began to turn slowly side on by the gentle push of the breeze now that they had stopped in the water.

Nearer to the shore, but still safely out of reach, the last few canoes also stop paddling. The men in them looked back fiercely, initially thinking about turning and returning to shore to engage in a battle. It was poor, unguided thinking and Parrish briefly wondered if their ineffective new Chieftain was just that, ineffective. But the men in the boats quickly spotted Parrish, his height an easy giveaway, realised who the man was and who all the men were and where they had come from. They just as quickly changed their minds. Deciding that discretion was the better part of valour, they started to withdraw, paddling away once more, but not before casting loud jeers back at the line of warriors angrily waving their fists and weapons at them from the shore. The laughter that came to their ears from across the waves did nothing to improve their demeanour.

Parrish just stood in silence. The anger of his men was plain but he also felt their dismay. Not so much at the fact that they could not fight these men or redress the great wrongs that had been done to their way of life, but to the plain realisation that these wicked people from the island across the water would not be punished at all for their terrible indiscretions and violations.

They were leaving untouched. Unmarked in anyway by the wrongs they had committed. The look in all his warrior's eyes said it all. This was just not right.

Parrish's shoulders sagged with the weight of this understanding too. It did not feel right. There was no satisfaction. No corrections of the wrongs perpetrated on his people and the Goddess. The fallout from this when everyone returned home was going to be long and unpleasant.

Just as he was about to turn his back on the flotilla of escaping canoes, trying to think of some pacifying words to mollify his men, a stray, cold breath of wind kissed his right cheek, stopping him in his tracks. And then came a second one. He looked away to his right and the dark clouds on the near horizon had deepened even further. Then everything went still. Unnaturally so. The wind dropped completely and the water out to the paddling canoeists settled to a flat calm. Everybody on the shore fell silent. Confused, baffled looks crowded onto their faces.

Tomps and Klud, standing either side of Parrish were confused too, but looked to their Chieftain. He would understand.

Klud opened his mouth to ask the question but the words froze on his lips. His Chieftain appeared to be staring out at the slowly moving away group of boats.

Parrish could feel himself going rigid. He tried to fight against it but could not. It wasn't the muscle screaming locking up he had experienced in the past but he knew what was about to happen. Almost of its own accord, his body started to march in an odd, stiff legged way out into the still water.

"What ..?"

Klud started, then as his Chieftain moved out into the sea, looked across at Tomps. The younger man nodded back and without further ado the pair splashed into the water after their Chieftain and fell in alongside either side of him, Tomps to his left, Klud to his right. The holy man, who was stood behind, also set off into the water. Everyone else along the shoreline just stared in amazement.

Parrish moved steadily out into the still water, pushing against the weight of it as he moved stiffly along. Klud and Tomps kept pace either side, close enough to come to their friend's aid should he need it, but far enough away from him so as not to hinder his progress.

Within a few dozen steps Parrish was almost up to his waist in water, Klud and Tomps almost chest deep. The holy man, being even shorter had to stop several paces behind. The water level was almost at the base of his ribs and he dare not go any further. He looked down at the water in dismay before looking back up. He gasped. From his position, looking at the backs of the three men, he could suddenly see a faint blue line of light, a barely discernible aura, appearing around the edge of Parrish's body still visible above the water line.

"The wrath of Dannu is in him!" he gasped in realisation.

Klud and Tomps heard, as did the men on the shore, but their eyes did not leave their Chieftain. The tall man's eyes still stared glassily out towards the distant canoes filled with the island villagers.

Parrish knew he was being controlled but this was not like before. He could still see and somehow felt the intentions of the force that controlled him.

Klud and Tomps, now unsure whether to stay or to retreat from this unnerving new phenomenon, stood open mouthed as Parrish raised his right arm in a stiff unnatural way. It pointed away to the dark clouds off to the east. The hand turned palm up and the fingers curled, beckoning the clouds forward.

The sky darkened almost immediately. The clouds roiled up quickly, quicker than anyone had ever seen clouds develop before and the air around them darkened. Everyone could now see Parrish's aura and there was a chorus of gasps.

The wind picked up and it could be seen as scudding ripples across the surface of the water. What was only moments earlier a flat calm began to chop up. Short, sharp little waves, then getting bigger as the strengthening wind took hold of them. The tops began to foam and little flecks of spume flew in the air.

Now the wind began to make itself heard and the dark clouds were rushing towards everyone, clearly being beckoned in by Parrish's silent call.

Klud was still watching his friend but Tomps was now gazing out at the canoeists. There were suddenly visible signs of panic amongst them. Shouts could be heard. Some people continued to paddle while others, seeing what was approaching, hunkered down in their craft, gripping tightly to the gunwales as the choppy seas made them bob about alarmingly. Sea water began to slop coldly into the boats themselves.

Piercing screams from some of the women could be heard, the sound carrying across the gap between the boats and the shore, a horrific counterpoint sound to the rising wail of the wind.

Then the squall was upon them. Rain, first in slow heavy spots, then with some force spattered into the surface of the Solent before sheets of water swept across the people. Parrish, Tomps, Klud and the holy man were immediately drenched, yet the silent warriors lined up on the shore somehow remained dry, just beyond the scope of the cloud burst.

The rain became a deluge and poured down before Parrish and his companions as a rolling grey sheet, temporarily blocking their view of the panicked and fearful Islanders in their canoes.

A single clap of thunder rent the sky. It was as if it were a signal and the rain abruptly eased. Parrish's halo shrouded arm dropped back to his side with a splash and he just stood there at stiff attention, waist deep in the choppy water, now just watching and waiting. He was still shrouded in his aura and could not move.

The squall moved away as fast as it had arrived and like a giant grey curtain rolled back to reveal a terrible sight. There was total disarray out on the Solent, now unveiled before the staring people of Dane-bre. Outrigger canoes were scattered about. Some were suddenly bereft of their occupants. Some manned by wet, dishevelled and terrified people, both men and women. And some were merely bobbing aimlessly about, upturned. The rounded bellies of their hulls low in the water all there was to mark the spots where people had gone to their deaths beneath the waves.

Everyone stared in shocked silence.

The wind dropped to a slight breeze and the sea calmed again to a gentle swell. Some of the people in the canoes, seeing the change remained alert enough to grasp this window of clear weather, picked up their paddles and set off towards the island as fast as they could. The rest took their lead and joined in. In a short time all the remaining manned boats were heading away towards the distant shoreline at best speed.

Tomps could not count that well but he could see that perhaps a third of the canoes remained bobbing and empty on the sea before them. He turned to Parrish, about to say something, when the tall man raised his left arm out of the water. He was still glassy eyed and staring out at the carnage but his hand pointed to the water a little way in front of Tomps.

"A gift from Dannu." Parrish said hoarsely, still not looking at Tomps.

Tomps, turning back looked at the still, dark water in front of him. A single bubble rose up from the depths and breached the surface with a quiet plop. Then another one followed by a string of bubbles before with a shallow, muted splash a body rose to the surface. A dead warrior, risen from the depths, floated face down before him.

Tomps stared at it for several long moments before tentatively reaching out. After a brief, reluctant pause, he grasped the body by the shoulder with his good arm and with surprising ease turned the floating corpse over.

It was the warrior with the broken nose.

Tomps mouth dropped open, then closed again when he realised he had nothing to say. He turned in amazement to his Chieftain, bowed as best he could while standing chest deep in water and said in quiet awe.

"I ... I thank you for it."

Parrish did not appear to have heard or even noticed him.

The young warrior turned back to the body. In a sudden instinctual moment he reached out, plucked the dagger that had wounded him from the belt of the corpse then, with a firm shove pushed the body away from him. It floated off a few metres then without a sound slipped slowly beneath the surface. In the blink of an eye it was gone from sight. Tomps looked back at his Chieftain but Klud now had his arms around his tall friend. The shining aura was gone and Parrish suddenly looked drawn and in pain. Tomps rushed to help his Chieftain and together with Klud they half carried, half towed the tall man back to the shore, the holy man proudly leading the way.

The warriors of Dane-bre made way for their Chieftain as he was brought ashore. They were not saddened at all by the decimation of the Islanders. They felt the punishment was just and well deserved. But they were stunned by the way the Great Goddess had funnelled and directed her wrath through their Chieftain. Yes, everyone called him Dannu's man. They had always known he was Dannu's man. But to actually see him as that. Wielding all that power and majesty. So much death and destruction. And almost it seemed with a mere wave of his hand. They wondered if, when he was being used as Dannu's instrument, there was anything he could not do?

They loved and respected their Chieftain but to finally be given the opportunity to witness the full power of Dannu flowing through him honestly frightened them. At Dannu's behest, it seemed the very elements were his to command.

But as Klud and Tomps helped the tall man up on to the beach and sat him gently down, he looked so battered and exhausted they understood it was a power that came with a price. And their hearts went out to him. He was their Chieftain, their leader and their friend. He loved the village of Dane-bre and everyone in it. His heart was theirs and so theirs was his also. He might be Dannu's man, but he was their man too.

They all went to his aid, the carnage out on the water beyond, momentarily forgotten. Gant organised a quick collection of dried wood and a fire was soon started. Helping hands peeled off Parrish's wet clothes and wrapped him in gladly donated woollen capes to keep him warm while his clothes dried out. The tall man smiled weakly back and settled down to warm up and recuperate from his fatigue.

Klud took charge.

"We will remain here for the night." He announced loudly.

"I am not injured," countered Parrish. "Just a bit cold, and a bit tired." To his men he looked anything but! "I will be ready to leave in a short while. Just give me a chance to catch my breath."

Klud stood over his seated friend. As a Chieftain Parrish could have taken that as an insult but he just looked up and saw his friend in his pomp. Clearly, he would brook no dissent.

"Parrish. My friend. You are greatly tired. I can see it takes a great effort to be the hand of Dannu. You must rest. We will watch for the rest of the day in case any Islanders return here, be it for help or revenge. A good meal and a good night's sleep will restore you and we will all set off fresh in the morning. I am sure Dane-bre will be safe for one more day, if it is the will of the Goddess. You always look after us my friend. Now give us the honour of looking after you."

Among the watching crowd, jaws dropped. Great words, and spoken to an even greater man.

At that moment Parrish could not, dare not argue with his friend. It seemed to him that there was suddenly quite a lot of personal development going on in his village, he mused. He smiled and nodded in agreement.

"You are wise as always, my friend. I will abide by your instructions." There was a pause before he added. "Just for today!"

There was a moment of stunned silence before the two men eyed each other sternly, then both burst out laughing.

Then everyone else smiled. The harmony of Dane-bre was suddenly fully restored in that moment.

The watching men's attention was swiftly returned also, as Klud barked orders to them and they all snapped too and set about their tasks.

26

The new dawn found Parrish fully restored. Klud was right, some food and a good night's sleep did indeed set him back on his feet.

It took no time at all for his men to have a light breakfast and break camp, clearing away not only what they had left but also the debris left behind by the Islanders only a day before. Finally ready to go, the men looked to their leader for the signal.

Tomps approached Parrish as they were about to set off.

"My Chieftain. I was wondering ..."

"Good man," Interrupted Parrish. "Keep it up. Yes?"

"For now the Islanders are away across the water. But what if they should return in force? We must be ready."

"That is a reasonable thing to consider. And I have the answer. Go and get Klud, Gant and the Holy one. I will send my warriors on a short way ahead and we will have a quiet talk together."

Tomps bowed and without another word dashed off to tell the others the Chieftain would speak with them.

Parrish waited till everyone was ready and stood set to leave. A sea of faces turned to him and he waved his arms.

"My brave warriors. Now we set off for home." He pointed westward. "Just follow the shoreline. I will be only a few paces behind. Go now, while I speak with my friends, and we will be with you in a short while."

There were glances at Klud, Tomps, Gant and the Holy one, who stood silent at Parrish's side. A few men wished they could be with them also but most were happy to be well away from Dannu's man and his companions. What they had seen the day before was still with them. There was a sea of nods then the crowd turned and walked away along the shoreline. A quick hubbub of discussion went with them.

The tall man turned to his four companions.

"My friends." Parrish smiled at the attentive men. "There is something you need to know. Share it with the others or not, I care not. But I want you all to understand what happened yesterday."

"We all saw what happened yesterday, my Chieftain." Tomps blurted out, not able to keep the wonder from his voice.

"You saw what happened, but you did not see what *really* happened."

The looks of confusion on their faces were almost comical.

"There is no need to worry, or to be on constant watch for any appearances by the island people for a long time to come. When the wrath of Dannu rained down on those people, it did not simply kill a lot of them. It killed some of them. Some she killed, some she left untouched. It was not the lucky who survived. It was the *chosen*."

The looks of bafflement grew from his companions. He understood he would have to explain it in its simplest terms.

"OK. Look. I saw what Dannu did. I saw it through her eyes. She thinned out the people. Like killing the old animals in a herd so the newer, younger ones can grow better and stronger."

There was a glimmer of understanding from Gant and the Holy one. Tomps was trying to figure it out while Klud, good old honest, straight forward Klud, looked on blankly.

Parrish smiled.

"She thinned out the herd. At least half the warriors were killed, including their useless Chieftain and Tomps own enemy." The youngster nodded in confirmation. "And she killed some of the island women. But none of the women bartered for at the solstice gathering. She made sure to keep the new blood." He turned to the Holy man. "And your two holy men also lived. They are to do the bidding of the Goddess and they have a long task ahead of them."

"To bring the Islanders back into Dannu's flock!" The little man suddenly understood.

"Yes. It will be many, many seasons before you will see those two at the great temple again. I honour them now for the great task Dannu has set before them." The little man bowed at that.

"We need not look over our shoulders for any sudden appearance of the Islanders. It will take a long, long time for the people over there to regain their strength in numbers. Yet while they are much less in number they are safe enough from hunting or war parties from other villages, protected as they are by the waters between them and everyone else."

Klud nodded. "I see." he said slowly. Parrish put his hand warmly on his friend's shoulder.

"Yes. And it also means that the remaining animals on the island can increase their numbers too. They breed and grow so much faster than people that Dannu's creatures will benefit too. Balance on the island will be restored so when the people there have grown in numbers enough to start hunting more, enough time will have passed that there will be plenty of creatures for their wants, but the holy men there will use Dannu's teachings to be sure they only take what they need. And so the natural balance is kept."

The looks on the Neolithic men's faces had slowly turned from confusion, through understanding and now to wonder. Such thinking. Forward thinking. Great thinking! They could not have even considered such powerful reasoning. Dannu is great.

Parrish let them all stew on these revelations for a few moments. Then he smiled again.

"Tell the others, or not. I care not, but now you see there is no need to worry about what is happening on that island. Dannu has begun a long task to put things back as they should be in that part of her land. Now do you see what happened yesterday?"

"Yes, yes." came a quiet chorus from his men.

"Good."

Parrish smiled again, knowing of course that his words would spread. From these four on to all the other warriors and from them to their wives. In no time at all everyone at Dane-bre would know and understand. It was what he wanted but it was not the done thing for a Chieftain to explain himself to anyone. So he was quite happy to let the village grapevine work for him.

He nodded to the four men and they naturally bowed back.

"Right then." His tone became more businesslike. "Let us be on our way."

The two days back to Dane-bre were thankfully incident free and stress free. Everyone was in good spirits and full of pride for their Chieftain. Whenever it came up in conversation, which was often,

Parrish would pooh-pooh their kind words and become embarrassed. This endeared him to his warriors even more.

Arrival back at Dane-bre also brought the pleasant surprise that the hillfort looked as if it had never been touched by the Islanders. The women had organised a complete tidy up and also attempted to rectify as much damage as possible.

Parrish praised them all for their efforts and the ladies giggled and bowed deeply. There were still tools to be replaced as soon as was practical. Some small building repairs to be done and a lot of stolen foodstuffs would need to be replenished. On that front Parrish had decided to allow his people a few days rest before sending out any hunting parties. He was happy to leave the details of that to Klud and Gant.

Of course, it did not even take a full day before the full revelations and details of the events on the shore of the undrinkable water were common knowledge throughout the whole camp. Parrish relayed his own brief version to Juli. She was amazed enough, but chats with the other women on their water collecting stints beyond the hillfort gave her ample opportunity to fill in all the gaps Parrish had left in his story. Her astonishment grew.

The other women of Dane-bre's attitude towards their Chieftain was much like their husbands in the way that a few ladies were envious of her closeness to Dannu's man, while most were happy to be led by the great man but keep what they thought was a slightly more safe distance from him.

A day later a small group of women were at the watering hole. It was Parrish's 'girls'.

Juli, Karin and Klud's first wife were refilling their skin bags and encouraging Anna to join in their conversations. She was still a little reluctant but those recent days when the village had been 'men free' had been useful for her in enabling her to finding her feet among the ladies of Dane-bre. They were very supporting of each other she found, much more so than in the still struggling village of Olann-bre. Daily life in her new village was actually easier and the women were so helpful she felt in their debt to them at every turn. They waved away her grateful praise every time it was offered. To them it was just how things were and she was now beginning to realise that it might just be her good fortune to be a part of the successful village of Dane-bre.

The four of them had just filled their water bags and started back when, as they emerged from the tree line, a familiar tall figure approached.

Parrish had taken the time to walk out to the edge of the flock, ostensibly just to have a friendly chat and share a few words with the warriors who were on sheepherding duty. Past experience had told him how monotonous a posting it could be and although he had absolutely no idea about animal management, he felt he should at least show an interest and be supportive of his men even when they were doing menial work for the benefit of the whole village.

Spying the little female group as it emerged from the woods, he smiled inwardly to himself then approached.

They all automatically bowed and also automatically bunched closer together. He eyed them warmly, then spotting the new face amongst the group said simply.

"All right, Anna?"

Startled at being addressed directly, she stuttered.

"Yes... I ... I am well, my Chieftain."

Parrish replied with a flat face. "Good." But one corner of his mouth curled up just as he turned and walked away.

"Did ... did I say something wrong?" Anna looked on at the tall man's receding back, rather dismayed.

Juli looked the new girl in the eye and smiled.

"No. He is not displeased." she knew her husband well enough. Karin and Klud's wife shared a smile. "He is just satisfied that you called him MY Chieftain and not just 'the' Chieftain. He was beginning to wonder if you would ever see Dane-bre as your new home."

"Oh! But I am just a girl, not even from Dane-bre. Why would he even think about me?" Anna paused, looking at the faces around her. They waited in silence while she thought on, then began to smile herself. "It is true then. He really does care for everyone."

There were knowing nods from everyone else.

"Now you see what we all see" said Juli. "He is truly special. There is much more to Dannu's man than just what you see before you."

Anna now understood too, and then a great curiosity suddenly welled up in her.

“Yes, I begin to see. I would very much like to know more about *my* Chieftain.” she smiled and raised her eyebrows in question to Juli.

“Ah. There is only one person who can really answer that.” said Parrish's wife with a knowing smile. Karin and Klud’s wife nodded again in agreement.

Now everyone was smiling.

27

Klud bristled.

"You dare approach me unbidden and speak without permission?!" he almost bellowed.

"Please ... forgive me." Anna cowered, bowed, but pressed on. "But I was told that the great Klud of Dane-bre would know."

Klud paused at the clumsy attempt at flattery. Not quite realising how much his great friend Parrish had influenced him over the years, his curiosity won out over his natural warrior pride. There was a pause before he decided to act and a tense silence followed before he said slowly.

"Know what? Told by who?"

"I ... several people told me this." Her pause before answering told Klud that she was not about to name names, even at the order of a warrior. This Anna girl from Olann-bre had some spirit, but he was a warrior of little patience.

"Told you WHAT?"

Anna flinched but bravely held her ground.

"That you were the only one who could tell me all about ...Chieftain Parrish."

Klud couldn't help it. In spite of his rising anger at the bare effrontery of being boldly approached unbidden by a mere woman, and even being asked a question, a grin split his features. How could this slip of a girl know that his great friend was his favourite subject?

"Parrish?" His tone became even. "So, you want to know all about the Chieftain?"

Anna nodded and bowed again.

"I ... I do. He brought me here. And he ..."

"Yes. He did." came the interruption.

The bluster had gone from his voice and Anna looked up in surprise to see the much feared and respected warrior now looking at her with an almost benevolent understanding, finish her sentence.

"He brought you back from the dead."

Klud spoke more softly than she had ever heard him before, and he nodded in agreement with his own words. Anna looked puzzled now but Klud simply pointed at the ground beside his fire.

"Sit." It was a command but sounded more like an invitation. She duly sat and to her surprise he dropped down beside her. Taking her courage in both hands she dared to look into the man's eyes and found him looking intently back. But there was no anger or indignation there at any sort of disrespect. This most feared of Danebre warriors was smiling softly! An almost conspirational smile, as if to a comrade. Before her very eyes he had turned from a battle hardened warrior into a wise and knowing sage.

"He brought you back from the dead." He repeated, speaking as a teacher would to a pupil. "And I can tell you girl, you are not the only one." Anna was all ears now, her fear forgotten. Klud saw the keen interest and nodded in understanding. He explained. "I was there and saw when he jumped head first into the deep and brought you back from the bottom of the river." Anna could do nothing but nod. Klud smiled at that.

"Did you know that his wife once fell right to the bottom of the defence ditch? Her legs were so badly broken that they were bent in all the wrong directions. She too was dead. But he just took her away to his hut. No one saw what he did there but he brought her back from the dead too." The girl's eyes widened. Klud enjoyed this reaction to his tale.

"And I saw him go out into a blizzard and carry back a young Tomps when the boy was dead from the cold. And what a warrior and friend that man now is. And Tomp's daughter was born dead and he brought her back too."

"B ... born dead?" Anna gasped, amazement plain on her face.

"Yes." But Klud was on a roll now and did not expand on this staggering revelation. "Also, when Narn's eldest son was killed, struck down by the power of Dannu, Parrish blew his own breath into the boy's mouth and he came back to life. Back from the dead. I saw it with my own eyes." Even Klud had to remind himself how amazing that had been. Anna's mouth hung open. He took a deep breath.

"And I too have been brought back from the dead. I was a prisoner in a distant village, waiting to be killed by their Chieftain, and Parrish came for me." As if to drive home the point, he repeated it, almost as if he himself could hardly believe it either. "I was *inside* another village. And he came for me, alone, at night. Crossing the land faster than it can be crossed by a mortal man! He was not even slowed by the village's walls and ditches, no different to these." He waved an arm wide to indicate Dane-bre's own surrounding walls. "He passed straight through this far village, unseen, and walked right into their shrine hut! And brought me back from the dead!"

"I ... I am sorry." gasped Anna. "I did not know any of this."

"Of course you did not." Klud waved away the apology. He smiled again at the girl, which she still found unnerving, and addressed her almost as an equal, gratified at her rapt attention. He decided to continue to expand his tale. "These are all truly great things that he has done, but that is only one side to Dannu's man. Yes, we call him that when he cannot hear us, as I am sure you do too. And that is why you want to know more about your Chieftain, yes?"

"How could I not!" replied Anna, transfixed by the words of this heroically tattooed warrior. "If you would honour me with more, I would ..."

Klud laughed at the thinly veiled begging for him to continue. As the sound died away his hand went to his face.

"See this?" He fingered his badly broken, miss-shapen nose. "He gave me this." Anna's eyes widened again. "I attacked him. He could have killed me with no effort to himself, but he did not. Now he is my Chieftain. But more than that, he is my greatest friend. I wear this injury with honour!" he smiled as his audience of one shook her head in wonder. She couldn't pull herself away and Klud was now fully into his stride. To talk about his great friend and Chieftain was a true joy, and he intended to make the most of it.

"But now, you must hear the tale of Dannu's man from the start. Girl, are you prepared to hear a long and strange tale?"

"Oh yes." breathed Anna eagerly.

Klud smiled broadly, not caring who might be watching, settled back and gathered his thoughts for a moment.

"From the start then." He took a deep breath and looked out and away, over Anna's head, over the conical roofs of the roundhouses and on past the palisade wall that surrounded Dane-bre, staring off back into the past.

"It had not been a very good spring, but one fine day a tall stranger clad in odd clothing just walked out of Dannu's land, bringing the warm sun with him ...."